Piano Teacher

The Piano Teacher

LYNN YORK

A PLUME BOOK

PLUME
Published by the Penguin Group
Penguin Group (USA) Inc., 375 Hudson Street,
New York, New York 10014, U.S.A.
Penguin Books Ltd, 80 Strand,
London WC2R 0RL, England
Penguin Books Australia Ltd, 250 Camberwell Road,
Camberwell, Victoria 3124, Australia
Penguin Books Canada Ltd, 10 Alcorn Avenue,
Toronto, Ontario, Canada M4V 3B2
Penguin Books India (P) Ltd, 11 Community Centre, Panchsheel Park,
New Delhi –110 017, India
Penguin Books (N.Z.) Ltd, Cnr Rosedale and Airborne Roads,
Albany, Auckland 1310, New Zealand
Penguin Books (South Africa) (Pty) Ltd, 24 Sturdee Avenue, Rosebank,
Johannesburg 2196, South Africa

Penguin Books Ltd, Registered Offices:
80 Strand, London WC2R 0RL, England

First published by Plume,
a member of Penguin Group (USA) Inc.

First Printing, March 2004
1   3   5   7   9   10   8   6   4   2

Copyright © Lynn York, 2004
All rights reserved

LIBRARY OF CONGRESS CATALOGING-IN-PUBLICATION DATA

York, Lynn.
The piano teacher : a novel of Swan's Knob / Lynn York.
p. cm.
ISBN 0-452-28477-5 (trade pbk.)
1. Women music teachers—Fiction. 2. North Carolina—Fiction. 3. Church
musicians—Fiction. 4. Organists—Fiction. I. Title.

PS3625.O75P53 2004
813'.6—dc22   2003055375

Printed in the United States of America
Set in Simoncini Garamond
Designed by Leonard Telesca

for
Ann Gregory York

and

in memory of
Evelyn Walker Gregory

All of one's life is music, if one touches
the notes rightly, and in time.

—John Ruskin

Chapter One

The whole thing got off to a bad start when Miss Wilma unceremoniously ran over a squirrel in the Strongs' driveway, right in front of the porch. She had been going over her prelude program, the standard wedding fare, Handel, Bach, a little Vivaldi, and she didn't see the squirrel at all, just felt a sudden small bump under her tire. When she walked up to the house, she confirmed it. There he lay flat, his little squirrel blood running across the driveway.

Surely Lily Strong has someone who could take care of it, Wilma thought, and rang the bell. She was let in by a small woman wearing a uniform from the Robert E. Lee Hotel in Winston. Lily had no doubt called in a dozen or more of these people to pull off this wedding of the century. Inside the house, it was dead quiet except for the clinking of silverware being counted in the kitchen. Miss Wilma walked on through the hall, resisting the urge to tiptoe. The living room, just to the left, was painted English-gentry green and filled with elaborately reproduced furniture. Over the fireplace hung a somber portrait of Franklin Strong, who looked like a minister instead of the proprietor of a chain of nursing homes.

She passed by the dining room, which was all set up to display the wedding gifts. There was enough china and crystal for four young women, but of course every bit of it was for Lily's only daughter, Martha. Martha was a sweet girl, but mousy. As a young child, when Martha had first started taking piano lessons, Wilma had had difficulty just getting her to actually strike the keys hard enough to make a sound. That was what you got when you had a siren for a mother. Poor Martha. If Lily had noticed Martha's tendency toward cringing shoulders or limp hair, she showed it only in her concerted efforts to prop Martha up. This elaborate garden wedding was a case in point.

Miss Wilma figured Lily had bought her house years ago as a stage setting for this day: her daughter married at home in front of the whole community. Lily's house was a notch up from all the others in Swan's Knob—a full five acres just on the edge of town, two stories, at least fifteen rooms, separate garage, pink brick. Wilma just hoped that poor Martha would not end up looking like a homely doll set down in the middle of all the festivities. Lily herself had married Franklin in the standard fifteen-minute Methodist rite just like everyone else of her generation. Wilma had been right there in the church. They had been friends—Lily and Frank, Wilma and Harry. They had been friends in a life that happened a million years ago. It was all long gone now, gone from the day Lily moved to this house, further gone since Harry was dead.

This was not the time, however, to dwell on any of it, which was one advantage to being an organist. You could just play and put all the rest of it aside. She went out the back door and looked around at the setting that the *Swan's Knob Gazette* would describe in tremendous detail on Sunday: a lovely formal rose garden with a raised back veranda, framed by four colonial columns, each wrapped with ivy and white bows. Lily had borrowed folding chairs and several green canopies from Snow Funeral Home. Lily and Grace Snow were great friends. Above all things, today's elaborate arrangements were for Grace and the rest of their crowd. Lily would be complimented right on into the fall over each and every detail. Wilma was glad that she no longer bothered with the Garden Club, and she had never played bridge. This way, she could safely avoid most of the frivolous chatter that these women survived on. She would not have to hear another word about how beautiful the back lawn looked, how pretty the flowers were, how appealing the bride and her maids.

Lily had arranged the chairs in rows facing the veranda. There were small bouquets at the end of each aisle. A wide white ribbon stretched across the front seat that was apparently reserved for Lily. Wilma herself had not had the opportunity to be the mother of the bride, not that she would have required a six-inch-wide grosgrain ribbon. Still, it was an image that you carried with you when you raised a daughter—something you thought about when you braided her hair—that someday the two of you would plan a wedding, that you would rush around for months to this store and that to find just the right veil, the gloves, the perfect dress. You would worry over tuberoses (Would they open in time for the ceremony? Would they go brown?). In her daughter Sarah's case, it had all been done before Wilma knew about it. Everything— engagement, wedding, honeymoon—all in one day, apparently, and just as well since Sarah was already expecting at the time. Just as well, too, that Wilma had not been invited. Whatever ceremony there had been had occurred at some kind of beach carnival.

It was a far cry from the little tents that dotted the expanse of the garden, sheltering buffet tables, punch bowls, wedding cake. It was all quiet and clean and white. Miss Wilma could hear Lily's cupid fountain on the far garden wall, and closer, the buzzing of bees.

Hidden behind an assortment of potted plants was the organ, also borrowed from Snow's. Miss Wilma had not been insulted by Lily's request that she arrive two hours in advance of the service. Her preparation time was important to her, and the organ in question had given her trouble at a recent funeral service at

Snow's. She wanted to make sure that the treble register had not been damaged by the transport. She began to arrange her sheet music, thankful to have remembered her clothespins—a trick of the trade that would save her if a breeze came through. She was thankful she didn't have to go to all this trouble on Sunday mornings. She could almost play a church service in her sleep by now.

From inside the house, Wilma heard a short shriek, followed by the clippedy high-heeled run of Lily Strong across the kitchen floor. A few moments later Lily was standing at the back screen door talking to someone inside. "Well, find a shovel and get it off the driveway, Shelton, then get a bucket to rinse the pavement and do it fast before the guests start coming. I've got to go talk with my organist."

My organist, Wilma thought, it is just like her to classify me in that way. But as Lily emerged from the house, she looked toward Wilma like an old friend in search of commiseration. "Lordy," she said. "Can you imagine one of these folks from the Robert E. Lee Hotel ran over a squirrel, just squashed him right out in front of the house, two hours before the wedding, and just left him there for everyone in town to step in." She shook her head, but not a hair of the elaborate French twist moved. Lily was a disciple of Cherie's Beauty Shop, where most every client emerged with voluminous hair, even though that look had died with Elvis a few years back. Lily's hair was jet black, always had been. Despite the extra height of the arrangement befitting the occasion, Lily was no more than five feet two or so. Everything about her was tiny. Even now with her long white-enameled fingernails, her hands looked liked they belonged to a doll.

Less than two hours before the most important occasion of her life, Lily Mae Alabaster Strong was ready. Wilma could see that she had completed her full makeup regimen, which was regarded in town as a bit overdone. She wore very sheer ice-blue stockings and dyed blue shoes. She had thrown on a red velour zippered robe, which could be traded for her mother-of-the-bride gown at the last moment. Lily began thumbing through Miss Wilma's music and then turned to survey the garden, her eyes darting around to check on each station. She looked back at Wilma and started speaking—"This looks good, oh I love this piece, oh lovely, and make sure you give us a real good and loud fanfare for the bride's march . . ."—but she could not remain still and turned to the garden again, her gaze landing on no object for more than an instant.

"And what are you doing with Cynthia Trolley?" Lily said absently.

Cynthia Trolley was the new voice teacher in Swan's Knob, the apple of everyone's eye since she had gone around telling every ambitious mother in town that her daughter sang like a nightingale or some recent Miss America. They were working on a joint spring recital, and Wilma was tired of her already. "Well, she's going to sing 'O Promise Me,' " Wilma said evenly. An unoriginal choice, but better than some folk song.

"And 'The Lord's Prayer,' of course." Lily watched a thin black man in waiter's clothes come out the back door carrying a tray of champagne glasses. "Careful, Shelton," she yelled as he maneuvered down the flagstone steps. "If you break those, we won't have enough."

"Not that I know of," said Wilma. And she hadn't brought that sheet music either.

Lily turned back to her, puzzled. "Well, we discussed it specifically. It's to go right after the vows. You've got to talk to her, Wilma. Remind her. This is all I need. Another disaster." Lily's eyes came to rest unblinking and wide on Miss Wilma for just a moment before she resumed her survey of the backyard.

"Let's back up here a minute," said Wilma, thumbing through her stack of music to make certain she hadn't brought the piece. "This is the very first I have heard—"

"For God's sake, Shelton, not like that." Lily's head had developed a little tremor, and now she really did look like a china

...ng from a rough toss across the nursery. She marched ...ay across the yard within shouting range of poor Shelton, who had acted on the unfortunate notion that the champagne glasses should be laid out in neat rows. "Lordy, don't you know how this goes? Stack them in a pyramid. This is a wedding. It needs to be decorative." Lily stood with her arms folded on her chest for a moment until she was satisfied that she had been understood and then walked back to Wilma and rolled her eyes. "He was probably the one who ran over the squirrel," she said.

Wilma worked to keep a neutral expression on her face. "Lily, about Cynthia and the—" she said.

"Oh, just get it done, Wilma. You and Cynthia have all the talent in the world, and I know you'll do just fine," said Lily, backing away. "Now it's in your hands, dear. I'm going up to pull my dress over my head and cry over my sweet Martha."

As the red velour robe disappeared into the house, Wilma saw that in Lily's mind Wilma was no different from some magician you found in the phone book for a child's birthday party. Damn Cynthia Trolley. She had a lovely voice, but honestly, where was her professionalism? Last week after some nagging, Wilma had persuaded her to run through "O Promise Me" but she had never mentioned "The Lord's Prayer." She'd just have to talk to her when she arrived. And where was she, by the way? It was nearly noon and the more eager guests would be coming by 12:30. At the opposite edge of the garden, she spotted the top of someone's head just beyond the privet hedge. Thank goodness, she thought, but it turned out to be Clem Baker and not Cynthia who walked in the garden gate. Clem was one of the local police deputies, and he was wearing his uniform, so Wilma guessed that Lily had hired him too—for parking cars or guarding Martha's wedding gifts. Who knew?

Clem was a polite young man, had a clean honest face marred only by a bushy blond mustache that made him look like he might sneeze at any moment. "Morning, Miss Wilma," he said as he mounted the back stairs like he owned the place. Wilma thought for a moment that he was going to barge right on in, but instead he just paused and held the screen door to allow Cynthia Trolley—finally, thank God—to make her way out the back door. She did not look like a woman who was now over forty minutes late for an engagement. She was as unruffled and fresh as one of Lily's floral arrangements.

"Good morning," she said as if she were practicing her enunciation. "Lovely day for a wedding!" She smiled broadly at Wilma and then at Clem, who was still hovering around the back door.

"Good, you're here," said Wilma. "We have a little under an hour until the guests arrive. I've already talked to Lily and there are a few things—"

"Oh, isn't this just lovely," said Cynthia. "Just beautiful."

"She said that you had discussed singing 'The Lord's Prayer.'" Wilma could feel herself flush.

"And the columns with all the flowers all wrapped around them. So romantic . . ."

"Yes, it's real pretty. Now, please, can we . . ."

"Of course, Miss Wilma. I'm sorry. I am such a sucker for romance." Cynthia laid her music down on top of the organ. "Yes, I am going to sing 'The Lord's Prayer,' but I didn't bother you with it because I am going to sing it a capella. So, if you want, I'll just warm up a bit and then we can try 'O Promise Me.' Just give me a C chord to start."

Had Cynthia mentioned this earlier, Wilma might have tried to dissuade her. A little accompaniment didn't hurt anyone, especially outdoors. But as it was, she was glad finally to get the show on the road, so she just turned on the organ and provided the chord. Clem Baker continued to hover for a few moments, which Wilma found vaguely distracting. Cynthia, however, sang without much visible effort, uninhibited by the quiet of the backyard or the bystander. Midway through the scale progression, Wilma saw Lily emerge from the house, now decked out in her full mother-of-the-bride costume—a flowing periwinkle gown with silver sequins covering the low-cut bodice. She floated over to Clem, undoubtedly ready to give him her last-minute instructions as well. Cynthia was finished with her scales now. As Wilma pulled out her well-used copy of "O Promise Me," she saw Lily lay her tiny hand on Clem's chest and cock her head to one side as if asking a question. Clem frowned in response, but followed Lily and her big dress into the house. Lily would terrorize the entire town before the day was concluded.

The audience departed, then, Wilma lost herself in her rehearsal with Cynthia. It went well enough, so that by the time the ushers began to bring in the first guests, Wilma was oddly refreshed and clearheaded and felt the familiar creep of adrenaline as she began her prelude. Between her selections, Wilma enjoyed the parade of guests. The widows first (as usual, since they had time on their hands), all clustered in a pastel-chiffon bouquet, wearing hats like they were visiting the queen of England. The hats must have been Mamie Brown's idea. She was usually the ringleader, and her hat was the most elaborate—peach to match her suit with clusters of roses and even a little veil. It must have been waiting a long time on the top shelf of her closet.

A small line formed at the side of the garden where people waited for ushers to seat them. Henry Lynch, the police chief, waited impatiently for an usher, then followed his wife, Sally, down the aisle, looking uncomfortable out of his uniform. Their friends Clyde and Susie Erath were right behind them. Susie looked just lovely in a blue silk spring dress with a little string of pearls. More and more people began to arrive. Lily had invited a large percentage of the townspeople.

Most of the faces were familiar—women from the church in their Easter outfits, men looking slightly reluctant, as if they might be asked somehow to stand in for the groom. There was Roy Swan, a middle-aged bachelor, looking around to determine what refreshments were planned for the reception, doubtless hungry since there was no one to feed him, even though everyone knew he had more money than God. His family had owned

Swan's Knob itself apparently, going back to the last century. As the last in the family line, he had inherited the whole mountain and Lord knew what else, though he spent most of his time with the Rescue Squad. No one greeted Wilma, of course, since she had a job to do, but people seemed to be enjoying the music. Agnes Blalock, one of her former students who now taught fifth grade, even nodded her head slightly in time with the music as Wilma played "Jesu Joy of Man's Desiring." Of course, Agnes had played a simpler version of the piece, which appeared in the John Thompson Third Book.

Wilma spotted Doris Moody, the Strongs' maid, just as the wedding party was lining up in back. Wilma was sorry she hadn't seen Doris earlier in the day. She was the aunt of James Moody, the very best piano student of Wilma's entire career. When Wilma got the chance, she liked to take a few moments to brag on him, and Doris was at least as proud as she. Doris had worked in the Strongs' house for years, had probably had a big hand in raising Martha. It didn't look like she would be sitting down, though. It was hard to know if that was her choice or Lily's, though Lily really ought to have asked her to sing. Wilma had never heard her, but she knew that Doris helped fill the pews every Sunday at the little AME church that was over near Dobson. James was often her accompanist, said she could take the roof off the church with gospel and Handel alike.

As the last guests were seated, Wilma got the sign from the usher and pulled out her music for the mother of the bride: "A Mighty Fortress is Our God." Wilma had attempted to steer Lily toward something less somber, might have even tried to sneak in Handel's "Entrance of the Queen of Sheba," but Lily had insisted on "A Mighty Fortress" after hearing Wilma play it at a funeral. Wilma began the hymn, and Cynthia joined her at the verse as Lily stepped down the aisle on the arm of a handsome usher. Wilma thought that Cynthia was singing a bit too loudly and she seemed to push the tempo a bit, but Lily was enjoying her walk, her head turning from side to side, acknowledging the crowd like the queen. At the front she stood as if in prayer, her head bowed toward her little altar as the usher removed the white ribbon from her seat with a flourish. It floated briefly in the breeze over the heads of the guests in the front row.

Wilma pulled out her copy of Wagner's *Lohengrin*. Behind her, Cynthia whispered, "Oh my, that little boy is looking green." Wilma saw the skinny groom marching out, barely visible behind Reverend Creech. The poor boy swallowed continuously, his Adam's apple bobbing up and down in his collar. When he made it to the front of the aisle and turned around, Wilma began playing the first section of the bridal march. A chain of the bridesmaids wound up the aisle and filled the front of the veranda, an elaborate statement of lavender. Everything was in place. Wilma paused to reset her stops for the bride's entry. Lily rose slowly and the crowd followed. Wilma had a sudden, mischievous inspiration, an occurrence so rare in her life that she could not resist it. She let forth from her organ an elaborate and ridiculously extended fanfare appropriate at best for Westminster Abbey. A moment later, she thought better of it, but it was too late. Wilma looked out for signs of laughter but was surprised, as she often was, to see that many things are lost on those who think highly of themselves. Lily's chest rose higher with each note, and in the back, her husband, Franklin, took on military bearing. Even poor little Martha seemed to gain height as Doris billowed out the train of her dress, and she and her father stepped down the aisle toward her mother's ultimate triumph.

Wilma played the traditional *Lohengrin* march, as she had a million times before. Father and bride walked nicely toward Lily's altar. Then, without warning, Wilma's organ seemed to shift registers, and underneath the march of triumph she heard the unmistakable tattered rhythm of a music-store snare drum: *Boom chicka boom chicka boom chick-chick*. Wilma scanned the switches on the organ like a pilot whose airplane was going down. Everything looked fine. She tried to increase the volume on the chords of the march, but found that the tin snare played louder still. Mercifully, the bride had reached the altar. Wilma somehow managed the last chords and took her hands from the instrument in humiliation, but the organ, damaged by the insult of transport and a hundred renditions of "The Old Rugged Cross," showed no mercy and continued its song, *Boom chicka boom chicka boom chi*— until Cynthia thought to lean down and turn off the power switch.

It is finished, Wilma thought. She was unable to move for fear of looking out beyond the potted plants to see the piteous expressions on their faces, frozen for fear that somehow she would set it off again.

✑

Roy Swan pushed back the sleeve of his suit and tipped his glass under the nearest stream of pink champagne thrown out by a cupid, feeling silly and oversized as he did so, happy that no other guest was close enough to get splashed. He took a big sip. Though the liquid was still somewhat chilled, he would not call it champagne at this point. For the life of him, Roy could not fathom who might have invented champagne fountains and why. It couldn't have been a European—those people had too much respect for the grape. He felt a certain identification with the wine maker since he dabbled in the area himself. A poor fellow had spent a lifetime perfecting the art of making still waters bubble, then along comes some fool to put it through a mile of plastic tubing and ruin it all.

Roy filled his glass again. It was small, after all. He turned around to see who he might want to talk to and who he might want to avoid. Even though he had no profession to speak of, unless you counted wine making or being a volunteer fireman, people always seemed to want his views on things. He supposed this had to do with his money, though he had not made a dime of it himself. People were standing around close to the area where the chairs had been set up, waiting on something. He wasn't quite sure what. This wedding was not like the ones he usually went to. Those were done in under an hour—fifteen minutes for the church, thirty minutes for punch and nuts, the bride and groom cut the cake and that was the end of it. Here, he saw, there would be more. Little tables dotted the backyard, each one with some kind of food on them. He had seen ice at one, for seafood maybe or fruit, and across the yard he could see a red heat lamp, which meant roast beef for sure.

He was the only one so far who had ventured toward the champagne, which made no sense to him. The crowd over by the chairs started to shift up toward the back veranda. Roy saw that the wedding party had come out and was standing in a line. Right. This was what they did in the fellowship hall usually, where you had to go by and wish everyone well before you had your refreshments. He was glad he had not helped himself to the food yet. Thankfully, a few other men were also ignoring the protocol of greeting the newlyweds and were making a beeline for the champagne fountain.

"What do we have here?" said Clyde Erath, fifth-term mayor of Swan's Knob, tucking his tie into his shirt. "Is this some kind of punch?"

"No, it's champagne, Clyde," said Roy. Clyde had not seen much of the world. "Bubbly."

"I saw you over here, and I thought you might have the right idea," said Clyde. Roy wondered how many other people had noticed him drinking his champagne. He generally considered himself a well-mannered person, but once in a while he would make some error, out of ignorance mostly—that and the lack of a woman in his life to whisper into his ear, someone to give him a little clue about these unfathomable rituals like his mother had when he was growing up. He had to give her credit, she had crammed a lot of manners into twenty-five years. He could negotiate most things just fine, but after all, he was almost sixty, and she had been dead a long time. There was always something new. Her basic theories, though, still applied. She had believed above all in kindness. She knew just what to say to make a person feel good.

If she had been present today, for instance, she would have known what he should say to Wilma Mabry. To him, Wilma had made only the smallest of errors, leaning on the wrong key and making the drums beat during the wedding march. But Roy could tell by the way that her face had gone blank and her neck had flushed red that this little incident had just about killed her. He had watched her instead of the bride during the rest of the service, and as far as he could tell she did not move a muscle the whole time the couple was saying their vows. She didn't even play the organ when the trembly voice teacher sang "The Lord's Prayer." By the end of the service, though, she seemed to get hold of herself a little and played just fine without a single drumbeat as the couple marched out. Roy scanned the crowd for Wilma now. As he did he noticed Chief Henry, out of uniform for once, approaching the champagne table. Henry was the last person he wanted to talk to. He was going to mention that awful July Fourth parade. Roy was never signing up to direct the thing again. Here it was the end of May and he was already sick of hearing from everybody about it. He refilled his glass and moved to the outside edge of the crowd. Some people had finished with the receiving line and were starting to filter out to some of the food tables. He couldn't see Wilma anywhere. Not far away, he spotted the voice teacher, Cindy somebody, but Wilma was not with her. Maybe she had left.

"This stuff isn't half bad," said Clyde, coming up beside Roy and holding his glass in front of his face, "but I'd put your Christmas scuppernong up against it any time."

"Well, thank you, Clyde," said Roy. He was glad to know that someone actually drank his home brew. He gave out a lot of it over the holidays. "But I don't see as there's much to compare. This is light afternoon wedding fare, whereas my wine is a bit heavier and kind of sweet." Clyde was probably not the best judge of wine. His florid face and rotund body made Roy think the old boy didn't turn away much of anything in the way of food or drink.

"Sweet is the word," said Clyde.

"Sweet?" boomed out Chief Henry's voice as he stepped up on the other side of Roy. "You call this champagne sweet? After tasting Roy's scuppernong wine?"

"Naw, Henry, it's Roy's wine we were talking about," said Clyde. He stepped in toward Roy a bit, and Henry did the same, so that they were standing in a little circle, blocking Roy's view. "Lord God, Chief Henry," Clyde said, "what's your man doing here?"

"What?" said Henry, looking around. Roy saw then that Deputy Baker was just behind them, helping himself to the champagne. Roy could not for the life of him figure why Lily would have invited Clem Baker.

"Deputy Baker," said Henry, putting on his chief's voice, "get over here, son."

Clem walked over sipping his champagne like he was born at a garden party.

"Deputy Baker, what are you doing?" Now Henry would put on a show for Roy and Clyde. Roy was in no mood for it or for Clem Baker, the rascal.

"I was invited, Chief," said Clem, gulping a bit now as if he might be booted out in a moment. A bit of foam settled into his mustache. "I had a little job during the ceremony guarding all of the wedding goodies, but now I'm off duty and Lily, Mrs. Strong, told me to enjoy myself. And that's what I'm doing, sir."

"Son, you can't enjoy yourself. You're in uniform. You can't be drinking."

"Listen to your chief, son," said Clyde. "It doesn't look right.

Several people will stop me before this wedding is over and say, 'Clyde, has it got to the point where we have no police force at all? Are they all a bunch of drunks? Do we need to lock our doors in this town?' I've got to answer these questions. I'm the mayor." As far as Roy could tell, Clyde's chief job as mayor was to butt into everybody's business, using his office as an excuse. Other than that, Clyde collected the insurance premiums on the policies that he had sold to everyone in town and played golf. "Roy, I'd think you'd be worrying too. The town's got your name on it, after all."

This was not the first time Roy had heard this. It was his cross to bear, he reckoned, but one of these days he was going to change his name—or the mountain's. "I don't think this is really the place . . ." he started to say, but they ignored him.

"Well now wait a dad burn minute, Clyde. I'm not sure I like that remark about drunk police. I am truly off duty. Look, I'm wearing my seersucker suit. Sally insisted on it, let me tell you, and so if I have to wear this goddamn thing, I'll drink what I want, thank you," said Henry. Roy noticed that Clem had angled away from their little group and was circling back to the champagne. Roy stepped to the left slightly so that he could see around Clyde's big head. Where was Wilma?

"Oh, now, come on, Henry, I was just making a point." Clyde had drained his glass and gathered up Henry's and Roy's so that he could get them all more.

"Well, let me tell you I plum-t deserve a drink after all the carrying on at my house this morning—what tie I was to wear, what socks, for God's sake, and did I like her hair. Should she carry gloves—Sally asks me this, like I know. Roy, old boy, you just don't know how lucky you are."

Roy smiled as best he could. He heard about this great luck of his all the time, always from a married man.

"So tell us the news, Roy," said Clyde, returning with the glasses. "How's the plan for the parade coming? Are you going to let all of us old veterans march on the Fourth?" Clyde and Henry had both served in France. Roy's time in Korea barely registered in their book. Roy thought by now he had seen most of the crowd, and he still could not locate Wilma. He started looking for another way to exit the group.

"Just make sure those Vietnam vets head up the rear," said Henry, leaning in. "Let them wear those worn-out fatigues, whatever, but I don't want to get into it with them this year. Except Clem, of course, he can march with us. He still respects the uniform."

"I'd like to join you," said Clyde, "but as always, I have to ride in a convertible. It's the mayor's job. I'll wear my uniform, how about that?"

"Excuse me, boys. Nature calls," said Roy, and he left them there and headed up toward the house. They were deep enough in not to notice his leaving. Roy was not going to spend the next few months talking about the marching order for the Fourth of July parade. It was 1980, for God's sake, and all the wars were equally over with at this point. As far as he was concerned, they just ought to line up the fire trucks, the Rebel High School marching band and all the pretty girls in town and just let them go on down the street. What else did you need?

On his way into the house, Roy managed to slip into the tail end of the receiving line, hoping to do his duty in short order. Most of the talking was done on Lily's end of the line, with the bride and groom required to do little but smile and shake hands. Lily, who always looked tinier up close, pressed Roy's hand and said, "What do you think of my champagne fountain, Roy? I know you are the wine expert."

"Mighty fine," was all he said. Through the years, Roy had heard many wild rumors about Lily, but it was only recently that he had stumbled upon something that resembled proof of her behavior. Thankfully, there was no way that she could know about that. Even so, it was simply amazing that she could stand up on her porch, mother of the bride, batting her eyes at her guests, not betraying the least glimmer of shame or sadness, not looking pale for a minute about the treacherous path of her life. Surely, as sure as the smile on her face, she had to endure the unsuitable snare drum of her own heart. He did notice when he shook her hand that she had a hard time looking him right in the eye.

At the end of the line, he kept on walking and slipped into the back door of the house. It didn't take him long to find a little bathroom tucked under the front stairway. The room was close quarters for his large frame, and he had to be careful not to knock over one of the shelves of figurines that hung on the wall right by the toilet. He was rinsing his hands when he heard footsteps in the hall, a woman's heels tapping quickly across the wood. He thought he recognized the step and hurried to dry his hands on a tiny gold-trimmed guest towel. By the time he got out of the bathroom and down the hall to the front door, it was too late. He walked out onto the porch and caught only a look at the taillights of Wilma's LTD as it sailed down the driveway. He felt a queer pang of disappointment: he had missed his chance.

Roy headed back down the hall, just in time to see Lily's maid, Doris, herding Deputy Baker toward the front door. "I don't care what she says," she said, taking the champagne glass out of his hand, "you ought not to be here at all." Doris had run the Strongs' house for years, and Roy wondered if someone ought to make her the mayor, because she sure had an effect on the deputy. He fairly well trotted out to his patrol car.

Roy went back to the garden and got himself a roast beef sandwich. He sat down at a table at the far corner of the yard. Now all that was left was to wait for the bride to cut the cake.

He was ashamed to admit it, but as far as Wilma Mabry was concerned, it all came down to pound cake. It was an embarrassing fact that the key to his heart really did turn out to be his stomach, not something a little lower, as he had always imagined. He comforted himself that he was not sweet on Miss Wilma for the *sole* reason of her pound cake. It had led him to her, though. It had all happened at a Wednesday-night potluck at the church. Roy had loaded his plate carefully, a little bit of everything. The women tended to watch what he took, so he just put a little dab of each dish on his plate—that way no one was insulted. Still, they would remark on it, what a wonderful appetite he had, wouldn't he come over for supper sometime—this from Mamie Brown, a plump widow of two years who, lacking eyebrows, drew them on her face with some kind of pencil.

That night, he cleaned his plate and then wandered back up to the end of the table that had the desserts, where Grace Snow insisted on finding him a clean plate, said he couldn't eat dessert on top of fried chicken crumbs. Wilma had been right behind the table, slicing her pound cake in precise wedges. She looked up as he began to survey all of the selections: brownies, Mamie's red velvet cake that tasted like medicine, cookies, banana pudding, Jell-O molds galore. Wilma was not the type to fuss over someone. She was not going to insist on putting a piece of cake on his plate. Roy had known her for years, and he had not thought much about her one way or another, and he did not at this moment, really, he just said, "That looks mighty fine," kind of putting an accent on the end of the sentence, hoping for a bigger piece, truth be told. He lifted his empty plate toward her. She obliged with a nice friendly smile, though he only got one of the standard pieces that she had cut already. Later he thought of it: Mamie Brown would have cut off a quarter of her cake, would have given him a piece that buckled the paper plate. For Wilma, that just was not necessary.

It was not this particular thing, though, that did it. None of this had done one thing to his heart, not in the least. It had started to happen when Roy tasted the cake. That little piece of pound cake tasted, he would swear to it, just like his mother's. The cake was all the good that he had thought was gone from this world, that impossible combination of a sweet crust on the top, a moist yellow inside, and just a hint in the center, the barest hint, of what his mother called a sad streak, a place where the cake had fallen, a dense sweetness where it had failed to rise. He had eaten slowly, collecting the crumbs on his fork. Then he left everything else on his plate and sought her out.

"Miss Wilma," he had said when he found her at the coffee-pot, apart from the other people in the fellowship hall. "I have to tell you that that was the best pound cake I ever put in my mouth." Better, he thought, for a bachelor man not to mention his mother.

Then she just looked at him, looked carefully, though, as if she understood somehow just how good he really meant. It was what she said back that did it finally. She said, "Well, thank you, Roy. You know it's the simple things that I like best. And really, I think they're the hardest things to get right."

When she had said that—Roy could still not explain it—he had felt the hairs on the edge of his scalp—those little hairs on his neck and around his forehead—he felt them stand up straight. It felt so funny that he had to reach up right there in front of her and feel them, try to smooth them down. He heard himself laugh, making a sound that was not quite familiar, and say, "You have got that right, just exactly right."

She smiled slightly, and he saw that she had not detected anything abnormal, hair or otherwise. She went on back to her seat and that was the end of it.

The bride and groom were making their way over to the wedding cake now and people began to gather around the table. From his seat, Roy could still see the top two tiers of the cake above the heads of the crowd, a white skyscraper with two unknowing confections standing on the top. The guests quieted a bit, waiting for the moment, and then Roy heard a mild twittering go through the crowd, gone over to laughter, then to sighs as the couple fed each other, carrying on in a way that was fitting only for the young.

As for Wilma, Roy had taken the past six months to think about it, and no ordinary courtship would do. She was not a woman that he could pursue like a schoolboy, he had seen that immediately. Roy had been sort of arranging things a bit so that he could see her. And when he did—during the church service at the organ or in town, walking to the school—he saw so much more than he had seen before. Roy saw that he liked her bearing, her straight back and even steps, the way that every movement seemed to have a purpose, a divine economy. She was—and he had thought for hours about this word—a handsome woman, not mannish in any way, but possessing a beauty that came from forthrightness. Though others might prefer someone who was not fairly on past fifty, he saw that in her a little age had brought out a subtle skin tone that seemed to him to radiate off her face and hands, those hands that were always moving, strong and supple hands giving way to forearms, to elbows, right on up into her choir robe. He had thought about several oblique approaches to her—town committees, mutual friends, a stupid plan for a Fourth of July celebration—but nothing had seemed exactly right. So he had done nothing about it really. He had gone back to his life of dabbling: tending to his investments, helping out the Rescue Squad, documenting some of the local history. But then, just two weeks ago, quite out of the blue, his little history project had produced a surprising discovery. It was then that it had occurred to him: what he had found was a windfall of fate. If he played it just right, Wilma would see him in a whole different light.

Chapter Two

Of all Miss Wilma's students, James Moody was the prize. He was the proof of her system, proof of the almighty hour of practice each and every day. From age eight, he had pursued his study of the piano with a kind of dog-eyed diligence, eager to do her every bidding. She could see promise in his face—a serious brow, an artistic mouth, burning eyes—and she could tell just by the way that he addressed the piano, James Moody wanted perfection.

When he played, he would raise his elbows and hold his arms away from his torso, as if only his fingers were worthy of approaching the instrument. Some days he worked so hard that Miss Wilma would catch him literally hammering the piano, the sound obliterated by the effort itself. James spent every Tuesday afternoon of his childhood on her bench, though she was never quite sure how his family managed. They were black folks who worked just about the smallest tobacco farm in the county. She would have taught James for less than the others, would have done it for free, but somehow never found a way to make the offer.

In those ten years of preparation, ten years in which her own life changed no more than the ticktock of a metronome, James had taken in every morsel she had to offer, and would on occasion produce a phrase, and increasingly a page or two, that were so close to right that she could swear that she had dreamt it out of him. During this final spring, the time had seemed to Miss Wilma to be all too short and suddenly almost gone. In the week before his audition for a music scholarship to Greensboro College, Miss Wilma worked and reworked James on every measure of the chosen piece. It was Frederic Chopin's Etude Op. 10, No. 12 in C Minor, the "Revolutionary." She forbade James to listen to any records of the piece, but she herself played Rubenstein's version incessantly in her living room and in her sleep. She used each practice to rid James of any unclean thought or misconceived movement. She reviewed with James in a frenzy the correct position of the bench, its distance from the keyboard, the weight on the foot pedal, the angle of the wrist.

She could remember this very confidence that she could see in James Moody—it had visited her during her own youth. It had been conceived in her fingers as they learned to dance across the keys and to make the music that poured out note by note as graceful and true as the composer meant them. Confidence had grown in her, threatened to unravel the soft strands of the cashmere sweaters that her mother knit dreaming only of a nice husband for her daughter. In the practice hall at college, she practiced hour after hour as a quiet ambition crept up and rode her back. She felt there the presence of future audiences, baffles for her grand instrument that rang out across the world, across the ages grander and more potent than any idea that her father posed in a lifetime of botany lectures.

So Wilma understood James Moody's strength. She knew what he was after. As he inched toward her ideal, she allowed herself a loud scratchy voice and brusque movement in their sessions. She strode around the room, pacing the beat and shouting until the child waiting for the next lesson time ran from her front stoop.

On this last Tuesday, the day of his audition, there was to be no lesson for James, but Miss Wilma prepared carefully for the final run-through. She had chosen to meet James on the stage of the elementary school auditorium. Though it was not the big concert hall that she had always imagined for herself, the auditorium had been her domain for many years. She had lessons during the school week for the young ones on the stage, and each spring she held her student recital there, filling the place with every parent in town. Miss Wilma used her key to unlock the back door and walked down the aisle, the dark wood releasing its scent to her footstep. She was ten minutes early, and had forgotten to bring the sheet music for Sunday's choir anthem to occupy her time. She was forced, then, to do nothing more than choose a creaky seat in the second row and wait.

Miss Wilma had scheduled this last session in the auditorium, hoping for inspiration in the hall's high pressed-tin ceiling, its faded stage curtains, and in the wonderful resonance that sound produced on its walls. She was hoping that in all this near grandeur James would be filled up and overflowing with the beauty of the music and with a sense of anticipation about the performances in his life to come. But as she sat without so much as a scrap of paper to doodle on, she was struck suddenly with the airless silence of the place. In two minutes, she was as fidgety as a first-grader and longing for any sound, even the relentless bass line of "Prince Polliwog's Dance," a piece she assigned each year to the student with the most plodding fingers. There were men and women all over Swan's Knob with "Prince Polliwog" sheet music in their piano benches, some of them now quite successful.

Those who escaped "Prince Polliwog," those who happily played Mozart or Brahms—there must be hundreds by now— even those would still have their scale books. Miss Wilma issued every student a cardboard score-lined scale book at the first lesson. She kept a supply on hand, fifty cents apiece, ordered from Strains Music in Winston. She began that first lesson by penciling in the notes of the C scale. She added a scale every week, major, then minor, then on to standard chords—first, third and tonic—

lesson by lesson over and over, child after child, year after year. She wondered if her old students thought of her still when they heard a Bach Invention on the radio or sang a hymn in church. Maybe for them she lived solely within the moldering pages of the scale books, tucked away in a piano bench. She wondered if they remembered anything about her, anything at all beyond the marks she made across their sheet music, if anyone in town could actually think of her in her kitchen fixing breakfast. "Here comes Miss Wilma, the piano teacher" or "There goes the organist for our church," they would say, and never "Good morning, Mrs. Mabry," as would be proper.

Just then, thankfully, James Moody wandered down the aisle. She noticed that he had grown taller recently and seemed embarrassed by it. He had his head and neck hunched down on his shoulders. One look at him and Miss Wilma feared that she had chosen their meeting place unwisely. Perhaps he too was feeling the silence of the place, and maybe the accumulated terror of a decade of recitals. She saw immediately that it was her job, just three hours before his audition, to abolish all of his misgivings, to inspire him, if she could. She launched herself out into the aisle, snapping the seat up against the back. She snatched the music from James's hands and dramatically ushered him to his place at the piano.

"Remember what I've told you about this etude and the master who wrote it," she said. "Imagine him, James, imagine him creating this piece, composing his 'Revolutionary,' as his beloved Warsaw burned. Now, play this piece with your hands and with your heart. Play as if your own home is gone forever—and you live now only in the music."

He began. Miss Wilma sat back down and allowed herself for the first time to hear the whole of what she had wrought. The piano, a baby grand Steinway purchased by the school five years ago in an auction, had been tuned just last week, and in James's capable hands music soared from its open lid. The sound was to her a glory, a manifestation of her ear, a reflection of her sense of the world. She felt for just one moment that some part of her might burst into a million pieces and fly off with that music.

Halfway through the second page of the piece, James began a passage of chords marked *con forza* that had given them months of difficulties. The notes were altogether correct, but when she heard them, something changed and Miss Wilma found herself in terror, as if she were in one of those dreams where she was standing naked in the middle of a party without a proper invitation. She began to hear what the jury would hear at James's audition— too slow here, an awkward phrase—tiny faults, but was it at all good enough?

It was everything as they had practiced, yet somehow each measure of notes began to accumulate like lead in Wilma's chest. She looked down at her own fingers—neatly clipped nails, wedding ring from her dead husband. They were just beginning to curl with age. James played on. It was too late, too late to make any correction, too late to tell him that it was entirely possible that his ambition might not get him farther than the next county, too late to warn him that no one, almost no one, was ever allowed on a real stage, too late to tell him that maybe the best he could ask for would be a teaching career with one brilliant, transcendent student. One great student to send on his way.

He finished the piece, gracefully removed his hands from the keyboard and folded them in his lap. His torso was perfectly straight now, his head erect, waiting. Miss Wilma wondered with her new loss of faith what she would say. She pictured him, years hence, with his shoulders permanently hunched over a tractor wheel, humming Chopin's melody as he rolled home to supper. She stood and jerked herself out to the aisle and up to the stage, swinging his sheet music. She saw on the face of this boy the expectation of all his years with her: "Now. Now," it said, "praise me. I have done what you've asked, and it was never, never good enough until today and now you praise me."

In that moment, she could not. She looked down at the tattered sheet music. It was soiled with the sweat of a thousand practice sessions and covered with ugly pencil marks, annotations she had made in a year of lessons.

"We have time," she said, "if we hurry, to get a clean copy of this music so that your judges won't see this mess. If you'll come on to my house, I'll get it for you." She closed the tattered pages and put them under her arm. By the time she looked back up at him, all of the expectation was gone from his face. She could not recognize the look that had replaced it.

James Moody did not take her up on her offer, and it was just as well, since when Miss Wilma got home, there they were, the two of them. They were sitting on her front steps, like they had been out for a short walk and thought they'd stop for a rest on the stoop. Her house could have been a public building, whatever. They didn't look like they were waiting for anyone in particular. Neither stood up or waved as she pulled into the driveway. It had been close to three years since Wilma had seen her daughter, Sarah, and her little granddaughter, Starling, even though they talked on the phone every month or so. Now, here they were. Wilma tried to get a good look as she climbed out of the car. Since she had reached her thirties, Sarah looked more like an adult, even though she was thin as a reed and still dressed like someone in college—frayed blue jeans, a Mexican shirt with little dolls embroidered across the front, silver rings on every finger and an arm full of bangles that clanked together as she pushed her long straw-colored hair behind her ears. She smiled faintly as Wilma came up the walk.

It was Starling who had sense enough to get up and hug Wilma. Starling was her given name (better than Sparrow, Wilma supposed). Even though she was not much over ten, Starling was approaching puberty. The local girls her age looked younger, but they were wearing smart khaki slacks and polo

shirts these days, while Starling was stuck with her mother's bohemian tendencies. She had the hips to hold up her peasant
skirt, though, and she would soon need to be wearing a bra
under that T-shirt—though judging from her mother's appearance that would not be a priority.

"Well, surprise, Mother," said Sarah without enthusiasm.

"My goodness, when did you get here?" said Wilma. "Is everything all right?"

"We just got in on the bus," said Sarah, standing finally, accepting Wilma's hug.

"The two of you?" said Wilma, noticing finally that Harper
had not come with them. "You took the bus by yourselves? All
the way from New Mexico? Wasn't that awful, didn't it take
days?"

Sarah laughed at Wilma like she was a confused child. "We
were fine, Mother, really. Who would bother us?" she said, gathering up their collection of bags—literally bags, Wilma saw, not
the blue Samsonite with the matching train case Sarah had received for high school graduation, but the kind of things you'd
find at an Indian store—woven blankets made into valises,
painted straw satchels, a fringed pocketbook.

"Well, come on in," Wilma said, putting her arm around Starling. Her hair was braided down the back in the same way that
Wilma had once done Sarah's, except the end was tied with a
rawhide strap trimmed with feathers. "I'm so glad you're here. It's
such a delightful surprise."

Wilma picked up the straw satchels and walked with Starling
into the house, with Sarah bringing up the rear with the rest of the
bags. Starling put her hand out and rested it on Wilma's forearm,
the way an old friend might, and said quietly, "We couldn't call
before we came, Nana. Mom said if you knew, you wouldn't let
us come on the bus, but it really wasn't all that bad except for a
few guys snoring last night and gross food."

"Well, let me fix you something, honey. What would you like?

I don't keep much food in the house since it's just me. How about some patty sausage and eggs?"

"Sausage, yuck, Nana. Just an egg burrito."

"Burrito?" said Wilma. "Honey, how about some toast?" The poor child had been out in Santa Fe, New Mexico, for most of her life, influenced by every culture but her own. Sarah taught children in a little private school, while her husband Harper was busy collecting the songs of the Indians. He had anthropology training along with his degree in music and had spent over five years on this project. It was sponsored by the Smithsonian Institution, but Wilma had a time explaining this to anyone in Swan's Knob.

Sarah and Starling started in on the toast before Wilma could finish scrambling the eggs, both of them buttering an entire bread slice and eating it without bothering to cut it in two. Wilma stirred a few more eggs and stood watching them out of the corner of her eye. Sarah herself looked a little peaked. She had inherited the dark circles under her eyes from Wilma, an unfortunate legacy, but Wilma thought Sarah's circles looked a little darker than usual. Wilma put the scrambled eggs on their plates.

"So you've finished the school year, I take it?" she said, aiming for a tone that did not sound nosy.

"Yes," said Sarah. "We start the year in mid-August, so we're done a little early. How about you? Did we get here in time for the big recital?"

"It's on Sunday night," said Wilma, "and I still have some music to rehearse before the Sunday service, so I'm afraid I won't be a very good hostess for a few days. That is, if you're going to be around."

"Well, I thought we would stay a few days. It's been a while since we were here," said Sarah, carefully.

"That's great. I'm glad you could come, really," said Wilma, pretending that this was all completely normal, Sarah and Starling traveling across the country to her doorstep unannounced. Wilma had learned during Sarah's adolescence that it just didn't pay to ask the obvious right up front. Sarah got her secretiveness from her father, who would always clam up if you cornered him in any way. He would pretend that Wilma was overwrought, when all she wanted to do was ask simple questions like, "Where have you been? How much did you drink? What happened to you?"

Wilma had learned over the years to disguise burning questions as small talk. It mostly had to do with your tone of voice. "It's good to see you," she said. "And Harper, how's he getting along? I suppose he had to stay behind and work," wondering if this was at all possible.

Sarah stared at Wilma suddenly over Starling's head, with her little deer look. Bingo, Wilma thought.

"I guess. Yes," Sarah said, coloring just the slightest bit around her temples.

"I see. Would you like more toast?" Wilma said. Sarah had left him, left him and come home. Lord knows what he had finally done. Wilma did not want to know. That explained it though. That explained why Sarah was not saying anything about their coming out so unexpectedly. Who could talk about a man in front of his own child? Most likely, Starling had not been told.

"Well, the two of you stay as long as you like," she said over Starling's head, catching Sarah's eye, trying to convey all of her understanding. She spent the remainder of their short meal in silence, signaling her trust and sympathy. This was not easy with Sarah in such sudden and close proximity, so Wilma tried to think of her as a cherished student—like James Moody, seated now at a piano in a recital hall down in Greensboro. Children ended up out in the world, that was all there was to it. Once a child raised her hands to the keyboard and began that first measure, there was nothing more to be done, even if every note was wrong.

She suppressed a sigh and ordered Starling to follow her

upstairs, where she busied herself with their rooms. She threw open the windows to accomplish a day's airing in an hour, destroyed the order of the linen closet, snapped sheets, hung out towels and prodded Starling to get ready for bed. She could tell from Starling's bag that Sarah had surely packed in haste, or perhaps had left Starling to do it. Starling seemed embarrassed when Wilma began going through it to find her pajamas, so Wilma abandoned the search and pulled out one of her own gowns. When Starling pulled the pink chemise over her head, Wilma could see that it wasn't much too big for her. She had grown up so much since Wilma had last seen her. She wondered if she was keeping up with her piano.

Sarah, to Wilma's eternal dismay, had been an indifferent piano student. Her interest had peaked at the end of fifth grade when Wilma had given her a fairly advanced and showy recital piece, "Wedding of the Winds." Sarah had learned it beautifully, but when it came time to play the piece in the spring recital, she had rushed through the final section like a mad elephant through grass. Wilma had scolded her afterward in the wings of the stage. That had been a mistake, because from then on Sarah had complained over every piece of music that Wilma set in front of her. She spent her lesson time riding the pedals, galloping through the music like she was trying to win a race. She practiced less and less, and seemed unaffected by Wilma's nagging. Even her father's quiet admonitions were of little influence. By high school, she was embarrassingly less accomplished than her peers, unschooled really in classical music, given to playing boogie-woogie when she did finally sit down at the piano.

Harry had told Wilma, "Let it go, hon. She's moved on to other things." She hadn't listened to him, because he had been in bad shape by then, half lit up most of the time, so what did he know? Wilma fought another sigh as she tucked Starling into bed and smoothed her shining hair that was the color of summer wheat, just like her mother's. There had been a lot of unpleasantness in those days. "Live and learn, doll. Live and learn. Move on." That was the kind of thing that Harry would say now, if he could. It was his way of being sensible about everyone's life but his own.

∽

Now that she had left the high desert and come home, Sarah could feel all the parched tissues in her body slowly absorbing the moisture that lurked in the mountain air and in the soil, and she felt for the first time in weeks like a being that belonged on the earth, the subject of gravity. It was a silly notion, but she had been nearly weightless for weeks, wandering around the house at night, riffling through piles of magazines and clothes, intending to sort through them, intending to straighten things out, but losing interest in her task midstream, lying exhausted on the cluttered couch and waking up to a bigger mess than ever.

Here in her mother's kitchen, there was not one speck of dust and there was the blessing of order, an order that Sarah could not for the life of her create in her own home, though she had been witness to this order and its maker for her whole childhood. Somehow it was beyond her. In this house, she knew that every little thing was in its place, that there was a process, a sameness to the way that her mother did everything. Just now, Sarah could hear her upstairs getting ready for bed, every step in sequence, every movement the same, from the first button on her gown to the half teaspoon of lotion she rubbed on her hands before she turned out the light. A lovely simple clockwork.

Of course, this safety, this normalcy was what had driven her crazy during her last year in high school. Her dad had been gone by then, escaped, she used to think of it, permanently excused from the dinner table. Though he must have been terribly unhappy to do what he did finally, she remembered him as someone who could always lighten things up, sneak up behind her mother, goose her bottom and make her squeal "Harry, honestly!" in mock anger. He would blow into the front door some nights without warning and yell, "Put on your shoes, girls, we're going out to dinner." After he died, they did not go out. Wilma made their meals on a strict schedule from a set of ten menus that never varied, except that on occasion, when Sarah complained loudly enough, canned peaches were substituted for fruit cocktail, meat loaf for baked pork chops.

In those days, Sarah would come in from her dates to find Wilma waiting for her, sitting at this kitchen table, teacup to one side, sheet music in front. One night, half drunk and mussed up from a night parking out at the Ararat River with Greggie Cranford, Sarah snuck up to the back door quietly, hoping that her mother had gone on to bed for the first time ever, sparing her the once-over and the post-date chat. All the lights in the kitchen were blazing, but when she looked through the window over the sink, she saw her mother slumped over the table with her head canted unnaturally to one side. Sarah could still remember the immense fear that gripped her ever so briefly until the rattle of the door awakened her mother.

And it was still a comfort, and a mortal pain in the ass, Sarah thought, to have someone to wait up for you. She could hear her mother's slippered steps to the bathroom now, the water running for a time, the door opening, the light over the sink turned out, more steps down the hall to check on the child, Starling this time, more steps (lighter now) to Sarah's room. A pause as Wilma wondered when Sarah would come to bed. Sarah was just sitting there, experiencing an odd childlike happiness when she heard her mother coming down the stairs. And boom, just like that, she felt that old irritation, that adolescent leave-me-alone creep up the back of her neck. She fought this feeling—she had just arrived, she hated to start the bickering. She braced herself—if only, if only Wilma wouldn't ask her anything else, if only she could skip the once-over again. Her mother came into the room nonchalantly, and then faked a look of surprise when she saw Sarah still sitting at the table.

"Why, I thought you were in bed," she said. "I was coming down for a little glass of water."

There was a stack of Dixie cups in the bathroom upstairs, so this was a little lie. But instead of prickling her, this pretense somehow washed away all of Sarah's irritation. Wilma's face was smooth with a careful innocence except for a tiny set of furrows across her forehead. Sarah had those same wrinkles. And she knew the feeling, she had it every time she let Starling go off with her friends at the state fair. More than once she had found herself lurking behind her child, watching her buy candy apples from a dirty vendor van. Even now she held her breath when Starling crossed a street, though she had long ago learned to look both ways. This was what you did for your child—you held your breath even as you let her go out there—this was how you loved her, how you willed her to be safe, to make her way in the world without falling down and getting even a little bit hurt. She could see all of this now on her mother's face, and as if knowing, Wilma put her hand up across her brow to rub out the signs. Sarah thought she saw her mother's jaw quiver slightly, as if she wanted to speak but stopped the words by sheer force of will. Her mother was holding her breath, not quite sure even what manner of danger her child was in. Instead of busting wide open and asking Sarah what was wrong, she simply took a deep breath and said, "Is there anything I can get you, honey? Anything at all?"

"No, but it sure is nice to be home," Sarah said finally, meaning it for once and wondering when she might tell Wilma the rest.

⁂

Wilma made tea and Sarah at least let her put it down in front of her. She shuffled around the room a while longer and saw finally that Sarah had discarded her espadrilles under the table, tucked her feet up in the chair, and taken a few sips. On the phone over the past year or so, their conversations had grown rather thin and careful. It seemed that most any of the town news that Wilma related irritated Sarah in some way. Now that she was here, Wilma wondered suddenly what they could safely discuss. She put a few shortbread cookies on a plate and put it on the table. Then she started the dishes.

Sarah looked at her absently and said, "Don't worry about us, Mother, we're family, no need to be our little hostess." She gave a quick laugh when she said the word "hostess," a light sound that stayed mostly in her throat.

Wilma tried to think of just what Sarah meant by that: our little hostess. All she had done was put a few cookies on the table. Why was that the kind of thing to make a clever remark about? Wilma had put on an apron when she had come into the kitchen earlier, maybe that was it. The apron was just a plain little check, nothing fussy, nothing like some that she had seen with appliquéd fruit or rows of lace.

"Well, we have to eat," said Wilma, "then I do have dishes to do unless you want to eat on paper plates. I put on this apron most every day, you know."

Sarah laughed again and said, "Mother, I only meant sit down, relax."

"You're the one that must be tired," said Wilma, hanging her apron in the broom closet. "Did you have to walk to the house with your bags after coming all that way on a bus? It still lets off in front of the dimestore, doesn't it?"

"Yes," said Sarah, "we were going to walk, but Clara Stone saw us from her counter and offered to give us a ride home."

"Well, that was nice of her," said Wilma. Clara saw and heard just about everything in town from behind her cash register. "And what did she have to say?"

"Mostly she wanted to know about us, about living in Santa Fe," said Sarah. "Wanted to know what it was like to live 'amongst the Indians,' if you can believe it." She used that same half laugh again. It was dismissive, like Clara was so stupid that it was hardly worthy of a whole laugh. Sarah went on: "I answered her as best I could, trying hard not to shock her with any real knowledge of the outside world. Then she caught me up on all the news about Wanda. She was in the class behind me, remember?"

"Oh, yes," said Wilma, getting up to put water on for more tea. Wanda Stone had beautiful long fingers and a romantic flair. What had been her senior recital piece?

"Well," said Sarah, "it seems that Wanda has gotten herself in a bit of trouble, moving to Atlanta, marrying the wrong man. Now she's home waiting for her divorce to come through."

"That's right, she came back around Easter. I've seen her up at the dimestore." It had been Debussy, a tricky prelude with lots of triplets in the left hand against right-handed couplets. "She's apparently had quite a hard time of it. There are all kinds of rumors—affairs, an abortion, some kind of run-in with neighbors in Atlanta. But I must say, she doesn't look any worse for wear," said Wilma, trying to sound worldly.

" 'No worse for wear,' huh?" said Sarah, and here came the laugh again.

"For someone like poor Wanda, this is a traumatic turn of events," said Wilma.

"Well, sure, now that she's back here," said Sarah, "working at the country club pro shop, making change for the coke machine, selling golf balls. Definitely traumatic. Wasn't she some kind of golf pro in Atlanta?"

"I think so. I hear she's a good golfer. Well, I am sure there are some ladies here in town who could use a good golf clinic. Besides, honey, her mother is here. Lots of people prefer to live near their families, close to where they have grown up," said Wilma. The kettle was beginning to make noise, and Wilma got up and walked toward the stove. "There are opportunities in this area, plenty of things she can do."

"Bullshit," she heard Sarah say behind her, just loud enough so there was no mistaking. Wilma pulled the kettle off the burner.

When she turned around, Sarah was almost smiling at her, and Wilma understood that Sarah had not meant for her to hear the word at all: bullshit. *Harry,* she said (silently, as one speaks to the dead). *Harry* (calling him as she did ten times a day), *I am going to take your advice.* She said, "I am really happy you and Starling are here, whatever the reason."

"Do I need a reason?" said Sarah softly.

"No, you do not," said Wilma, wondering why nonetheless. "I am just surprised, that's all. What if you'd gotten here and I was off on a trip? What would you have done then?"

"A trip right before the spring recital?" said Sarah, arching an eyebrow.

"Well, maybe not," said Wilma, "but if I had known you were coming I could have at least stocked up on burritos." She smiled to signal that she had made a little joke, but Sarah did not laugh as she would have if Harry had said such a thing. Harry could always produce a wisecrack that would diffuse the darkest tragedy. In these fifteen years since he had been gone, they could have used some wisecracks, she and Sarah.

"That sums up the reason that I didn't let you know I was coming," said Sarah, raising her voice to sound just like the schoolteacher she was. "You always make such a production of things—aprons, luggage, bedclothes." She tapped on the table-top, as if typing additional grievances too numerous to list aloud. "It's just too much, Mother."

Wilma wanted to arch her own eyebrow. So they were back to the apron now, and all puffed up about it. All this in an effort to disguise the real reason Sarah had come running the whole way back home.

It was late in the week before it occurred to Miss Wilma that she had heard not a word from James Moody. She had been busy rehearsing her other students for the recital and rushing home to make dinner for Sarah and Starling. For the most part, the two of them had been content to stay at the house. Starling seemed to enjoy playing alone in the back garden. Sarah was even less talkative than the night she arrived. She spent most of her time sleeping. Wilma found herself wishing that she was the kind of woman who could take to *her* bed over some minor incident, suffering until someone would coax *her* downstairs. In the end, though, she really didn't have the patience for it. Instead, she just banged around the kitchen wondering why James had not thought to call her, why at least his mother had not picked up the phone, though in truth she was not the type for such a courtesy.

Throughout the years of James's lessons, Wilma had seen Cheryl Moody at each of the spring recitals, but otherwise only a few other times when she came to pick up James in her husband's truck. She was a rather expressionless woman, tired looking. It was amazing to Wilma that the woman had produced such an energetic son. James practiced relentlessly and arrived at lessons ready to take on the world. Was it possible that James's ambition was all his own? As far as her music was concerned, Wilma had tended to her own little flame of ambition at James's age. Her mother had not discouraged her. She wanted things for her daughter: She wanted her to have an education that would provide the proper sort of finish on a girl, wanted to make sure that Wilma knew how to be a proper hostess, how to fix her hair—each talent, of course, aimed at the pursuit of a suitable husband. In this context, then, a certain musical ability was a pleasing trait.

On the other hand, Wilma's father was a man made practical by decades of teaching botany. He was opposed to encouraging pipe dreams in children, which meant that he would have dismissed any notion of a concert career. Better to have a trade to fall back on than to waste time cultivating meager talent. Her father made it clear that Wilma needed to think about finding some steady means of support—like teaching. In those days, teaching and just a few other jobs were reserved for young women to "fall back on," which was what you did if you wound up unmarried, you fell back. She saw now that her father had little faith in her abilities: to play a piano, attract a husband, choose her own life. Still, she had quietly labored at Guilford College, quietly hoped, and, she thought, received encouragement from her professors.

She had in fact performed as a piano soloist at the Eastern Music Festival, just before her senior year. She had played well and was so pleased with herself and even felt pretty in the strapless blue gown that her mother had sewn. Afterward, at the back of the hall, she saw her parents standing with her teacher, all of them smiling with pride, all of them knowing at last what she had become, a concert pianist, a performer with a promising future. Her teacher turned to her father as she approached them. "She will make a fine piano teacher," he said, loud enough so that she knew he meant for her to hear. No compliment had ever fallen further from its mark. She thought for a moment that she would cry like a child and ruin the front of her dress. Then, already well bred, she recovered. Her professor was correct, of course. A concert career was one in a million. Even Harry had said this to her several times over the years. Still, she might have had some minor success with regional orchestras. She might have gone on a bit.

Perhaps she was just being a snob, or maybe even a bit prejudiced, to notice Cheryl Moody's thin housedress, the old pickup, and to think that James Moody did not have people who wanted the best for him. Maybe they, like her father, were just a little wary of James dreaming too many dreams for himself. Even so, she could not help but hope beyond hope on his behalf and she could not help but worry about that scholarship jury. Maybe he simply hadn't heard any news yet. Maybe he just didn't want to tell her that he had been turned down. Surely not. She would not even think about that. She could not bear to think that his performance in the recital on Sunday would be his swan song.

She had just put away the last dish from the dinner she had

made for Starling and herself when Sarah drifted down the stairs. She looked positively transparent to Wilma, her skin so pale you could see every little vein on her face. She didn't speak as she came into the room, but went straight to the refrigerator, a habit that Wilma remembered from her adolescence. She waited until she had the door open and her head half buried inside before she said, "Harper called this morning. He's on his way."

As far as Wilma could remember, it was the first time in four days that Sarah had mentioned his name. Wilma did not know what to think. Maybe she had read too much into the situation, maybe she should have asked to begin with, maybe he was expected the whole time.

"Oh, fine," Wilma said, "he will be along after all. When will he get here?"

"I'm not sure," said Sarah. "Sometime in the night. Just leave the door unlocked."

Wilma fought her irritation. She was dead tired, but who could sleep with the porch light on and the front door unlatched?

When she finally lay in her bed, Wilma was at least grateful that she had something to stew about other than poor little James's outcome. Of course, arriving at her house in the middle of the night was the kind of thing that her son-in-law did routinely. Harper made it a private mission, it seemed to her, to break with convention, happy to disarm those around him. Harper and Sarah had been married ten years now. Their wedding—if you could call it that—was just six months before Starling's birth. Everyone in Swan's Knob knew this, of course. It was exactly the kind of arithmetic that was popular in a small town. No one had said much to her at the time, apart from a few muted attempts at sympathy from one or two women in the church choir. To Wilma, premarital sex was not altogether appalling, but she had just always had the nagging sense that the pregnancy had somehow rushed Sarah through the best part of her life. She reminded herself that Harper was not all bad.

He had the kind of charm that worked on just about everyone at first, although Miss Wilma figured that his apparently overwhelming sex appeal was reserved for those of another generation. Harper was no taller than the average woman really, though she had to admit he had a beautiful, soul-searching kind of face dominated by those deep-set dark eyes. She supposed he still fancied himself the sensuous jazz-musician type since he covered up the rest of his face with a thick beard and mustache. Wilma had hated beards and most any other form of hair on men ever since she was compelled to trim up her father's beard during the few years between her mother's death and his own. She associated beards with the sickly sweet smell of pipe tobacco that always lingered around her father.

Thank God the trend for facial hair and pipes had skipped a generation or two. Her Harry's cheek had been smooth even at midnight, as smooth as if he had just dried his face from a shave. She rearranged her covers a bit and propped her head against the pillow. She let her mind dwell on Harry then, tried to hold on to the thought of his smooth cheek, the sway of their bodies together as they danced. She tried to hear Artie Shaw's orchestra play "Our Love is Here to Stay," to remember the feeling of his hand on her back, breathe in the scent of his sandalwood shaving soap, hear just the cadence of his breath, and then, to think no further than that, to drift off to where he was waiting.

It was no use. She could not conjure him when she was compelled to listen to every car in the street, when she wondered again what kind of idiot would come all the way from New Mexico and time the whole thing so that he was driving over the Blue Ridge in the dead of night.

Strangely, the traffic on the street seemed to pick up—Miss Wilma wondered if she was just imagining that it did. Still, even on Main Street there were usually few people out past midnight.

Then she heard the siren. It was because Wilma considered her-self a thoroughly sensible woman, because she had not in her life given over to hysteria or fantasy, that she could not ignore the overwhelming premonition that occurred to her the second she heard the sound. The siren told her: Harper was dead. Dread in her heart, she got up and looked out the window, but she couldn't see anything. She put on her housecoat and ran downstairs and out the front door, pausing to turn off the porch light in case Larry Welks next door had also been awakened. By the time she got down to the sidewalk, though, she felt a bit silly. She was bare-foot and had not bothered to button her housecoat. She tiptoed to the curb and craned out to look down the street toward town. She could see as far as the library. It was quiet again. She was get-ting to be a foolish old woman, she thought, borrowing the trou-bles of the whole town. Harper was probably drinking with truck drivers in Knoxville, and surely one of the town's four policemen— Clem Baker, probably—had set off his siren by accident. He would have hell to pay if he woke up Clyde Erath or anyone else on the council, but Miss Wilma would not be the old biddy who made the complaint. The things that run through a middle-aged woman's mind in the dark. Foolish.

Her feet were getting cold, and she had turned to go back in when she saw the blue light of the hearse. It rolled down the street in the quiet, rolled right up to the block without a sound. It passed her in slow motion, so that she could see the polished black paint, the gleaming trim. She could make out Ronald Snow inside with his son Ronny, both of them sitting up straight and of-ficial, not saying a word. The hearse passed on down the street and into the night. She began to shiver. Harper had never been a good driver. He had been so close, they would say, so close to his destination. She hurried up the steps and into her den to call Grace Snow. The Snows ran the funeral home. Their hearse dou-bled as the town's ambulance. There would be no one to answer at the police station and surely no one would recognize Harper or his car. Grace could tell her what happened. She dialed. Grace was asleep, of course, but being the wife of a man who tended to all of the dead and dying in town, she was accustomed to late-night calls.

"Hello?" she said with a croak. "Hello?" more plainly.

"Grace, it's Wilma Mabry. I'm afraid it's my son-in-law, Harper. He was driving from New Mexico, and I wonder if there's been a wreck. I saw Ron and Ronny go by in the hearse, I just wondered," Wilma said.

"Where did your son-in-law wreck, Miss Wilma?"

"Well, I'm not sure. That's why I called you. I heard the sirens."

Grace sounded confused. "Is this on top of the shooting tonight?"

"I don't know. That's why I was calling you. I thought maybe you knew. But you say a shooting, Grace?"

"Yes, dearie. A policeman shot. Ron just got a call a few minutes ago. He didn't know if they needed an ambulance or a hearse, so he took Ronny and called the Rescue Squad too."

"You don't know about any wreck?"

"No, honey, I haven't heard a thing about it. Those sirens weren't for you. It was Clem Baker, honey, something awful's happened up on the bypass."

"No," said Wilma. "Oh, no, surely not." She pictured instantly Clem's jaunty walk up Lily's back steps, his nice "good morning." "Is he all right?"

"I don't have a single detail. Ron just pulled on his pants and left after the call." Grace was fully awake now. "Wilma, I knew your daughter and Starling were back in town, but I didn't know that your son-in-law had joined them. He's not been home yet tonight?"

"He's just *arriving* tonight, Grace," Miss Wilma said as pointedly as she could. She made her apologies and got off the phone, feeling flush on her neck and face. Borrowed trouble. Poor Clem

Baker. She hoped he was okay, and she wished to goodness that she had thought to wait a few minutes before awakening the most talkative woman in town. It was not so much that Grace talked too much, it was that no detail about the dead or their kin was too sordid for her to discuss with her friends. Ron was a second-generation undertaker and the soul of discretion, but Grace was known to tell most of what she knew. Not many people liked to eat with Grace—you never knew when you might hear about some swollen corpse.

Wilma went back to her bed. She must have somehow got to sleep because when she heard Harper at the front door, it was getting light already. She blamed him for it all. She blamed him for still being her son-in-law, for her near-sleepless night and for her foolishness on the telephone. As he woke up her daughter in the next room with a lascivious laugh and several loud kisses, she wondered if, in the end, a wreck would have been altogether as tragic as she imagined. Wilma prayed that Starling would not wake up to hear the muffled thumps and creaks now coming from her parents' room. Or maybe this was all as common as a lullaby to her. Miss Wilma wanted to jump from her bed and clomp around the house so that she could not hear their noises, but she was afraid that her movement would only acknowledge what she could hear, then Harper was sure to mention it later in the day, just to get a rise out of her. She lay quietly. In her head, she played Chopin's "Revolutionary Etude" loudly and a bit faster than necessary.

Chapter Three

Onstage, twelve-year-old girls were twirling parasols and singing "I'm Just a Girl Who Can't Say No" at the beginning of hour three of Miss Wilma's annual spring piano recital, lengthened this year since she had combined forces with the new voice teacher. It seemed to Harper that the event was attended by every soul in Swan's Knob, with at least fifty percent compelled to suffer the entire ordeal, having one or more child under the tutelage of Miss Wilma's mighty hand. The women in the audience were gently nodding their heads and smiling up at the grinning girls in silly hats on the stage. It was getting hot in the auditorium, and Harper could see that most of the men were sleeping, trusting their wives to wake them for their own children's performances.

The irony of the lyrics and the lilting innocence of those who sang was lost on the crowd. Harper wanted to crow and double over with laughter as the pubescent girls bounced around the stage—"a terrible fix," indeed. He wondered what the daddies here would do if they found their little girls saying, "Come on, let's go." He looked over at Sarah to see if the scenario struck her as funny, but she nodded her head along with the rest. He could see through the windows that the sun was getting low, with light filtering through the new green leaves of old trees outside. He loved the otherworldliness of the dry, sun-colored New Mexico landscape, but he realized now that he had never stopped missing the trees. In front of him, seated by the windows, another person stared out. The light shone on her hair. Harper watched her for a minute as she turned back to the stage, and he thought he saw a smirk, quickly erased, just as the girls onstage finished their song. As the audience clapped, Harper was sure he saw the woman laugh out loud, then she put her fingers to her mouth and blew a loud whistle. He could hear it over the clapping and saw several in front of her turn around. She merely smiled at them as the audience settled in for the last student's solo. The performer was the boy Harper had been waiting to hear, the one that Miss Wilma had sent to Greensboro College for his scholarship audition. She had mentioned him casually, but with pride, several times. After suffering through two hours of plunking and plodding, Harper was eager to finally hear one who was considered the best in this town.

The student—James Moody was his name according to the program—was black, a fact that Wilma had not mentioned. It was just like her, bending over backward, afraid of offending, when in Harper's mind this just compounded the accomplishment. There were not many black families in the area, and most of them were too poor to even think about a piano. James was a tall kid for seventeen, but looked comfortable in his suit and tie. He sat down at the piano and took his time settling in front of the keyboard. Harper saw that he was to play Chopin's "Revolutionary Etude." Not a bad choice if he could pull it off, though what were the odds, here in a town where the North Carolina symphony never held a concert and his piano teacher played two-bit weddings on a broken-down funeral parlor organ?

James Moody began to play. From the first measure, Harper knew that he was listening to a pianist of extraordinary talent. The sound that filled the auditorium was full and melodic, with James Moody's hands releasing music into the air where the elaborate sprays of runs and chords were suspended beyond their physics, inhaled by the assembled crowd. The sleeping men awakened and the restless sat still. For his own part, Harper sat in his seat transfixed in those few moments, unwilling to move in the slightest, wanting to hear everything that this young man had to offer. The piece was over and the audience was on its feet clapping on and on for James Moody before it occurred to Harper: Did Miss Wilma know what she had here? Had she any clue at all? Harper thought that she did, maybe so. She had taught him these years, and what a fine job she had done. But then, he thought, what had she said about his audition—Greensboro College. That place would fall far short of this kid's reach, he was certain. God, who did he still know at Juilliard? Maybe it was not too late to get him an audition.

James Moody stood on the stage with his hand resting on the aging Steinway, taking small bobbing bows and looking over at what must be his entire family, a group of nine or ten, assorted older people, parents, siblings, all with the same smile, clapping and waving to him. Just as the applause began to diminish a bit, Harper heard one of the men shout out "my boy," and he saw James Moody smile for the first time as he left the stage. As people settled back in their seats, a younger child with yellow ringlets peeked her face out beyond the stage left curtain and started to wave to someone in the audience. She was quickly jerked back behind the curtain. Miss Wilma then walked out and placed her music at the piano to begin the final number. This would be another wretched choral piece, Harper decided, featuring that overly perky voice teacher. He turned his attention back to the pretty whistling woman by the window. She was watching the stage, her face turned in profile to Harper. He could not discern her age. She was seated beside an older woman, who could be her mother or her aunt. The seat on the other side of her was vacant. She wore a simple blouse with a round white collar, slightly prim, but her hair was cut stylishly, with the front longer than the back and the right side slinging down over her face a bit. Her skin was olive and the hair was short in back, exposing her neck with a small curl lying just in the middle. He took a deep breath as if to take in her scent from the distance.

Beside him, Sarah shifted in her seat. Harper looked over and saw at once that she had seen him looking—seen him again, she would say, looking without even bothering, she would say, to hide his attraction, sniffing like a dog. Onstage, Miss Wilma began hammering out a jaunty rendition of "Yankee Doodle Dandy." All of the students, lined up by height, began to march onto the stage carrying little American flags. Toward the end came a few older girls twirling batons. It was altogether more than Harper could bear. Thankful he had chosen an aisle seat, he made a quick wave to Sarah. He got out of his seat giving her no time to respond, and headed for the back exit. He would deal with any consequences she had for him later.

Downtown Swan's Knob had little to offer a global wanderer unless he needed a grilled cheese sandwich or the kind of serviceable shoes old ladies wore. Harper liked to think of himself as a person who was hip to street life—a traveler able to savor the scene whether he was in New York City, Santa Fe or Ile de la Cité—but architecturally speaking, the four-block downtown didn't have much going for it, unless you compared it to the suburban strip malls that were sprouting all around the more prosperous North Carolina cities. Still, Harper thought as he passed the Coach House Restaurant with its front planter boxes full of pansies, there was some value in a place where people still walked down the street instead of driving up to an asphalt parking spot. If he lived here—perish the thought—he would run into his friends (and his cousins, his kin were all over this county) at the Coach House, he could stop in and chew the fat with the old hew-haw that ran the hardware store, flirt with the soda fountain girl at Surry Drug. When you thought of it that way, this podunk town was not so different from his old neighborhood in the

Village. After all, hadn't he spent most of his days within four blocks of his Bleecker Street apartment? He had to laugh over this thought as he tried to think about where he might find a beer in this town. In Greenwich Village, you could stumble from bar to bar and never touch the ground. Tonight, he was just hoping to find that dank little pool hall open. And here it was squeezed between Wall Hardware and the drugstore—Squirrely's.

The entrance to Squirrely's was uninviting, just a narrow set of wooden doors and a small storefront window painted black and peeling, but Harper was thirsty. A dingy light came through the bare spots in the window, so Harper knew that the place was open, but he could not see who was inside. The setup looked haphazard but was probably carefully designed to block the view of any woman who came down the sidewalk. Most 'men, of course, would walk on in without giving it a moment's consideration, but on this side of the world, no woman was welcome in a pool hall, not for a minute. Such an absolute social norm would have saved Harper considerable grief in New York and out in New Mexico. In those places, anyone and everyone could turn up in a bar, which was where the trouble usually started for him. Despite any intention on his part, there was always some thing of beauty that caught him unprepared, unguarded, and far away from a town like this one where every set of eyes was worn by a judge.

He had forgotten. This was not Greenwich Village and not Santa Fe, not by a long shot. In this town there remained harvest queens, righteous veterans, corner spittoons, pink teas, hayrides, and absolutely no sense in anyone of what was passing by unheeded in the great world outside. And though even President Carter wore his hair long these days, Harper had weathered more than a dozen comments about his hair and beard already, and he expected his visit to Squirrely's to bring a few more. He entered the dark hall, the unfamiliar door slamming loudly behind him. The room was near dark except for a glaring light focused over the pool table. A ball, mishit by a rattled player, bounced off the table.

"Good one, Curly," said a dark-haired man as his opponent cursed and bent under the table in search of the ball. Everyone else looked at Harper.

"Excuse me, ma'am," said the bald bartender. "Can we help you? Oh, wait a minute, boys, I am clean mistaken. 'Scuse me, son, have a seat right here."

Harper tried to amble uncaring up to the bar and found a vacant bar stool that had been recently repaired with electrical tape. He sat silent, figuring that in this place there was no need to order. He half smiled like a guy in a western. The bartender pulled a beer from the rusty cooler. Harper asked for a glass without thinking and was immediately sorry. The man hunted behind the counter a bit and produced a curved sort of mug meant for an Irish coffee or some other fancy drink. In Harper's hand, it was greasy, like it had been used by someone eating a hot dog.

He put the beer to his lips and nodded briefly to the others at the bar. The man beside him was drinking a Coke and sweating. He was a large man with half a head of hair and a bit of a belly pressed up against the counter. "How do. It was hot as hell in that auditorium," the man said. Harper knew then that he was in and that they would let him stay and drink his beer in peace.

He took a few long sips and looked around. On the wall behind the bar was a calendar with a picture of last season's Swan's Knob football team, the Blue Rebels, all suited up, helmets on their knees, framed by a dozen cheerleaders. "Hey man, could I take a look at that?" he asked the bartender, who pulled the calendar off the wall and handed it to Harper.

"There they are, the whole bunch of those lazy-ass boys. Seven and four, and there's the laziest one of all," said the bartender, jabbing a short finger at a blank-faced freckled boy in the front row.

"Oh now, Tommy's just fussing to keep from bragging," said

the man with the Coke. "That's his boy Rusty—a real talented running back. He'll take the team to the state finals next season."

"Looks like a killer to me," said Harper, hoping that he had made an appropriate comment. To Harper, this team was a portrait of rural adolescence—half boys with big hands, half men held back a few grades. The cheerleaders looked like they belonged with a team from a different school altogether. They posed like models with toes pointed, legs lifted in a kick. Harper was startled to see that among them was the woman from the recital. He had assumed that she was years older, could not imagine her cool beauty in the halls of a high school. The bartender—apparently a proud father—waited in front of him to return the calendar to its place of honor. Harper handed it back.

He wandered over to the pool table, careful not to disturb another shot. As the game ended, he picked a cue off the rack and tried to catch the eye of the winner. "Anybody got the next one?" he asked. The dark-haired guy with a crew cut shrugged and began racking up the balls. He was wearing what looked like a vest left over from a tour of duty in Vietnam, but by Harper's estimation he was no more than twenty-five, far too young to have actually seen action. He looked over at Harper, then quickly set up his cue and broke the balls. None rolled in. A good sign. The guy lit a cigarette with fingers that were as big as sausages, way out of proportion with the rest of his body. He took a large drag from the cigarette and nodded at Harper. His turn. Harper surveyed the lay of the balls and decided to go for a short corner shot. He carefully leaned over the table, took his shot, missed. The cue ball just bounced off the felt. Damn. He reared back off the table, whipping his cue into the air. The stick hit the light with a clink and the whole thing began to swing on the pendulum hanger, throwing crazy light over this corner, then that, over faces and smoke, like the beam of a searchlight in the dead of night. Harper reached up and grabbed the rim of the lamp to stop its swinging. For the second time, all eyes in the bar rested on him.

He ducked his head and stepped back into the shadow. He'd let the other guy take his shot. This was almost worse than the damn recital—everybody watching everything he did—except at least this place had beer.

His opponent set his cigarette on the side of the pool table and took his time this go-round, positioning himself for the shot. The ball banked neatly off the felt and dropped into the corner pocket. Then the man turned back to Harper and gave him a crazed grin, like someone out of that *Deliverance* movie (and here Harper had assured all of his Santa Fe friends that the guys like you saw in that movie didn't exist anymore). The man held his gaze on Harper in some kind of macho contest that Harper could not even begin to fathom.

"Whew, you gittum, Avery boy," called someone from one of the shadowy corners. As "Avery boy" ambled back around the table looking for the next shot, Harper got a look at his vest. It was the real thing, all right. He had seen plenty back in the early seventies, but most people left those mementos in the backs of their closets these days. He wondered what this guy's story might be. Maybe it was his older brother's vest. He and his buddies were shit-faced, that was for sure. The boys in the cheering section did look old enough to have been in Vietnam, and what's more, not a one looked like he had gone for student deferment. The whole lot of them leaned unsteadily against the back wall. The man they were whooping at, Avery, had eyes that were all pupil, black as the night in any jungle. Jesus, maybe the guy was old enough, maybe he had been there. Looking at those eyes, Harper wondered if he and the boys were using a little something besides Pabst Blue Ribbon. Harper hoped to hell that he had not wandered into some informal Vietnam veterans' club—because he had less than no credentials for them. About the only thing he could say, and he'd have to be careful even these years later not to sound too smug, was that he had a lucky number back then, 316. That would be his lucky number for the rest of his life. But still, he'd avoid the whole discussion if he could. He sure didn't want to have to talk about deferments, or even the draft lottery, in this crowd.

In the end, he decided that the beer buddies up front were safer than Avery and his boys, so he just concentrated on one beer then another as he finished out the game, losing horribly, not caring, and returned to his seat at the bar. The same guy next to him, this one too old to have been in Vietnam, was still sweating and still nursing the Coke, only the liquid in the bottle looked nearly clear to Harper. Harper leaned over to him and said, "Mighty interesting looking Coke you got there."

The man smiled. "Yep. It'll do the trick, if it don't make you blind first."

Harper had not seen corn liquor since his teens. He said, "Oh blindness, hell. That's just what they tell men about anything women don't want them to do. And I'm talking more than mash here. 'Don't do it, sonny boy, it'll make you blind.' I see fine, my friend, how about you?"

"Since you're calling me your friend, I reckon you want some too," said the man.

"Wouldn't hurt," said Harper.

"Well, all right," he said, motioning down the bar. "Tommy, this boy here needs him one of them special Co-colas." He turned back to Harper. "My name is Roy Swan. You're Miss Wilma's son-in-law, aren't you? I saw you at the recital."

"Yes, sir," said Harper. "I am her very unworthy son-in-law, Harper. Harper Chilton."

"Unworthy?" said Roy. "What did you do?"

"Nothing to her liking, that's what," he said.

"Hum," said Roy, silent for a minute, sipping out of the bottle. "But you don't live around here, do you?"

"No," said Harper. "We live in Santa Fe, New Mexico."

"What for?" said Roy. "You from around there?"

"Nope," said Harper. "Actually, I'm from just down the road, outside of King."

"Really," said Roy. "What's happened to you, boy? You lost your accent."

The bald bartender put a pale Coke down in front of Harper and stood in front of him expectantly. Harper hoped that the Coke would cut the taste of the liquor a bit. He took a small sip and swallowed quickly. By the time the fire reached his stomach, he realized that the liquor had been mixed with maybe three teaspoons of Coke. The rest had been poured out and replaced with corn liquor. Harper could not speak. Roy seemed to notice this and said, "This boy Harper is from King, Tommy. Your older boy Virgil might have played him in football. How old are you?"

Harper swallowed again, and hoped that his vocal cords had recovered: "Thirty-one," he managed.

"No," said Tommy. "Virgil is only twenty-eight. You'd have missed him, and excuse me, but unless you were the kicker, I don't believe you played football."

"No," said Harper, ignoring the comment. "But my younger brother Jimmy did, played halfback." Over the initial jolt, Harper took another sip and this time felt something about his entire body begin to relax down into the seat.

"Jimmy, Jimmy Chilton," said Roy. "I don't think I remember him."

"Oh yeah," said Tommy. "I do. Hell of a player." He walked toward a customer signaling him at the other end of the bar.

"So, who'd he play for in college?" said Roy.

"He didn't go," he said. Harper sipped his drink again and held it up to the light. He was getting into territory best left alone. "This stuff isn't half bad, after a while. Little cloudy, though."

"Well, it ain't no fine wine," said Roy. "Chilton, Chilton. That sounds familiar to me. I wonder if I know your Daddy. What's his name?"

"Wallace," said Harper. "Wally Chilton."

"Wally, hell yes. He's on the Rescue Squad down there, isn't he?"

"Oh yeah, he was on it for years," Harper said. Shit, he thought, he's going to know all about Jimmy.

"I think I've met Wally. I was a volunteer fireman here in this county back a few years ago, and I believe I've met him. Sort of a short fellow, isn't he? For real bad wrecks out here on Highway 52, they sometimes would call us in from three counties. Really, we'd be crawling all over one another. There were some bad wrecks from time to time. I remember one was so bad that the car was totally mangled, I mean messed up beyond all recognition. In fact it turned out to be the car of one of the men on the Rescue Squad with his own son in it, and he didn't even recognize— Ah, damn, son. I have a damn big mouth. That was him, wasn't it? I didn't remember until I was right on top it. Damn. I am sorry. Here, have another drink. Shit, me and my big mouth."

Harper was amazed at how quickly the room had become blurred. He should have seen the path of the conversation sooner—like a bad position in a game of chess—he could have steered Roy away. But maybe this was not possible. In his life and in his family's, all paths led to that night. He drank again and looked over at Roy, who was hunched over the bar, sneaking looks at him, wondering what he might do or say. "Don't worry about it, man," Harper said. "It happened. It happened."

Roy let a few minutes pass and said finally, "Lord, we've all had more than our share around here. You've heard about last night, I reckon."

Harper was thankful that the man seemed ready to change the subject, that he didn't find a way to ask him any more. "A policeman got killed, yes," said Harper. "I heard, and actually I saw the car and all the Rescue Squad cars when I drove into town. That's too bad. Who was it got shot—Barney Fife or Andy?"

Roy didn't laugh and looked around to see who might have heard. "The man's name was Clem, Clemont Baker, and don't you go making jokes. Every one of these men here has spent most of the day going back and forth between this here bar and the police station. That man over there at the pool table, the man that just whipped you at pool, is Avery Spivey, Clem's brother-in-law. Avery's twin sister, Ava, was Clem's wife. The three of them grew up on the same road. They were friends since they were kids. Clem was sort of like Avery's older brother. He and Avery both survived their time in the service. Clem was in the army, spent three years in country in Vietnam.

"And Avery?" Harper was curious.

"Oh, Avery joined the army too, volunteered, which probably sounds strange to someone your age. I think he was still in boot camp by the time we pulled out of Vietnam. Ended up on the grounds maintenance crew down at Fort Bragg. Anyway, they were good friends, Avery and Clem. So, it just kills me to think about this. Here Clem gets himself home safe, marries Ava, joins our little police department, and then one night he's out on the bypass and someone just empties out his gun on him. Can you imagine? Some sucker empties the gun and then bends down and searches his body for more bullets, reloads, and shoots him one more time just for the fun of it. Boy, something like that ain't never going to happen to Barney Fife. This ain't Mayberry, this ain't no Mount Pilot, never was, not any town close to it. So don't you go making jokes about a policeman who died in the line of duty." He lowered his head and spoke in a whisper, "Even if the man did get shot with his own .38."

"Damn, now it's me who's said the wrong thing," said Harper. "I meant nothing by it, man. Really, it's just a terrible thing. Do they know who did it?"

"That's what this crowd is waiting to find out," said Roy. "Chief Henry's done turned them out of the station a couple of hours ago, when they brought in a suspect—some longhaired Indian, can you believe it? They found him still camping out down by the river, just sitting there with a bunch of rocks in his pockets. Don't know where he come from, what he's doing here."

"An Indian, you say? What do you mean an Indian?" said Harper.

"Well, an Indian—dark skin, thick shank of hair down his back, silver jewelry all over. Everything but the feathers."

Harper began to gulp the remainder of his drink, hoping it would melt the thick place in the back of his throat. It had to be. Roy was talking about Jonah Branch. It had to be him. Jonah Branch had hitched a ride from Harper all the way from Santa Fe. Harper had carried him across the country in his car. What was he doing in this town? Harper had left him at a truck stop over the mountains in Virginia. How had Jonah made it to Swan's Knob before Harper? How had he had time to kill Deputy Fife?

Harper heard the rattle of the bar door behind him and saw the other men snap their heads up to see who was coming in. In spite of himself, Harper turned around as well and saw a group of five or six men led by a stocky man in a policeman's blue uniform. Just inside the door, the man stopped and let the others pass him. He looked at the expectant crowd, and Harper thought for a moment that the man would cry, but he just shook his head slightly and walked toward the bar.

"That's the chief," Roy told Harper quietly. "Henry Lynch."

As the chief approached, the man sitting beside Roy got up and took his hand, said, "Ah, Henry," then moved down the bar a bit, giving the chief his stool. Harper's bottle was empty, but it didn't seem quite the time to ask for a refill. Tommy put a beer down in front of the chief. Harper caught his eye and raised his empty Coke bottle. Tommy took the bottle from Harper and replaced it with a beer. Maybe Tommy was laying off the still liquor out of respect for the chief, but after the sting of the liquor, beer tasted like dishwater. The chief pulled long and hard on his beer, oblivious to the crowd drifting toward him. When he put the bottle down, he glanced over his shoulder, sighed and cleared his throat.

"Well, boys," he said loud enough for most everyone to hear, "here's what we've got. We still have the suspect, a thirty-year-old male Indian, in custody. We've spent most of the afternoon interrogating him, and right now the SBI men are going over the whole thing with him again. There's no question in my mind but that we'll have us a formal charge by morning."

"Henry, maybe you ought not to arrest him," said a man down the bar. "Just turn him loose. We'll take care of him, yes sir. What do you say?" The man laughed and the men around him joined in, sort of huddled together, slapping the back of Clem's brother-in-law, saying to him, "Don't worry, Avery boy, we'll take care of him." For his part, Avery seemed stunned by the chief's announcement. As the other men jostled him, he swayed back and forth a bit, and Harper thought for a moment that he might fall, but finally, Avery managed to lift his fist in the air and shout, "Shit yeah, we'll get him."

Harper could see that this was mostly a lot of bar talk, especially at this time of the evening, but still it put a chill down his back. Nothing like the confines of a small town to bring him to the brink of paranoia. Shit, and not two days back. Maybe this was not the same guy from Santa Fe. It couldn't be.

He leaned forward on the bar to try and hear what Roy and Chief Henry were saying. The bar buzz had grown so loud that Harper couldn't make out a word from the chief, but Roy said, "Lord, Henry, what are you thinking about? There ain't nothing about this boy but his looks that says he did it. You ought to turn him loose and get to work on finding out who did this."

The bar was crowded now, and the energy in the room was a little scary to Harper. For about two seconds he wondered if he should ask about the suspect, find out the name, maybe tell them what he knew. He noticed that the men now stood in little groups, circling the members of the chief's posse. Avery and his buddies were right in the middle of it all. Things could get ugly.

"Be careful with your hunches," Roy was saying to the chief, "or you could have more trouble. Maybe you ought to find out just how he got here. That could be the key. Maybe he had help. Maybe his fellow criminals left him behind."

Harper tried to make himself very small in his chair. Roy must have noticed the shifting, because he stopped what he was saying and turned to look at Harper.

"Look, Henry," he said. "This boy just got into town, too. He's from Indian country out there in Santa Fe. Maybe you ought to take him in too. Harper, this is Henry Lynch. Chief Henry, they call him. Henry, this here is Miss Wilma's son-in-law, Harper Chilton."

"Chilton," said Chief Henry, "Chilton. You kin to Wally Chilton?"

"His son," said Harper.

"His son?" said Chief Henry. "Well, I seem to recall, the Wally Chilton I know—"

"Lord God, let's not go into that again," said Roy, shaking his head at the chief.

"Real sorry about your officer," said Harper in the most respectful tone he could muster. His stomach was tingling and he felt a wave of what-the-hell kind of honesty welling up in his chest. It was time to head on out.

"You from Santa Fe? That right?" said Chief Henry. "Well, I'll be. It's an invasion. This Branch fellow we got across the street has a license with an Albuquerque address. Isn't that close to Santa Fe?"

"Branch fellow." It was him. Jonah Branch was being held in the murder of a policeman, and Harper was the dead meat in the getaway car. He was only half drunk, which was suddenly to him not close to drunk enough, but he was too drunk to stay any longer. One wrong word and it would unravel before him.

"Albuquerque?" he said, finding his Piedmont drawl. "Well, I reckon it's in the state somewhere. To tell you the truth, one town out there looks pretty much like another." He tipped up his beer to finish it and waved to Tommy.

"That's close enough for me," said Roy. "Go on and lock him up, Chief Henry." The two men laughed.

"I think I'll pass for now, but don't leave town, son," said Chief Henry.

"Well, gentlemen," said Harper, putting his money on the bar. "I'll take that as my cue. My wife always likes me to come home before I get arrested."

The men inside were still laughing when Harper got out on the sidewalk. The lights were burning in the police station across the street. He could see several men walking around in the smoky front room. He moved on as quickly as he could past the dime store, Wall Hardware and the Coach House Restaurant, all dark. He reached Church Street, crossed over into the residential section of town. One, two, three houses with dark windows, silent porches. He broke into a run.

Chapter Four

Sarah was bone tired, with the kind of sinking feeling you get only in the first months of pregnancy. She was tired enough to drift off without one more thought about Harper, and she was almost there, but she heard a car pass, thought she heard a door slam, and her heart just beat her eyes back open, put her mind back down the path of waiting, waiting. Waiting for Harper. She had waited for him a thousand times in darkness and in daylight, on Saturday night and Sunday morning, on street corners, in bars, and in bed, especially in bed. It wasn't so much the waiting, she knew the outcome—he'd come home, they'd have fight number 248, penalty assessed, the silence of a few days, followed by mournful music, followed by some kind of capitulation. This she knew—it was like some rare composition in the repertoire of purgatory. She had ceased to fear it. What she never knew and what she really feared was what she had missed—his life, the life of Harper playing fortnightly, acts committed in their entirety while she waited.

There was a time when she liked to think he was out doing things to feed his art—hanging out in the halls of rare old jazz with near-dead blues singers, pulling his trumpet out and jamming until dawn. During the early days in New York, long before their exile to Santa Fe, she would lie in her bed, waiting for him, and she would conjure an East Village nightclub, Harper on a smoky stage, and she would have him play a tune for her, the sexy lady at the back table. It would be like some quiet bedtime story you repeat to a child. When he returned, she would be sleeping. She would wake up docile.

By the time they beat it out to Santa Fe under the cloud of an ongoing dispute with fellow musicians, her little fantasy movie would not run through the projector—the film would jump off somewhere about the time Harper took the stage and explode on-screen into a sea of women's faces, each one made up hip with half-closed eyes and frosted lips. In those days, the East Village was a pretty small place—just like anywhere once you get in the middle of it—and often, she had encountered the women in the life of Harper. They were not blues singers, though in consoling herself she noted that they looked like death in the full daylight. After a while, she quit looking into the faces of women as they walked down the street and concentrated on shoes.

When Sarah wanted to know something about a person, she would look down at their shoes. A person could dress up in any old outfit for the day, but their shoes were in their closet for a while. You could tell by looking just where a person had to walk and how they got there. Some people got so used to their shoes that they went right on wearing them right down through the soles. In New York, she'd seen high heels half sawed off by the sidewalk, lopsided by their owner's gait. One day, she'd spotted a girl just come up from North Carolina disguised in screaming purple-and-red hot pants, only she was wearing the Capezios her mama had bought her for college dances. Harper, as always, adapted better and faster than anyone else, and when she pictured him during those years in the Village, his squared-toed stack-heeled shoes peeked out from his wide pants, one foot pointed to the right, knee bent, hip cocked.

Sarah for one had never grown accustomed to a heel of any size, which she attributed to the brogans her mama bought her every fall at Belton's Shoe Store. By the time she was ten, Sarah had a longing for shoes unlike any of those serviceable models found in Belton's. She wanted slim shoes with thin leather and tiny straps—shoes she could use for the delicate walk of a young lady. She wanted a life that was not possible in brown suede brogans. They spawned kneesocks and sturdy legs, the kind of legs that forever ached in a pair of heels.

Sarah turned over. She knew that lying awake for Harper did her no good, but here she was. She put her hands behind her head and tried to pretend she was lying in the sun on her back in a field, warm and safe, but as she pictured the sky, she saw oddly her pink balloon—full of helium and tied with a string by Mr. Belton himself, a small consolation for the shoes that anchored her to the street. He had tied her balloon to her wrist so that her arm was buoyed as she and her mother walked down the sidewalk to the house. Halfway home, the fall sun had made her warm, and she stopped to take off her sweater. At that moment, the string slipped from her wrist and the balloon rose silently to the sky. It was gone by the time her mother, marching down the block, had missed her and turned around to see Sarah stopped, looking vacantly at the trees. To Wilma, prizes for children—balloons, candy, ice cream cones—were unnecessary and were used only by the weakest parents. She had said nothing about the lost balloon. Sarah thought now that maybe she had not even noticed that it had flown away, or maybe she had noticed it and decided that a ten-year-old should simply take the mishap without a fuss. Whatever, she had asked only that Sarah catch up to her and move along home so that she would not be late for her next lesson.

In those days, Sarah had a child's naive capacity to comfort herself and could think of the balloon as drifting and drifting way up high over the town and over the country and over the earth and finally flying up to God and the angels. She had made it through her childhood like that, but tonight back in her old bed, she saw the balloon going higher and higher, then bursting into a thousand pieces in the sky.

Sarah rolled to her side this time, whipping her head around too fast and feeling a wave of nausea. Ignore it, she thought, if you just let it go for tonight, for tomorrow, soon you can deal with it. She tried to breathe evenly, but the nausea startèd again, beginning at the nape of her neck and spreading down to her stomach. She thought she felt a flutter way down deep. Probably her imagination. She counted: ten weeks, maybe eleven. It was possible.

Just then she heard the back door and Harper's footsteps. She looked: a few minutes after midnight. Not as late as he could have been, but then there were fewer places to detain him in Surry County. She heard him on the stairs: he mounted quickly and without his characteristic sneak-home tread. She thought maybe he was going to roll out a revised breakfast table act ("Oh, did I wake you, my dear, it wasn't very late, I was out with the bladey-blah blah"). She was about to bury her head under the pillow when Harper rushed into the room and closed the door behind him. With her eyes accustomed to the dark, Sarah could see him lean back against the frame, still holding the knob, gulping breaths.

He craned his neck into the darkness and broke the silence of ten thousand nights: "Sarah, are you there?" he said. Sarah was so startled that she bolted up in the bed before she knew it, making her head swim and her vision blur as her husband launched himself onto the bed and put his head down in her lap. His worn cowboy boots hung off the end of the bed and he kicked them back and forth like a small child having a tantrum. Out of instinct, Sarah grabbed his head and held him like he had fallen out of a tree and skinned his knee, rocked him like she knew how to fix it all. They sat there for a long time.

"Well, Sarah, I've really done it now," he said finally. "And it's nothing like what you would have imagined. Nothing. Anything you might think about: some woman or any of those kinds of problems. Well, it's not what you think, but I figure that doesn't matter. It's the karma of it—I deserve it, you see. It's all real clear that I have brought myself down this road, and now I will be made to pay. Big time."

In the next silence, Sarah thought about the currency of the payment. She could not fathom the offense, but this rare, in fact unprecedented, midnight confession spelled millions demanded from her own public humiliation account.

"I am going to jail," Harper said dramatically. "I know what you think. I haven't even been here long enough to get into that kind of trouble."

"Drugs?" Sarah said—if not some sexual mishap, what else remained?

"Lord, no. This is worse, Sarah—accessory to murder, honey, and this wasn't any barroom mix-up."

"What are you talking about?" Sarah said. "Back in New Mexico? What happened?"

"No, Sarah, I'm telling you it was right here. Clem Baker."

Sarah leaned over and cut on the light and turned toward him. "The murdered policeman?"

Harper buried his head on her lap. "Turn off the light. Cut it off and let me get through this."

Sarah turned off the light. Harper rolled over and faced the window. She could see his profile in the faint light, his beard resting on his chest.

"Remember when I came into town last night. It turns out that I drove in right after that Baker guy was shot. I passed right by the Rescue Squad. I didn't think anything about it really—I mean I felt bad for the guy and his family and all but I didn't think any more about it until tonight when I was down at Squirrely's. Those old boys were talking, you know how they talk, going on and on over all the details about how Clem got shot and the number of bullets and the kind of gun and the fatal wound, on and on and on until I was half listening. Then they started talking about the guy they caught and put in their little jailhouse. They said it turns out it was an Indian who did it for sure and weren't they going to string him up and all. Started nudging me, saying maybe you know this fellow, Harper boy, since you just came from Indian country. Well, you know me, I was about to fire up my lecture on whatever I thought these local yokels need to know about how big this world is and how many people there are, some good, some bad, some white, some black, some red—but being in Squirrely's, I decided to hold my tongue for once. These old boys went on about how this man had hair even longer than mine and all braided up, lacking only the feathers or he would have been Tonto, on and on like that. Finally, I worked it in to ask his name. Jonah they say, Jonah Branch.

"Sarah, do you remember Jonah Branch? The photographer who always exhibited at Minga Wood's," said Harper. Sarah felt her face go on fire at the mention of the name. Why had Jonah ended up in Swan's Knob? She knew the answer, and it made her heart jump.

"Here's the weird part, Sarah. I picked up Jonah Branch back in Santa Fe at the Texaco on Cerillos Road. He had a little pack with him and said he needed a ride. Said he was taking a little vacation. When I told him where I was headed, he said he thought the East was as good a place as any. He was good company, didn't talk much, but seemed like a good listener. We drove the whole way together until a truck stop just before the Blue Ridge Parkway. The fog got a little hairy for me so I stopped for a cup of coffee, got to talking to a few people, and when I turned around, he was gone.

"I figured he had gone his own way and never gave it another thought and I never dreamed he would show up here. Somehow it's my fault he came. He must have done it, you see, because of what I told him about this town. What exactly stoked him off, I don't know. I told him about your growing up here and your daddy and Wilma and her church choir and all the good old boys, ignorant as hell, and told him about what it was like to grow up in a little town, all the little celebrations in the year, and hell, I talked about Swan's Knob and how I grew up down the road in King. Then I got to talking about what I saw in the pueblos, about the rituals of the seasons, comparing how his people see it and ours. Hell, I don't know what I said, but something in it must have set him off, because the next thing he did was go right up on the bypass and shoot Clem Baker up and down. And it was me, Sarah, me who brought him into town."

"Did you talk about me, Harper?" Sarah said. She was trying to catch her breath, to understand just what had happened. Jonah had come. What had Harper told him? What did Harper know?

"What?" said Harper.

"About me, did you talk about me," said Sarah. "What did you tell Jonah about me?"

"Oh, I don't know, one thing or another—the usual stream-of-consciousness road talk, babe. What does it matter? I am fucking doomed, doomed by all of this, not two days in this damn state. I can't even talk anymore." His burden dumped out there on the bed, Harper pulled off all his clothes, draped an arm and a leg across Sarah. He relaxed his body, was asleep in less than a minute and never noticed in the least Sarah's heart leaping in her chest, pumping blood enough for her, her baby, and maybe for the rest of the town.

Eventually Sarah tried to push Harper onto the other side of the bed, but he kept sagging back down on her. Finally she poked him with her knee until he groaned slightly and rolled over onto his stomach. Once she got loose, there was nothing to do but leave the house. She slipped her clothes back on and grabbed her sandals. She found her mother's keys on the kitchen counter, closed the back door without a sound, and coasted the car out of the driveway.

She managed to start the cold engine of the LTD once she had backed it into the street. She headed toward the center of town and was stopped at the light in front of the library before it occurred to her what she was doing. She was looking for Jonah. He had come for her after all, come the whole way to Swan's Knob. That much seemed clear, though the rest was a cloud. She slowed down as she passed the police station, though she had no idea what she was expecting to see. A single light shone through a window in the back. Surely most everyone had gone home, but Sarah could not help but imagine that Jonah was in there right now, being questioned by a bunch of good old boys. She pulled the car over to the curb and was considering going up to the door when the light in the back went off. She felt a little guilty relief. Everybody must have gone already, the last guard was going to sleep. Nothing she could do tonight.

As she rolled on down Main Street, she tried to think of Jonah back in the jail, sleeping that sleep of the innocent, as he always did. For her part, a bit of coffee seemed in order now that she was up and out, but the closest open restaurant was likely a good thirty minutes away in Mount Airy. Too far. By default, she settled into the old route she and every other teenager had worn out every Saturday night of high school: down Main Street, left at the Primitive Baptist Church, right on the bypass past a few of the remaining mill houses, past the mill full of cars for the third shift, past the drive-in that was showing *Kramer vs. Kramer* this month, down off the bypass onto the end of Main Street. She tried to sort out what Harper had told her back in the bedroom. It was a nightmare, it could not be real. Sarah tried to think about Jonah in the flesh, in Swan's Knob. If he had arrived with Harper, where had he been for the last twenty-four hours? She turned left into the parking lot of Setzer's drive-in. It was long closed for the night. Two white hamburger wrappers blew like tiny ghosts across the asphalt in front of Sarah's stopped car.

If Jonah had come for her, why hadn't he just come to her mother's house? Where had he been when they arrested him? She could not think of a single place where he might have gone. Hell, she could scarcely remember what she had done all those years growing up there. Had she done nothing but drive around this circuit?

Sarah turned out of the parking lot and started back down Main. There was one place left to go—down to the Ararat River. This she remembered. It took just fifteen minutes. She remembered each turn, each curve in the country road. She had never been to the river alone, but she and every other kid in Swan's Knob had grown up on its banks. In the summer, there were rope swings and secret swimming places up and down the river, neatly organized by grade and social status. The places had names like The Vine, Naked Gulch, and Cling Peach. In the winter, there were fires on the bank, snow forts, and once a drowning under the ice. For the high school kids who could beg or borrow cars, the dirt road running parallel to the river was known as Ararat Heaven, breeding ground to the stars of Swan's Knob High. Sarah rolled down her window and drank in the late-spring air, the light of the night's full moon.

As she approached the bridge, she could hear the rush of the river. She pulled off onto the dirt road and slowed as weeds beat against the car. She parked the car facing the river, right beside a little camp area that had been her high school hangout. The badly tuned LTD engine whimpered for a few seconds before finally dying. Sarah got out and walked around to the little clearing. It was all the same—a big fire ring with river rocks placed all around the border, logs and stumps for seats, cigarette butts and a few beer cans scattered around. Sarah sat down. The sound of the river filled her body. She welcomed its washing, rested until she felt her breathing match the current. She concentrated only on the sound for a few minutes. It occurred to her that maybe this river was where Jonah had ended up today. He was always at home outdoors and this was a place that would please him. Maybe he had spent last night camping right here. She tried to piece together the few things that Harper had said. Maybe he had gotten it wrong, at least the part about Jonah and the murder of Clem Baker. That was a mistake. It was all some small-town mistake, charges drummed up by ignorant sheriff's deputies. To them, Jonah Branch probably looked like a criminal. He was a tall man, built all of sinew. His hair lay down his back in a braid. He wore ancient blue jeans, shirts of indifferent origin, carried a duffel even in Santa Fe.

He had come for her. This she knew for certain. Harper had said that he had met Jonah by chance, that Jonah wanted a ride to nowhere in particular. That was his way, she knew, to make you think it was all your idea. She knew he had set out to one place in particular. But he had not made it to her doorstep. She wondered what had propelled Jonah's journey—she wondered what he knew or sensed about what had happened to her. And now he was in jail.

She found she could no longer sit still. She stood up and walked up the little wooded trail to the bridge. When she got out to the middle, she leaned out over the wooden rails. The noise of water was louder here, and in the moonlight she could see white-caps in the places where the river passed large rocks. Just on the other side of the bank Sarah could see the light of a campfire, then on a bit farther downstream maybe a candle or two, and she thought she could hear laughter and girlish squeals. God, the air felt so good, so full of the river. "Yaah," she screamed down to the water, "yaaaah," her voice swallowed up. "Yaaah." It was the kind of thing Jonah would do. It was the kind of thing she could do when she was with him. It felt good in her throat. She tried a few more screams then switched to a laugh.

She was still laughing when she saw the outline of a car just on the far side of the bridge, not fifty feet away. Before Sarah could shut her mouth, the back door of the car swung open and the dome light flashed on. For a moment Sarah saw the head and torso of a woman, bare-breasted, arms outstretched, holding her white shirt wide open. The woman did not see Sarah and did not move to close her shirt, but looked down at someone in the seat. It seemed to Sarah that the woman began to laugh. Sarah squinted in the darkness and then she saw that a young man had half fallen out of the car and was scrambling to get back in. Finally he got himself upright and closed the door. It was dark again.

Sarah stared at the place where the light had been and strained to hear any voices. She wondered if some comedic vision had been visited on her, but she could scarcely fathom what it meant. Children, they were, just kids exploring in the dark. She herself could remember one night by the Ararat with a boy who had sky-blue eyes and the hands of a magician. If she had dared to open her shirt to show him her breasts (she had not), she was certain that he would not have fallen out of the door of his Mustang.

She turned back to the water. Presently she heard a car door slam and an engine start up. She looked over and was blinded by the sudden beam of headlights. The car roared and popped into gear, and some little high school boy screamed his daddy's car over the bridge. Sarah's eyes adjusted to the darkness once again, and it was then that she could make out the white shirt. For just a moment, it seemed to cross the bridge on its own, billowing on the body of the breeze. Then Sarah saw that the young girl wore it. She ran past Sarah, oblivious. Sarah could see the taillights of the car, waiting a hundred yards down the road. Over the bridge, the girl slowed to a studied walk and made her way back to the car. Just before she reached it, the passenger door was flung open and Sarah could see the boy inside sit himself upright, grip the wheel and face directly to the front. He did not check the girl's progress. Finally the girl climbed in the car and closed the door, and the car rolled off with Sarah's own bare memories down the dirt road.

Sarah lingered on the bridge for a while then, watched the few little lights down the river go out and the place go quiet. She felt calmer now than she would have imagined. Maybe it was her sense that even though Jonah was in the jail, he was at least nearby. Tomorrow she would help him straighten the whole thing out. She headed back toward the car. Halfway down the trail, she spotted another light, a flashlight this time, shining near her old campfire area. Didn't kids have curfews anymore? Sarah slowed up and tried to make a lot of noise so that whoever it was would hear her coming in time to leave or at least cover up. She reached the end of the trail just in time to see the back of a boy—or more of a man, from the looks of his shoulders—running out of the clearing and past her car toward the road. For an instant she wondered, against logic, if she had found Jonah. But no, though the man was close to Jonah's size, Sarah could see that he had short hair and wore some weird vest over his T-shirt. A local, no doubt. His date had long since made the road. Sarah could not even hear her footsteps, just the bushes beating against the man's pants, then the car door, quickly followed by the starting of some souped-up engine.

Just another date night down by the Ararat River.

∽

When Wilma got down to the kitchen that morning, he was sitting in the back on her concrete arbor bench. Though she wondered later why she did not scream with alarm, her first feeling when she looked out her sink window was curiosity: There was a young man cross-legged on her bench, munching on a few wild strawberries pulled from the back alley. Maybe it was his comfort, and his complete lack of self-consciousness for trespassing into Wilma's yard, that made her have little reaction except to watch him without fear of her own discovery.

He was barefoot, his sandals lined up in front of him. He was brown from head to toe and the white of him—his teeth, his T-shirt—gleamed in the sun. He wore some kind of necklace tied with rawhide and a silver cuff on his arm. Wilma flushed suddenly at his beauty and then wondered how long ago, if ever, she had so admired a creature. Just then a bird flew past him and he turned to watch, smiling up at it, and Wilma saw the rest of him. The hair that had looked clean and well trimmed from the front was not cut in the back. It was a real shock of hair, a black ponytail pulled up in a silver clasp and falling to his waist. Wilma found her breath gone, and as he turned back she jumped to stay out of view, but it was too late. He had seen her. He waved at her window, hopped up, and was opening the screen door before she could even begin to run or call out. Instead, she did the opposite and just went to unlock her kitchen door as if he were some kind of kin. Funny, she thought, it was unlocked already. She pulled it open, and he stopped at the threshold and straightened himself.

"Good morning, Mrs. Mabry," he said in a tone more formal than his attire. "My name is Jonah Branch. I am a friend of Sarah's from Santa Fe." He offered her his hand, the one where he had the silver bracelet. Wilma looked at it as she shook his hand. It was a solid silver cuff, thick and carved with Indian symbols.

She said before she thought, "You're an Indian," then blushed.

He laughed at this and she looked up at him, straight on, and found herself laughing too. "Well," he said, "I guess part of me's an Indian, Mrs. Mabry. Some parts, after all, I guess you'd say two parts Anasazi and another ten that are Irish, Polish, whatever. Everyone in this town has asked about my ancestry."

"Around here about half the county's got some Cherokee blood," she said, by way of making up for her remark. She dropped his hand finally and stepped back. "Sit down, won't you? Sarah's not up yet so I might as well fix you breakfast."

She walked over to the counter and fumbled for her apron, wondering how she found herself hostess to a barefoot Indian in her own kitchen before seven o'clock in the morning. *Harry,* she called, *have you sent me an angel? Have I let a stranger in my kitchen?* No answer, of course, but she felt better instantly. She pulled butter and eggs from the refrigerator. She didn't dare ask the young man what he'd like—she was sure not to have it. "Are you in town for long, Jonah? Sarah didn't remember to mention your coming to me, not that it's any problem whatsoever. She and Harper should be up in a minute, once they hear us down here banging the pots. I can offer eggs scrambled, fried or boiled. Which would you like?"

"Scrambled. So Harper's still here?" he said.

"Oh, yes, he got here just a few days after Sarah and Starling arrived. It seems this is my season for visitors."

"I know when he got here. I caught a ride from him in Santa Fe. I've just been held up a few days by the police downtown."

"Police?"

"Yes, ma'am, your police force of two—recently reduced from three, I take it, in some local blood feud. Surely you heard about the shot policeman."

"Clemont Baker, of course, I heard." The butter in Wilma's pan began to smoke. She pulled it back off the flame without a potholder and heard the sizzle before she felt her palm start to burn. She ran to the faucet to run water on her hand. "Damnation, I've burned myself. Jonah, would you hand me the butter right quick?"

"Mrs. Mabry, forget my breakfast and fix that hand," he said.

"That's what I'm trying to do with the butter," she said. "It's the best remedy I know of."

"What would a bunch of fat do for a burn? Don't you have an aloe plant out in your garden somewhere? The juice in the plant will take the pain right away. May I see?" He gently grasped Wilma's wrist and turned her arm to make her hand turn toward the light. He bent down over the palm.

"Second degree. You're going to have some blisters."

He bent closer and blew a trail of cool air across the red streak in her palm, then lightly touched the skin around it. The singular occurrence of intense pain or unfamiliar gentleness was almost out of the realm of Miss Wilma's experience, so their sudden combination, to her embarrassment, made her sink down a bit as if every joint in her body was weakened.

"Whoa," said Jonah. "Why don't you sit down over here a minute and let Jonah the fry cook finish the breakfast." Wilma sat down, took the wet cloth Jonah offered, and watched him clean the blackened butter out of the frying pan and begin again.

"I can't imagine," she said. "I've cooked eggs in that old black iron skillet for . . . for . . . a number of years now"—since before you were born, she thought—"and I have never grabbed the handle without a rag or a potholder. I guess I am just not awake this morning, or else I was too busy listening to you. What were you saying? Right, the police officers downtown."

"Yes," he said, "they were holding me in your police station. 'Suspicion of murder,' they said. Very official, those boys, for such a small-town force."

"Murder?" she said. Why had she let this man in her house? Wilma wondered how she could get upstairs to get Sarah and Harper.

"Yes, can you believe that kept me for two days? Took them until noon on the first day to even let me know what they thought I did. Then they must have had ten people taking turns questioning me, over and over, the same thing."

A suspected murderer was now serving Miss Wilma her breakfast, gently placing the plate in front of her, buttered toast and all. She was happy that she had gotten dressed before coming to the kitchen this morning. She looked down and realized she still wore her slippers—they would not do for running.

"So they let you go. Did they say they had cleared you?" Wilma said evenly.

"Well, they did not say and I did not ask. But of course, Mrs. Mabry, I had nothing to do with this. Surely you must know . . ." He stopped and looked directly into her eyes. "Well, ma'am, I apologize. It dawns on me now that here I am in your kitchen, and you could not possibly know. I apologize, please go get your daughter, and she will vouch for me. You do not have a murderer in your kitchen."

"Maybe I will go check and see if Sarah is up yet," she said. As she climbed the stairs, she noticed that she could travel fairly quickly in her bedroom shoes. She hustled down the hall and opened the door to Sarah's room, not even thinking to knock. Harper lay naked in the bed with bedclothes pooled around his ankles. Wilma looked only long enough to confirm that her daughter was not in the bed with him, then pulled the door to and ran to the bathroom. No Sarah. She checked Starling's room, her own. No Sarah. Wilma began knocking as loudly as she dared on the door to Harper's room, holding on to the knob.

"Harper. Harper. Wake up. I have a problem here." She waited until she heard the bedclothes rustle and barged in just as Harper sat up in bed. She turned her head. Pulling up the sheets to cover himself had not been Harper's first priority.

"I need you to get up and come downstairs. There's a man here who says he's a friend of yours and Sarah's from Santa Fe. He started out real polite and just now says they held him at the police station on suspicion of murdering Clemont Baker. I have no idea about this except that he's down there right now eating breakfast. And where is Sarah? I thought she was in here with you. She is nowhere upstairs."

Harper blinked and scratched his chest. He looked idly about as if Wilma might have missed seeing Sarah in the room somewhere. Wilma marched across the room to the window and looked out to the driveway.

"Harper," she said, "my car is gone."

She could see that Harper would be of little help in this situation. He was slow in waking, and the way that he sat immobile, she could tell he had yet to grasp the vital facts of the matter.

"Harper," she said, trying to make the orders concise, "get up, get dressed, and try to think for a minute where in the world Sarah has gone. Now think. I'm going to change my shoes. Wait for me right here. We've got to figure out how to get this guy out of the house, and then we'll go downstairs together. Hurry. Lord knows what he's doing down there."

"Who?" Harper managed, finally breaking the surface of consciousness. "Who's down there?"

"Your friend from Santa Fe who's accused of murdering Clem Baker. Jonah something, a guy with a ponytail. Wake up, we've got to think here, son."

She went to her bedroom, tore open her closet and took frantic inventory of the shoe pockets hanging there, locating in ten seconds a pair of yellowed Keds last worn two years ago on the Fourth of July. She kicked off her pink scuffs, which catapulted into the back of the closet, and wiggled her feet into the stiff canvas. As she crossed the hall, she was surprised to find Harper somehow fully dressed, looking grim and oddly purposeful.

"Miss Wilma," he said, "I don't know what this dude has told you." Harper's speech came out double time and had the pitch of a teenage boy. "First, are we talking about the same guy—sort of chiseled, scary eyes, black hair down to here, is that him?"

"I think so," she said. "You knew him in Santa Fe."

"Hardly at all, hell, no," said Harper. "Let me tell you. I only vaguely met the guy around at an art gallery opening or some other party. I ran into him on the way out of town, and I gave him a ride. He came all the way with me to North Carolina, and I let him out at the turnoff at Highway fifty-two. Wilma, did he tell you that he is still a suspect? Is he out on bail this quick?"

"I don't think so," said Wilma. "He says the police just let him go. Good God, you don't think he broke out?"

"I have no idea," said Harper. "Wilma, what is he doing downstairs?"

"He's making breakfast," said Wilma, feeling foolish. "He just looked so . . . harmless when I saw him sitting out in the garden, and he said he was your friend."

"I barely know him, like I said, beyond your standard road

talk, Wilma. And what do you think this is going to look like, him over here in your cozy kitchen? I will be implicated, you know, I am the link here. I brought him to town, he killed the sheriff and now he's in your house hiding out. I'm next—accessory to murder, I'm up a creek, Wilma, and you're letting the murderer cook you breakfast."

"Son, that makes no sense whatsoever," said Wilma. She had never seen Harper so unnerved. Strangely, the sight of him shivering in the hall brought to her a necessary calm. She would get this Jonah out of her house, and then she would find out where Sarah had gotten to.

"I think, Harper, now that I've had a few moments to catch my breath, that the best way to handle this is to just treat this man as you would a guest who doesn't know when to go home. So now, let's just be cordial but fairly direct and mention how much we've got to do this morning—which is true. My Lord, I have a lesson in a few minutes, then the funeral." Miss Wilma was not sure that Harper was listening. "Now, Harper, are you with me here, son?"

"Why don't we just call the police?" Harper said.

"Well, he's in the room with the phone, for one thing. For another, I don't want Chief Henry telling the rest of the choir that he found a suspect sitting in my kitchen. Now we can do this with no problem. Just don't ask too many questions, and if he stands up, you stand up—then, you go on over to the door and open it like you'd love to chat further but you've just got to run. Once he gets out on the porch, you close that door—but don't slam it. When he hits the walkway, you lock it, and we'll go from there."

"Really, Wilma, I don't think we need to be so nice. Just tell him to split."

"This has nothing to do with being nice. I just think sugar works better than salt." Wilma noticed that Harper was barefoot. No matter, that was his business. She was not going to tell her grown son-in-law to put on his shoes. "Now you come on." Wilma walked down the stairs and down the hall toward the kitchen, careful to assume a casual pace. As she entered the room, she said, "Look who I found just getting up." Jonah was sitting at the table eating his eggs, but he stood as she came in and wiped his mouth. Nice manners, again. He looked down the hall to see who was coming, and Wilma turned to see that Harper was not there.

"Well, Harper was right here behind me. I guess he's a little slow this morning." Had he jumped out a window? She looked back over at Jonah, who was still standing. His dark eyes were open wide, unblinking. He reminded her a bit of that groom at Lily's wedding, a little nervous and excited. Her initial impression returned. This boy looked more like the living statue of David than a small-town murderer. She finally heard Harper's jeans swipe across the hardwood as he shuffled down the hall. He didn't look at her, but walked right over to Jonah, and said, rather rudely, "Man, what are you doing here?"

"Right now, I'm having breakfast." Jonah glanced back at her, then looked down at his plate. "I'm sorry to start without you, Mrs. Mabry, but the eggs were hot."

"That's quite all right," said Wilma. "Cold eggs are just terrible."

"Man, *what* are you doing here?" Harper was not following her plan. As she stood there looking at Harper's back—his thin T-shirt, thin body, pale skin—Wilma could not help but compare the two men. The result did not favor Harper.

"Well, really, I came to speak to Sarah," said Jonah. "I think she will want to talk with me too." Wilma saw him color slightly and look past Harper toward the hallway. Now she was beginning to understand, but she could see that Harper was still lost.

Harper said, "It so happens that I would like to talk to her too, man, but she must have split sometime during the night. So she's not here, and if you were thinking she would help you with bail money or bus money, man, think again."

"I came for none of that," said Jonah, a little nervous, Wilma thought, but resolved.

"Word to the wise: don't wait for her," said Harper. "The police could always change their minds and arrest you again. If I were you, I'd be on the highway with my thumb up." Harper stood without moving and stared at Jonah.

There was a moment of quiet tension. Harper meant it to intimidate Jonah. Maybe he thought Jonah would just turn and leave. But Wilma knew Jonah was no man after bus money or any other way out of town. What had landed on her doorstep in the flesh was the third member of a genuine love triangle. Jonah was not about to leave. Wilma thought that maybe she should be ashamed, maybe she should be appalled—but to her surprise, she felt a little bit of a thrill. Good for Sarah, whatever it was. She had never been a mother who wanted to live her daughter's life. But today, just for today, she decided, she would meddle—just this once, because Sarah was out, because Sarah would surely not want this young man to leave.

She changed her plan. In the continued silence, she threw a look at Jonah to let him know that Harper was a man of appalling rudeness, and that she was embarrassed by his mentioning the police.

"Now, Harper, perhaps your friend Jonah needs some more coffee. Why don't you sit down yourself. Maybe Sarah will turn up soon."

Harper looked dazed and responded with a slight whine, "But, Miss Wilma, don't you have a student coming soon? And don't you have that funeral to get ready for?"

"Why yes, but don't mind me," she said, "just enjoy your breakfast." Harper regarded her with utter confusion as she walked over to the coffeepot and reached for it with her right hand. At that moment, she noticed that she was still clutching the wet rag. She pulled her hand back and grabbed the pot with her left hand. As she began making the rounds to pour, she flexed her right hand down by her side. It was throbbing and the palm felt stiff.

"How's it feeling?" said Jonah.

"Well, it hurts a bit but it'll be all right," said Wilma.

"My God," said Harper, seeing the burns, "what happened? How are you going to play the funeral?"

Wilma stopped and held her hand up to her face. There were two large rows of blisters, one across her palm and one across the middle joints of her fingers. It had not occurred to her. She had done some real damage, and she wondered how she could explain it sensibly. She decided she would not. "It's just a little burn. It's fine. I'm just perfectly fine, but I do need to get dressed before my lesson," she said.

Chapter Five

Sarah heard the rush of the river before she even opened her eyes and sat up immediately. She could not recall deciding to sleep in her mother's car last night. She could remember only sitting on the passenger side, leaning her head back against the door so she could see the stars.

According to the dashboard clock it was seven o'clock. Harper would be sleeping. Her mother would be up. Sarah decided that whatever panic she felt, she would check it. Maybe no one would miss her for several hours, especially if Wilma didn't need her car. Even then, maybe they would figure she was out to do an early errand. She could hear her mother, "You could at least, at least have let us know." And she would say, "For heaven's sake, Mother, I am a grown woman." And Wilma would say, "Under my roof . . ." And Sarah would say, "Mother, that may have worked in high school . . ." Forget it, forget it, she thought, you let her do this. On the other side of the county, out in Santa Fe, or halfway across the world, she could still hear her mother—the Wilma tape was running.

Sarah got out of the car. Her immediate mission was to locate a good bush. She found some Kleenex in the glove compartment and headed toward the river. She was done in two minutes, and after some deliberation, buried the Kleenex. She laughed as she walked up the path: She could not recall peeing outdoors in her lifetime, and in fact as a child she had steadfastly refused on a number of occasions.

The beauty of the morning and the freshness of the air made it altogether too nice to return home. Sarah stretched in the sunshine, looked at the river and the distant line of the Blue Ridge beyond. She could just make out the small pass that was Fancy Gap. In Fancy Gap, just before the parkway, there was an old roadhouse restaurant, backed up against the rock. They had biscuits and ham and grits. God, she was hungry. She remembered this hunger from her pregnancy with Starling. During the second or third month, there had been a two-week period when she could not get enough to eat, and everything, everything tasted just great. It would take her less than an hour to make it. She jumped in the car and started the engine, threw the car in gear and stepped on the gas. She was looking backward to turn the car around in the road, but the car lurched forward. Sarah felt a large jolt accompanied by the *kabam* of an impact. When she looked forward, she saw that she had run into a tree, and lucky thing it was, too, for it had prevented the car from rolling down the bank into the river.

"Shit," she said aloud. She looked down to confirm she had at least one foot on the brake. She used the other foot to put on the parking brake. Then, carefully, carefully, she put the car into reverse, rocking the gear arm in its place to make sure this time. She released the brake, and with her knees shaking, she slowly put on the gas. The car shook slightly, then rolled backward onto the road. Sarah stopped, put the car in Park and rolled down her window. She took a few deep breaths, threw it into Drive and then roared down the road. Good God, she thought, how long would it have been before they found me? And what would my mother have thought? A suicide for sure. Another suicide. It would have driven Wilma crazy. She'd say, "Why, I knew that things were not perfect in her marriage, that she had come to visit me for a reason. I had no idea about her pregnancy, how could I have? And why in the world would that be a problem for her? She did not seem distraught. Sarah has never been difficult, and really who would have known?" In town behind Wilma's back, they'd whisper, "Another suicide. Poor Wilma. It does run in families, you know."

Whatever drawn-out speculation, whatever bridge-club explanation, Sarah was certain that Wilma would settle on the wrong story. All the more reason, Sarah thought, to avoid landing facedown in the Ararat River. Despite her present state of confusion, and even if that were her choice, she'd scarcely take her mother's prized LTD with her. That would have been seen, she knew, as a final insult—far worse to wreck the car even than to desecrate Wilma's sacred rosebushes.

Sarah concentrated on her driving as she traveled through Mount Airy and began the winding climb up to Fancy Gap. As she rounded the first overlook, she was grateful she had come, for the mountains were at once strange and familiar to her. The round hills were dark with trees, and at this hour there was so much fog that only the landscape around the road was visible. The rest was cloud. The car leaned into the curves of what felt like the last mountain on earth and cut through the passages carved in its side. When she reached the top, maybe she would find the right atmosphere for thinking, an ancient and clear air to sort the whole thing out.

Fancy Gap was not the top of the Blue Ridge, it was the first pass across a range that reached into Virginia and Tennessee. The TipTop Diner was just before the entrance to the Blue Ridge Parkway, a touring road that wound across the chain through most of North Carolina and its neighboring states. When Sarah pulled into the parking lot, she remembered that she had no purse or wallet in the car. She located five dollars in her jeans, then rummaged through the glove compartment again for loose change. She found a few dollars' worth in a plastic key chain wallet, and at the last minute grabbed a small desk calendar given out by Swan's Knob Bank & Trust.

The restaurant was half full. Sarah could smell the country ham on the griddle and the fresh biscuits. A few locals sat on stools at the counter and the half dozen couples were eating in leatherette booths. No one she recognized and no one anxious to catch her eye. She was directed to a small table next to the window right behind two women about her mother's age, each wearing one of those horrible polyester pantsuits. She sat down with her back to the women and the rest of the crowd. As quick as the waitress showed up with the coffeepot, Sarah ordered the largest breakfast they offered. While she waited for her food, she pulled out the calendar. She wanted to figure it up one more time.

"Good thing we didn't try to get the men up here with us this morning. Philip was downtown half the night. He'll sleep through the funeral if I don't get home to wake him up."

Did people do anything around here but eat and go to funerals? The woman was just behind Sarah, and she was too loud to ignore. Sarah had to re-count the weeks several times. She could pinpoint the cycles of her body fairly well, and this put her just at twelve weeks along. This was the fact, and in itself not so upsetting. She had always considered birth control more of an art than a science. The second calculation was more troubling.

"I know that this is a terrible thing, to have a policeman shot in our little town. And Lord, I feel so bad for his wife and little boy." Sarah ducked her head down. More people from Swan's Knob, of course. "But I tell you, these men are carrying on like they are all in the middle of some Greek tragedy. Some fool set off the volunteer fire siren in the middle of the afternoon yesterday, and Philip almost ran out of the house without his pants."

The waitress brought Sarah's breakfast at the same time that she served the ladies behind her, so the women were mercifully quiet for a few minutes. Just because Sarah hadn't recognized them didn't mean that they wouldn't know who she was. She slid the calendar into her lap. She had been over it before, her last night with Jonah had been March 15—this she remembered distinctly because he had teased her about the Ides of March, beware the Ides of March. For Harper, she was not certain—in their married life, sex was not an event that she marked. It was more of a basic commodity. She could no more remember when she last had potatoes for dinner. However, she was quite certain she would remember if she had given up potatoes altogether.

And here was her problem—the ultimate gray area—a week or two on the calendar she could not truly account for, a week in which she could not say who had fathered her child. She believed she could endure anything except for this uncertainty. A vital fact that was likely unknowable. It was the uncertainty that she was determined to hide.

"And what about this longhaired man from Mexico, Emily?"

"New Mexico, honey. Not Mexico," corrected the quiet friend.

"Whatever. Randall says he wonders, with all those folks here for the wedding, that maybe, just maybe . . ."

"Shhh . . ." said the friend faintly, and there was silence on the other side of the booth. Sarah continued to eat and even signaled the waitress for more coffee, hoping she hadn't been caught listening, or worse, identified.

The woman resumed, but dropped her voice so that Sarah could only hear bits of what she said. "There was . . . visiting . . . and then you saw her dress in front . . . so much of that champagne . . ."

Sarah was glad when she finished her breakfast, for suddenly the TipTop felt just like downtown Swan's Knob—altogether too public. The women were onto another topic now.

"Well, I've seen the car myself," said the friend. "The word's been going around town for months. Just this past Saturday, in Surry Drug . . ."

Of course. This was a county where you had to watch even

what you bought in the drugstore. And it was the very last place on earth where you would want to make a decision about the course of your life. She would go somewhere else, maybe back to Santa Fe, and wait in silence until the baby was born with Harper's nose or Jonah's eyes. Or she could go down to her mother's house, pick a story now and stick to it. She could make a case either way.

Or maybe, just maybe, she could refuse ever to discuss the matter, go off and live alone with her children on a mountaintop and tell her neighbors that her children's daddy was dead. Shot dead in a blood feud.

Wilma had provided sex education to Sarah in much the same way you would provision a small child for summer camp. Sarah had come home from seventh grade one afternoon to find an entire kit for womanhood laid out on her chenille bedspread: a box of Kotex sanitary napkins, the requisite white belt, a stack of wax paper bags with printed blue edging and the words "for disposal," and a book entitled *What Every Girl Should Know*. Her mother had put a little bookmark in front of the chapter entitled "The Cycle of Conception." On the bookmark, she had written, "Please read this part carefully!" and Sarah saw she had underlined various passages about how easy, how very easy it was for a girl to get herself in trouble. God, what did her mother think happened in seventh grade? Her mother wouldn't even let her shave her legs, which was going to keep her a virgin forever anyway.

Sarah had not started her period yet. Her friend Becky Small said that it was because she was so skinny, that skinny girls have fewer hormones, which was how the whole period thing got started. Sarah plopped down on her bed and flipped through the book to see if maybe it contained some information that she didn't know yet, though that was unlikely. For example, she wondered (and who could you ask?) if a blow job actually required any blowing at all. This was something she really might need to know at some point—though not in the near future because, eew gross, really.

There was a little diagram in chapter two that showed the changes that happen to a girl's body when she becomes a woman. Sarah opened her closet door so she could stand in front of the full-length mirror. She looked at herself sideways, then in the back and then the front. Thank God for her long hair, because otherwise she would look like a boy. She had no waist to speak of, and of course she was flat as she could be, despite a training bra and a shirt that had little pleats down the front. She sucked in her stomach and pushed her hands up under her rib cage so that her shirt formed a tidy bustline. Now, that didn't look so bad.

"Sarah," her mother said from the doorway. Sarah jumped. Her mother was always sneaking up on her.

"What?" she said, now busy inspecting the contents of her closet. She could see her mother from one corner of the mirror. She was standing at the doorway, a basket of fresh linens on her hip.

"I was just wondering if you had any questions about . . . well, you know, those little items that I left on your bed. Any questions?"

"No," said Sarah, "we covered everything in health last year."

"Well, you're getting older and I thought you'd be needing a few of those supplies pretty soon now," she said, smiling a little at the mirror.

"Thanks, Mom," said Sarah. Her mother was hovering in the threshold now, wanting to say something more. Sarah's red shirt had fallen to the floor of the closet. She picked it up and fished around for an empty hanger.

"Make sure you read that part I marked," her mother ventured. "You are living proof, you know, that it only takes *one time*." The "one time" had enough syllables to make a little tune. "Literally, honey, once. Do you understand what I mean?" Sarah looked for something else that needed hanging up, anything to stop a conversation that included her parents' having sex. Gross, totally gross. "And I told you about cousin Mindy. She was only sixteen."

"You know, since I am getting older and everything, how about buying me a razor?" said Sarah. "My legs are disgusting."

"Honey, best to wait. You know once you start that, there's no going back."

Sarah turned around to argue, but her mother had started back down the hall.

"And honey," her mother said, already at the top of the stairs, "put those things away before your dad gets home. There are some things men would just rather not see."

∽

Maybe he still had a buzz from the pool hall home brew. Maybe he was still recovering from Wilma's harsh reveille. Whatever it was, Harper was in a fog. Coffee. Definitely coffee was required before speaking with this Jonah character. Luckily, Jonah himself didn't seem to have anything to say either, and thankfully Miss Wilma had taken her songbird act upstairs so there was a little time of silence in the room. Harper stuck his nose into his coffee cup thinking the steam might help. Jonah was loading dishes into the sink now like some brown nose, and after a few minutes, asked him: "Eggs?"

Harper wanted to ask Jonah, this Jonah Branch, whoever the hell he was, exactly why he was offering Harper eggs here in the kitchen of Harper's own mother-in-law, but that seemed almost beside the point at the moment. Harper decided this guy was somehow generally pissing him off, was making him mad as hell just standing in the kitchen, and Harper could not think why that was. He was normally a peaceable guy—had even been told he was a sweet drunk—so he could not figure out why he would like to knock this guy silly out into the yard.

"No eggs. I'm not hungry," he said. "But, man, you've got to fill me in. What is your deal? I left you up in the mountains, and the next thing I know you turn up arrested down here."

"I was just camping out by the river," said Jonah, bringing his coffee over to the table and sitting opposite Harper. "Pretty little spot. I can't get over all the green around here. I met some local high school kids. They dropped me off there, and I was just cruising along, watching the river, and boom—next thing I know, some local cops are coming out of the bushes, putting me under arrest. I thought it was some kind of joke, at first—you know, them calling me Indian boy and kemosabe. Then they started talking about the murdered cop, and I knew I had hit a bit of trouble. Pretty soon, I'm in a damn cell and these guys are bustling around that little station like they are on to something big. I kept waiting for them to straighten the whole thing out, but no, these guys were scrambling around, not telling me anything. They'd bring their buddies in and let them look at me, like I was some kind of zoo animal. Then they'd go whispering in the next room. Pretty soon, here they'd come again, pulling me out of the cell to ask me more questions. What was I doing in town and what was I doing camped out near the bypass at that time of night and who did I know here and what did I see and what did I have against poor old Clemont Baker. All day yesterday. Then some kind of state cops came in and they put me back in the cell. That was even worse. It was a real tiny room, with a toilet and the only light coming through a little window in the door. Every time they'd come by to check on me, the room would get darker. Spooky as hell. It's hard not to start getting paranoid after a while." Jonah's voice was low and mellow voice like some FM station announcer's. The effect was a little too pretty for Harper's taste—just like the rest of the guy and his raven ponytail, Jesus—and Harper wished that he would quit looking at him so intensely as he talked.

"There must have been a dozen men in the station late last night. It was getting real eerie. I didn't know what they might do. You hear those stories and you don't believe them, but these men last night were talking real low, then got louder and louder and I couldn't really make out what they were saying. And finally, they all left me alone and I went to sleep. Then early this morning, they just came in and let me out. They gave me no explanation, and man, I didn't ask them a thing. I just put my wallet in my pocket and walked out. I went up and down Main Street a few times trying to figure out which direction Sarah's house was in and finally I ended up here. So far, I'll tell you, I haven't seen much of that Southern small-town welcome that everybody tells you about."

Somehow, Harper found himself short on sympathy for the guy. "So they let you go," he said. "Why haven't you split town?"

Jonah got up and went back over to the sink again, keeping his back to Harper. He didn't answer right away. He turned on the water, let it run for a few seconds, then turned if off and stared out the window over the sink. "There's no reason to leave right now," he said. "I mean, the cops didn't say they wanted me to go."

"It's a free country, man," Harper said. "So what I'm asking is, why in the hell would you stay? I have been here before, and let me tell you, there is nothing, nothing to keep you."

"If that's true, then what are you doing here?"

"Sarah. This is Sarah's hometown. We covered this in the car on the way out here. When Sarah split New Mexico last week, I figured that she was headed to see her mother."

"You didn't say she left without telling you."

"Yeah, well, she did. I didn't even know she was mad at the time. I just got home one night late, and she and Starling were gone."

"So you followed her here. Well, how did it go, have you patched things up?"

"I guess so. I mean I haven't really talked to her about it, but when I got here she let me back upstairs, if you get my drift." Jonah turned around suddenly when Harper said this, and Harper gave him a sly little smile just to let him know what he meant. "Yeah, man," he said, "she was waiting all right." This was not strictly true, but Harper was encouraged when he saw Jonah blush under his tan at his remark. He pressed further: "God knows what little peccadillo I committed to make her run. Could have been any of a number of little things—a late night, a bad rumor, a talkative redhead. But I guess it doesn't matter now, she's forgiven me for whatever it is." Harper wondered why he felt compelled to invent these college-boy remarks for Jonah. In truth, most of his sins had been committed years ago—he had done nothing, nothing at all, to get himself in hot water for at least six months, maybe a year—but all of these things were totally off the subject. He said, "But the question is, why are you hanging around?"

Jonah turned back to the sink, suddenly very intent on washing his coffee cup. "I thought I would wait around and see Sarah," he said. His tone struck Harper as carefully casual.

"And then what?"

"I thought she could show me around a bit. You know, the places she told me about: the Ararat River, the Knob, the soda fountain at the drugstore," Jonah said.

Harper was suddenly awake. "The Ararat, the soda fountain? I am not getting this. Was Sarah at a few shows at Minga's gallery without me? Because I can't remember seeing the two of you talking." Harper would have noticed. Sarah didn't talk much about herself, and her hometown was not the first item on her party chatter list.

"Sarah did work at the gallery last summer, you know. Maybe we've spent a little more time together than you thought," Jonah said, now with a tone that was not at all casual. Then he looked straight at Harper again. Harper was struck again by the absolute beauty of the man's face. Each feature was distinct, and his eyes were an iridescent green like some exotic cat. Harper was not exactly sure how to read their intensity. Anger, somehow, pride, and maybe a sort of possessiveness. Then he knew.

Harper bolted out of his chair and opened his mouth to tell the guy to get the hell out of the house. But then it occurred to him: it should have been clear much, much earlier. Everyone knew, everyone, everyone, Sarah, certainly Jonah, and Wilma—Sarah had told Wilma, and Wilma had asked Jonah to stay. It didn't ever matter to Wilma that her daughter had committed adultery, that her new boyfriend was suspected of murder, that she let this man into the house while Sarah's daughter, his daughter, slept upstairs. Oh God, Starling. He wondered if she knew too.

∽

Sarah tucked her tired body and her raggedy calendar back into her mother's car. *Just one time.* It was funny how her mother could latch on to some particular phrase and then find a way to bring it up again and again until all meaning was lost. Sarah would do everything she could to push the words away, but they always stuck around and played over in her head like some catchy jingle from the radio. Still, she had to admit, there was something in the warning. Wilma had that second sense about Sarah, always had. Just like that little woman's kit—Sarah had needed it in earnest just two weeks after her mother had laid it on her bed. Now, how had Wilma known that? That was what Sarah was after, some kind of second sense, finally, about her own situation. Maybe she would drive along the Blue Ridge a bit. The ramp to get on the parkway was just across the road from the TipTop. It would be quiet up there, she could think. She could go back and see what she had missed. She settled in the seat and took the road north.

Sarah had grown up hearing the story of her parents' first date. It was her father who always told it. There had been a fraternity mixer at Wake Forest. Her mother had gone over to the party from Guilford College with her best friend, Sally. Sarah could almost recite the story.

"That was the year I was president of old Delta Sig, and my

buddy Preston said he had me a mighty fine setup. Mighty fine.
Mighty fine."

She did not have a story to tell Starling about her first date
with Harper. There had been no actual date, for one thing. In
their circle at Guilford, dating was not really done. Couples simply showed up together in the commons one Sunday morning
wearing the same brand of mussed hair and everyone knew.

Of course, Sarah had noticed Harper the moment he began to
hang out with her gang of friends, all regulars at one long table
in the commons just across from the preppy voice majors.
Though he wasn't very tall, he had a way of arranging his torso
across a chair to maximum effect. One day he just sat down next
to Sarah.

"God, I just had a physics class that blew my mind," he said to
her, and it was clear that he was speaking only to her and not to
anyone else at the table. It was the first time they had actually spoken, though they had been watching each other for weeks.

"God," she said, "as if German lit isn't enough," referring of.
course to the fact that they were both taking a twentieth-century
German lit class. Rilke, Kafka, Mann—completely dark and
mind-blowing.

"Oh, man, it all ties in. That's what makes it so totally amazing. It's like you wish you were high for the class. We were talking about this guy Heisenberg. Get it? Another German. You just
know he hung out with Kafka, man." Harper had transferred to
Guilford from some big-deal school up north. A number of rumors floated around about exactly what had transpired. He
played in a jazz trio off campus.

"Really?" Sarah was able to listen intently, containing her excitement at this turn of events. She was happy that by chance this
morning she had put on her purple long-john shirt that made her
look a little like Joni Mitchell.

"On the night we met, your mother was wearing her pearls and,
as I recall, a very nice blue cashmere sweater. I knew the minute I

laid eyes on her. It was love at first sight, baby doll, love at first sight."

"So get this," Harper said. "This Heisenberg comes up with this thing called the Uncertainty Principle. He was trying to describe the location of an electron as it whizzes around the nucleus of an atom. And he just couldn't do it. So what he comes up with is this theory—and this can hardly be physics—what he says is that when you attempt to measure the world, to know one thing for sure, you destroy your ability to know other things."

"Wow," said Sarah. This was the kind of discussion she always thought she would have in college.

"It's like philosophy. What Heisenberg is saying is that the world is totally uncertain. Voila." Harper flipped his hand in the air like a magician just finishing a trick. "There it is—no use arguing—it's all reduced to an equation." Sarah could see that some of her other friends were also watching this little performance, but Harper focused on Sarah like she was the only one at the table.

"*I tried my best to impress your mother, pulled out my fancy shag routine and all. I swirled her and twirled her across the whole dance floor until I twirled her right into Preston Everly, who was drunk as a skunk and dumped a glass of purple jesus bathtub punch all down your mother's pretty sweater. After that, there was no way Wilma could dance with anyone else. Hey, hey, hey. She was marked.*"

Harper took Sarah's hands and looked at her in a way that made her feel like she was bathed in a white light. She pictured herself with chiseled features looking just like Joni Mitchell on the cover of her album *Blue*. Harper leaned in and whispered, "There is no way to predict what will happen. So I say, let's get in our measure today, while we still can. Let's take one path and destroy all the others."

Sarah was not completely naïve. She knew there was a big leap here, from logic and science right into Harper's bed. Sarah had seen him with other girls. She had seen him kissing Janey Foscue in the stairwell of Davis Hall, had watched him nuzzle another girl through a symphony concert. She was sure there were other things that had happened in more private circumstances, and she would imagine these scenes in Harper's bohemian dorm room involving jazz and poetry and candles. Sarah didn't care. She wanted to be next. To hell with her mother's fertility curse.

When Sarah finally got her chance that night with Harper, she was, technically, a virgin. She had her mother to thank for this. There had been plenty of chances to remedy the situation, going all the way back to her make-out sessions down by the Ararat River. Maybe the warning about poor cousin Mindy had somehow reached her, or maybe her mother and father's courtship story was programmed in her brain so that nothing else would seem right.

"Don't ask me how, but somehow, someway, I parlayed this little purple jesus mishap into a big ole kiss out on the porch later on in the evening. . . . And that's when I got her, my doll baby. Isn't that right? Just one kiss and she knew too. Isn't that right? You shake your head now, baby doll, but that's not what you did on that night, no ma'am."

On her first night with Harper, Sarah sat weightless on his bed and watched him light a patchouli stick and two half-burned-up candles that sat on a record crate by his bed. As he lifted her shirt over her head like she was a child, she felt her fears all burn away and drift like smoke from the patchouli, fragrant and harmless through the air. She had been right about the jazz—Stan Getz, if she was not mistaken.

"Look," she had said as they sat facing one another, sharing a joint donated by his friends down the hall, "it's no big deal, but I guess I haven't actually done this before." She used a casual tone, as if this state of virginity was due to some random carelessness on her part.

For all her efforts to toss it off, Harper held on to her confession like it was a teacup as delicate as an eggshell. He took her face in his hands, called her "precious, precious," and he pulled her to him skin on skin until there was not even a molecule of air between them. She thought that maybe it was the pot or maybe the patchouli or maybe, just maybe, it was the kind of love that would last a lifetime. And though the reality of a man, naked, standing before her with all of his parts was a kind of funny, funny surprise, she found that over time—over what seemed like a long time— she warmed up to the whole idea. And then they traveled beyond the idea and interlaced their bodies—fingers, elbows, necks, her breasts, his long hair and hers—an alchemy of mingled scent and touch. And that really, in the moment when they had all said that she would cry, she did, but not for pain or for sorrow of what was lost, but over what she had found, immeasurable and sweet. And in a little while, she cried again over just the sound of Harper sleeping, breathing in her ear.

If she could stop the car for a few minutes now, she might be able to stay in that moment. She wanted to find some piece of the mountain where she could still feel the warmth of Harper's breath on her neck, still feel excited about what was to come, where she could live in her twenty-year-old body without the tired dread of real life as it had unfolded. She took the first paved road off the parkway. The road was narrow and steep at first, then it leveled off and dipped down into a small valley. She half hoped to drive into some lost Appalachian civilization where people said "holler" and "settee" and played old-timey instruments on unpainted porches. She crossed a wooden bridge that spanned a small stream and slowed the car as the road began to wind up the other side of the hill. The light flickered green through the leaves. The trees grew thicker with each switchback, with small pools of light falling across the dark loam of the forest floor. At the top finally was a wooden sign with shrubs neatly arranged around it. Skyline Lake, it said. Up ahead, Sarah could see a clearing. As she drove into it, she realized that she was at the top of a mountain.

In the valley on the other side was a golf course with a large hazard pond in the center. Several groups were already playing. She could see brightly colored pants and shirts in the distance. Around the edge of the course and up the side of nearby hills were little clapboard bungalows. It was all newly planted, brought up from the Piedmont, and she knew she would find no fiddlers here. She looked for a place to turn around and took a road to the right that ran along a ridge, hoping to find a driveway where she could get the car turned around, but all of the driveways were very steep and the road continued to narrow. Finally the road ended with a large yellow hazard sign marking a cliff. Sarah stopped the car and got out. From this vantage, little of the golf course was visible and she could see out over the mountains, all the way down to the Piedmont, it seemed. She forgot the mountain suburb all around her. One comfortable old hill after another waited in the distance, clear into the horizon beyond. Sarah climbed up onto the front hood of the car and settled her back against the windshield.

During her first fall with Harper, they had spent many evenings outside under the trees on North Campus. In the cooling weather, their crowd would haul blankets and books out to the lawn and hang out late until the campus police ran them off. Someone would bring a guitar, there would be bottles of sweet wine and skunkweed passed all around. Harper would lead Sarah to a quiet part of the crowd and sit down right behind her. He would wrap his arms around her and pull her back to lie on his chest. In the half darkness, he would press his beard into her neck and whisper to her, whisper anything at all, and he would pull the ends of her shirt up out of her pants and just lay his hands softly on her belly, just leave them there not moving for a while, making her think what he would do. She would be still, only breathing. She would not see anything around her, she would feel only his touch. Then she would move slowly under his hands, and he would know, and he would pull her tight against him and move his hands over her breasts, over her belly, and down into her pants.

There was a point, she knew, when she did not care who saw, when she did not even know. In those days, she would lie with her whole body on top of him on the lawn. It was a time of full possession, when everyone else was a mere spectator. It was a time when the half-burned candles left over from other lovers held no meaning for her, because she was sure that they were gone forever, null and void. In the sweaty sleepless hours in his room, Sarah knew that they owned each other, that there was no return to the other world. She could remember herself in those days, unable to bathe her own body without thinking of him, unable to sleep and even to dream alone, wanting to find some ritual, any rite to circumscribe their love. Though it made her grown-up self ashamed almost to recall this, she remembered looking into his eyes while they made love, thinking that she saw his very soul and hers.

Sarah heard the bang of a screen door close by, closer than she would have imagined. There were no houses at this end of the street. She sat up a bit on the car hood and peered out over the hill. Through the trees she could see another house sitting on a street that had been cut in the side of the mountain just below. She could see mostly the roof and a little driveway where an older man in a yellow Ban Lon sweater was wrestling his golf clubs out of the trunk of his car. Even though the car was a land barge with a trunk big enough for four complete bodies, Sarah could hear him grunt and curse as he tugged at the bag.

"For Pete's sake, Sammy, just leave them in there." His wife stood behind him now, her hand over her mouth, laughing, Sarah thought. "Honey," said the woman, sounding more amused than annoyed, "just leave them. We'll fit the suitcases in the backseat. We'll be up here on the weekend anyway."

The man said nothing, continued to grunt. Finally, the golf bag came free. It flew out of the trunk, catching him off guard. He fell backward and the bag landed on top of him. Sarah could not make out what he said, cursing maybe. Some of the clubs fell out of the bag, clanging in the driveway. Sarah could see the bright colors, their club covers and other unnecessary accoutrements, all knit by the wife. They were bobbing up and down as the man shook the bag, struggling to free himself.

"Oh, Sammy, honey, are you hurt?" said the wife, running over to him. She bent down and began tugging on the carrying strap, trying to free her husband. She was a small woman, dwarfed by the man's golf bag, and wore a bright red pantsuit with a matching scarf in her hair. Even at this distance, Sarah could see that she wore more makeup than Wilma would wear in a month, and from the sound of it, high heels. She was strong enough to pull the bag off her husband and help him up.

For all of this, Sarah suddenly felt like a Peeping Tom and made herself small on the car, though of course the car remained big as ever. She felt like a child about to witness her parents' argument, for now, this woman would be scolding her husband over the mishap. Sarah hated to hear it, really. In her childhood house, these scenes had normally occurred at a time when her father was in no condition to defend himself, which was the point of the argument. Down in the driveway, the man in the yellow golf shirt was checking himself out, brushing off his pants. He turned to his wife and Sarah found that she was holding her breath, but the couple just stood facing one another for a moment, and then Sarah heard their mingled laughter roll out over the mountains.

This was unknown territory, this landscape of laughter on a random morning, and for a moment Sarah was taken up by their mood. She was the child of Sammy in the golf shirt and his wife in the red pantsuit. Sammy and his wife began loading their car with suitcases and grocery bags again, oblivious to her car parked on the road above them. Sarah tried to see herself in Skyline Lake in thirty or forty years, tried to imagine what kind of Sammy would be by her side, but she could not picture herself tolerant and laughing in a red pantsuit.

At the end of their enchanted first semester, Harper had talked her into going with him to New York. After telling enormous lies to her mother, they had headed north in a van with six other friends. Harper was a veteran of the city, having spent two years in what he called a "creeped-out" music school before transferring to Guilford College. He had lined up a place for everyone to stay in, an old warehouse building somewhere in the Garment District. As they rode a metal-frame elevator up to the third floor, Sarah wondered if they would be sleeping on a factory floor, but they landed in a largely empty loft with enormous photos on the walls and grubby kitchen appliances in the corner. They dropped their belongings in a heap and left the loft on foot.

Sarah never loved New York when she lived there as much as she did during that first day of trekking through the streets with the wind blowing through her North Carolina coat, the city lights set off by all the Christmas glitter. Harper ditched the rest of the group and led her through the streets of the Village, then to Midtown to see the big tree at Rockefeller Plaza. They blew through Macy's and Saks and head shops and East Side florists. By late afternoon, they found themselves standing in the middle of Central Park with snow flurries swirling around them. They opened their coats and pulled their bodies together, stood chest to chest with the fabric wound around them and their arms holding each other. Sarah thought then that she had been transformed, that she was no longer a girl from a little town in North Carolina, that she had been singled out and then made a part of a whole new place, a place where Harper led her and she had followed.

Sammy and his wife, with a purse to match the red pantsuit, drove away finally, and Sarah decided that it was time to leave as well. She climbed down off the hood and got into the car. When she turned the key, the engine started briefly, then died. She tried again and the engine only sputtered. She tried again, checking the dashboard gauges. The damn car was out of gas. She would have to find a phone and call a gas station. Maybe someone was in one of the nearby houses or maybe there was some kind of clubhouse where they had a pay phone. Of course, she had no money, having emptied her pockets to tip the waitress at breakfast. She wondered if she could find a country gas station where they would take her word on a gallon or two of gas. She looked around the car for anything that she needed to take with her. Nothing.

It occurred to her that Sammy and his wife might have some kind of gasoline stored around their little bungalow. Sarah locked the car and walked over to the embankment. It was too steep. She turned and walked down the road until she came to the turnoff, then headed down the hill and into the next street where Sammy and his wife lived.

Chapter Six

By the time Miss Wilma got herself bathed, her injury was making itself known to her. She had kept her hand out of the bathwater and changed the cold washcloth several times, but still, the imprint of the stove's burner throbbed across her palm. She found it hard to go through her routine without getting anything on the burn. It made her clumsy enough to spill bath powder all over the floor, which she tracked across the room when she went to her dresser to get her good slip and stockings. By the time she got to her makeup, she was perspiring so much that her rouge lumped on her cheek. The left-handed application of mascara, heavier than usual, made her face look wide-eyed and oddly asymmetrical. She rummaged in her drawer and found the lipstick that she reserved for dark winter days. The bright red seemed to straighten her face a bit.

On her way to the closet, she tiptoed over to the door and opened it a crack to let some air in. She could hear that Harper and Jonah were still talking in the kitchen. She couldn't hear what they were saying, but their conversation was carried on in normal tones. She wondered how long it would be before Harper figured it out or Jonah told him. She wondered herself what had gone on between Sarah and Jonah. Maybe there was nothing to it at all and she had made it up in her own mind. That's probably what

Sarah would say. "Honestly, Mother," she would say, "you always think the worst of me. How could you imagine me with another man? This is what your mind does when you've deprived yourself all these years." And Wilma would reply, "Sarah, I am not accusing you, darling, only giving you a little bit of credit this time." Or more likely, they would say nothing about any of it to each other. Sarah would not talk about her intimate life with Wilma these days, hadn't in many years, and in truth Wilma would not dare to bring it up.

She pulled her green linen suit with three-quarter sleeves from her closet and laid it on the bed. Longer sleeves might rub against her hand and make it worse. She added a fitted silk cream blouse that dressed up the suit enough for the afternoon's funeral, if she was careful not to wrinkle the skirt before she got to the church. It was hard to say just when and how in Sarah's eyes she became more of a barely indulged distant relative than a mother. It had happened before Sarah's wedding, that was for sure, since Wilma had not been invited. Sarah had called collect from a pay phone to give her the news. "You're not going to believe this," Sarah had said, giggling like the teenager she had been just two years before, "we're married." Wilma could hear calliope music in the background, the sound of someone else's laughter and maybe the smack of kisses. "Harper and I." This stung, like the burn did now on her hand, as did the news two months later that there was a baby on the way.

Wilma tried to tie the attached collar into a bow under her chin. By the time Wilma knew that she would be a grandmother, Sarah was already four months pregnant. She had skipped her graduation ceremony, left for New York City just after her last exam. No time to come by Swan's Knob. Once Sarah was gone, their phone calls became brief. Wilma would want to know so many things, but would somehow hate to ask, so there would be a silence and then Sarah would say she had to go get their clothes from the Laundromat down the street. When Starling was born and for months afterward, Wilma wanted so much to go to see her and would have even ventured the trip to the city alone. She waited and hoped for the invitation, sent Sarah's own rocking chair in a crate, but no invitation came and she could not, though now she wondered why, bring herself to ask.

She was finished now and it was time to get on with her day. Despite the poor makeup job, the woman in the mirror, standing there, sixtyish in her green linen skirt and silk blouse, looked very organized. In the mirror, even the damp washcloth in her burned hand looked like a simple handkerchief, held as a ladylike precaution against sorrow or unforeseen perspiration. For some reason this morning, her very orderly appearance disappointed her, like rain just before a picnic. But this was not a morning to moon at her reflection like a teenager, it was time for her lesson, though she had not heard the front doorbell. She walked out into the hallway and stopped to listen. She could no longer hear the men talking, but someone was washing the dishes in the kitchen. Starling's door was still closed. She would undoubtedly sleep until noon.

Wilma wondered if she should be worrying about Sarah. Funny. Since this morning's revelations, Wilma had somehow suspended her concern. She felt that maybe Sarah had been taking care of herself for quite some time. Wilma went down the stairs and across to the music room without bothering to check on whoever might be left standing in the kitchen. She looked out the front window and found her ten o'clock pupils, a pair of seven-year-old twins, sitting on the stoop. Jonah sat between Lindy and Lou with his hands on his knees, elbows tucked against his large torso. All three had their heads bent, giggling like best friends from the second grade. Wilma tapped on the window and the girls snapped their heads around, wide-eyed. On seeing her, their giggles were gone. They hopped up in unison and trotted with straight backs up to the front door. By the time they filed into Miss Wilma's music room, their gaits had taken on a gravity that stopped Miss Wilma's heart, that made her want to shout, "Go on out and run and play now. No lessons this summer. We'll see you in the fall," but they were already seated at the bench, their two sets of braids falling neatly down their backs, their scale books open to F Major. Wilma reminded herself of the big wonderful smile yesterday on James Moody's face after his performance at the recital. He had not heard anything from the scholarship committee, he said, but he thought that he had played well and everyone on the jury had clapped for him. Maybe all of his practice, summer, winter, spring, and fall, would pay off soon. Wilma looked at the subdued twins with their serious little faces, considered what might make them smile—the boogie-woogie, perhaps—but in the end said only, "Begin."

∾

The street where Sammy and his cute tolerant wife had their mountain house seemed deserted—few cars in the carports, curtains closed. When Sarah reached their house, she marched right up the drive like a neighbor going for a visit. There was a sign out front hanging on a colonial lamppost. It must have come from Sammy's workshop where he had spent several fall evenings burning out the letters. His wife had painted it then in blue and white. LUV HUT, USA, it said. There was a little heart at the end. Red. The plain lovey-doveyness of this sign in front of the sweet little house made Sarah want to cry. At the same time, it welcomed her. She was a person who could barely enter her own mother's house without knocking, but here, somehow, here she felt free to walk through the carport and up the stairs to the screened-in porch. It was not even locked—another sign of welcome. She walked across the bright putting-green carpet. The utility closet was unlocked as well. She found the chain and turned on the light. The closet had a slightly metallic smell of mountain mold and was filled with pots, lawn-chair cushions and a few grasshoppers. No gas cans. Not even a lawn mower.

What Sarah really needed now was a phone. She did not think that Sammy and his laughing wife would mind if she tried the doors and windows, so she circled the tiny house, but everything was locked. Sarah sat down on a white wrought-iron chair in the screened porch. She was tired, really tired suddenly. Somehow walking up the hill in search of the clubhouse or some other place seemed insurmountable. After a few minutes, she began to feel the cold metal through her jeans. A phone. She looked at the entry at the other end of the porch. It had a door with wood on the bottom half and glass panes in the top. If she broke just one little pane, she could reach her hand in and unlock the door. Her daddy had done this once. Being sober in the light of day, though, she thought she could avoid slicing her arm badly enough to have dozens of stitches. If she was careful, she could avoid getting blood all over this woman's floor.

Sarah made herself get out of the chair for a closer look. Maybe the woman in the red pantsuit wouldn't mind one little broken pane if she knew the whole story. She cupped her hand up to her forehead and pressed it to the window so that she could see in. The door opened onto the kitchen, which had a spotless linoleum floor. She would sweep up the glass. There was a small tarp covering an outdoor grill. Sarah took it off the grill cover, folded it double and wrapped it around her fist. Then she held the rest of it securely over her arm and tapped at the glass with her fist.

She could not remember now exactly why her father had broken the glass in their kitchen door. She recalled only the sound of glass echoing through the house all the way up to her room upstairs. She ran downstairs and found her father standing in the kitchen, dripping blood on the floor. She remembered later her father's sheepish smile as he walked in with a Wall Hardware bag, which held some caulk, a replacement pane of glass, plus a few more. "In case," he said, "that crazy old bear comes back again."

Sarah closed her eyes and punched hard. The glass fell out in one clean piece and then shattered when it hit the floor. Reaching the lock was easy, and the air inside was warm. A blanket of stillness lay over the house. Sarah had never entered a corner of the universe as an intruder, and she was surprised that she felt nothing but the calm beat of her heart as it followed the tick of a distant clock.

She stepped over the glass, through the pristine kitchen and into the living room. It was a room designed for comfort. Every piece of furniture was padded in some way, covered with earth-tone fabrics and piled high with afghans and pillows. The room was dominated by enormous windows facing the mountains. It was the same view that she had seen from her car. The sun was stronger now and she could see the mist literally rising up off the mountains. Two recliner chairs, one slightly smaller than the other, sat at the far end of the room, facing the window. Sarah could picture the couple spending their afternoons in these chairs, him listening to a ball game maybe, her reading a book, chatting sometimes, sometimes holding hands. Sarah laid down on the couch. She felt a little like Goldilocks for a moment, lying in Baby Bear's bed. The view was breathtaking from this position. It was like she was resting in a cloud. Here, away, far away from anything she owned, anything she owed, she felt in full possession of herself, so clearly apart even from the decision that she must make. She felt the rhythm of the hills around her, the song they sang as the curtain of mist lifted. She knew that she was straying from her purpose, but the phone could wait, and she wondered, would Sammy and his wife really mind?

✍

The sink full of sudsy dishwater was a strange comfort to Harper. His submerged hands relaxed under the water, warmed his shivering body, and he washed the dishes slowly to make the task last. He wanted to stand there and stare out the kitchen window undisturbed forever. He did not even want to turn around. He heard Wilma come down the stairs and cross to the front of the house. She opened the front door and he heard for a second the laughter of her students on the porch. He could heard a deep laugh continue after Wilma's step stifled the students'. Jonah was still out there. Harper knew that he should be reacting in some way, taking the situation in hand, dealing with it. But shit, he couldn't think of a thing to do about it.

He started to work on the frying pan and tried to shuffle through the last few months in Santa Fe. Had anything been out of place? Their lives, he knew, had no kind of routine, no one day was like any other. There was no time that they got up every day, no time they went to bed. They ate meals together once in a while, and those were nothing fancy, each person finding something to eat in the refrigerator, grabbing a fork and knife and sitting down and getting up at random. In Miss Wilma's house, he noticed, even this morning, Wilma had put out her placemats and set the table. He had not asked for so much as a set of matching jelly glasses from Sarah, and for himself he expected to come and go as he pleased. Other than some objections when Starling was a baby, Sarah had seemed to go along with this arrangement. These days Starling was old enough to keep her own schedule, to be home alone. Now that he thought of it, he remembered pulling up in the driveway near dusk recently and seeing the house all dark. He had been surprised to find Starling sitting on her bed with her room lit only by the glow of an incense cone. He tried to remember, had he talked to Starling that night? Probably. Maybe. What had he said?

Sarah must have come in later. He wondered, how had she seemed, how did she look, what was she wearing? He couldn't remember a thing, and shit, why would he? Just a plain old day, like the rest of them. He could not be certain that he had even looked squarely into Sarah's face. Had he really been paying attention in the least, he might have seen something there in her expression, might have said, hey, Sarah, what's going on? Maybe one extra gesture, one extra question might have made her take his hands and sit him down and tell him, tell him everything.

Like hell she would have.

She had been careful to make sure that he didn't know a damn thing. Why tell him? Why not make him drive her fucking boyfriend across the country first? Why not just split in the middle of the night and let her egg-cooking boyfriend lay it all out for him? Why not let the Indian stud spell it out for him, chapter and verse, in her mother's kitchen? Maybe that's what all of this Jonah business amounted to—a long plot of revenge. Sarah's vengeance on him. But for what?

It was difficult for him to add it all up. To compare his multitude of small sins, truly peccadilloes, with this whopper of a blow. So far, it looked like she had gone way overboard her first time up. If it was her first time up.

Harper heard Starling shuffling down the stairs. He had exactly three seconds to dump his thoughts into the dishwater and get his shit together. He rubbed his eyes on his sleeve and tried to cop a casual stance, but he found that when she appeared, he was choked up by what he saw. It was as though he had not seen her for a really long time. She was wearing an old T-shirt with kittens on it that she had worn since grade school paired with very short jean cutoffs. She grunted slightly in Harper's direction and began to butter a piece of cold toast, her tangled hair concealing her face. Harper swallowed hard and dried his hands. "Honey, don't you want me to make you some fresh toast?" he said, managing a fairly normal tone.

Starling gave him a confused look, but dropped the toast on the counter. "I guess so, sure," she said and sat down at the table. Miss Wilma's students had finished their scales and were moving on to the assigned piece in their John Thompson book. Harper, he told himself, just hang on to the music, cling to the notes. The students played together at the piano, and Harper could hear immediately that one child had practiced more than the other. The other child finally stumbled badly and lost her place, creating a syncopated tangle. Miss Wilma stopped them.

Starling watched him make the toast, looked around the kitchen at the rack of dishes he had just finished. "Where's Mom?" she asked. Harper was given a few seconds' reprieve as the students began to play again. Starling rolled her eyes. "Oh God," she said, "will this go on all day?"

"No, babe, Wilma has a funeral this afternoon, so Plink and Plunk may be her last students," said Harper. Keep up the patter, he thought, you're fine. He put the toast on a plate, poured a glass of milk, and put it in front of Starling.

"Butter, please," she said. Miss Wilma had a special dish for butter, with a little dome and everything.

When he put it on the table, Starling giggled and said, "Since when did I ever drink milk?" He dumped out the milk and poured some juice.

"And a knife?" She smiled, enjoying the new game.

"Babe, you are a lot of trouble," he said, "just like that mother of yours."

Starling concentrated on her toast for a moment. "So is Mom sleeping again?"

"At ten o'clock? No, babe. You know your mother is a morning bird."

"Not since we got here. She's been sleeping day and night. So where is she?"

He was obliged to answer. He considered mumbling something about errands, multiple errands that could take a while, but this tack could get him into trouble later on. He chose the minimalist approach, and said, "She went out. I'm not sure when she'll be back."

That was enough. Starling looked at him, evaluating his expression. "Did you guys fight? She didn't head back to Santa Fe, did she?" Her voice lost its teenaged timbre as she spoke, sliding up the scale to the squeak of a ten-year-old. She bent her head down until her chin touched the ratty kittens on her T-shirt.

Seeing her, Harper felt like putting his own head down on the table and crying for them both. "Santa Fe? I seriously doubt it, babe. For one thing, she's in Miss Wilma's car. For another thing, this is your mother, honey. Has she ever taken off across the country before?"

It was the eyes of the teenager and not the child that glared at him now. "Okay," he said, "I meant, she'd never take off without you, babe. Sarah is not about to leave you here, leave us here"— he lowered his voice—"with Miss Wilma. Look, maybe she's gone for a drive. She'll be back in a little while. You'll see." This last bit seemed to work to some degree. Starling got up to make herself more toast, swaying her head a bit in time with the tumbledown waltz being drummed out in the sunroom.

"How about you and I play a little later today once Plink and Plunk have cleared out?" she said. "The keys on the piano at home are such a mess lately that I haven't been playing anything but violin." She was right—most everything above high C was sticky and half of the rest was out of tune. Harper had meant to see about that months ago, but it had just slipped past.

"Sure, babe," he said, vowing to himself to do it today and to really pay attention to her this time. Harper wondered how much she knew about her mother's situation—very little, evidently. He wondered what she was going to think about Jonah's presence in the house. It was hard for him to judge just how much she could put together at her age. Who knew, maybe Jonah was already an old family friend to her.

✍

Sarah could picture Sammy's wife—a woman who remained unperturbed through thirty-five years of bad habits, a woman who would rather laugh at small faults than run them up a flagpole, this woman whose shelves were full of romance novels and

god-awful blown-glass birds and silhouettes of women in bonnets—
Sarah could picture this woman sitting down beside her in her
red pantsuit, saying, "Well, of course you had to get in the house
somehow. You needed a phone." Then they'd have a long talk
about all those important minor topics that she and her mother
could not get to: how you could cry over any little thing at the
wrong time of the month, how she had once cried over a student
reading her own haiku, how there was no sound more terrible
than the sound of glass breaking, how some days it was difficult
just to swing your feet off the bed, how hard it was to look back
and remember just exactly how someone had looked the last time
you saw him, the very last time just before you left the house and
came back and he was gone.

Sarah had told Harper the whole story about her father that
first day in New York. Somehow, it was easier to talk about so far
from home, as they walked the streets of the Village. She had
begun the tale offhandedly: the old story of drinking—"your father's drinking," her mother called it—late arrivals, slurred ex-
planations, the smokestack wheezing of a man passed out in the
kitchen. She told Harper these things in a tone that did not be-
tray the weight of the events. To her, it sounded like an ironic
book report on a biography of Tennessee Williams. Sarah told
him that few people had known, few had guessed, because no
matter what happened, her father had appeared in his office the
next morning at Frederick Mabry and Son, Accountants. He was
Harry Mabry, the son, starched shirt, adding machine ready to
go. The broken window and blood all over the towels in the
bathroom, they were just the work of "that crazy bear, sweetie."
Sarah had told Harper these things in just the way her father
would tell his own story—so far away, so in the past and now
done with that Harper had listened as you would to any childhood saga, casually, with half an ear, his eyes trained on his surroundings.

He led them finally to a little park, to a special little bench where he had played with his now-famous friends right on the street. He was about to name them and launch into his own recollections when Sarah pulled him back. "What happened," she said, "what happened was that he got worse and worse, then just when we thought he would never get better, he seemed to be suddenly happy again, almost like himself, like he had fixed everything in his mind. Then, one morning when I was at school, he went out back just after my mother had left the house. While I was in algebra, he went out back and shot himself with his deer rifle. Through the head."

Sarah was embarrassed by the obscenity of the words. She saw each blunt detail as it steamed out of her mouth and settled down into the empty cold park.

Harper had said, "God, babe, I am so sorry," and pulled her close. She thought now that he had not been sorry, for sympathy, regret, remorse were all beyond him then. He had held her for what he judged to be the proper interval, then he had indeed launched into his music buddy story, filling up her silence with a rush of words and hand motions and little tunes trumpeted through his lips. And after a while, he pulled her up off the bench to lead her on.

At the time, she remembered, she thought Harper's one moment of silence ran deep, with her sorrow profoundly acknowledged at some corner of his soul. This had produced a momentary relief, but by the end of that night, it occurred to her: truly her sorrow had been dumped out there on the ground without so much as a layer of dust to cover it. Harper pulled her away from the park, had promised her festivities beyond her imagination.

Sarah laid back on the couch, stuffing needlepoint pillows behind her head so that she could still take in the view. She was engaging in what her mother called wallowing in the cold soup, a term original to Wilma that meant dwelling unnecessarily on unpleasant past circumstances. Sarah thought that her mother considered vast portions of her own life so unspeakable that even thinking about them was unwise. Certainly this theorem applied to Sarah. But for today, Sarah was here in the house of Sammy to wallow away, and for today she would think about the Village Palace, a place she had not thought about very often over the years.

On the single night she had been there, the Village Palace resembled no famous place Sarah had ever seen. There was nothing more than a small sign hanging on a brick arched alley to mark the entrance. Inside, it was comfortably dark, smoky, and full of people in all description of trendy black clothing. The band was between sets, or maybe, Harper told her, they hadn't started yet, it was only ten o'clock. From the entry, Sarah could not see a single vacant chair or even a place to stand, but Harper waded through the crowd to the most raucous group in the place, leaving Sarah a few paces behind. There were eight or ten men and women clustered around two or three round tables. Most looked older than Sarah. When they saw Harper, they swarmed him like someone raised from the dead, ruffled his hair, slapped his back. The women—every one of them—rushed forward to kiss him. When he remembered to turn around to bring her into the crowd, the men looked her over frankly and smiled back at Harper. They seemed friendly enough, all faintly rumpled and smoking like a bunch of frat boys. This hint of boyishness, however contrived, made them seem approachable to Sarah and she smiled at them. The boys were always the easy part. They smiled back in a way that told her they would forgive her little North Carolina notion of the world in about two minutes, especially if she would just call one of them "sugar."

The girls—or more properly from the looks of them, the women—were an entirely different matter. As a group they had stepped back perceptibly as Sarah had stepped in beside Harper. With one look, Sarah could see that whatever smiling she had already done had been a mistake. Each woman wore a world-weary expression that Sarah could not put on without practicing in a mirror. These women had on *outfits,* not like those her mother would wear, but *ensembles.*

Two chairs were produced from somewhere and placed at opposite ends of the table. Everyone sat down and went back to their conversations. Sarah tucked her hair behind her ears. Who were these people? The guy sitting on Sarah's left began to speak so rapidly to the man across from him that it sounded to Sarah like some foreign language. Two women to Sarah's right, one with long brown hair, the other with short hair pulled behind her ears, regarded her briefly then turned back to one another. As a way to calm herself, Sarah tried to mentally place these women in the Foundation Department at Belks or on a dorm floor with juice-can curlers in their hair. Impossible. At the other end of the table, Harper was talking to a brunette with a face right out of *Vogue*—black eyeliner in a perfect oval surrounding each eye, thick enough to be seen at a distance. She wore a thick coat of gray shadow on her lids. Harper seemed to know her well, laughing now with her, leaning over to catch something she said. The man beside Sarah had a perfectly trimmed beard and some kind of British safari jacket. He handed her a juice glass and poured red wine from a carafe on the table.

"So," said Sarah, resisting the urge to leave her place and stand beside Harper, "you all must have known Harper when he lived in New York before."

"Well, it is hard to avoid knowing one another," said the man (he was actually smoking a pipe), "when you're at Juilliard. It is a rather small group, when all's said and done."

"Juilliard?" said Sarah, realizing that she had used all three syllables and then some. The wine did not taste half bad. The man smiled but managed to keep his lips curled around the pipe.

"Yes, Ju-llie-yard," said the man, "the music school."

"Yes, I know what it is," she said. Harper had just not told her.

Sarah remembered little else about their conversation except that the man had continued to fill her glass and had continued to speak to her in a condescending but appreciative manner, as if he found her quaint and amusing. For her part, Sarah found that she could not resist obliging him. Through the evening, her accent became more pronounced and she began to tell stories about fatback and cows and other things she knew nothing about and to field questions about life in a South that resembled Mayberry more than any other place, a little town built on a back lot in Hollywood. She entertained the young man, and he began to wave his pipe around and laugh heartily and say over and over, "How completely amusing." As she began to lose track of the wine, she noticed that some others were listening, too—even the women, though Harper (damn him) was otherwise occupied and did not look once in her direction. She remembered thinking clearly just before she got completely lost that she had stumbled into what she least expected in Manhattan—a small town as provincial and isolated as some mountain hollow. She remembered thinking before she lost all thought and speech that she hoped here too in this small town that folks would show kindness to a stranger, for the last thing she remembered before she forgot everything was that Harper and the eye-shadow lady stood up and left the nightclub together.

Sarah saw the trees begin to sway as a breeze whipped through the little valley. She felt chilly suddenly by association. It was May, nearly June, but the mountain house felt cold. She got up off the couch and started to pace the room. The idea of Harper leaving her there in a strange bar in an unfamiliar city late at night with virtual strangers still made her madder than hell even all these years later. She had reminded Harper of the incident over and over for the first five years, pointing out other women with harsh makeup, comparing his latest indiscretion with that night and once telling the whole story to a dinner party of near strangers.

Early on Harper tried pitifully to defend himself—he and the woman had only gone out for some air, had come back and Sarah was gone, but eventually he had banned the incident entirely as a topic of conversation.

When he spoke of the evening to friends, Harper called it the night they had caught Thelonius Monk at the Palace, said he was trying out incredible new material that Harper had never found on any record. For her part, Sarah could not remember the music at all. She did not know if Thelonius Monk had come on after she had left with the guy with the pipe, or before, during her whole Southern fatback routine. In fact, to this day she remembered not another thing. To her, there was Harper out the door and the next thing she remembered was a headache, pain preceding full consciousness. She had opened her eyes to totally unfamiliar surroundings.

She was lying on her side in a bed in a dark and tiny room. She had waited calmly for a few moments, expecting the recognition to come. What came to her was that she was in New York City, nothing more. She turned onto her back and discovered that Harper was curled up beside her. They must have crashed in the apartment of yet another friend. She thought back, as much as her headache would allow, to the night before. Nothing, except that he had left her. Well, she thought, looking at the stained ceiling, at least he came back, but damn him for leaving.

Involuntarily, her knee popped up and struck him in the back. Damn him. He groaned and turned over to face her. Sarah looked over, then leapt out of bed. The sleeping man was not Harper. Sarah stood for a moment shivering, realized that she was naked from the waist down, and began to search the room for her jeans. She found them in a dismal pile, commingled with someone else's. Still standing, she struggled to get the pants back on, but her balance was not good and she was forced to sit down on the bed. As she pulled at the left leg, she studied the person in the bed. It was the man with the pipe. Surely she could not have been so stupid.

She picked up her shoes and opened the door—the room was so small that she could barely open it halfway without hitting the bed. She slipped out, but stopped short at the edge of the outer room. It was nearly as small as the bedroom and was literally filled wall to wall with sleeping people. In the semidarkness, Sarah thought she recognized several people from the Palace, men and women, their faces distorted with sleep, collectively emitting the vapors of a stale nightclub. Sarah quickly identified the bathroom and tiptoed in. Once inside, she ran the water and performed a quick inventory of the damage done. As she had feared, the headache was the least of it. She waited a while until the water got hot and then she washed up as best she could, not thinking about what had happened—with luck, she would be eternally spared the memory. She thought instead about how she would get out of there and onto the street and away from the city.

She found her purse hanging on the bedroom doorknob, but her coat was not with it. Forget it, she decided, get out of here. The human obstacle course on the floor was her first test, and as she plotted her path, she saw that Harper slept among them, face-down on a worn-out couch. When she walked by him, she briefly considered waking him, but rejected the idea. Damn him. Near the front door, she saw his companion from the night before curled up on a beanbag chair. She was wearing Sarah's coat. Without a moment's thought, Sarah bent down, grabbed one lapel and tugged until the woman's arm came out of the armhole, then tugged again until the woman rolled on the floor and Sarah could pull the coat off her other arm and free the entire thing. At this point, the woman woke just enough to rub her left eye and to stare up briefly at Sarah, who smiled down into the woman's pale, smudged face and walked out the front door.

On the street, Sarah found that getting unlost was easy as pie in New York City. She ducked into the nearest subway and studied a map until she found the route to Penn Station. She did not even have to go back to the surface before she was safe on the train south. Though she arrived near suppertime, in her mind she was back at her little liberal arts college before any of them even woke up, while they all still laid dead to the world in New York City.

If you had asked her that night, she would have said that she would never see Manhattan again. But in Sarah's life, biology had done nothing but play tricks on her. By early fall, there she was, bathing Starling in a rusty sink where the water took a full five minutes to get warm, up on the third floor, surrounded by fewer square feet of New York City than the place of the man with the pipe. She had never known the man's name, had never seen him again. Sarah forgave Harper in her rush to forget, in her rush to get on with their life together. As her own small concession to circumstances, she had allowed him to lead her back there, to the city of his dreams, at least for a time.

Chapter Seven

Miss Wilma used her key to let herself into the back of the church. She stopped in the choir room to collect her robe, organ shoes and hymnal. Then, carrying her whole collection, she entered the sanctuary through the back. Out of habit she closed the door silently and tiptoed up to her place behind the choir loft. The organ nook, with its single beveled-glass window, had been her domain for twenty years now. It was as familiar as her own bedroom, and what with choir practice, Sunday service, and ceremonial days like this one, she had spent nearly as much time in it.

She was seated at her organ tying on her shoes before she looked out at the rest of the church and saw that Ronald Snow, Jr. was in the middle of his own preparations for the funeral. Ron prided himself on running the best funeral home in the county and performed his duties as if they were a God-given right rather than part of a small-town funeral business handed down from his daddy Ronald Senior. From all Wilma had seen, he put on a nice funeral, treating even the poorest of kin with dignity and running the proceedings with military correctness. Even his mode of dress had a precision that bordered on fussiness, sleeve cuffs showing just one-half inch, tied knotted just so. The only unseemly element of his countenance was a full head of red hair, the color made more brilliant in contrast with his translucent complexion and pale gray eyes.

Ron had rolled Clem Baker's casket to the front of the church aisle and adjusted its placement along the chancel rail until it was centered. The casket was an elaborate mahogany model with intricate handle fittings, and Miss Wilma wondered who had paid for it. Ron locked the wheels into place and opened the top half of the lid. He scanned the contents with a professional eye. He turned his head to the side a bit and frowned, seeing something he didn't like. He pulled his handkerchief from his pocket, licked the corner and began to gently dab, like a mother whose child has a dirty mouth. He stepped back, checked his work, stepped up to make some other adjustment, then closed the lid and straightened his own tie. As he turned around to lift a spray of flowers from the front pew, Miss Wilma—suddenly feeling like an old maid on a party line—rattled her music on its stand. Ron startled and dropped the spray.

"Why, Miss Wilma, I didn't see you there," he said, blushing up to his hairline.

"I'm sorry, Randall, I just this very minute walked in and you were busy with the flowers so I didn't want to disturb you," said Wilma. Ron bent to pick up a dozen red carnations that had fallen across the communion rail. The spray looked better without them. Wilma despised carnations more than anything and had not allowed the florist to use even one on her Harry's funeral spray. "I'm sorry I startled you. Will those be all right?"

"Oh, I can fix these in no time," said Ron, recovering rapidly now. Miss Wilma realized that she had not spooked him at all. He had just been embarrassed to think she might have seen him rummaging around in the coffin.

Miss Wilma went on about her business, arranging her sheet music for the service, flexing her burned hand to keep it from getting stiff. Thankfully, funerals were a lot easier for her than weddings. They were usually hastily assembled, and there was not a bride and her mother to fuss over every blessed detail for months on end. Wilma was generally left on her own to select the music. She had found over the years that is was best to use old familiar hymns. Handel, Saint-Saens, Bach—the pieces she would prefer for her own service—sounded cold to most people. To them, they were without emotional weight, and really, people came to a funeral to have a chance to cry. Today there would be plenty of that—Fred Surratt from the Baptist church choir was coming to sing and his old gospel style was sure to get folks going. He had told Miss Wilma that he would sing "In the Garden" and the ever-popular "The Lord's Prayer."

Ronald and his son Ronny—Ronald Snow, III—were now bringing flower arrangements of every description down the aisle, filling the front of the church. The warmth in the sanctuary propelled a sweet, deathly scent into every corner. For Wilma, the association was instant, overwhelming and as inevitable as her own inhaling. She leaned back on the bench, allowed herself one deep breath's worth of recollection of Harry's funeral. It had been in exact keeping with all of the town's most dignified traditions, she had seen to that. Closed coffin, of course, given the circumstances, with a simple spray of yellow roses, a short eulogy, family burial. Most difficult for Wilma was the question, the big question, that had loomed conspicuously over the entire proceeding.

Though it was undoubtedly a major topic of speculation for some months, everyone had been afraid to ask Miss Wilma, unless you counted the careful inquiry of Reverend Creech when he had come to call. He had kindly avoided asking her outright, but said, "I suppose we shall never know *why* this happened to Brother Harry," and paused to see if she would be forthcoming. In her new widowhood, she found, she need not reply. Miss Wilma wondered though if the people of the town collectively concluded, as she had, that Harry's real reasons for killing himself— good, bad, indifferent—died with him. What hung around after all was said and done, after these fifteen years, was a suspicion, widely held, that what he had done might have been prevented by a truly attentive wife. Of course, this was what she believed.

She had replayed it a thousand times, that morning when Harry had killed himself. She had tried to think carefully about every word over breakfast, tried to see a sign, but she could see only his head with the one shiny bald spot bent over the *Journal Sentinel*. Coffee, a little buttered toast, just as usual. He had skimmed the front page, gone on to sports and business, one of a million days.

She could not recall what they had said, but she still wondered if he had known, as he sat at that table, that he would load his gun in just one hour, that he would kill himself so soon after Wilma left the house that she heard the gunshot before she was halfway to school. She pictured him rushing away from the table the moment she closed the kitchen door, transformed suddenly into a man with a single purpose, into a man who did not care about the news or his breakfast or the one he had shared it with for twenty years, a man who would not care about anything again.

There had been clues, though. Wilma was certain of this—if not on that singular morning, then certainly in the days and weeks preceding them. There had surely been clues, even if she had not been conscious of them. She had realized this when she heard the sound. It stopped her cold in the middle of a stride right on that sidewalk in front of Janey Blalock's house. She could point out the exact spot, the very crack in the sidewalk where she heard it, *pop,* a sharp report, but not as loud as you would think. *Pop,* and instantly, all of the unheeded, unnamed, and unimagined clues clung together like metal filings on a magnet, and Wilma knew sure as the world what had happened. She had only to turn around and go home to claim the body.

It was just in the past several years that Wilma had been able to recapture the clarity that took hold of her in the two minutes it took to retrace her steps, cursing the navy-blue spectator pumps that prevented an all-out run. Harry had for months, of course, been drinking from dawn to dusk, beginning probably from his first visit to the bathroom, where he had a bottle hidden under the sink, ending there too. There was liquor at his office, and no one between clients to stop him since his father by that time had been dead for months and out of the office for over a year. No one to stop him, she had thought, not even his wife, who knew about all of the financial troubles caused by his father's will. Not even me, I did not stop him, she had thought, I did not stop to comfort him in those months when he came home late and drunk and sweaty. What had she done instead? She had cut corners, that's what she had done, made sandwiches on paper plates for Sunday dinner, stayed late at the choir practice so that Harry would come home to a dark house. She had pretended to be asleep some nights. She had switched him to wash-and-wear shirts. All little things that must have added up for him. *Pop.* And she knew. She had let him go long before he let go of himself.

As she had rushed down the street in the complete and utter stillness of a workday already begun, she knew that she had utterly fooled herself. She had believed that her silence and her tolerance had been the best gift she could offer to Harry. Now she knew that silence had been wholly insufficient, a sign of treachery, not love. As she climbed the front steps, nearly breathless, she prayed, Lord, make me a worrywart, make me a woman with a sick and morbid imagination. Lord, let me now make a fool of mine self and let me burst in upon mine husband on the toilet, with his pants at his ankles and the sports section in his hands.

She had run to the kitchen and up the back stairs and found the bathroom door standing open. Inside, humid air and then a drip, drip, drip-drip of the shower nozzle. Her job in the past months had been to find breakfast foods most suitable for a hangover. It had been her job not to ask many questions about Harry's meetings down in Winston, where the restaurants closed late. It had been her job not to think too much about the situation, to smooth over the rough spots at home, when Sarah asked difficult questions of her father and when his soiled clothing smelling of gin and even (if she had not imagined it) bad perfume. It was her job to smooth over these things, to ride out the storm, to uphold her standards, to save her home and to wait for the worst to pass. Wilma had run from room to room looking for Harry, finally calling out, "Harry, Harry, where are you? What have you done?" It was the last time she would speak to him out loud.

In the end, she had looked out her bedroom window onto her garden and caught an aerial view of what her husband had done—the bald spot long gone, the ultimate and most terrible smoothing over.

Wilma took one more deep breath and then pushed it all right back out. The funeral flower perfume was nearly undetectable now, just like any smell if you breathed it long enough.

There was no practicing to be done until the soloist arrived, so rather than sit in her place and stew in her own cold soup, Wilma rummaged in her bag for the mail. She was glad she had taken a few minutes to run by the post office to get it. As she flipped through the bills and ads that had accumulated in her box, she began to wonder how Jonah and Harper were getting along. She hoped at least that Starling's presence would keep a lid on things until Sarah returned. The mail looked routine: a light bill, a muted thank-you note from Lily with a check, a Davis Department Store statement. At the bottom of the stack was a manila envelope with Wilma's name and address typed on the front of it. No return address. Wilma pulled open the flap. What in the world was this? She tipped the envelope over and a stack of photographs slid out, fluttering off her lap and down into the foot pedals of the organ. Wilma bent down to retrieve them, and when she did, she caught sight of one that had landed faceup beside her right foot. Good God! Wilma bolted upright, her feet striking the F and B pedals. A startled minor chord darted out into the church. She quickly sat back down and threw her hand up to wave off Ronald. "Oops," she said to him, and he returned to the flowers.

Wilma turned off her organ and swung her body around so that her legs dangled off the back of the bench. She pointed her toes so that they reached the ground and stood up. She turned and was so riveted by the pictures that she could scarcely pick them up. They were black and white and the focus was fuzzy, but it was all too apparent that they were pictures of a naked man and a woman, caught in the act. Wilma made herself gather every one of the pictures and check around her immediate area for anything she might have missed before she sat down in her side chair to look at them. What in the world was someone doing sending her pornography? There was just no reason. She settled herself down a bit and took a good look at the photographs. There were about a dozen in all. Wilma had to flip through them several times before she got a good idea about what she was looking at.

They were really not pornography, not in the sense of being smutty pictures. The photos had been taken by an amateur, because most were dim and out of focus. The more she looked, the more it seemed that this naked man and woman didn't have any idea someone was taking their picture. It looked like they had been out in the woods somewhere, lying on a blanket down in a little ravine. Maybe the photographer had stood up on a ridge with one of those telephoto lenses to spy on the couple. There was not any question about what they were doing. In one picture the man was on top, then in another, the woman. Then in one they must have been finished; the man was lying on the blanket on his back and everything, and it looked like the woman was sitting up against a tree.

Who were these people? Wilma could not really tell. In most of the pictures, they had their heads buried on one another. She would need better light and a magnifying glass. Wilma checked her watch. The soloist and everyone else would arrive any minute. Who would send her these awful things? She stuck her hand in the envelope. Maybe there was a note. Her fingers touched something just as she heard the booming voice of Fred Surratt at the back of the church. She looked to see that there was not a note but one final photo in the envelope. In this photograph, one face was plain as day. There was no time to do anything but stuff everything back in and close the flap before Fred made it to the choir loft.

As Fred greeted her, Wilma stashed the envelope in her organ bench, where it stayed through their short rehearsal, through the prelude when people came and came and filled the church and stood in the back and finally crowded the vestibule. As she played, Wilma's hand burned and burned and she was grateful to feel it, for despite anything she might have told herself about that envelope, Wilma felt somehow attached to it, culpable—as if it would brand her, mark her, just for sitting on top of the bench that contained it. She felt this most keenly as the plain wife of Clem Baker filed into the front pew in her navy dress, holding on to her little son, smoothing his hair. Wilma felt that she had fouled Clem Baker's wife and that Clem, hovering over them, would take the knowledge of her discovery to his grave. The image would not leave her mind, even as she played the man's favorite hymn. For Miss Wilma was sure of what she had seen and that was the ecstatic face of Clemont Baker.

She heard barely a word of the sermon that was offered up in the name of the dead policeman. She spent the entire service utterly still on her bench, not even bothering to move to her side chair when the sermons started, as was her custom. From behind the organ, she could see most every face in the church, two hundred or so chins pointed up toward the pulpit. In order to maintain her equilibrium in the light of what she had just seen, Wilma tried to study the range of expressions used for the occasion. About half of these people had been at the Strong wedding. The widows (cheerful headgear stowed away and traded for expressions of impersonal concern) sat halfway back on the right, just as they did on Sunday mornings. Roy Swan, the perpetual object of the widows' affection, sat safely behind the group. He looked genuinely sad. Grace Snow—wide-eyed to capture anything worth telling later—was in the back with Ron, who regarded the proceedings with a professional demeanor. Lily Strong had made it, Wilma saw, but had not brought Franklin. Wilma could not see what expression Lily had chosen for the day, since she had her head down, probably studying her manicure. Chief Henry and Tim Jessup, his remaining deputy, were both on the front row. They were pallbearers, of course. Henry sat up solemn and straight, but fished in his pocket every five minutes or so and brought out a large handkerchief and pretended to wipe sweat from his face. Behind him were four or five young bucks from the town, all friends of Clem's, Wilma guessed—a car mechanic, a clerk from the hardware store, a few farmers' sons. They were wearing the expressions of those newly informed about mortality.

The sermon was delivered by an elderly minister from the Bakers' childhood Primitive Baptist Church way out north of Elkin somewhere. It was longer, less learned, and far more emotional than anything Wilma would expect from the church's resident Reverend Creech, who had been relegated to the scripture reading and a few prayers. Wilma tried to concentrate on the sermon, to ignore what she knew to be the truth, but she was unable to stop herself from watching Clem's wife, Ava. Though she had been composed and resolute to this point, Ava began to dissolve as the old man's voice got louder and louder, testifying to the sanctity of Clemont's life and the damnation of his killer. It was as if the preacher's words brought to Ava Baker the news of her husband's death for the very first time.

She buried her face on the upright chest of the man beside her—her brother, it was, name of Avery—and if Miss Wilma remembered right, her twin. They did look alike, Ava and Avery, both with thick black hair and eyebrows, dark eyes, and childlike, shallow features. You would think to watch the two of them that they had been left alone in the world, though they appeared to have kin all around them, and Ava and Clem's little boy sat straight as a little stick, unheeded, beside his mother. Ava cried like a child herself. Avery hung on to her, looked like he was biting his tongue, biting real hard to keep from crying too.

Watching Ava and Avery, Wilma was sorry that she had not climbed back to her chair, where she could see only the minister. It was hard to look at them knowing what she knew. She could just not get over those pictures. Why did she of all people have to know about those awful woods, those awful things? What in the world did anybody think she would do with the information? She had to check on her own composure to make sure that she wasn't sitting in front of everyone making strange faces, like people do when they are walking down the street talking to themselves. She fought the urge to shift on her bench, uncomfortable now without a backrest. She hoped that most anyone in the church was so accustomed to seeing her there that they would not notice her any more than a light fixture or an altar cloth.

The old minister finished. He stretched out his right hand and went straight to the benediction. "Dear Lord," he said, then stopped so they could all hear the silence of the ages, "dear Lord, be with us today." Wilma silently thumbed through her hymnal to locate the recessional hymn, and peeked out again at the family. Avery was whispering fervently to Ava Baker's bowed head. He grasped her shoulders as if to pull her up out of her grief. He seemed to talk to her with an intensity that was unseemly for a time of prayer.

Wilma knew little about the Primitive Baptists. There was one church in Swan's Knob where they met every other Sunday for the entire day. With these people, maybe talking and carrying on was just part of it. The prayer ended and Wilma began the final hymn, "Precious Jesus." Avery stood up with the rest of the pallbearers—Chief Henry, Deputy Shaw, and Ronny Snow—and lined up beside Ronny, unsure what to do with his large hands, settling finally on tugging on the bottom hem of his short suit jacket. Miss Wilma noticed his scuffed-up brogans sticking out sadly from under his pants. As the men began to roll the coffin down the aisle of the church, he had to shuffle to catch up and get in step with them. As the coffin passed the second pew, an older couple—Clem's parents, or maybe Avery and Ava's—stood up slowly, the mother in a plain cotton dress, no tie on the father, just a shirt buttoned up at the neck. They waited for Ava to get to the aisle, then each of them took one of Ava's arms as if she could not make it on her own. They walked with her and her little son behind the coffin, down the aisle and out of the church. Country, just country, country people.

ↄ∕ɔ

Sarah felt better once she had called her mother's house. Though she had not been able to hear very clearly through the house's ancient telephone, Starling had sounded quite normal, not at all upset by Sarah's disappearance. Sarah had been brief.

"You're cool," Starling had said, accepting the few details that Sarah offered, and volunteering no information about the climate down the hill, though Sarah had gathered that Wilma was not at home. Sarah had promised only to be home by dinnertime, which bought her a little more time on the couch. She went back to the den, rearranged her pillows and laid back down. She began to feel a bit of that pregnancy sort of contentment, the kind that had you taking deep breaths and postponing the laundry. She was happy that she had called, and most happy of all that Starling had answered—the real Starling, the girl she had now instead of the little baby crying in the Greenwich Village apartment. They were two separate people, with the red-faced baby set way back in Sarah's mind along with the rest of her time in New York.

Sarah had little memory now of Manhattan's streets. When she thought about those first months of Starling's life, only the interior of the shotgun apartment remained hanging up there three floors off the ground. A creaky front door opened into the middle room, home of a beat-up couch and the precious stereo. To the left was a kitchen where each appliance had some kind of leak. Its only window opened onto an airshaft that let in the cooking smells and domestic disputes of a dozen other families. Back through the living room and tiny bath, the front room held Harper and Sarah's mattress, Starling's crib and Sarah's treasure, the rocking chair. The chair, Wilma's one concession to their situation, had been in Sarah's own nursery and in Wilma's. It had arrived on the day that Starling had come home from the hospital. They found it sitting on the front stoop in a wooden crate that served as their kitchen table for some time after. For all the trouble and expense she went to sending a crated chair to New York, Wilma herself never showed up in the flesh. After years of hounding her every move, Wilma was curiously absent during Sarah's first year as a mother.

Besides her baby, the rocking chair's familiar creaks and the sound of its runners across the floorboards were the only things that separated Sarah from utter despair. She spent most of that year by the front window rocking Starling. She wondered now if her mother had even a clue about this—certainly she would not have approved of the endless rocking, the endless holding the baby between nursings. During that time, Harper also slept through most of each day on the couch and spent his evenings playing his trumpet with this jazz group and that. Very little money made it into their apartment, so once Starling was a few months old, Sarah found a job at a private school. The school had a nursery spot for Starling and a vacant teaching position in English. Sarah figured she might still be teaching Wordsworth to the spoiled children of East Siders if Harper had not become embroiled in a dispute with Eddie Moonman Macon, the leader of the little jazz combo that Harper played with a few nights in various clubs in the city. "Artistic differences," Harper had told her, several weeks after the fact, once Sarah finally realized that Harper was no longer working. Of course, Sarah eventually discovered that the "artistic difference" was in fact Moonman's new girlfriend, a redhead who had been caught with Harper's hands in her shirt in the alley behind the Five-Spot after the last set of the evening. This apparently was the last straw for Moonman. And as it turned out, Harper was pretty much despised for one similar transgression or another by most other promising bands in the city. The work dried up and Harper began to sleep all day long in a deep depression that cured itself most evenings around sunset.

This whole life in New York was not something that Sarah had shared with her mother. If she had, there would have been two lectures waiting for her. Number one involved sleeping in the bed that you had made, and the other, a different twist on the same theme, involved the mortal dangers of "lying about." This kind of thing—sleeping in the daytime, rocking by the window, thinking too much—was a capital offense in her mother's book.

On the day after they had buried Sarah's daddy, Wilma had marched Sarah right out into the back garden, where they had spent the day ostensibly weeding, pulling out anything and everything that looked in the least offensive. Sarah had worked in the very back of the yard, in the peony bed, far away from the spot where her father must have fallen, but Wilma worked that particular rose bed with vigor. Sarah remembered that by the late afternoon, Wilma had thrown most of her rosebushes into the wheelbarrow. She had turned the backyard into a collection of severely pruned sticks, but that did not seem to matter. They had not for one minute laid about.

∽

When she had finished the postlude and turned off the organ, Wilma looked up to see Roy Swan still sitting in his seat, third window back on the left. He was leaning forward with his arms dangling over the pew in front of him, his hands clasped together. Wilma thought maybe he had stayed behind overcome by emotion, not wanting anyone to see. Roy had a soft heart. He was probably the one who had paid for Clem's fine coffin. Wilma gathered her things as quietly as possible. She made sure to get her secret envelope out of the bench. It was too big to hide in her handbag, so she added it to the top of her stack of sheet music.

Roy stood up and waved as she came down the steps of the choir loft. Wilma saw then that he was in no way overcome. In fact, he approached her with some eagerness. By the time he got to her, he was almost smiling, but the somberness of the occasion occurred to him finally, and he said, "Lovely service, Wilma. The music was beautiful as always."

He said this in respectful tones, though his full bass voice nevertheless filled the empty sanctuary and echoed off the walls. As he spoke, Roy lowered his eyes to look at Wilma's music collection instead of her face, a subtlety of breeding. Wilma had always considered Roy the best sort of gentleman. It was funny that he chose to spend his time with the men on the Rescue Squad and the fry cooks in the sandwich shop.

"This is not the time, Wilma, but we do need to talk," he said.

Wilma had forgotten. Roy had been after her to help plan a Fourth of July celebration—fireworks, music, some patriotic program on top of Swan's Knob. Roy, poor man, had no family left. He just didn't have enough to do. This event was just about the furthest thing from her mind at the moment.

"Roy," she said, "right now, I cannot even think past this afternoon. I have a house full of family, every one of them needing some kind of attention, and I don't even know what I'm fixing for supper tonight. Can we talk next week sometime? I think the whole thing can wait, don't you? Between us, we can come up with a plan in no time. It's just a matter of the posters and the punch."

Roy looked puzzled, but said, "Well, all right, Wilma. As I said before, this matter is entirely up to you."

"Up to me?" Wilma said, "You're the mastermind, Roy. I'm just the person with the music. You're the one to line up the fireworks, the permits, you name it."

"Fireworks?" said Roy. "Oh, the Fourth of July. Oh, we have plenty of time."

"Right," said Wilma, "that's what I just said." How old was Roy now? Sixty? Sixty-five? Surely he wasn't getting senile. "Well," she said, "you better go on if you're going to make the graveside, Roy. I've got to defrost a roast." It worried Wilma a little that Roy's mouth hung open as she moved quickly on down to the choir room. Good Lord, she thought, we are all getting old.

The day was heating up a bit by the time Wilma reached the parking lot, and of all things, Lily Strong caught up with her as she was fumbling with the rusty lock on Harper's car.

"Wilma, where is your LTD? What are you doing driving this old thing?" Lily said. The lock would not budge, so Wilma was forced to turn and look at Lily. For the funeral, Lily had chosen a black suit with lime-green stripes and brass buttons as big as her eyes. She had on her imitation Jackie Onassis sunglasses and a chiffon scarf tied on to preserve her hair from any wind that would come up.

"This is Harper's car. Sarah has mine. Aren't you going to the graveside service?" said Wilma, hoping to keep the conversation short.

"Well, of course I am, but I always wait a little bit so that I can pull my car into the cemetery last. They're taking him nearly to Elkin to some little country plot, so Lord knows what kind of mud will be in those driveways. I don't want to get stuck. Would you like to ride with me?"

"Oh, no, I have a houseful. I need to get home," said Wilma. It was the truth. She would rather go home than pull into a country cemetery in a large white Cadillac, Lily banging the car door shut, ten minutes late, in the dead quiet, the birds singing, all eyes turned toward them.   The lock on Harper's door was not working, so Wilma moved around to the passenger side.

"Well, before I go, hon, the reason I stopped over here was just to give you a little word from the wise men," said Lily.

"And what did these wise men say?" said Wilma.

"Well, you know full well there are no wise men, it's just an expression," said Lily. "What I was going to say is, what in the world was that convict Indian doing on your porch with the Elliott twins this morning?"

"Are you referring to Jonah Branch?" said Wilma, choosing an icy tone. "If so, Lily, he is no convict, he was only briefly questioned by the police, and for the record, he is only a small part Indian, which could be said for most of us around here, that is, if we know and own up to our true origin."

"Oh Lord, let's not get into that now," said Lily. "I was only saying by way of protecting you and your reputation that you have no business having that kind of visitor on your front porch. People around here are saying that he was involved somehow in this killing, whether they arrested him or not. Who knows if it's true? But, Wilma, even if it's all falsehood, I still don't think I would invite him in for lemonade, not with two little piano students sitting on the porch with him. You know their mother, you just tell me what Lois Elliott will say when she finds out. Three people mentioned it to me before I could get in the church door this morning, asking me what in the world he was doing there."

Wilma felt a sudden prickle of heat at the base of her neck. Knowing Lily, she had been the one to tell everyone else. "Surely not," she said.

"Well, yes," said Lily. "Hon, just tell me, what was he doing there? Have you taken on boarders?"

"Goodness, no. He is a family friend," said Wilma, hoping that would do. It would not.

"Wilma, let's not forget, hon, even though it is not a well-known fact, that I am also part of your family. Your husband and I did have the same father, even if he would never claim me." This was one thing that Wilma did try to forget about, and she in particular didn't want to talk about it here in the parking lot, but Lily would not be deterred. "So, hon, I know more about your family than any person on this earth, and I know you don't have no family friend by the name of no Jonah from no New Mexico."

Wilma noticed that Lily talked a little more like Lily Mae when she got upset. "Lily Mae," she said, for the name always made Lily mad, "I didn't say he was an old family friend, just a family friend, a friend of Sarah . . . and of Harper. Now please do me the favor of not blowing this small incident way out of proportion. If you keep talking, you'll get everyone going. You know that folks in this town can chew up some small tidbit and pass it along with one extra detail, and by next week they'll be saying I'm trading my piano students to the Indians. Please, Lily."

Wilma ducked into the passenger side of Harper's car and tried to unlock the driver's side door. The lock would not budge. Lily was pulling her own keys from her green purse. She said, "Hon, you know that I will not say a word but to defend you. I just thought you might appreciate a warning."

Wilma waited until Lily was in her car and out of the driveway. She made one last survey of the lot before she hauled herself over the stick shift to get to the driver's seat of the car.

She was glad to see when she got home that the house had not burned down. Wilma supposed that she should be grateful for small favors; however, an intact house filled with iniquities was, in fact, small consolation to a small woman in a linen suit trapped in a rusted-out Dodge Dart in her own driveway. She was at the end. She would die of heat prostration right out in front of her house before she would crawl over the console again. Miss Wilma laid on the horn and found the noise to be the most beautiful sound she had heard all day. She did not let up, not even once, until Starling came running out of the house, followed by her barefoot father.

Miss Wilma could only roll down her window two inches but it was enough. "Harper, you will have to get me out of here, the lock is stuck," she said.

"Well, why did you lock it?" said Harper. "The whole thing is broken. You'll have to climb out the other side."

"I will not climb out, I will not climb out here on Main Street," she said. "It's your car. Just get me out."

"Well, hand me the keys." He sighed, and she fished them out the cracked window. "Why you would even think of locking the car in this town is beyond me. Who would steal my car?" Wilma had an answer, but she didn't say it. Here was the reason: it was the difference between their generations. She would never leave a car without locking it. Period. For him, it was situational, you had to think who might steal what. Everything was situational, no right, no wrong, no do it this way. Too many decisions, and this was where it got you.

Harper put the key in the lock and jiggled the door handle. Starling stood behind him with her hand over her mouth—Wilma couldn't tell if she was appalled or laughing. Droplets of perspiration began to roll down her back inside her blouse. "Come on," she said, "I'm dying in here."

"If you were dying, you'd climb over the stick shift," he said as the handle finally creaked and released the door. "Now please don't lock it again."

"Don't worry. I do not intend ever in this lifetime to get into that thing again," she said, noticing that her own car was still not in the driveway. She was almost afraid to ask, "So, where is everyone?"

"Mom called," said Starling eagerly. "She got stuck up in the mountains and should be on her way home soon."

Wilma looked at Harper, who shrugged and said, "Starling talked to her right after you left. She had hung up before I got to speak to her."

"And our friend . . . ?" Wilma said, not sure about what to say in front of Starling.

"Asleep," said Harper, "in the back."

"Back bedroom?" said Wilma. Starling was staying in the back bedroom.

"No, in the backyard."

"He's sleeping in my backyard?"

"He said he didn't get much sleep in the jail, so he rolled out his sleeping bag on the bench under the grape arbor."

Wilma supposed she should thank her lucky stars that he had not chosen the front porch swing.

Chapter Eight

Sarah had to admit that after all she had finally had just about enough thumbing through dreary history. She pulled herself up off the couch and began to survey the rest of the house. She walked down a short hall that led to two bedrooms and a bath, the second bedroom converted to a little sewing room. In their bedroom, a windup alarm clock ticked on the dresser. The bed was covered with an ample chenille spread, a single enormous rose perfectly posed in the center. Of course, the woman had made her bed before leaving the house. As did Sarah most days. It was the one task that compelled her even when others did not, as though there was something sacred about it. Like a grave, a bed could not be left open. Housekeeping, Wilma would say, good Lord, it's just basic housekeeping.

Along the far wall was a large closet. By now Sarah was too curious not to open it. She half expected to find a row of bright red pantsuits, but of course there were none there, just a few summer outfits, a stock of high-heeled shoes. Sarah looked up at the top shelf.

"Aahh!" she screamed. A row of mannequin heads stared out at her with eyeless faces. The mannequins wore blonde wigs, each in a different state of styling—two perfectly coifed, another in disarray, one in curlers, for God's sake. "Shit," Sarah said aloud. Okay, they were only wigs, but why so many? She thumbed through the clothes in the closet then, knowing as she did so that the whole enterprise was getting a little weird. In the back of the closet, she found a bathing suit hanging on a lingerie hanger. It was a bright Hawaiian print, pink with white flowers. As she pushed it along the rail, it seemed unnaturally heavy, and then she saw. There was a large pad in the right bra cup, a prosthesis.

This sight, with the suit sagging there on its little hanger, listing to the right, took her breath away, made her feel tears coming up from the back of her throat, tears that came quickly for a woman she did not know really, for a woman whose house she had violated. Everything she had seen—the woman's click-clack walk, her hand on her husband's shoulder, the way she slung her pocketbook across her arm—rushed back at Sarah. She closed her eyes and collected up this tiny group of ordinary gestures. Nothing to do with her, nothing. She shut the closet door and tip-toed back to the living room, where the faint ticktock of the alarm clock followed her. A golden afternoon light poured out over the mountains and onto the twin chairs of Sammy and his precious wife, onto the glass-blown birds on shelves, onto the dust of a thousand days of the laughter in this room. The whole of it was random, of course, even the light. Sarah would tell herself this a hundred times, a thousand times, every time she thought about this day.

By the time Sarah met Jonah at Minga Wood's gallery, she and Harper and Starling had been in Santa Fe for several years. Sarah had picked out their life there. She was drawn by the landscape of the place, its sun colors and ancient winds, its otherworldliness. One winter day back in New York, when the heat in their apartment was not enough to warm the radiator pipes, Sarah had found the notice for the Smithsonian research project cataloguing Native American music, had convinced Harper to make a half-assed application, which was miraculously successful. It was she who had gotten up out of her rocking chair, moved them cross-country to a nice, tumbledown adobe, found a job at a private school and made herself virtuously busy. Santa Fe was so far from her upbringing that it might have been a foreign land, though Sarah had lived there, she fancied, centuries before. Her ancient self had molded its adobe bricks and paved its streets under the same clear light.

Sarah loved the crowd of artists that filled up Santa Fe and brought it life. Though she could not be one of them, she did love to inhabit their lives on the fringes. And so, soon she was working in her friend Minga's gallery during the summers and holidays. She had watched Jonah at gallery events from her post at the entrance for some time before they actually spoke. He was hard to miss, even in a crowded reception of pretty people jostling elbows and smoking cigarettes. He was the son of two cultures, Indian and Anglo, possessing the best of each, gunpowder-black hair, the copper skin, features derived from carved stone hills, these coupled with the surprise of green eyes. He had a graceful manner and confidence that made him seem to somehow quietly stand apart from any crowd.

He was a photographer, Minga said, of the highest caliber. His newest work was portraits of potters from the Santa Clara and San Ildefonso pueblos. Minga had been amazed, "dazzling," she said, clanking all her bracelets together at once. She planned a show for him. On the day he came to hang his work, Sarah watched him lean each piece against the wall and study the photograph as if to discern its place in the world. He was oblivious of everything around him—Minga, who sat talking about artifacts with a serious collector, the tourists wandering in and out tracking up the hardwood floors, Sarah behind the reception desk. As he placed the photographs, Jonah seemed most intent on his subjects, seemed to whisper to them almost, asking them where they should be hung, where they would be happy, maybe. Sarah had laughed aloud at this thought, and he had startled then, and turned toward her.

"Okay," he said, laughing too, "caught in the act. You've caught me talking to my pictures."

"No, oh no," said Sarah, suddenly feeling the need to straighten the brochures. "I was just . . ."

"Oh, I don't deny it, do I, Teresita?" He spoke to the photograph in his hands. "We must only worry if they start talking back." His eyes narrowed slightly right before he smiled at Sarah. "Could you help me for a moment?"

Sarah left the desk, glad for something to do. She was conscious suddenly of the way she walked across the bleached wood floor.

"Okay, just hold my friend Teresita here up against the wall, just above your waist, and let me check it from out here." He eyed the photo and then surveyed the rest of the portraits lining the walls. Sarah noticed though that he did not seem overly aware of himself, a welcome change from most of the artists and musicians that Sarah knew, who were preeners and performers more than anything else.

"They worry, you know, about these pictures." He approached Sarah and guided the frame a foot to the left.

"Who worries?" she said. "I think Minga is thrilled to have them."

He smiled again. "No, the people in the pueblo. They worry. They would deny it, of course, most of them live in this century just the same as you and me. But it's lurking there somewhere in the culture. That I have taken something of them away. That their spirits will be trapped in the image."

Jonah marked the top of the frame that Sarah was holding and moved to the next photograph. It showed a woman, her back bent with age, working on a water jar. The light shone on the woman's face and hands and on the vessel that she held. They were all of a whole, it seemed to Sarah, the jar, the hands, the face, a striking sameness in their color and texture, as if the potter herself was earth, tempered by fire.

"You have captured something," she said, looking up to find that Jonah was studying her and her reaction, "only I don't think that you have taken anything away." He kept his eyes on her then, as he might any of his subjects, she supposed, trying to see what the light would bring. She could not imagine in that moment that he would find anything worthy, anything that might shine in a photograph. There was nothing in her like what he had found in these other subjects. Right there, right under his gaze, she had known: she had been walking around with parts of her as hollow as a string of dried red chiles. A rista, red and brittle with seeds inside that rattled if you shook it.

⌒

All the way up the driveway and into the house, Wilma felt Starling's eyes on her, saw her looking with the concern young people reserve for the doddering old.

"Honey," Wilma said, when it looked like Starling wanted to help her up the stairs, "I am fine. I am nothing more than hot. I just need to get out of this wilted suit."

Starling shrugged and went back over to the kitchen sink. Wilma saw that she was almost finished washing a large pile of spring lettuce and was laying the leaves to dry on a dish towel. Farther down the counter were some potatoes that had already been scrubbed and a rump roast thawing on a plate.

"Well aren't you smart," said Wilma. She couldn't begin to think how this child had gotten this kind of training. Probably it was more of a survival skill than anything else. "Can I help you do anything?"

"No, Nana, just go upstairs and find some clothes that aren't wilted," said Starling, laughing. "I'll go ahead and put the roast in the oven. You just put it on three hundred fifty degrees and let it cook, right? Do I need to cover it or anything?"

"No, just put it in the oven. I usually salt it about a half hour before it's done," said Wilma. "Starling, honey, this is real sweet of you. Best thing you could have done. What did your mother say when she called, honey? Did she sound okay?"

"She sounded fine, actually, said she had gone up to the Fancy Gap diner to eat this morning and was taking her time about getting back."

"Did she give you a time?" said Wilma. She was impressed by the way Starling moved around the kitchen, breaking the clean lettuce into little pieces, then going right on and peeling the potatoes and cutting them into a waiting pot of water.

"No, she said this evening. She's usually home by dinnertime."

"You mean she's run off before?" said Wilma. It was out before she thought about it.

Starling frowned. "She hasn't run off, Nana. Why would she run off? She didn't sound like that when I talked to her. She sounded real calm. I think it's like she said, she just went up to eat at a diner, then she was driving around a bit."

"I'm sure you're right, honey. Don't mind me. I've just had a long day. I'll just go up and freshen up, and then I'll come back down to help you." Wilma felt bad for even suggesting that Sarah had run off. Here the child was perfectly content, and she had to ask the wrong kind of question. It was the kind of thing she expected Harper to do. That had been her day in a nutshell: every imaginable indiscretion.

When she got to her room, she thanked her lucky stars for the window air conditioner that she had installed two summers before. She turned it on and stood in front of it as she undressed. It smelled a little moldy, like it always did at the beginning of the season, but the cool air was such a relief that she didn't care a bit. She took off every damp article of clothing, then started over with clean lingerie. As she looked through her drawers for something comfortable to wear, an extreme tiredness came over her. Maybe if I just lie down for fifteen minutes, I'll feel better, she thought.

She threw on her housecoat, laid down on her bed and pulled the quilt up over her shoulders.

∽

There was not a single tea bag in this woman's kitchen, which was a surprise to Sarah. Sarah surveyed the rest of the cabinets— not much at all, a few spices, a couple of cans of split pea soup, a box of saltines, and a can of peanuts. Sammy and his wife must patronize the TipTop Diner more than most folks. In her own kitchen, of course, there was rarely anything that you wanted, since Sarah was a sporadic shopper at best. Starling had stopped complaining long ago when her mother brought tacos home from the neighborhood tienda. Harper was rarely home to complain either these days.

Now that she thought about it, Harper had simply faded away during the past year. It had been several years since he had committed any indiscretion bad enough to warrant a discussion, and in the absence of something to fight over, what did they talk about, really? She tried to imagine their last discussion—what had it been? When?

He asked her, she guessed, about her classes maybe or something about Starling. Those were her only pursuits, really, maybe a boring life to some people, to Harper maybe. Sarah, though, loved teaching, and loved the students she found in Santa Fe. They were a far cry from the East Side New York liberal offspring: They came to school bronzed, with braided hair and beads gathered from the country around them, conscious of neither breeding nor divorce settlements. They regarded mixed blood, native potters and D. H. Lawrence with equal acceptance. These children who came through Sarah's classroom, their sisters and brothers, nearly a decade's worth, had wholly occupied Sarah. And as Starling approached the age to be among them, Sarah had been consumed with her lively here-and-now. As she grew, Starling filled up more and more of her life—she was

Sarah's student, her companion, her child growing into her own person. Harper had intruded less and less. He had become, Sarah realized now, less of a thorn. By the time Starling was in school, he seemed more inclined to wake up in the proper bed. Sarah had noted with some relief that her friends gave up the practice of mentioning unfamiliar female names in her presence, signifying their importance by cutting their eyes in her direction.

For his part, Harper had worked along on his Smithsonian project, and by now it was as near completion as anything he had ever done. He had collected every native song within three hundred miles and had only to finish organizing his project. That part of the work—"the taming," he called it—he had scarcely begun, and in the past few months, Sarah realized that she had not even noted his progress, or lack of it. According to Jonah, who knew people in the village, Harper spent his days in the Santa Maria pueblo, where he watched others work in the morning, then hung out with them through the afternoon. Sarah had not asked Harper about it, had not bothered to inquire, for at the time it was just Jonah on her mind.

During the duration of Jonah's show at Minga's gallery, Sarah was always aware that Jonah was around. He seemed to fill up the space, soaking the light from the corners. From their first meeting, she could not be in his presence for more than an instant without drawing a large breath that could not be easily expelled. Being long past college and for God's sake married with a child, Sarah was unwilling and most certainly unprepared to acknowledge his effect on her, beyond that first sudden breath. She confined herself strictly to involuntary responses through weeks and numerous unavoidable encounters with him during that summer. Sarah's friend Minga had once used the back room of her gallery as a developing lab for her own photography. It was the lab and the prospect of using it without charge that brought Jonah back to Minga's that summer after his show was over.

Day by day, he put the lab area back in order, hauled in new chemicals, stowed away picture frame debris. Sarah stayed behind the gallery desk during the first few weeks, pampering the incoming buyers and tourists and quietly monitoring his progress from afar. Eventually Jonah brought in a thick black curtain, a velvet cast-off from a local theater group, and attached the curtain to a track on the ceiling. Finally he began to develop film in earnest, and Minga disappeared on a buying trip. Sarah was left in the quiet of the gallery, where there was no sign of Jonah's presence beyond the occasional sound of the curtain pulled on its track. It was sometime during this period that Jonah began to notice that Sarah was watching him. He wondered, he told her later, about her suspicious looks for days. He thought that she resented his presence and had decided that he was bad for business. Gradually, he told her, he thought he saw something else right around the edge of her gaze.

At the end of one day, Sarah ushered out her last customer and locked the gallery door. As she turned around, she was startled to find Jonah right in front of her. He was standing just a few inches inside her comfort zone, blocking her path.

"I thought you might like a tour of the darkroom," he said. She could only follow him to the back.

⁂

In the stillness of the graveside service, Roy found himself with the urge to shift around on his feet a bit. He could walk a long way, but just a few minutes of standing hurt his legs. He was glad to be in the back of the crowd where no one would notice him fidget. Fewer people were gathered here at the cemetery than in the church. The cemetery was a good thirty minutes out of town, north near Shiloh. It was set in the side of a little hill, the incline making Roy feel a little off balance, like he might slide off down the bank. He considered the land a real poor choice as a final resting place. The cemetery belonged to a little Primitive Baptist church that sat up on top of the hill. It didn't look much sturdier than a tobacco barn.

Roy noticed that most of the people present were from Shiloh. Some of the officials for the police or the town had come, and then there were a few of the idle curious. Roy figured that included himself. Snow's had not bothered to bring out their funeral tent, so the coffin sat right out in the sun. Roy should have gone over that with Ron when he called about the arrangements. It wasn't right. At least they thought to bring the green carpet to cover the fresh dirt and put down chairs so that Clem's family wouldn't have to stand and stare down into the grave. It was something Roy would not want to do.

His own parents had died long, long ago in a train wreck right outside of Baltimore. They had ventured north to visit his mother's sister in Philadelphia. Roy had been in the service in Korea at the time. They were buried before Roy had even known about it. He was happy in a way not to have the memory, but to this day he felt funny about the fact that he had returned home to find nothing left of them but a headstone with two names chiseled out and a verse picked out by Ron Snow, "My house has many rooms." Ron had started in on giving Roy the details about the condition of the bodies delivered to him by the railroad company, but Roy had stopped him. There was no sense in it.

Out here, the old local preacher was presiding. He had the voice for it, feeble as he looked, for as his voice boomed out across the hill, everyone else got quiet. Roy bent his knees a little and shifted his left foot up behind himself for better balance. He looked around at the nearby headstones and tried to replay his conversation with Wilma. She had obviously not had any idea what he was talking about. Maybe he had totally misjudged the situation. If so, it would not be the first time. Roy, old boy, you may have just fixed yourself but good, he thought, messed up yourself with the best little woman on the earth.

Roy was happy to bow his head for the prayer, and for good measure said his own that Wilma would not flat out hate him over the foolish acts of others. This reminded him that he had not seen Lily among the crowd, and as the benediction was finished, he began to look around for her. He didn't see her anywhere. As he walked to his car, he shook the hands of those acquaintances and friends he passed, not saying much more than a quiet how are you. His car was on the top of the hill next to the church. As he approached it, he caught sight of Lily sitting in her own car, blowing her nose. Evidently, she had not gotten out at all, but had watched the service from her front seat. Roy was not sure what he could say to her or if he could even look her in the eye. He was relieved that the moment she saw him she started up the car, backed it up fast and hightailed it out of there, right down the road.

Roy found the envelope on his driveway when he got out of the car at the house. He must have dropped it on the way to the post office. Good God, buddy, he said to himself, you are getting old. The envelope, so carefully prepared, had a tire mark down the middle of it. A few bits of gravel were embedded in the damp paper. The writing on the outside—it was addressed to Wilma— was blurred by the moisture, but when he opened it up, the letter inside was still dry.

Lord, what Wilma must have thought. No wonder she had been short with him. Roy folded the letter carefully and put it back in its envelope. He needed to think about what to do next. This time, he would try to think everything through a bit better so as not to make a complete fool of himself again. Fireworks, fireworks, she said. She must think he was dumber than hell.

All of this worrying was making Roy hungrier than a bear, so he went on out to the kitchen to see about something for supper. The kitchen always looked gray and deserted this time of day. He knew he was a grown man, getting up there at fifty-nine, sixty-something (never could remember exactly). Anyway, his age did not stop him from remembering the kitchen when it seemed mostly yellow and bright and filled with wonderful smells, and his mother was bustling around in her apron. He had kept up the house all these years—had painted the kitchen last fall even—and his housekeeper, Nellie, kept things neat as a pin, kept food in the house, waxed the floors. But it wasn't the same. In the refrigerator, Nellie had left meat loaf, potatoes, a pot of green beans. He could heat this up, and it would be fine. But lately, he had noticed that whatever Nellie left him for the weekend tasted like old sawdust in his mouth.

Roy went over and opened the pantry door. Here he had his wine, one bottle reserved from each of the years he had been making it—seventeen in all—and then a dozen of last year's vintage. Plenty to get him through to the fall wine-making season, but tonight, after the funeral and all, he didn't much feel like opening a bottle. His pantry also housed his growing collection of preserves and pickles from the women at the church, at least one jar from every marriageable matron. He wasn't going to count them. He saw, however, that he had nearly a whole shelf dedicated to Mamie Brown's Mystery Mountain Jam, a monument to the lady's persistence. Each time she slipped him a jar (in the fellowship hall, after a band concert, at his front door at Halloween), she would tell him with a wink, "I make every batch a little different, using just whatever fruit is ripe at the time. That's the mystery." Well, he sure wasn't going to eat jam for dinner. He could go down to the Coach House, have him a smothered veal chop and a salad, though he hated to insult Nellie by leaving the food. But that wasn't the point somehow.

He realized that he had come to believe very truly that whatever it was missing from his food, from his table, from his life, that Wilma could sure as the world provide it. It was pure foolishness that he would trump up this belief—he knew it was—especially at this time of his life. He had gone along just fine for so long, though it hadn't been much of his doing. His situation alone had provided most anything that a person needed, so really he hadn't ever had to ask for much at all. He wondered if in the big book of things this left him at all entitled. Of course, this was the most foolish notion yet. It was without any foundation. He might as well have been avoiding the cracks in the sidewalk all his life. Wilma of all people was going to do what she was going to do. He really was crazy with love to think that contemplating a local mystery could somehow throw them together the way he had in mind.

It was almost dark in the kitchen. Roy pulled a near-empty milk carton out of the refrigerator and dumped the milk down the sink. Then he stuffed a hearty portion of meat and beans into the carton and took the whole thing to the outdoor trash can. Something in him just had to give it one more try. Right or wrong. Plan or no plan. He would just ask her to come with him to dinner down at the Coach House. Somehow, by hook or by crook, he would make it right.

❧

Way off in the distance, Wilma could hear her phone ring. Sarah, it could be Sarah, she thought, but it was too far off for her to get to it, and she realized there were other people in the house. After a few rings, it did sound as if someone picked it up mid-ring, although Wilma couldn't hear any voices. She could smell the roast cooking. She sat up about the time she heard footsteps on the stairs and a little knock. "Nana, are you awake?" whispered Starling. "Telephone for you."

"I'll be right there," said Wilma, trying to locate her bedroom shoes beside her bed. "Is it your mother?"

"No, it's a man," said Starling.

"Did he say who?"

"Ah, a Mister . . . mister . . . it starts with an 's,' I think?"

" 'S'? Is it Snow?"

"I think that's it," said Starling.

"I'll be right there," said Wilma. Good Lord, Ron Snow was calling her. That meant either someone was hurt and taken to Baptist in his ambulance, or worse, someone was dead. She hurried down the stairs. Please, please don't let it be, she prayed. Starling handed her the phone.

"Hello, Ronald?" she said.

"Hello? Wilma? It's not Ron. It's Roy."

"Oh, Roy Swan." She was filled with relief. She had to stop doing this to herself. "Roy. How are you?"

"Just fine, mighty fine," he said, "and you, how are you?"

"I'm fine. Well, just about the same as this afternoon, but rested. I guess. I was taking a nap," she said. What was Roy wanting now? She rubbed her eyes, which were sticky. How long had she been asleep? Not very long, the roast was still in the oven.

"Oh and I woke you up. I am so sorry," said Roy.

"No, don't worry. I needed to get up." It was just starting to get dark. Out in the backyard, she could just make out Jonah's form huddled in his sleeping bag. A flophouse. Her home had become a flophouse.

"Okay, well, I apologize," said Roy. He cleared his throat. "I'm calling . . . the reason I'm calling here, calling you just to see . . . well, I know you have family there, but I know . . . well, I'm not sure but I figure—that they've been there a while, and I wondered if they could spare you."

"Spare me?" said Wilma. The sleeping bag was moving now and she saw Jonah sit up and look around the yard. "Spare me, for what?"

"Well, I wondered if they could spare you for dinner," said Roy. "I was going down to the Coach House for dinner, and it just occurred to me that maybe you'd like to come with me down there, if they don't need . . . if you weren't . . . if you didn't have any big plans." Jonah was out of the sleeping bag now, rolling it up. He would be inside soon, along with the rest of them. He left the bench and began walking around the garden, looking for something.

"Roy," said Wilma. What was Jonah up to? "I just don't know how I could do it. . . ."

"I understand completely," said Roy. "It was just an idle thought. We'll do it next time."

Jonah stopped in front of Wilma's rose bed, where most of the bushes were still just beginning to get leaves. He put his hands in front of himself. Wilma saw a stream of liquid arch down onto the flowerbed right into the root system of her Summer Damask bushes. He was like a man in the *National Geographic,* a pilgrim urinating in the Ganges, desecration of the highest order. Roy was still talking.

"Roy," she interrupted, "could you hold on just one minute?" She put her hand over the receiver and turned away from the window. "Starling, darling, has your mother come back, dear?"

"No, Nana, I haven't seen her."

"And your daddy, where is he?"

"He's been out doing something with his car, fixing the lock or something," she said.

Wilma got back on the phone. "Roy," she said without giving him time to explain any further, "the Coach House sounds just fine, but I will need you to pick me up if that isn't too much trouble."

"Why I wouldn't have it any other way, Wilma," he said, sounding awfully pleased. Wilma figured Roy was the kind of man that once something was on his mind—like this Fourth of July program—he could not think about anything else. Well, the Fourth of July or Labor Day or any other topic would be just fine with Wilma, just as long as she didn't have to host a dinner including a man who urinated on her rose bed, peed right over the very spot. It gave her shivers.

"Seven o'clock?" Roy was saying.

"Fine, see you then," she said and hung up the phone.

She felt a pang of guilt as she saw Starling proudly pull the roast out of the oven. "Oh, doesn't that just look perfect," she said. "I am sick, just sick, Starling, about this phone call. That was my friend Roy Swan who has a terrible problem that he needs to discuss with me. I am so sorry but I am going to have to go up to the Coach House with him and miss your lovely dinner. Do you mind terribly, dear?"

Starling shook her head and smiled. "No, you go on, Nana. You've been home every night since we've been here." Wilma looked at her closely—she seemed unaffected by the whole thing. Her own mother, Sarah, would not have taken it so well. Still, Wilma wondered what part of hell was reserved for a woman who told bald-faced lies to their granddaughters. Poor Starling, with her father, and now this situation with her mother, she'd been lied to so much. Wilma felt bad, but here came Jonah up the back steps. Harper would not be far behind him.

"Starling," she said, "I have got to get on some clothes. Honey, I will be back down in a minute. You are such a big girl to make such a meal for these men all by yourself. I'm sure your mother will be home to help with the dishes." At least one would hope, thought Wilma, that Sarah would be as good as her word to Starling. She would not deliberately mislead her own daughter.

Chapter Nine

Sarah had promised Starling that she would be home soon. The phone book was only a half inch thick and covered a dozen little towns. In the Yellow Pages, she found the number of a gas station in Fancy Gap. She called and explained her situation—the part about being out of gas. For safety's sake, she gave the man directions to her own car rather than to Sammy's house.

"Okay, ma'am," said the gas station man. "I know right where that is. I'll be there directly. Wendell is out in the wrecker right now, and I am here by myself. Just as soon as he gets back, I'll come on. Now you sure you don't need no wrecker? You sure you're just out of gas? Because if you think we might need it, I could bring the wrecker."

Sarah convinced the man that a wrecker was unnecessary and hung up. She was unsure exactly what "directly" meant in terms of time but figured she had a few minutes to put the place in order before she walked to her car. Getting the glass swept up was easy, but she wasn't sure what to do about the hole left in the door's windowpane. She settled finally on the back cover of the phone book, which fit nicely over the hole. What she hated most was the shock they would have coming into the house to find that someone had been there. It would be upsetting, she knew, sort of a creepy feeling, and they would have to search through the house to find out what was missing, and then they would call the police or the sheriff or the golf pro up the road and report the break-in, and then they would tell all their neighbors about it, and everybody would be frightened and decide that there was a crime wave in Sleepy Hollow. Sarah hated the thought of it. She decided it would help to leave them a note:

Dear folks,
I would like to express my sincere apology for having broken into your lovely home. If I have caused you distress, I am profoundly sorry. However, I have not done this without good reason. This morning, I was on a vacation outing with my husband, and we began to quarrel, I'm afraid, over my current pregnancy. Unfortunately, he became quite angry and made me get out of the car, and then drove off down the road and left me. I walked for a while until I found myself on your street. I passed by several other houses, but yours looked the most forgiving, so regrettably, I had to break a little pane of glass to get in and use the phone. Unfortunately, I will be unable to reimburse you for the broken glass as my husband drove off with my purse in his car. Please know that I have not disturbed your home in any other way.
My sincere apologies, Maude Adams

Considering what she had done already, Sarah did not think it was too bad to make up a good story for them. It was partially true anyway: she was pregnant and she was sorry and she did not have a purse. Maude Adams had been the name of her mean third-grade teacher, dead by now most likely. She left the note on the counter, where they would see it first thing. As she closed the door, she saw that the broken pane didn't look so bad, really. She had put the front of the phone book cover facing out, so that when they first came up to the stoop, they would see the picture of the pink rhododendrons with the Blue Ridge Parkway in the background.

As she walked down the driveway, she looked at the LUV HUT sign once again. It was hung on its little post with two eyehooks, and she noticed one of the hooks had come loose, making the sign crooked. She looked at the cunning grooved letters and the little red heart. As she reached up to straighten the sign, she made a little wish on that heart, and hiked on down the road.

When Sarah turned onto the next street, she was happy to see Wilma's car parked on the overlook. Where it would have gone, she did not know, but it was good to see the familiar green paint and its clean gray seats. The temperature had dropped a bit, so she settled into the front, put her arms around herself. It was afternoon now, the mountains were still beautiful. She had had her day, had taken most of it and had not even put Jonah on the ledger.

Their time together had been short, not more than nine or ten months now, and even then, their time had been really just a string of afternoons, a few evenings. This was part of the trouble. Sarah could not pinpoint the substance of it—she knew only that in Jonah's presence her heart seemed to swell, take on more weight, it would drop down into her chest. To even know that he was present at this moment down in one of the valleys in front of her, to know that he was nearby, made her aware at once of her heart beating.

That was the reason—or one reason at least—why she had left New Mexico, to find out what it would feel like to be well apart from him. Sarah had wanted just to think about him, under Miss Wilma's watchful eye, to be forced to reason through her actions while watching her mother walk around her kitchen, making a grocery list, living her own life under a tried-and-true method. Sarah did not need her mother's actual opinion, she had not planned to tell her a thing, she had just wanted to sit at the kitchen table and watch what Wilma did—she would know then, would know what to do about Jonah.

*   *   *

The day she followed him into the darkroom and Jonah closed the door behind them, Sarah smelled the fumes from the chemicals that sat in shallow tubs on the counter, sulfur and sweetness and metal all in one breath. The curtain was pulled over to one side of the room, revealing a small worktable stacked up with metal canisters. Jonah led her to the table, pulling a roll of film from his pocket.

"I shot these this morning up in Santo Domingo. They're nothing too important, just pictures of my friend Dan Eagle wrangling some of those big dough bowls he makes for the tourists. Let's develop them now and I can show you the whole process," he said. She watched him, watched his big hand palm the film, tried to listen to what he was telling her as he moved the metal cans around on the table. "It starts with developing the negatives. The exposed film has to go in one of these canisters. The tricky part is getting the film off the roll and onto a spool. For that you need complete and total darkness. Any light at all will spoil them." He walked back across the room and shut off the overhead fluorescents. A red light mounted over the counter stayed on. It threw a strange glow into the chemical vats. As Jonah passed by the light, it shone on his face like the first seconds of sunup out in the canyons, a perfect rock face chiseled out of the ages. He took his place beside Sarah, lined up the things he would need, explained each detail to her, chattering a bit—she thought—because she was staring.

Finally he pulled the black curtain across on its track. Sarah's eyes blinked and blinked, struggling to understand the dark. Jonah stopped talking then, and it was quiet, so quiet that she could hear her own pulse, she could hear Jonah breathe, could hear him part his lips. There was a moment, just a moment when Sarah thought she would see a spark, an inevitable arc of attraction between two forces. She held her breath.

Then she heard Jonah begin to work on the roll of film, prying off the top of the housing. The film rustled and clicked as he began to thread it along the developing wheel, describing again his motions. Sarah was breathing again by the time he said, "It's done," so she was not ready when he touched her arm, feeling to find her hand and place the spool in it. "Check this," he said. "This is how you know you've got it right. Now you get the spool into the canister." She groped around, found the top with shaking hands, heard him laugh as she tipped the canister over. Just as she managed to get the spool loaded in, she felt Jonah come up close behind her, stretch his arms around either side. His hands touched hers as he fit the lid down over the top of the canister. He pushed it down tight, then withdrew his hands, standing still right behind her, an inch away.

"Finished," he whispered, and before she had time to feel the word on her neck, he had turned her around, had spun her like a doll. Before she could even let out her breath, he was kissing her—finding her lips like they were his own, kissing her like they were both invisible, kissing her like they would never need the light or anything else again.

Another gust of wind blew up the mountain, bending the trees and leaves in its path. In New Mexico, the wind came to you without warning in short bursts of dust and red sand. Here, Sarah could see it miles away. When it reached her finally and blew into the window, it left moisture on her face. Sarah had the sensation that she could get out on top of the car and launch herself out into the valley, fly over its contour, glide all the way back down to Swan's Knob and alight in front of the police station. She wondered if she could walk right into the police station and somehow vouch for Jonah so that they would let him go.

She had to concede that the timing of her day trip was way off as far as Jonah was concerned. If nothing else, he was a friend who had needed her today—she was the only person around who knew him really, and she had left town. She had been so worried

about her own predicament that she hadn't spent a minute thinking about his. At least she knew that Jonah, the very picture of
easygoing, would not be overly distressed by the situation. If he
was still in jail, chances were that he was advising his jailer on a
cure for his bad back or a potion for sick houseplants. Maybe he
was already out by now. Maybe some reasonable person had
talked to Jonah, and Jonah made him understand that he could
never murder even a cat. Maybe Harper had gone down to the
police station and told them that Jonah had been with him in the
car on the night of the shooting.

Even so, Jonah had been in jail overnight, suspected of murder. Every person had a limit. By the time they let him out, maybe
he would want to do nothing more than hitchhike right back to
Santa Fe. Maybe he was already on the road, riding with a trucker
back up over the mountains into Tennessee, then Kentucky,
thinking about the steep footpath up to his little house on the
Tesuque hillside, the last bit of the path lined with ancient stones
he had found on his forays into the desert, perfect piles of rock
on rock, leading up to his single room, to his kiva—the adobe
fireplace, and the futon on the floor covered with the old Navajo
blanket, the futon mattress where they had lain together, completely still with the blinds shutting out the afternoon sun. Maybe
he was thinking, riding in that truck on his way home, about how
they would make love on his mattress, and how they lay so still together that they would fall asleep in the afternoon heat, fall into a
sleep so deep that they would be almost dead but dreaming and
how they would wake up drugged from dreaming in the heat and
moving with each other, moving in the drowsy heat on a mattress
that held them but did not give in underneath, but held them,
held the whole afternoon and the next and the next. Would that
be what he would remember, would that be what he would be
thinking as he barreled down the road away from her? She felt the
miles between them suddenly well up inside her and she found
herself sitting in her mother's car on top of a green hill crying be-

cause of the miles that she had just made up, and she found her-self wondering if he was rolling down some road crying too.

A large wrecker came racing up the road, throwing up a little gravel as it stopped. A tiny man in a large mechanic's coverall jumped down from the driver's side and walked up to her car with a springy step. "Woo-wee, you picked some spot here to run out of gas, little lady. Where in the world were you going? Not a soul lives down on this road here." He peered into her window. "Aw, and my goodness, you're crying. You didn't think I was going to let you set here all night, did you? Goddamn Wendell, that boy of mine, I've told him and told him not to take all day. I came up here the minute he got back. It's all right, now. I'll have you fixed up in no time flat. You just sit right there."

The man ran back to his wrecker, glancing back several times to check on her again. For some reason, the little man's kindness made some kind of dam break in her, and by the time he got back with the gas can, she was really crying, crying in a way that she would never cry in front of another person, crying about ab-solutely everything. She could tell that this unnerved the man a bit, for he cussed and railed against his tardy and sorry excuse for a son as he emptied the gas can into her tank. She was still crying when he cautiously approached her window and said, "Can you try to start it, honey? Or do you want me to get in there and do it?" Sarah nodded and bent over to turn the key in the ignition. "Now, pump your gas pedal there a couple of times," he said, and she did. The car started up. Sarah revved the engine.

"Now hold on there," he shouted. "Lordy, watch out, you'll go off the side of this here mountain." The man's eyes grew large on his tiny face. He was gripping the door with his fingers just inside the window opening and his whole body braced against the car. "I gotcha. I gotcha. Now, hon, please. I don't want to have to pull your nice car up out of this ravine here. Just put the car into Reverse and real slow, real slow, put on a little gas to back it up." The man waited until he saw that she had found the proper gear and moved back a half step. "Okay, hon, come on back, come on, come on back." Sarah eased the car up the road until her car was facing the wrecker. She stopped and put the car back in Drive. "Okay, whoa," the man shouted. "You wait right there and let me get my wrecker turned around and you can follow me down to my station."

∽

Harper pulled a few old tools out of the trunk and began to tinker with his car door's broken lock. His car was a Dodge Dart. It was about fifteen years old. He was the third owner and was as indifferent to maintenance as the rest. He didn't have a prayer of fixing the thing, it had been broken a good six months, but he had no desire to go inside. He had nothing more to say to Wilma, and he expected that Jonah himself would go in soon, looking to take a bath or borrow some clothes or buddy up to his daughter. He'd stay outside. It had been a long day, and so far he'd managed to maintain his cool. He had spent the morning nursing his hurt, trying to keep the lid on. In the afternoon he had worked on a little duet with Starling at the piano. If he was honest with himself, right now he was out in the driveway mainly to wait on Sarah, hoping she would pull up any minute now. He wanted to see her first, wanted a few minutes to talk to her before lover boy got his chance with her.

He still wasn't sure what he would say, but he had taken a good long look at the situation from as many angles as he could think of. He had to admit: If he pretended that he was some nosy neighbor, who could just see from the outside looking in, he was just getting what he deserved. But that wasn't the whole story. Sarah knew that, at least she would if she took half a minute to think about it. Sure, fidelity, faithfulness—the kind of things that kept you out of bars late at night—these qualities did not come naturally to Harper. Early on, especially in New York, he had not really taken any trouble to restrain himself as far as other women were concerned. Surely Sarah had not forgotten. They were living then in a place and time where not one soul used the word "adultery." To their friends in the Village, marriage was simply an incidental fact, and making it with someone was almost as quotidian as sharing a deli sandwich. This was not a concept that he would expect Miss Wilma or anyone else in this town to warm up to. Hey, he thought, that was why he and Sarah lived where they did. And at the time, Sarah had understood this, he was certain. She had shown she knew the score in a thousand ways—by her own actions and by her quiet acceptance of his. It had been beyond discussion.

As for faithfulness, fidelity, and for God's sake, love, he had married her, hadn't he? Just like that, no hesitation. On the very afternoon, what had he said? They had been sitting out on Guilford's commons on one of the first warm days with their faces tilted up toward the sun, and Sarah had told him about her baby. It's coming, she said, coming in fall. Like that, she had told him, with a flat voice, no trace of whining or pleading. It's coming. He had looked over at her to see if he could see that fact written on her face, but he could see nothing new, just a clean white face shining in the sun. Her eyes were closed, and there was no hint of expectation in her expression. Harper had closed his own eyes. In the brightness, he could see the veins on the inside of his eyelids, could almost see the blood running through them. Millions of questions occurred to him, when and where and how and why, what and what might we do about it, but then he looked at her again, a girl with little bony arms folded over her lap, serene and warmed by the sun. He could not bear to make a single calculation, he vowed not to ask one thing, but only said in some clumsy way he could not remember that maybe the thing to do, the thing that would cause the least hassle for them all was to go right then and there on that day and get married.

He could not remember how she had answered him, he could not remember much about the drive to Myrtle Beach, what they'd said, how they had found a justice of the peace and convinced him to marry them out on the beach. They had stood out on a stretch of sand just beyond the amusement park, right as the sun was going down. Sarah had been beautiful, he remembered that, and her lips tasted like salt when he kissed her. By the time it was done and the JP was signing the papers propped up on Harper's back, the ocean had receded into dark and the sand felt cold. Harper remembered climbing back up to the boardwalk and seeing that the lights from the rides had been turned on, hearing the music from the Tilt-A-Whirl and the kids screaming on the roller coaster. He and Sarah had walked through the park, smiling at each other, and Harper had felt like a holy man among the profane.

He did not allow himself a doubt or a single question until months and months down the line. And when he got around to it and really thought about it in detail, he had to admit that it was possible that the baby wasn't his. He was pretty sure that Sarah had been with Tommy Gotschall in New York, though he had never asked, and he was close to certain that the timing was right. This might have mattered to another man, but it did not to him. Not really. He was with Sarah, he loved her. He had married her and stayed that way. It was over ten years now. As far as he could tell, Starling looked nothing like Tommy. When he looked at her, Harper saw her mother's face more than anything else, and maybe a little bit of his own chin. He did not dwell on it really, and it did not seem important enough to discuss with Sarah. Starling was his now. He had raised her. That was all that mattered.

Maybe lately Sarah had forgotten some of this. Maybe she didn't count this kind of loyalty. Maybe she had held all of his little sins against him. Maybe all of his little wrongs had finally added up to exceed her one big mistake, if indeed she had even made one. Maybe the debt was paid and she was moving on. Somehow, Harper could not believe this was so. He had to believe that this Jonah fellow was just a passing thing to Sarah. Maybe Jonah was here just to make a nuisance out of himself.

Maybe Sarah would throw him out the minute she came back. This is what he had told himself all day.

He had convinced himself that if he could just see her first, things might be all right. He had planned what to say all day, but now he was wondering if it was a good idea to say much at all. Jonah seemed like the quiet type, full of soulful glances. Maybe that was what she liked. He didn't know.

A car passed by the house, slowed down and turned into the driveway. It was getting dark, so the headlight blinded Harper momentarily, but he walked on up to the driver's side of the car. Once he got past the headlight, he could see that it was not Wilma's LTD, but a late-model Thunderbird. The man from the bar, Roy, was driving. Harper hoped he hadn't come to follow up on their conversation from last night.

"Evening, son," said Roy, getting out of his car quickly. Before Harper could say anything, Roy had walked past him and was up the steps of the front porch. He rang the doorbell. He clasped his hands behind his back, then rocked up and down on his toes. Lights came on in the front rooms of the house. As Roy reached up to smooth his hair, the front porch light popped on. It seemed to startle him momentarily, but he recovered sufficiently to greet Miss Wilma in a booming voice as she opened the front door.

Wilma unlocked the screen door and unceremoniously charged out, letting the screen door slam behind her.

"Well, good evening," Roy said. Harper could not hear Wilma's response. She walked directly down the steps, leaving Roy to catch up at the sidewalk.

"No, I'm glad you called," Harper heard her say as Roy followed her down the front walk, with his hand waving hesitantly above the small of her back. Harper was unaware of any occasion since her husband's death that Wilma had gone out with a man on a date. From all indications, however, that was what she was about to do this evening. Why of all nights would she pick this one? As they neared his car, a horrible thought crossed his mind:

Could it be that this was no date at all, but instead was some meeting with the police concerning the murder investigation? This was not a good idea. What if the police learned that Jonah was at Wilma's house? She was sure to tell them. There was no way she could predict the awful consequences of this disclosure. He had to warn her.

"Miss Wilma . . ." he began.

"Oh, Harper, I didn't let you know," she said. "I am going down to the Coach House with Mr. Swan here. Roy, you know my son-in-law, Harper, don't you?"

"Miss Wilma, may I have a word?"

"Can we talk when I get back? I won't be but a little while. Bye-bye," she said and ducked into the passenger side.

Roy closed her door and said to Harper with a wink, "Don't you worry, son. I'll take good care of her."

As he watched them drive away, his only small consolation was that the police station was not their destination. He turned back to his car door, a totally futile occupation now that it was dark. Surely Jonah was inside by now, probably telling Starling what a nice room she would have at his place. He had to admit, though, that during his time with her this afternoon, Starling had seemed totally ignorant of her mother's relationship with Jonah. She had seemed to regard him as no one with any particular significance, had displayed no curiosity about him. Harper took this as a good sign, though it was possible that she was just playing dumb to spare him.

Another car pulled into the driveway. Sarah at last. Harper hurried down to the car. Sarah waved at him, smiled sheepishly. She had just turned off the motor and cut the headlights when a police car pulled up at the curb in front of the house. Harper's heart began to beat blood all the way up into his ear canals. A bunch of men got out of the car and proceeded in slow motion up the driveway. Harper saw that Sarah was out of the car now and standing by him.

"What's all this?" she whispered to him. He could only shake his head. The men halted in front of them, forming a semicircle. Harper recognized the chief, who said to him in an official tone, "We have reason to believe that a man by the name of Jonah Branch is on the premises. Is that correct?"

Harper could again only nod. He recognized several of the men from Squirrely's Pool Hall. Avery, Ava Baker's brother, stood with his hands clenched on his thighs. There was also a deputy, and several men in suits, probably the SBI. Sarah looked at the men, then back at him with increasing alarm.

"Will you please ask Mr. Branch to step out of the house?" said the chief. At that moment Harper heard the front screen door open and turned to see Jonah and Starling walking onto the front porch. All of the men hustled across the lawn and up to the porch, with the chief pulling his handcuffs from his back pocket.

"Jonah Branch," he said, fumbling with the handcuffs, "you are under arrest for the murder of Clemont Baker."

"Oh my God," Sarah said and ran toward the porch.

∽

What kind of mother are you, Sarah? This was all that would come to her mind as she ran up the stairs. The space in front of the door was crowded with the men, and on the other side of them Starling was plastered up against the house, her eyes wide open. The front two men stood like riot police, blocking her path. She grunted slightly as she tried to press between them and heard a voice finally say, "Let her through, boys." It was Chief Henry. She felt his eyes on her as she rushed over and put her arm around Starling's shoulders. Shame on me, she thought, to let Starling see this. Jonah, wearing a dusty T-shirt, stood barefoot before the men. He offered them his wrists like a man in a movie. As he did this, he looked over at Sarah with an expression that hid nothing about what had passed between them.

"Inside," she said to Starling, but Starling did not move. She was looking not at Jonah, but at the shiny handcuffs that clinked in the deputy's hands. The expression on her face was fascination more than fear. The men fumbled to open the cuffs and get them around Jonah's large wrists. "Inside," Sarah said, leading Starling to the door this time, "into the kitchen and stay there. I'll be there in a minute."

Sarah closed the door behind Starling. The men were leading Jonah down the steps now. Sarah wondered what she could do. "Chief Henry?" she said. He turned around to look at her but kept walking. She followed him. "I'm Sarah, Wilma Mabry's daughter."

"I know who you are," he said flatly. She had to walk quickly to keep up with him.

"I wish you could stop a minute and talk to me about what you're doing. I think you're making a mistake. There's been some kind of mix-up about this man you have here," she said.

"I don't believe so, honey," the chief said. "You best let this be and go on now back in the house." He passed Harper now, throwing his head back a bit toward Sarah to remind Harper to get his wife back up where she belonged.

Harper didn't acknowledge the gesture, but reached out to Sarah's forearm as she started to move past him. "Just be cool," he whispered. The men put Jonah in the car, the dome light shining on his stone face. He looked back plaintively at Sarah in the driveway until the last door closed, and the car was mercifully dark. The deputy started the car, and as it rolled down the street he turned on his red light, broadcasting the arrest into the front room of every house.

Sarah could no longer remember exactly what she expected to accomplish by coming back to Swan's Knob. It was like she had brought home some small science experiment that proved lethal when the general population was exposed. In Santa Fe, on those carefully appointed days, she would drive home from Jonah's flat with the whole afternoon still lingering on her skin. In the empty house, she would turn on the shower, put every piece of clothing in the basket, and get a long scrub with her loofah. By the time Starling got home, Jonah would be long gone. Sarah could be Starling's mother, the kind of mother Starling's friends wished they had, the kind of mother who would understand and fail to nag them about their wardrobe or curfews. She and Starling would work on their sweater loom or talk about school. Jonah would be another life altogether. It had been odd, so far away from Santa Fe, to see him here, to see his brown hands, to see him stand two feet from her daughter, like some unknown contamination.

Sarah found Starling in the kitchen pulling brown-and-serve rolls out of the oven. Somehow in the next half hour, Sarah would be called upon to provide some kind of truth to her daughter, some kind of explanation about where she had been, what had happened. She was, even after her daylong trek, wholly unprepared for this, so she felt a rush of gratitude and love when Starling said only, "These rolls got a little burned on the bottom. Do you think they'll be all right?"

Starling had spent time outside today, Sarah saw. Her sweet face had a pink glow that made her absolutely breathtaking. She was so unspoiled in that moment with her burned rolls and her apron, Sarah wanted to rush over and hug her tight. "Oh, honey, they look fine to me. I'm sure they'll be just delicious. Where's your grandmother? Upstairs?" At least her mother had not been required to witness an arrest on her front porch. Dinner was almost ready. As usual, above all things, come what may—missing daughter, police, murder—her mother had been certain to get dinner on, although she must have asked Starling to set the table. The utensils had been carefully laid on the placemats, but they were all backward, with the fork on the right and the napkin under the spoon. The effort was altogether sweeter than the correct arrangement would ever be. She hoped that Wilma wouldn't rush around fixing things when she got back downstairs.

"Nana's not here. Lucky you," said Starling. "She went out to dinner, just in time to miss your friend getting busted. God, are you guys in trouble. Wilma's going to croak. Why did he get arrested anyway? I couldn't understand what the policeman said."

"Why did she go out to dinner?" said Sarah. "She made this dinner here."

"No, I made dinner," said Starling. "Nana got a phone call from some man, Roy someone, and just ran upstairs and changed her dress. Go get Dad and let's eat. We'll all be sitting around the table here when she gets back. We'll just pretend we don't know what happened to Jonah. By the way, what did happen?"

Sarah didn't answer and went to look out the front door. On her way home, she had pictured her mother sitting in a glider on the porch, waiting, crying maybe. This speech she had prepared: "Mother, I am really sorry for causing you pain and worry, as I have done throughout my whole life. But, Mother, I have some problems, some very adult problems, which if I can say in a kind way, are not your concern." This she had gone over several times, anticipating her mother's worry, her relief. She had even imagined that her mother would take one look at her and have a sudden psychic vision—that she would just know that her daughter was expecting a child and that she would cry out to Sarah from her glider, and as she did, the baby would jump inside of Sarah, and she would run up on the porch and sit with her mother and they would take off their shoes and use their bare feet to push the glider up and back and then they would talk there, they would talk about all the things that had happened, they would go over it all. These things she had played out as she drove down the mountain.

She had planned nothing to say to Starling or to Harper, which seemed rather stupid now, thoughtless.

Out in the driveway, Harper had moved finally from his spot and now seemed to be sitting inside his car. She heard a muffled hammering, which stopped when she called out to him. After a few seconds, he emerged from the passenger door.

"Starling has made dinner," she said. "Better come on in." Harper climbed up on the porch and started to walk past her. She grabbed his arm. "Harper," she said, "she's asking. She wants to know what's going on."

Harper looked at her, met her eyes for the first time in ages. "Well, tell her," he said quietly. "Just tell her, tell us, what happened."

Chapter Ten

"I don't know if you like a salad before dinner, but they have a real nice one here," Roy was saying. "Reba Beth was telling me the other night that she and Franklin have this special machine that shreds the lettuce real fine, kind of fluffs it up and makes it crisp at the same time. Anyway, I highly recommend it."

Wilma could tell that Roy was mostly just talking, afraid of any kind of silence. Surely he had seen her here before, and surely he knew that she and everyone else in Swan's Knob had eaten just about everything on the menu.

"For dinner, I do like the veal cutlet. That's nice. Or the chicken and dumplings—but they may not have that tonight—I think Reba Beth only makes that on Tuesdays."

Now that she was sitting here with Roy, Wilma was beginning to question the advisability of accepting his last-minute invitation. It seemed to her, in all, that this day had started well before she could put her feet in her shoes, and it had just picked up speed from there. One spur of the moment after another. *Harry,* she prayed, *just shut your eyes, if you have them.* Harry would not want to see her, in the back booth of the Coach House, sitting across from a man sweating in the effort to impress her. Without more than thirty seconds' thought, easy as pie, she had put on her lipstick and gone out on a date. A date. There was nothing else to call it. This was after fifteen years of nothing, fifteen years of not even thinking about any living man on earth. She was totally un-prepared.

"Roy," she said as she saw Reba Beth coming over to their table, "you seem to have so many ideas about this menu, why don't you just go ahead and order for both of us."

Roy blushed with pleasure and made a big show with Reba Beth, saying, "Well, tonight, I think *we* will start with one of those salads, blue cheese dressing for me, and is that all right with you too, Wilma?"

Reba Beth looked down at her order pad, but Wilma caught her pressing her lips together to hide the smile. Roy didn't notice and went right on with ordering every little thing. Wilma felt a moment of real panic—what had she been thinking? She had no business being there. It wasn't just that she was worried about Sarah. She was just in a panic about whatever life she had left back there, back a few days ago before something had started making the world spin so fast, making everything pick up speed and spinning everything she knew about way off in the distance, too far away to return to now.

She looked out at the crowd in the restaurant. It was full of people who knew both her and Roy, and she thought she saw a few of them turning around to look in her direction. Worst of all, there was Grace Snow, out with Ron and Ronny. Wilma saw Grace steal a glance at Wilma's corner. Then she turned back to her table and leaned over the vinegar and ketchup toward Ron and whispered something. Wilma could tell that she was the topic. For the first time in her life, Wilma wished that she lived in New York City. She could not stand for every little thing she did to be observed by the general population.

She realized that Roy had stopped talking finally and was look-ing at her with a gentle smile on his face. Involuntarily, she smiled back. "Roy," she said, "did you just ask me something? I apolo-gize, I have just had a very long day."

"No, I didn't ask you a thing," he said. "You just looked for a minute there like a deer, fixing to run up out of this booth. Are you okay? Do you need to go . . . would you like to be, you know, the ladies' room is right over there."

"No," said Wilma. "I'm just fine for the moment. Just feeling a little guilty, I suppose, for leaving all the family behind, especially with Sarah gone all day."

"Where'd she go?" said Roy. "Wasn't that your granddaughter who answered the phone? Did Sarah leave you to watch her? And Harper's there too?"

"She just needed some time off. She'll be home by the time I get back," said Wilma, less sure about it than her tone implied. She wondered now if she hadn't left the house just to make certain that she wouldn't be around to see the scene when Sarah returned to both Harper and Jonah in the house. A pretty pickle for sure.

"Wilma, I wanted to talk to you about this afternoon, after the service."

"The Fourth of July?"

"No, no, that's the point. This afternoon, I wasn't talking about the Fourth of July at all. There's been a little mix-up, and to tell you the truth, I'm not quite sure about how to talk to you about it. It's kind of delicate."

Now Wilma felt herself blushing. There was a pause as Reba Beth brought them their salads. Wilma just didn't think she could take any kind of declaration of love—not tonight, not sitting in the Coach House with half the town watching. Roy pushed on.

"It's about the photographs, Wilma. The ones that you got in your mail today. Do you know the ones I'm talking about?"

Wilma nodded and sucked in her breath. She was thankful no one was in the booth behind Roy.

"It was me that sent them to you," he said.

So this was what this little dinner was all about. It was not a date at all, but something else, probably the payoff in some town-wide practical joke.

"Land sakes, Roy, what were you thinking?" said Wilma, louder than she had intended. Roy turned around this time to look at the folks in the restaurant and smiled sheepishly back at them.

"Now, Wilma, I don't blame you for being upset. But you've got to let me explain," he said.

"If this was some scheme to get my goat, well, congratulations, you have it," said Wilma. "But let me tell you, if you have nothing better to do than play mean pranks on widows, then you are a sorry excuse for a man. Here, I thought that you were . . . Just forget what I thought."

"Wilma, this was not a prank. I would never do such a thing. Just let me explain."

Wilma stared at Roy, who took a bite of his salad, made sure to swallow it, then whispered, "Okay. I take it you got a look at the photographs?"

"Well, of course I did, how could I avoid it? Someone just sent me a plain manila envelope, no return address, no warning, no nothing. Wouldn't you open it? I was in the church of all places, sitting up at my organ. Why, I almost fell off my bench. It's lucky I didn't break something. That would've been a scene, wouldn't it? Miss Wilma lying in the choir loft with a broken leg and pornographic pictures of a dead man spread all around her."

Roy stared at her a minute and then he began to laugh.

"You think it's funny?" she said.

"Not at all," he said, laughing harder. "It's really not one bit funny. But think a minute, really picture it. Lord, what would everybody say?"

"That I had lost my mind," she said, "which is not very far from the truth."

Roy laughed again. "Wilma, let me just tell you that of all the people I know on this earth, you are the most sane person among them. Now I mean that sincerely. Really, I sent you those pictures because you do have such a good head on your shoulders. And I want to assure you that I did not mean to alarm you when I sent those pictures. As a matter of fact, I sent you a letter explaining the whole story."

"Letter? There wasn't a letter. I know because I looked for one."

"Well, that's part of the mix-up. It seems that I dropped it out of the manilla envelope on my way to the post office."

"Mighty convenient, Roy Swan. But I still don't understand. Why in the world would you send me those photographs?"

"Well, it's kind of complicated, Wilma, and somehow, I think if I tried to tell you, it might come out wrong. Would you mind if I just gave you the letter and let you read it?"

"I suppose," said Wilma. This was most confusing to her, because she had always thought of Roy as a gentleman, and it pained her to know that he was passing around those terrible pictures. Roy pulled a small envelope out of his sports coat and handed it to her.

The envelope wasn't formally addressed; it just had "Wilma" written across the front in a fine old-fashioned hand. It was a little damp and water-stained. Wilma sure hoped that Roy hadn't cried over it. The inside was dry. Roy had written the letter on expensive formal stationery, heavy paper with his initials embossed across the top. "How many of these did you hand out?" said Wilma.

"Just one," said Roy. "Just take a minute to read, please."

Dear Wilma,

It is my fervent hope that you will read this letter before you look too closely at the enclosed photographs. Please, please be aware that they are indeed offensive. For this, I apologize and beg that you do not think too badly of me. I am sending them to you because you, of all the people I know, are the individual who is most worthy to decide what is to be done with them.

In case you cannot tell or do not want to look too closely,

*the two paramours are Clem Baker and none other than Lily
Mae Strong. . . .*

"Lily Mae?" said Wilma. "Are you sure, Roy?"

"Wilma, you saw the pictures, don't you think that was her?"

"Well, I didn't get a thorough look in the church there. I did
see right away that the man was Clem Baker. I mean, his face is as
plain as day in one picture. Truth be known, I felt very strange sitting in that church with the man's coffin not thirty feet away, looking at pictures of his . . . But the woman, I couldn't tell who it was
right off. I was planning to come back to my house and look at
them with . . . to look at them in better light. But Lily? Roy, she's
got to be twenty years older."

"I know, I know. Just read on, please," he said.

She could tell that he was watching her for her reaction as
she read, and she was worried about what else she was about to
find out.

> *Yes, ma'am, Lily Mae is the one. She is at it again. I
> know that this knowledge is sure to bring you suffering—to
> remember that Lily had similar dealings with your own hus-
> band, that her wickedness caused his death, and that her
> reign of misdeeds continues. For bringing you this grief
> again, I apologize.*

> *But in these photographs, I believe is some kind of proof,
> some kind of evidence of what Lily has become. Exactly
> what they prove, what awful act they foretell, I cannot say.
> You know her better than I do. I thought it was right that
> you be her judge, that you be allowed to exact your revenge
> on her if you so chose.*

"Roy, you have got some of this wrong. I don't want to go
into it right now, but where my husband and Lily Mae were
concerned, there is a lot you don't know," said Wilma. Roy

regarded her with a kind smile again, which irritated Wilma this time.

Beyond him, she saw Chief Henry and some other men walk into the restaurant. They looked around for a table, but when Chief Henry saw Wilma and Roy, he headed straight back to their table.

"I know all of this must be painful, and I would never dream of bringing it up . . ." Roy was saying. Wilma pulled the letter up to her chest and smiled at Roy. "Why look, we've got company," she said.

"Evening, Miss Wilma," said Chief Henry, looking as grave and formal as a man sent to the mother of a fallen soldier. "I'm afraid we've had to pay a little visit to your house. Now, there is no cause for concern, but I did want to let you know. You see, we got a tip that Jonah Branch was hiding out there this afternoon, and in light of some new evidence that came to our attention, we went over there and arrested him just a few minutes ago. Now, he came along without any struggle at all, and no one was hurt in any way. In fact, he came right on out on the front porch, so there was no chance for me or my deputies to get even a speck of mud across your living room carpet."

"Mud?" said Miss Wilma. "You arrested that poor boy on my front porch? For what?"

"For the murder of Clemont Baker, ma'am," Henry said, all official.

"Henry, the man did not kill Clem Baker. Surely you know this. He is not a criminal. And for that matter, he was not hiding out in my home: he is a houseguest, and I'll thank you to return him," she said, wondering if they had turned on all their red lights and led Jonah to the patrol car in handcuffs.

"Now, Miss Wilma, don't you go getting upset. This is just police business. We're just following where the investigation leads. You tell her, Roy."

Roy looked at a shiny new gun strapped around Henry's gut and cut his eyes over at Wilma. "Henry," he said, "I believe I told you the other night that I thought you were barking up the wrong tree. And if you have put this big criminal in the jail, why are you wearing your gun in the Coach House?"

Henry reached down, then reddened a bit. "Aw, shoot, I just wore this to the arrest and forgot to take it off. Don't worry. It ain't loaded. Those SBI boys just hustled us out of the station, so they could talk to the suspect."

"I thought you decided that he was not a suspect the other night," said Roy. "Isn't that why you let him out?"

"Well, I wasn't for that," said Henry, "but those SBI boys said we had to. They have changed their tune now, let me tell you, and it's all because of some evidence that me and those boys found this afternoon." Chief Henry pointed over his shoulder at a far table, where Wilma could see three men: Guy Thomas, a part-time policeman who worked second shift at the mill; Tim Jessup, the regular deputy; and Avery Spivey, Ava Baker's twin. All three were smoking and talking with quiet animation, pretending that they were just too busy with police work to see how everyone in the place was looking at them. Wilma could tell they loved their little spotlight, though. They had the new, straight postures of re-cently gained importance. Tim was in his police uniform, Avery was wearing what looked to Wilma like some hunting vest made out of military material, and Guy Thomas was in his mill clothes.

"What's the Spivey twin doing hunting evidence with you?" asked Roy.

"Well, I've deputized him for the time being," said Henry.

"Can you do that?" asked Roy, sneaking a cute wink at Wilma. "I thought they only did that in the movies, just before forming a posse."

Henry laughed. "Oh, you love to make fun, don't you, Roy. Well, I am not about to get up a posse. I was just shorthanded, on account of Clem, you know, and Avery just kind of fell in with us when we started investigating, being ex-military and all. I'll tell you what, he's motivated, after taking care of his sister."

Henry sandwiched himself into the booth beside Roy, who did not seem pleased with the development. Henry missed his expression, though, and ducked his head down to confide the remainder of the information: "Here's how the arrest went down. I promise you, Miss Wilma, before I'm through, you will be thanking me for getting that man out of your house and away from your daughter. And from the little one, she's your granddaughter, right?"

Wilma only nodded. Sarah must have gotten back just in time for the whole thing. What had she done when the patrol car arrived? Wilma felt a little queasy when she thought about Starling being there.

Henry ducked his head down and said, "Here is the way we cracked the case. I decided that we should go back out to the campsite, out where we originally apprehended the suspect. I told the boys there to go over it with a fine-tooth comb, which is what we did. You know Avery was in the service for a few years before he came back to the mill. He says he had some special training down there at Fort Bragg and such and he knew how we should divide the site into quadrants. So each of us took a piece, and looked real close, and what do you know but Guy come up with something. Something important, which tied the suspect to Clem Baker."

"What was it, a confession note?" said Wilma.

"Well, I ought not to say," said Henry, "since you do have some involvement in the crime. They have cautioned us against spreading news around town, contamination, they call it. Can you believe that?"

"It seems to me," said Roy, stealing a wink at her, "that Miss Wilma does indeed have a right to know what you found, Henry, since you have been arresting suspects on her front porch and telling people that she was involved in the crime. She has a right to due process, the right to meet her accuser, the right to full discovery under the law."

"That does make some sense," said Henry, "and I can't see what it would hurt for you to know. What we found was a cigarette lighter, lying right in the campfire ashes, had Clem's initials on it plain as day. I rest my case."

"Did you check it for fingerprints?" said Roy.

"Law me, Roy, you ought to be one of us. That was the first thing the SBI wanted to do," said Henry. "They said the test was inconclusive—which means that they just found a few smudges, could be Guy's from picking the thing up, could be the Branch boy's. That don't mean nothing, though. It was found at his campsite, in his campfire ashes. That was enough for the SBI."

"Excuse me, Chief Henry, can I bring you some supper, too?" said Reba Beth, setting big plates in front of Wilma and Roy.

Mercifully, Henry began getting up out of the booth. "No, I better get back on over to my table," he said, and then, all official again, "Now, I caution you folks about talking to anyone about what I have revealed."

The eyes in the restaurant followed Chief Henry back to his table. Any further speculation, Wilma saw, would be aimed at him and his investigation. No one looked back over at Wilma and Roy. The smell of the veal cutlet and gravy reminded Wilma that she had scarcely eaten all day. She was hungry. She looked over at Roy, who was watching her with his hands in his lap. The minute he saw her pick up her fork and knife, he did the same. They ate a few bites without saying a word. Finally, Roy began to shake his head and smile.

He said, "I tell you the truth, I did not know that Reba Beth had commenced to offer a dinner show on Thursday nights. I don't know about you, but I'd just as soon have done without it."

"Dinner show?" said Wilma. "Oh, you mean Henry." She began to laugh with Roy in spite of herself. "Well, I don't see it as funny. He's locked up an innocent young man. You and I both know that."

"I am not sure what I know at this point," said Roy. "What is this about Jonah Branch being your houseguest? As far as I know, they found him camping out down at the Ararat."

"He was, I guess. He just came to the house this morning, after Henry let him go. It seems that he is a friend from Santa Fe."

"Whose friend?"

Wilma began, "This is a little vague in my mind."

"Well, we just had to stop by and say hello to you two," said an oozing Grace Snow as she bore down on their table and grinned elaborately.

Oh, hell's bells, thought Wilma. Roy, however, looked in no way embarrassed. In fact he grinned back at Grace rather proudly, like Wilma was some kind of prize debutante. Ron Snow stood just behind Grace and put his hand on her arm like he would like to steer her away. "Hello, Roy, Miss Wilma," he said in a more dignified tone.

"Well hello," managed Wilma.

"With all that's going on at your house, I am certainly glad to see you finally taking some time to kick up your heels." Grace's eyes were dancing. Only someone like her would consider a little dinner at the Coach House something to smirk over. Wilma felt her neck begin to turn red, and it must have been visible, since Ron gave Wilma an apologetic look and began to propel Grace toward the door.

"Have fun, you two," said Grace, departing with a little three-fingered wave. For just the briefest instant, Wilma had the impulse to respond with a vulgar hand gesture that she had seen several young people use over on the freeway in Winston if she didn't get her car out of their lane fast enough. Thankfully, the urge passed quickly. At a moment like this, it was no wonder to Wilma that she had made few close friends in her life. Grace was an example of someone who thought that just knowing you gave her the freedom to take drastic liberties with your privacy.

Roy, bless him, waited until Grace and Ron were out the door before attempting to talk to her. "You were saying . . . about the friend from Santa Fe . . ."

"Oh, yes," said Wilma, happy not to have to react to Grace's comments. "It seems that he knows both Sarah and Harper." She was tempted to tell him the whole story, but in truth, she didn't actually know much of anything. She wanted to talk to Sarah first.

Roy was busy cleaning his plate with the speed of a man accustomed to eating alone. "So you, yourself, don't know him very well. Do you know how he got mixed up in this?" he said.

"I don't think he had one thing to do with it," said Wilma. "He was just a stranger who came into town at the wrong time. Have you seen him? To a person like Henry, anyone with long hair and a few days' beard growth is bound to be a killer of some sort. Now to me, it is obvious that this man wouldn't hurt anyone. But that's beside the point. What we need to be thinking about, Roy, is these photographs. Maybe Henry ought to see them."

"Whoa, there, ma'am," he said. "Wait a little minute. We need to think long and hard before we give the pictures to anyone. No telling where they might end up. They could cause all kinds of uproar in this town."

"Now you say," said Wilma, "after blowing me off my organ bench."

"I have apologized, in writing," said Roy, "but maybe you didn't get to that part yet. Go ahead and finish the letter."

"I'll tell you, I don't really want to pull it out again in here, Roy," she said. "For all we know, Mr. Official over there might take it upon himself to confiscate it."

"I see your point," said Roy, wiping his mouth. "Then how about dessert? You know, their pecan pie—"

"Why don't we just get Reba Beth to fix us some coffee to go," said Wilma, taking a few last bites.

∽

Sarah followed Harper into the kitchen, where she was able to do little but plop down at the table. She felt like a ghost, almost transparent, with all the blood gone out of her, unable even to let anyone know she was there. Starling flittered about the kitchen, a little mother hen in training, excited by the porch drama and maybe nervous about its effect on her parents. Since she had been a toddler, Starling had been one who could sense alien energy in the air, seemed to soak it up. She ran from stove to table, glancing every ten seconds to Sarah's place with a winning smile. Sarah saw sadly that Starling wanted nothing more than to make things right. Starling had thrown a tea towel over her shoulder, as Wilma often did, and carried the meat platter to the table with a careful pride. Harper, seeing her, became suddenly jovial. Chattering, pulling out her chair, making an elaborate show of placing his napkin in his lap. Starling giggled, and Sarah worked to put a smile on her face.

When they all settled at the table, there was a little moment when everything was quiet. Wilma's grandfather clock ticked in the living room, bugs hummed out in the yard. Sarah looked down, half expecting to hear her own father clear his throat the way he did just before saying the blessing. When she looked back up, she saw that the three of them, their little family, were collectively a bit uneasy now. Maybe it was the weight of the events of the day. But more likely, Sarah thought, it was that they had embarked on an unfamiliar ritual. The occasion was made even stranger since it was staged in her mother's kitchen. It was the room where for every evening of Sarah's youth, six o'clock on the dot, there was a forced march through dinner. Sarah and her father were there with Wilma, heads up, backs straight, pleasant conversation, left hand in your lap young lady, Harry must you slurp your soup. Perhaps there was something to be said for it—its rigor, its safety, always safety first.

Sarah saw no reason not to give it a try. Dinner. It was a simple thing really. She had seen her mother do it under the most adverse conditions. "Well," she said, picking up a bowl of peas and passing them to Harper, "doesn't this just look wonderful. Why, Starling, you have done yourself proud."

Starling and Harper looked at each other and began laughing, and Sarah saw that she had taken it a bit too far.

"Nice accent and very funny," said Harper. "That's pretty good, but I wouldn't do that right to your mother's face."

"Yeah, weird, Mom, you looked just like Miss Wilma for a second when you said that," said Starling, who was raising a large cleaver over the shriveled roast.

"Don't call her Miss Wilma," said Sarah. "Can I help you with that, honey?" She was relieved that she had at least made everyone laugh.

"It's okay. I'll do it," said Starling, sawing off a thick slab. "Give me your plates."

When Starling handed Sarah her plate, she began to work on her food, each item either overcooked or undercooked by half. She watched Harper as he took a bite of mashed potatoes that managed to be both lumpy and watery. They smiled at each other as they had over a thousand little things that Starling had done since birth.

"So what did he do wrong?" said Starling.

Sarah made an effort to swallow what was in her mouth. "Who?" she said. Wilma lesson number one, denial. Feigned ignorance that there was anything to discuss.

"That man, Jonah. What did he do?" Starling said.

"Nothing," said Sarah. Lesson two, dismissal. "It's a big mix-up. He hasn't done a thing."

"Then why did they come to get him?" Starling said.

"They think he was involved in something, but they're just wrong," Sarah said.

"Well, what?" said Starling.

"What?" said Sarah.

"God. Mom, what was it that they think he did?"

"Don't say God," said Sarah. Lesson three, turn the tables.

"Don't say God?" said Starling.

"Starling," said Harper, sounding rather fatherly, "several nights ago, a local policeman was shot out on the bypass. Somehow the police decided that Jonah was involved. And they're going to talk to him about it."

"That's right," said Sarah. "It's just some small-town mix-up that should be straightened out by morning." Thankfully Starling went back to her dinner.

"So how was your adventure?" Harper said to Sarah, evenly, she thought, and without irony, like he genuinely wanted to know.

"Fine," said Sarah, "the mountains are always beautiful."

Harper looked over at Starling, who was chewing. "So, where did you go?"

"Up to Fancy Gap," said Sarah, "up on the Blue Ridge Parkway."

"What did you do up there?" said Harper, still casual, though he had already asked more than a month's worth of questions.

"I went up to an old diner, had a major breakfast, then I drove around," she said, finding it suddenly a little hard to finish a sentence with only one breath. She wondered if she sounded at all normal, if she had any chance of convincing at least Starling that it had been a routine day. "I got back so late because I had a little trouble with the car. Ran out of gas. You know me."

"You could have called us to come get you," he said, kindly again, but looking straight at her, "then you would have known Jonah was waiting."

"I did call. I told Starling where I was, when I would be home," she said, trying herself to sound kind.

"Who is he?" said Starling.

Harper and Sarah looked at her.

"Jonah," she said. "He said he knew you in Santa Fe, but I don't remember him. Who is he?"

"A friend of your mother's, Starling," said Harper with a little edge in his voice. He had never referred to her as "your mother" before. "Sarah" it had always been, just "Sarah." He knew about Jonah then. Knew at least part of it.

"A friend, from Minga's gallery," said Sarah, studying her plate again, afraid of the silence, afraid of the next question. Starling kept eating.

When Sarah looked up finally, Harper got jovial again—stretching it a bit, Sarah thought: "I'm glad you've had an adventure. We've always been quite the merry wanderers, you and I. Maybe we need to do that again, now that Starling is older. I was thinking myself about that today. About trips, just tripping on out there. When is the last time we did that? When you think about it, our wedding day just started as a day trip, and look where it's landed us now. Remember, Sarah, we just took off, we took off on a whim. Didn't tell anyone. God, that was great. What do you remember about that day, Sarah?"

She remembered that it was not a whim. She remembered that on that morning on the quad she was scared out of her mind, remembered that she had loved Harper fiercely, that she had been terrified to tell him she was pregnant. "What do I remember?" she said. "Wow. Let's see. I remember that it was just a beautiful day in Greensboro when we started out. We had been sitting out in the sun, so we had just minimal clothes on, cutoffs and T-shirts, I think, you were wearing your Grateful Dead tour shirt. Could I have a roll, please?" Why had Harper gotten them onto this topic?

"You got married on the beach, right?" said Starling.

"Yes, we did," said Harper. "It was at sunset. We spent the better part of the afternoon trying to find a justice of the peace to marry us. Finally we found one not two blocks from the arcade, had a little sign in his window. Remember?" said Harper.

Sarah nodded. This she could not vouch for, really. Her chief memory of that day was the feeling of unbelievable relief and a kind of wonder at what she was about to possess.

"Did you have flowers around your neck?" said Starling. "I saw that in a movie."

"I don't think we had flowers," said Sarah.

"Hell, no," said Harper, waving his arms broadly. "We didn't take time for flowers—we were on a mission. When we got to that beach, we just kicked off our shoes and ran out into the water splashing and laughing until that old JP just motioned us in. Remember?" He smiled at Sarah.

"Oh, yeah, said his supper was waiting," she said. At that hour on the coast, the light fell softly on everything. Sarah had been too young to be scared, too young to be anything but wholly taken in by the glow of Harper's face. Just like him to remind her tonight of all nights. Damn him for bringing it up, but at least Starling had been diverted. It was a story that they had told her many times, though not lately. Now came the little game.

"Who was there?" Starling said, on cue. "Was Nana?"

"Oh, no," said Harper.

"Grandma and Papa Chilton?"

"Oh, no," said Harper. "No one but the justice of the peace, some man we stopped on the beach as a witness and Sarah and me."

"And me, where was I?" Starling said, knowing the answer but wanting to hear the little rhyme. "Where was I?"

Harper said, "You were there, little darling, you were there, but you were nothing more then than a star in the sky, looking down, looking down on us like a spy. And you said to yourself, 'There they are, they're my folks.' Pretty soon, you came down, down to the ground and here you are, our little darling, our little Starling."

Sarah had to smile at Starling, but she could not manage much more than that. The next little star seemed to be tumbling in her belly, rejecting the food she had just eaten.

"I have dessert," said Starling, enjoying the moment now, enjoying their simple family meal. "I cleared out Nana's strawberry patch. I hope she won't mind."

∽

Once he cupped his hand around her elbow and helped her fold herself gently into his front seat, once he had closed the door and she sat there in his car safe and perfect on his leather seats—soft like butter, the salesman had said—once he had her all alone sitting in his car on the dark side of Main Street, Roy stood on the sidewalk and just looked in at Wilma, stood and looked until she stared back after him like he was some kind of fool. "Like butter, like butter," was all that would come to his head as he walked around the car to his own door. He knew it was only a car, the same car that had brought them to the Coach House, but somehow there in the dark, things had gotten all charged up and he wanted to start up his Thunderbird and drive, drive way on out somewhere like a man in a movie.

By the time he got in and got his key in the ignition, his fancy thinking had tied his tongue up again, and he realized that he had not spent enough time planning what actually ought to happen next, apart from the obvious, which Wilma supplied before he even had the car in gear:

"Well, you better get me on home. They'll all be waiting," she said. Wilma did not sound very charged up herself, but Roy couldn't tell for sure. He had noticed before. Sometimes she acted all gruff and businesslike just before her eyes got real wide and a little watery around the corners. They were alike that way—crusty outside, mush in the middle.

"I don't think I can let you go yet," he said. "We have some more to do, some more to talk about at least. You have got to finish the letter before we go back—just in case I got something wrong and I need to explain some more."

"I can read the letter just fine when I get home, Roy. I have people there," she said, shifting her legs around, crossing her ankles, then uncrossing them.

"So you said this afternoon. But, Wilma, I think we really need to talk—looks like there's no one in this town to work things out except you and me," he said, hoping to make his voice sound substantial but likable, kind of serious, like the guy on *Gunsmoke*. He looked over at her for effect, but swerved the car a bit in the process. Wilma noticed and gripped the door handle, but she didn't say anything about it.

"Well, I suppose I don't have to read it, you could just tell me the rest," she said.

"I wouldn't know where to start," he said. "Let me just pull over a minute and turn on the map light." The grammar school was right off down the street to Roy's right, and it seemed as good as anyplace for some privacy. He pulled in the drive and rolled the car along the gravel road that led behind the school to the athletic field.

"Goodness gracious, Roy, there isn't a streetlight in sight. I don't know how you think I'm going to read this thing," she said, businesslike again.

He rolled the car to a stop and clicked on the map light on the front console. A soft light fell across her face and down onto her lap. She rattled around in her purse to find the letter, then held it in the light. There was silence for a few minutes, which made Roy feel a little nervous. He flipped on the radio and turned the dial away from his country station before she could hear it. There was nothing but loud static for a few seconds, then he hit a station with a clean signal, must have been Mount Airy. He could tell by the announcer's voice that it was some teenager rock-and-roll station, but he didn't dare risk more grating static. Wilma was now holding the letter all the way down on her lap, watching him fiddle with the radio, not reading at all.

"Roy, as much as I hate to admit it, I cannot make out much of your lovely handwriting in this light," she said.

"Well, I never was much for the Palmer Method," he said, "You're not the first to single out my shaky hand."

"No, it's not your writing. I have just left my glasses in my other purse," she said. "Why don't you read it to me, if you don't mind." This disclosure seemed to have cost Wilma something, though Roy couldn't think what. He didn't take the time to think about the words he was going to have to read before he nodded and took the letter from her hand. The map light was dimmer than he imagined on the paper and he was forced to lean over toward her, holding the paper in a space just between her lap and his face.

"Where did you get to?" he said.

"I'm not sure," she said softly from somewhere very close by, about six inches from his forehead. "Just go from the beginning." He did not move his head to look at her. He just began to read, assuming the low and gentle tone, he hoped, of a kindly country lawyer reading a will:

Dear Wilma,

It is my fervent hope that you will read this letter before you look too closely at the enclosed photographs. Please, please be aware that they are indeed offensive. For this, I apologize and beg that you do not think too badly of me. I am sending them to you because you, of all the people I know, are the individual who is most worthy to decide what is to be done with them.

In case you cannot tell or do not want to look too closely, the two paramours are Clem Baker and none other than Lily Mae Strong. Yes, ma'am, Lily Mae is the one. She is at it again. I know that this knowledge is sure to bring you suffering—to remember that Lily had similar dealings with your own husband, that her wickedness caused his death, and that her reign of misdeeds continues. For bringing you this grief again, I apologize.

But in these photographs, I believe is some kind of proof, some kind of evidence of what Lily has become. Exactly what they prove, what awful act they foretell, I cannot say. You know her better than I do. I thought it was right that you be her judge, that you be allowed to exact your revenge on her if you so chose.

If you wonder how these photographs have come into my possession, let me tell you that no one but me has seen them or knows that they exist. I am certain of this fact, since I myself took the photographs and developed them. Before you think that I have become Swan's Knob's Peeping Tom, let me tell you what happened:

As you know, I am embarrassingly, somewhat a man of leisure due to my family circumstances and over the years, I have developed a keen interest in local history and genealogy. I must admit that I spent quite a bit of time wandering these parts, gathering little bits of history, names and dates and so forth. A few weeks ago, I was out off 681, north of Dobson visiting an old family cemetery that dates back to the 1700s. This cemetery is in a beautiful spot on the top of a gentle hill on land that was owned early on by the Lowell family. I was up on that hill on a beautiful May morning, it was warm and the birds were singing, and I was photographing the headstones—the light was at a perfect angle so I could get the names and dates just right. After a little while, I thought I heard a woman laughing. This spooked me just a little at first, being in a cemetery, but it became clear to me quickly that the laughter was coming from down in the valley somewhere, though not too far away. I didn't pay any attention at first. I kept on making my pictures. But the laughing continued and after a while I thought I might have heard a man laughing too, and to tell you the truth, my curiosity just got the most of me. I couldn't see anyone from where I was, so I walked around the side of the hill until I

*thought I could see some people down in the woods below
me. Now here is the part that I'm ashamed of: last Christmas, I bought myself a telephoto lens—one of those things
that lets you take pictures of things from a distance. I use it
for football games and things. I pulled that lens out of my
bag and put it on my camera, just thinking I would take a
look down in those woods and see what was so funny. Well,
now you can see what I saw. I must admit again, that after I
figured out who it just might be, that I did creep down that
hill a little bit to get a better angle. I am ashamed of myself
in one way, but in another, it occurred to me even as I was
taking them, that these pictures might be of some small service to you and your peace of mind.*

*Of course all of this happened last week, several days be-
fore Clem died. I will tell you frankly that I do not know
now what to think. It is for this reason that I wanted to lay
the matter into your capable hands. It was my first thought
to call on you and to relate my story in person. Since Clem's
death, I must admit that I have lost my nerve, and thought it
best to let the pictures speak for themselves. If you would
like to discuss this matter with me, I am at your service any
time of the day or night. If this is something that you would
like to lay to rest, I will respect that decision. We need never
mention it again, and I will go to my grave, alone in the
knowledge of what I have provided to you today.*

*In closing, Wilma (for calling you Miss Wilma as if you
were some silly old maid piano teacher has never seemed
right to me), let me again say how I hold you in the highest
esteem, higher than you can know. If I can be of service to
you in any way, please call upon me.*

*Your humble servant,
Roy*

As he read, Roy was aware vaguely in the background of some kind of rock-and-roll music on the radio with a young, young man wailing about some herd in the grapevine. The sound was so inappropriate for the sentiment of his words, he could scarcely read them. As those final sentences came out of his own mouth, Roy was struck by the schoolboy nature of his feelings for Miss Wilma and for the altogether foolish circumstances that had brought him to write the words and then to read them to her in a car overlooking a baseball diamond—"highest esteem," indeed. Maybe this was what happened to bachelors who somehow got off the path during their youth—they tucked themselves away only to become old fools with leather seats. He was barely able to raise his head to face her. When he managed finally, he was surprised to see that she was looking right back with her eyes open as wide as he had ever seen them and as soft.

If he had ever had an impulse in his whole damn life, one struck him now, and he was just one second from acting on it, but somehow he let that one second pass and then another and then in one second more, he was never sure quite how. Wilma started to giggle. It was a contagious thing, and it got him started too. Pretty soon they were laughing like children and he wondered if somehow she was laughing at them both, he wondered if she was laughing because they were people well past fifty, who were sitting in a car well past dark, parked behind the school looking at an empty baseball field, listening to teenager music and reading love letters to one another. He hoped that was what she was laughing at, because it was so damn funny and because he could not stand it, not for one minute, if she was laughing, just laughing only at him. He wondered. So after they finished laughing, he did it. He just acted on his impulse and he kissed her right there. And then he had his answer.

Chapter Eleven

As Roy pulled the Thunderbird into her driveway, Wilma tried to sit in the seat next to him as if everything was a-okay, but in truth she felt turned upside down, as if she had come home from the Coach House Restaurant by way of Australia. True, this was her house, this was her driveway, but in the space of an evening, there had been this outing and this man, Roy Swan. How different the name sounded now, Roy Swan. It was both strange and familiar. And then just ten minutes ago—was that how long it had been?—he had kissed her, kissed her in the car by the school yard. Kissed her. Roy was a man she had stood next to a thousand times, at church, at the school, but now here he was, his aftershave was filling the car with a lovely heady scent that she had never noticed before. Here he was sitting beside her, thinking who knows what, remembering that kiss maybe.

And now, now it was hard to think of anything but that kiss. It was all new, her life, completely new and hard somehow—she had to admit that, hard—because everything, everything would have to be formed again. For instance in just a moment, she would be required to stop thinking, to stop all thinking about that kiss. That was the first order of business, no more, no more focusing on his lips. Forget it. One kiss. Silly woman, it was one kiss and she would just have to get used to it and go on, and in fact, go on immediately, because of course the first thing required would be for her to get out of the car and go into her house. Though she had a very distinct system for entering her house (depending on the time of day and degree of darkness—porch lights, floodlights, keys in hand), somehow this did not cover the present circumstance. Here was her old beloved bungalow blazing like a Christmas tree, full of people, her own kin. On any other night of her life, she would be thinking now of the people inside, of what they were doing, she would be thinking of the lights that burned in every window, she would be thinking of her electric meter and her Duke Power bill come June 15.

But she did not give a flying buttress.

In truth, her mind was on just one thing, or maybe just one more of the same thing, since Roy was fidgeting now beside her, and she knew beyond all doubt—unless, and this could be the case, she was just a silly woman—she knew that maybe he had the very same thing in mind, but wondered, as she did, if they should kiss again here in the car or wait until they got on the porch.

Wilma detected then a marvelous and frightening feeling rise up—though she could not pinpoint its exact origin—this feeling, this plain wanting. This feeling was strong, and by now it had lodged itself squarely in the center of her body and seemed to bloom out to every extremity (*sorry, so sorry, darling Harry*). She wondered briefly where all of this had hibernated all this time, how she had hidden it even from herself. Roy made no move to get out of the car, which was good, because as much as she wanted to kiss him, she did not want to be seen kissing him on her porch. In Swan's Knob, this would be tantamount to a billboard out on the bypass saying, "We are acting like a couple of teenagers." She sat there another few seconds, him fidgeting, her trying not to fidget, and then she had a radical thought: She turned in her seat toward him and leaned forward slightly and that was all it took.

This second kiss was even better than the first. The first one had been nearly over before Wilma's brain caught on to what was happening. This second she felt full on her lips and then with her whole mouth. Roy seemed to approach the entire operation with a kind of reverence, which only charged the thing further. After all of these years without anything much more than a pat on the shoulder, this kind of kiss—with their tongues, their very breathing so entwined—it was wonderfully obscene. It made her want to press closer to him, to put her hand on his neck, which she did without being able to think first whether she should. Roy paused to look at her and began again and she found her hand around his waist and his arms around her, and she marveled at the ease of this, the fineness of suddenly getting something she had forgotten that she wanted.

She was aware finally that she was in her own driveway and that this kind of thing was on a pretty short fuse. She leaned back slightly but was not quite willing to separate her mouth from his. He understood though and gently finished it. She was glad that neither of them had one thing to say, that in the end it was easy to get out of the car and easy to walk together up to her porch and to say softly to each other, "Good night."

Once she was inside, she paused and peeked through the little windows beside the door so that she could watch Roy go back to his car. He walked with his hands in his pockets, whistling maybe. She watched until his car disappeared. She would have preferred to be alone for a bit and mull things over, but she could hear the voices in the kitchen and she smelled some part of the dinner that had been burned. Funny how her mind had wandered away completely from their whole strange situation. It occurred to her that she had seen her LTD parked in the driveway just now, so Sarah was home. She could not fathom what kind of dinner they might be having given everything that happened. For once, she would have preferred to go on to bed, but that would not do. Best to ignore everything she knew about everything and walk on in the kitchen like it was any other occasion. She checked herself in the hall mirror first. Her hair was a little flat on one side, and if they were paying attention, they would notice that her neck was a little flushed, but she figured they would have other matters on their minds.

Everyone was laughing when she came in, and Starling was up at the counter spooning strawberries onto coffee cup saucers. She saw Wilma first and smiled.

"Well, you've caught us, Nana, you've caught us red-handed," she said.

Harper and Sarah turned around surprised. They hadn't heard her come in.

Wilma smiled at Starling, resisted the urge to put her hand on her neck. "Well, what have you done now, Starling? Did you turn the roast to charcoal? I do smell something burning."

"No, the roast was super. I burned the rolls a little bit, though. But I am using up all your strawberries. I hope it's okay. Do you want some?"

"Oh, no, dear, I've had my dessert," said Wilma, and dessert it had been. She felt her neck flushing again. "You know, I do have berry bowls for those. They're right up in the cabinet behind you." She wondered now what difference this could possibly make, really.

"These plates are fine. I'm almost done," said Starling.

The entire scene struck Wilma as rather cozy, but she couldn't tell if Sarah and Harper were just trying to keep the lid on in front or Starling, or if in fact all was well. By the looks of Sarah, it was not the latter. She had that slightly deflated look again.

"Aren't you going to sit down, Mother?" said Sarah without much enthusiasm.

"No, I'm going to bed directly. It's been a long day. I just saw my car in the driveway and wanted to check on you and make sure you were all right," she said.

"Oh, I'm fine," said Sarah quickly, "perfectly fine. And, Mother, I am sorry that I borrowed your car without checking with you."

In the middle of the night, Wilma wanted to say. You were gone all day and left me to clean up your little mess here. "As long as you're all right, dear," she said, deciding that this was really what she meant after all. "But I'm afraid that your friend Jonah did do some waiting around, and we just weren't sure what to tell him." She looked pointedly at Starling, who was busy with the strawberries. "Downtown just now, I ran into Chief Henry."

"Yes, we were all here when the Chief came to—" said Sarah, looking at Starling. "We were just talking about the big misunderstanding. How the police don't know the whole story."

"I'm not sure anyone does, dear," said Wilma. "Maybe you all can fill me in on what you know later."

"After I go to bed," said Starling. "You know, I am ten, nearly a teenager. You could talk in front of me now. They do most times at home. I was here, you know, I was on the front porch when they busted him."

Busted. Arrested. Right at dinnertime, thought Wilma. Everyone on the street home. And Lord, poor child, right there. It was a terrible thought, but Wilma was just all out of gas. "Honey, there is nothing about this situation that you need to know. Good Lord, I think I've heard enough about it tonight myself. Eat your strawberries. I'm going to bed."

She walked over to the sink and looked in at the pots. No one had bothered to run water into them. Oh well. "Good night, all."

She retreated to her room though she was not ready to go to sleep. She changed into her nightclothes and powdered her feet. After seeing Sarah and Harper at the table, she had to wonder if she had read the situation correctly earlier in the day. Maybe Jonah was just a friend—who knew how these things went these days?—or maybe he was her lover and this was all okay with everybody, or Lord, maybe it was all three of them involved somehow. This she couldn't quite picture, surely not Sarah, though she wondered what she really knew about her anymore. Her Harry had always said there was no telling what really went on in a marriage with the drawn curtains late at night.

She had to admit that after seeing Roy in private tonight she would never think of him in the same way again. He was certainly a gentleman. She would never have gone to the Coach House with him otherwise, and he was kind, now that she thought about it, in a very nonshowy way. Always on call to help at the high school booster club, raising money for the Rescue Squad, giving old people rides to church. Funny how she had not really seen beyond this all these years, had not thought about what kind of kisser he would be, what kind of lover. . . .

Downstairs she heard the water running and quiet talking, with Starling laughing occasionally. Maybe Harper and Sarah were just being cordial until they got Starling in bed. Really, none of it was her concern, except that it was her after all who would be around town long after the rest of them had gone. Given that state of things, she would prefer that she not be known as the one person in the county who extended hospitality to a murderer. No matter what Chief Henry found at the river, she was convinced that Jonah was guilty of not much more than adultery, if that was even considered a crime anymore.

She located Roy's letter and the envelope of photographs. Her impulse was to read the letter again, but as she looked at his beautiful script, she could think only about the way his neck felt, the little prick of the tiny hairs. She drifted there for a moment, and caught herself doing so and wondered again what would happen to her now that all of this—best to call it what it was—this desire had been awakened. She must simply march past it for now, quit replaying the kissing over and over in her mind.

Her first order of business, then, was to recheck Roy's photos to make sure there had been no mistake. She sat down at her dressing table, turned her makeup light on high, and pulled out her strong reading glasses. She flipped through the stack until she came to one that showed the woman most clearly. She just looked at the whole thing for a minute. She would focus on the details when the shock wore off a little bit. She could not quite put her finger on the full effect these images had on her in this moment. The couple was lying on some kind of quilt or blanket under a large tree. The ground was not completely flat. There was a little rise there so that in the photo the woman's torso was propped up slightly like a necklace in a jewelry case. The man, Clem, was astride the woman. The woman had her arms stretched up over her head and her legs wrapped around his waist. Wilma could not help for a moment thinking of herself in this position—though she wanted to snatch the thought back once it occurred to her. Still, Lily—if this was actually Lily—was about Wilma's age. Wilma moved the picture closer to her face. The dark hair, the tiny hands, the pale skin, these were all of Lily's traits. Wilma looked at the next picture down in the stack. In this one, the woman had thrown her head over to one side and you could see the profile. Wilma bent down close. Sure enough. Lily, making love to Clem Baker.

Wilma did not know who to feel sorry for: Clem; his little wife, Ava; her Harry in his grave; even Lily herself. Lily had grown up under terrible circumstances. Her mother had been raised far up in the mountains by ignorant people and had been sent down to Swan's Knob by her own parents to work in a yarn mill. Lily's mother had caught the eye of Harry's father, who was the accountant for the yarn mill at the time. She had come to beg him to stop sending all of her paychecks back up to her parents. Harry's father befriended her, kissed her in the office, impregnated her in a storage room. He had abandoned her altogether by the time Lily was born. When he moved out of the mill to start his own accounting practice, he never spoke to Lily's mother again, though he knew—Harry said—he knew the whole time what he had done. Lily's mother was too proud and stubborn to ask him for a thing. She moved to Winston-Salem, where she worked for Reynolds Tobacco for the rest of her life.

There was a quiet knocking on Wilma's bedroom door, and then a muffled, "Nana, Nana?"

No time to stash the photos. "I'm getting dressed, sweetheart."

"Okay," said Starling, sounding six and alone in the world.

"Start getting ready for bed, Starling, and I'll come tuck you in in a few minutes." Starling was the one who was losing out in the situation. It was always the child who got lost in the shuffle. And here, her grandmother, who should be an ally, who should be a help, was in her room mooning over her new boyfriend and rehearsing the sexual indiscretions of the whole county.

Lily had certainly received no help from her disgraced mother, but she was not one to go quietly. What she lacked in pride she made up for in ambition. As soon as she was old enough to understand, she began to visit Harry's father in his office and to inquire about his legitimate family, which by this time included a wife and Harry, just one year younger than Lily. Harry was never sure of the details, for none of the story came to light until after his father's death, but somehow Lily had wheedled some money for schooling and other things from Harry's father, including an introduction to Frank Strong. They were married not long after Wilma and Harry and for a time lived on the street right behind them, just on the other side of Wilma's rosebushes. They had been good friends then, part of a little group in town of six or eight couples, newlyweds, then women waiting out the war together, then young parents. After the war, they were apt to go up for swimming at Hanging Rock, for picnics on the Parkway, for dinner at the Starlight in Mount Airy. They had been good friends, Frank and Lily, Wilma and Harry. Harry had not one inkling that Lily was his half-sister, though Lily could have—and Wilma thought, should have—told him.

Wilma put the pictures down and turned to Roy's letter. She was again struck by his writing, sweetly formal, quite different from his speaking, most of the time. She started to read it again

and was caught up in the sweetness of him, that kind and wonderful sensibility that she had seen in him tonight. It occurred to
her that it was possible that she was fooling herself entirely. Was
it Roy who had done this to her or had she just been smitten by
the first man to look her way in fifteen years?

"Nana," Starling called out from her room.

Wilma put on her slippers and found her silver-handled brush
and comb. She went into Sarah's old room. Starling was sitting on
the bed in Wilma's old nightgown, with her mother's yellow hair.
Little pieces of it had gotten loose from the braid and glowed in
a frame around her completely untouched face. Sarah's room, but
not Sarah. Of course. God, time had passed. The force of this
simple truth made Wilma want to sink down to the floor where
she stood. She could blink three times, and while she was not paying attention, her life would be over.

"How about if I brush your hair a little bit?" she said, sitting
next to Startling.

"Sure," said Starling. She turned around and tipped her chin
in the air so that Wilma could reach the braid. Wilma unwound
the feathered band, unfurled the braid. Starling seemed a bit
sleepy and was content to sit without talking.

Wilma was wholly content to simply pull the brush through
Starling's hair. Every motion was long ago memorized and soon
she began to hear the words that Roy had read to her in the car.
Of course, the entire situation and the way that it had come up
was very strange. Something else had been bothering her, though
the last part of the evening had pulled her mind from it. But it
came back to her now. What bothered her most was Roy's impli-
cation that she had some sort of score to settle with Lily. She did
not, really. Lily had indeed caused her the worst kind of grief, but
only because her very presence in the world grieved Harry most
of all.

Harry had been the most loyal of sons, coming home after
Wake Forest and joining his father in his accounting firm. He

worked with his father and their six clerks for his entire career—
taxes and trusts and bookkeeping—until the day that his father's
health prevented him from working further. Harry had worked
on then, worked as his father's health declined, as Wilma took
him into their house and nursed him between piano students.
Through all of those years, through all that time working at desks
that faced one another, through nearly a year when his father
could scarcely get out of bed and grew cross with Wilma when
she tried to feed him—through all that time, Wilma never heard
a word of disagreement between them. And so it remained until
the day he died, and they took him up to Snow's, and to the cemetery, and buried him, and Harry cried—the one and only time
Wilma had seen him do it—Harry cried as he left the grave.

On the day that he found his father's will in the office safe,
Harry phoned Wilma mid-morning and asked her to meet him
for lunch at the Squeezebox downtown. Wilma hated the
Squeezebox—the real name of the place was the Luncheonette,
but the nickname fit since inside it was no bigger than a living
room, just a fry grill surrounded by a counter long enough for
ten stools. Wilma hated to eat there during the lunch crunch,
with all the men in town elbow to elbow eating chili dogs with
onions, but that morning, something in Harry's voice told her
to go on down there without asking anything further. Wilma
had arrived just before noon, so that there were still two seats
at one end of the counter, and thankfully Harry came in right
after her.

It was there, not two feet from a grill full of sizzling pork chops
and fried baloney, that Harry told Wilma about his father's will
and the letter that came with it. Tommy, the owner's towheaded
smart-aleck son, was working the grill, and he eyed them as he
flipped the meat, hoping for some little drama that he could tell
folks later.

Harry knew enough to keep his voice low and his head up.
"Well, Dad's left us a surprise in his will. It's a doozy," he said,

smiling in a way that made Wilma think maybe he'd found a secret savings account or some old stock certificates. She ordered a
coke and a slaw dog.

"It looks like after all this time that I actually have a sister," he
said, the smile still stuck there on his face. "Or a half-sister—
someone who's been right here with us all these years. It's Lily.
Can you believe it? My sister." He had turned red, that real
ashamed red, as if he was the one who had done the wrong.

"We just had drinks with her at the country club," said Wilma,
like that was relevant. She could smell the pork grilling now.
Tommy brushed butter onto Texas toast and loaded on the chops,
all done with the two of them for the moment, checking out the
beauty parlor wash girl at the other end of the counter.

"There's more," said Harry, and he spilled the rest in a rush,
as if the velocity of the news would blunt it: how his father left the
bulk of his estate to Lily—his money, his house, and the worst
blow, half of the business. Harry was instructed to liquidate all of
the assets and turn over the proceeds to Lily. Wilma guessed that
she heard all of this well enough, but it was the kind of thing that
she couldn't really take in right away—something didn't add up
quite, there in the middle of lunch hour. She couldn't do much
more than sip her coke.

"The accounting firm, Wilma. I have to buy Lily out of her half
now," Harry said, chewing. He spoke without the slightest intona-
tion, like he might be talking about the weather. "He left me a letter. Said forgive him, please. Forgive and help him pay off this one
final debt." How Harry could sit there on the stool and eat his
pork chop sandwich, talk about his whole life's work falling down
around him, well, this was beyond Wilma. She was not sure all of
what she felt—she was sorry, so sorry. Up to this moment, she had
been still mourning the dead man, it had scarcely been a week.
Now, she cursed him too, cursed what he had done. She felt so
bad for Harry, just awful, awful, and wondered what in the world
she could do for him. She looked at his hands then, the hands of

a serious professional man. He had both hands around that sandwich, she saw, mashing it, just mashing the thing to death and then she looked at his eyes and saw why he had called her, why he could not tell her at home. His irises were open so wide that she could see only black. She had thought she understood then, understood why they were not at home with this news. Of course. This way, less fuss. The worst had happened, bringing it all home to her tonight would not make it better.

"Are you quite certain that you've understood this all right?" she said, trying her best to toe the line, to sound levelheaded, to keep her bottom lip from trembling. Her hot dog was stone cold and she was not about to eat it. "Can we fight this?"

"No," he said, finishing his sandwich without spilling a thing, wiping his mouth, catching Tommy's eye for the check. "Dad was right. He owes her. I had a father. I belonged to him for my whole life. Now Lily will get what is left."

Starling relaxed her head down into her neck, getting drowsy. Wilma finished brushing her hair and helped her climb under the covers. "What will happen to Jonah?" said Starling. When Sarah was small, she had also asked these kinds of questions right before bed. They were always things that had been following her around all day, unspoken. Always tough to answer.

"I'm not sure, honey. Things are very confused right now. Maybe they'll get straightened out in a few days." It was as close to the truth as she could get tonight.

"But what was he doing here? He's from Santa Fe, you know." Starling sat up in the bed a bit. "He's Mom's . . . he's a friend of Mom's." Starling looked at Wilma carefully to gauge her reaction. Wilma felt the strong temptation to lie mightily—anything to protect Starling from all the mess. Starling looked at her now with a wise look that was out of place on a child, and Wilma saw that to deny the circumstances would only break that tiny sprout of grown-up knowing in Starling.

"You're right, he is a friend of your mom's, honey," she said, tucking her in. "I'm not sure why he's here, except I guess he came to talk to your mom." There. That had been easy enough. Starling curled up in her bed, and Wilma turned off the light. In the hall she could hear that Sarah and Harper were still sitting at the kitchen table, still talking. There was no shouting, and thankfully Wilma had not heard any glass breaking—though she wondered why she had even been listening for that. She closed her bedroom door and went back to her dressing table.

Wilma had assumed through the years that this story about Lily and Harry, or at least some form of it, had been passed through the community. From Roy's letter, however, it seemed that maybe people had gotten the wrong idea. This, Wilma knew, was really Harry's fault. It was the result of his extreme discretion in handling the matter. Harry told no one but Wilma about the will for several weeks after he discovered it. Even Wilma did not fully realize until much later what the news had done to her husband. Eventually Harry took the will to a lawyer in Winston and began the sad business of liquidating the estate, selling his father's house, his stock portfolio. It was not a vast fortune, to be sure, but it would have been enough to change their lives for the better, enough to send Sarah to college without a scholarship, to make Wilma's piano lessons less of an economic necessity, enough to retire in comfort. Instead, Harry struggled to keep the business that had been his life's work. He pulled all of their savings from the bank and took out a loan, and finally managed to purchase Lily's half of the accounting firm. Only when he had completed every sale, had converted each and every asset to cash and had tallied every last dime in a neat column of figures in a leather ledger bearing the firm name, Mabry and Son, did he call Lily.

The evening he came home from his meeting with Lily, he poured himself a large bourbon, and as was his custom, he sat down at the kitchen table to talk to Wilma while she finished making supper. Wilma noticed that he did not put the bottle of whisky back into the cabinet, but set it beside his glass. Perhaps he had done the same thing many times before, but that night after his meeting with Lily, Wilma had noticed it and counted the drinks for the first time (three before dinner, two after).

"How did it go?" she asked.

"Fine," he said. "Lily was surprised."

"That's all?" she said. Harry was usually a great storyteller. It was unlike him to make her wheedle it out of him.

"She said she was grateful to him, grateful to our father. She called him that, 'our father.'" Harry looked up at Wilma, slowly replacing his glum expression with a completely brave and pitiful grin. The first drink was gone. "So what do you think, doll? Can you see any family resemblance?"

In just that moment Wilma finally took the whole thing in. The whole tacky, sordid, conception-in-a-back-room situation. It just burned her up. Selfish, selfish old man. She had changed his sheets every day. "What could he have been thinking?" she said.

"Along the brow," said Harry. "Have you noticed? Lily and I have the same forehead." Half done with drink number two.

"Did he say a word to you? Did he even tell you he didn't like the job you were doing? Any clue at all?"

"'Our father,' I can't get over the way she said that, reverently, you know, like the beginning of the prayer," he said.

"Well, she sure got what she was praying for," said Wilma.

Looking back, Wilma thought she might have been kinder. She might have seen past Harry's bravado, past his usual jokes, might have risked just a few of the right questions, might have said something just sad enough so that they could grieve together, but this was not their way.

Wilma turned off her makeup light but left her old boudoir-fringed sidelight burning. She picked up the little sterling frame that had been on her dressing table since before her wedding. It was one of her favorite pictures of the two of them, taken just after Harry had come home from the Pacific. Handsome boy, and remarkably young. Wilma had heard how many boys returned from the war shell-shocked and ruined, but Harry had been the same boy that danced with her all night at the Delta Sig mixer at Wake. When he proposed, he had said, "Can we forget the war? It's over, let's go on, let's get married." She had never asked him another thing. It seemed so silly now—what a waste not to know. But from the beginning, their love had been forged, tacitly, on smooth sailing. Surely this could not have been all wrong. They had sorrows, just like anyone else, and the fact that they did not wallow in them did not mean that they did not feel them deeply. Silence could be more eloquent than anything else, couldn't it?

Besides, when Harry first got in trouble, when he started leaving bit by bit, the indications were not drastic—a little reticence to discuss the matter, a few more jiggers in the glass—all perfectly natural in her book. What she could see now was that Harry had died gradually from that very day, from the "our father." It had happened right before her very eyes.

Wilma looked at her twenty-four-year-old self in the photograph, wearing the blue cashmere twin set that had been Harry's favorite. She had worn it the night they met, had tucked it in her closet when he went to war, and had put it on for that homecoming date. It was probably moldering away right now in a box in the attic. She wiped the dust from the frame's glass with a cotton ball. A pretty girl and her beau in their old-fashioned frame. *Good night, sweetheart. Good night, doll.* She tucked them behind her perfume bottles.

If she were completely honest with herself, Wilma had to admit that in those months after the funeral, her chief concern had been what people might say. She had assumed that Lily would find a way to slowly leak the details of the will. In response, she simply kept her head up high, and was grateful that polite people would simply not discuss the matter with the principals, namely Wilma and Harry. It did surprise her that some loud-mouth like Grace Snow did not find a way to insinuate her way into a discussion, but when this did not occur, Wilma was not one to borrow trouble. From what Roy had said this evening, the facts of the will were not known around town. Lily had somehow been persuaded—by her husband, Franklin, or by Harry or by a once-in-a-lifetime bout of good sense—to keep quiet about the matter.

It was an amazing feat, really, especially in such a small town. As for the money, people had assumed that Lily and Franklin's money came from Franklin Strong's family, though as Harry's father probably knew, it was long gone. Wilma would have thought that this would have ended their friendship with the Strongs, considering Harry's hurt. Within the year, Lily and Franklin moved to the large colonial on the edge of town. However, Harry had kept up with Lily, out of dogged loyalty, she supposed, checked in on her from time to time, though Wilma could never understand it. For her part, Wilma could not continue to think of Harry's father or of Lily in the happy sunlight. She could not bear the thought of all the time that had gone by—all of the weekends during tax season, the nursing and feeding and sheet changing that goes along with an old sick man—that Harry's father had not said a word. She thought too about all of the opportunities that Lily had: late-night parties, small dinners and their children playing on the playground together.

Wilma thought that in all that time, Harry's father might have said, "Look here, Harry, there's one small detail—that woman there is your half-sister. I abandoned her mother in my youth." Yes, and Lily might have said, "Hey, friend, this is a bit awkward, but now that we know each other, I need to tell you that Harry and I have the same father." She would have thought it might have come up. For her part, she could do nothing about the dead old man, but she certainly did not intend to be best friends with his illegitimate daughter. It was during this time, this time when Harry continued to see Lily and when she absolutely refused, that people may have gotten the wrong idea. They may have assumed, given little information and wild imaginations, that Harry and Lily were romantically involved. Lily was after all a notorious flirt. It was true, of course, that Harry always had a soft spot for Lily, this for all the years he had known her. He always lit up when she came out onto the patio of the country club to meet Franklin after a round of golf, always jumped to light her cigarette after dinner (Wilma could picture this now, Lily bending over just a bit too far for her neckline). But the thought of them together, honestly, it was too creepy to even consider. There was even a word for it, a word which Wilma would not even utter in her mind.

However, even in retrospect, it did fairly well peeve Wilma that beyond the secret indignity of near poverty that she had endured over the years, there was this: Everyone in town thought Harry had run around on her before he died.

Wilma folded the letter and looked at the photograph of Lily and Clem one more time. Even now she couldn't find it in herself to be more than a little bit mad at Lily. Lily's chief crime was inopportune birth—no fault of her own—and her secondary offense was keeping quiet about it. Wilma could scarcely blame her for that. As for seeing her buck-naked out in the woods having intercourse with a man substantially her junior, well, that—that on its own was kind of pitifully funny. It would be even funnier if Wilma didn't know that the man had died just a few days later. She couldn't imagine that Lily killed him—from the looks of the pictures, she must have had a pretty good thing going, and one thing about Lily, once she had ahold of something good, she didn't let go, that was for sure.

Wilma thought she heard the kitchen chairs scraping on the floor. Maybe Harper and Sarah were on their way upstairs. Wilma got up from her dressing table and made her way across to her bed. *Good night, Harry. Good night, doll.* As she removed her robe, she noticed that the piping on part of the collar was coming off. It had been that way a while, but she knew now that she better go on and get it fixed. Or no, maybe she would just go out and buy a new one, with a gown to match. In blue, powder blue, maybe, and for Pete's sake, why not black? She looked good in black. With a little low light, a little perfume . . . She began to blush right there in her own bed. One little date—if she could even call it that—and she was planning out her lingerie. One minute she was talking to her dead husband, remembering his accountant hands, his dancing at the Delta Sig mixer, the next minute she was contemplating sex with another man.

She had not heard a word of gossip about Roy and any woman in town, but she was certain that he wasn't a virgin, not that she had any business speculating. She thought again about the kisses they had, those two. Those were not idle, aren't-you-sweet little kisses. They were the kisses of an experienced, mature man. She knew that he had traveled a great deal over the years, he certainly had the means. He had been in the army as well, in Korea. And perhaps, there had been some girlfriends in Winston, discrete liaisons, certainly. . . . Wilma pulled herself up out of bed and stamped over to get her Jergen's lotion. Utter nonsense, all of this speculation. This would lead to foolish behavior. She had seen it before in women of her age and even older, usually those newly widowed and feeling a bit lost in their empty old houses. They'd show up at a covered-dish supper or any other how-do-you-do batting eyes over every eligible man alive. Why, she'd seen them do it to Roy himself.

He probably had an entire pantry full of widow-woman jam. She would bet ten dollars that he had at least one jar of that foul Mystery Mountain Jam that Mamie Brown made out of the overripe figs that fell in her yard from Lucille Whitehead's tree next door. Wilma couldn't think why he hadn't taken one of these widows as a wife, the way they made over him, up and down the fellowship hall— "Come right over here, Roy. I've made that banana pudding that you like so much, and look, I have all this ham left over, why don't you just take it home for your supper tomorrow night."

She would not be doing that, no sir. She would not stand in line with her casserole.

Wilma climbed back into bed and rubbed the lotion on her hands. Sarah and Harper had still not come upstairs. She felt bad for Sarah—she had some explaining to do. If Sarah was having an affair, she was not handling it very well, from Wilma's point of view, but what did she know? She couldn't even explain her own behavior tonight. What did she know about what Sarah was facing? Still, she couldn't figure out why Sarah felt compelled to play the whole thing out on her own mother's front porch. Wilma had to chalk it all up to part of her job as a mother—her child's problems were her problems. If your daughter's Indian lover turned out to be a convicted murderer, well, that would be your lot in life too. It seemed to her that Roy was at least willing to help her figure out who did actually kill Clem Baker, but she was still not so sure she wanted to know the real truth. If it wasn't Jonah who killed Clem, and she was pretty sure it wasn't, if it wasn't Lily, which she was pretty sure about as well, then it still was liable to be somebody who knew something about her story, the one that had started with Harry's daddy and ended with Harry's death, right outside her window, right out in her rosebushes.

Good night, doll. Go to sleep, Harry, if you sleep. Good night, doll, good-bye.

Chapter Twelve

*H*arper worked to maintain the cool that he had copped over dinner. Starling had gone to bed, and all of a sudden Sarah had taken an intense interest in getting her mother's pots and pans perfectly clean. For his part, Harper had enough to do just trying to keep the giddy family thing floating in the air over them, trying not to dive down into the resentment that was boiling like mad in his gut. Down there, there were little bubbles that wanted him to shout: "You did it, didn't you, Sarah? You've been fucking him, haven't you?" Instead he said softly, "Honey, does your mother have any kind of booze in the house?"

Sarah turned around from her place at the sink, up to her elbows in suds. "If she does, it'll be in the bottom of the china cabinet."

Harper walked into the dining room, treading as lightly as possible, but still managed to make the crystal clink on its shelf. He opened the cabinet doors, causing another round of clinking. He found an ancient bottle of wine, sediment sitting on the bottom, some cheap brandy, cooking sherry, and a half-full fifth of bourbon. He brought the bourbon back into the kitchen, along with two glasses from the Seattle World's Fair of 1962. Sarah was drying the pots now. Harper sat at the table and watched her as she emptied the entire dish rack, stowed away the last glass and turned, reluctantly it seemed, to look at him. She did not look good, he noticed for the first time—not that she wasn't beautiful, she would always be that. But somehow under her tan she seemed completely fragile, like it was an effort even to hold her features in some kind of order on her face. As she looked at him now, he thought for a moment that she would cry, and he wondered truly what emotion was dammed up there behind her eyes. Sorrow? Pity?

He began pouring the bourbon out in two glasses. "Do you want ice?" he asked. She shook her head and sat down. She was looking at him still when he took a long sip of the bourbon, looking at him in such a familiar way that he was able to say, quietly, without even a hint of anger, "So you did him. Okay. You did him, I figure, more than once, maybe for a while now. You did him. Let's just start out with that and move on from there."

"I *did* him?" she said. "That's all you want to say about it?"

"Well, yes," he said. "What else?"

"I'm not sure," she said. "It seems that there is a little more to it than that."

"Like what?" he said.

"Well, for one thing," she said, "I guess I'd want to know any thought you might have about it."

It was true then. He had known it, of course, but . . . shit. "My thoughts. Let's see," he said. "I'd say what's done is done. Move on."

"Just like that. Move on. End of Story," she said, her voice flat but her eyes burning into him.

"Yeah. The end. Unless, well, unless of course you have some other idea." He could not look at her now. The glasses had a picture of the Space Needle and some other domed building. He concentrated on swirling the liquid in his, flooding the bottom deck of the Space Needle.

"Some other idea? Like what?" she said. Waited. "I said, like what? What is your great idea for me?"

Harper kept his eyes on his glass, felt her gaze.

"Harper? Are you there? Or have you moved on already?"

That forced him to look up at her finally, and when he did, he saw that she was regarding him in the unblinking manner reserved for their conversations about Harper's own indiscretions.

"Look," he said, "I am not the asshole here. Why are you accusing me?"

"I am not accusing you of anything. I am simply amazed that nothing, nothing in this world can faze you."

"I am fazed, Sarah. Believe me. This guy saunters into your mother's kitchen this morning, drops the bombshell over coffee. I am fazed, man." Somehow his glass had been drained and he poured more.

"What did he tell you?" she said, her tone accusing Harper again.

He was not going to get a break here. It didn't matter that the shoe was on the other foot. "He said very little, Sarah. Look, he didn't ask for your hand or anything. Let's just say it was apparent to all what had come down between the two of you."

There was a quiet sarcasm in her voice: "And what did he say exactly—what was it that came down?"

Your shoes under his bed, he started to say, your treasures in his cove, but he stopped because this was not what he wanted to say to her. He was at that point in the bourbon when the liquor was just starting to taste good, when he could feel it warm his stomach. It made him want to confess something, anything. Sarah was looking at him, looking at his hand on the glass.

"Sarah," he said, hoping she could hear the echo of the past decade in his voice. "Sarah. I don't want to talk about Jonah and what you . . . I don't want to talk about him. Here is what I want to ask: Why did you leave Santa Fe and come here? Surely you didn't think that he would follow. Surely you knew that I would. And I did. Remember? I did. I followed you here. Remember the night I got here? Here is what I want to know: Do you remember when I came into your room before dawn? Do you remember that first hour?"

She said nothing, but seemed to regard him more gently.

"That hour, Sarah, that hour is what we are, you and I. Not just making love, beyond that. That hour, meeting there, above everything else. Sure, we have put our shoes under other beds. I grant you that. Both of us."

She narrowed her eyes.

"Okay, I might be more guilty of that than you, in some ways. Let's not forget, tonight we're talking about you, babe. But that's beside the point, really. Sarah, I have taken some time to think about this today. I just think that we have to move way beyond all of this crap. I have always thought we agreed on this. This is not our parents' world, where sex has got to have a label on it. Adultery, copulation, promiscuity, premarital whatever. Come on. We are way beyond that way of thinking, aren't we? I know you see this."

Her eyes met his for a split second then traveled back down to his drink. He was getting nowhere—it was like the first ten bars of a solo break with a new band. He looked right into her eyes and got nothing back. For a moment, he got that sinking sensation that tells you that everything is lost. That was the moment to stand up and walk out, but for the life of him, he could not. He got out of his chair and walked around to her and sat on the edge of the chair next to hers. He reached into Sarah's lap and grasped one of her hands, a fist, really—it felt like a baseball in his hand. He felt the same rush that he got standing up with his trumpet, first number of the set, no one in the club listening yet. "Here's the thing, babe. I'm not trying to cop anything here, no kind of excuse for you or for me. What I'm saying is that we can forget all about it. No you did, no I did. Forget it. Forget his name. Think about us, babe. Last week this time, everything was all tangled up—things between us had gone so bad that I didn't even know about it, you took Starling and split back here, I turn up to find you. I turn up and what, what happens, babe?"

"Sex?" She wrinkles her face up, like she's giving him a reprimand, but behind that he thinks he sees a little smile.

Here was his chance. The big solo.

He was up to jam, man, he was launched. He just had to follow the changes right on out there, dwouda-dwoodle-dee-dee even if he was going up-tempo and blowing his horn in the wrong damn key, dee-deedum shit. Launched. The time for thinking is done, dee-deedum, he had to go: "Way beyond sex, babe. More than that. More than any word. There in your room, not quite dawn. I can make out the white of the pillow, I can see just the bare outline of your face. I come into your little bed, get in gently beside you before there are more than three strands of light through the window, just when I hear a little bird sing, I am there beside you and I reach out, and before I can touch you, as I reach out, I know. I know what you will do. Quiver. It is a perfect A played on an open string, a whole note, four counts."

"Sex," she said, quarter note, F sharp.

"More than sex, I just said. A symphony, a whole conversation." It was quiet then. A dog barking blocks away. He was still holding her hand. The fingers were relaxed now. They were longer than his, elegant.

When he looked up, she was almost nodding. She said, "More. Somehow I don't think that's the point. More than sex. What we need is something other than sex, something else that holds us together." She noticed her hand now too and withdrew it gently.

"We have more, much more. We did from the beginning. Look at the way that we got together. Can you have forgotten? You have to answer here."

"No," she said weakly, "I haven't forgotten. You saved me from disgrace."

"Not at all," he said. "I cannot believe you think of it that way."

"How else?" she said. "I was pregnant. You married me."

He was suddenly angry now, but not sure why, though it pro-pelled him on: "And that saved you from what disgrace? The dis-grace of being unmarried? The disgrace of having Tommy Gotschall's child?" Though they may have somehow discussed this possibility early on, it had been a decade since either of them had spoken of it. Harper was not sure now why he had crossed the threshold.

"Tommy Gotschall?" Sarah said vaguely.

"Tommy Gotschall. My friend from Juilliard. Good God, Sarah, the man from that night, the man from the Palace, the man who could be Starling's father." Tommy Gotschall, Starling's fa-ther. It was a mistake, he knew at once, to have said it out loud, because it made him wonder if it really could be true.

Sarah began to cry. "Tommy Gotschall," she said. "I never knew his name." The bourbon was all gone, except for the three fingers in Sarah's glass, still untouched. Sarah held her lips to-gether tightly.

"Tommy Gotschall," she said again, as if she were trying to commit the name to memory.

He had been an idiot to say anything. "I only bring it up now, babe, to let you know that it doesn't matter. It never did. You don't know it was him for sure, do you? I mean, it could have been me, right?"

"Yes," she said. "I wanted it to be you, but I never knew for sure."

"Well, you do now," he said. "Starling is mine, in every way that counts. And really, babe, check out her nose. It is mine, the same little bump in the middle and everything."

"And her ears, too," Sarah said, wiping her eyes, "I have al-ways thought her ears looked just like yours too."

"There you have it," he said. Dee-dee-duh. Dee-dee-duh. He thought he could feel a little hope hanging in the air, but some-thing else, something like a cloud seemed to move across Sarah's face.

"Jonah," she said. "Oh my God, Jonah. What are we going to do?"

It was more than hope, Harper had more than hope, that was Jonah's cloud. Sarah was already worried about how Jonah would take the sad news: Jonah was history. Harper was thinking now about that moment at the end of a fine long solo run, when the whole band joined into the fray, that moment of joy and relief when the band flooded the room with music and the crowd clapped long and hard for his solo. He was hearing this, hearing the whole scene, as he said, "Let's not worry about that tonight, Sarah. You can tell him later, much later." Dwouda-dwoodle-dwoodle-dee-dem-dee-dem-dwee, dwee-dum.

"Tell him what?" she said. "We don't need to tell him anything. He's in jail, for God's sake. Locked in a cell downtown at this very minute."

"That's beside the point," said Harper, hearing the dog bark again, hearing the faucet.

She wrinkled her forehead, put that accusing look back on her face. "I'm not so sure," she said. "You could get him out. That is the point. You could, but you won't."

"How?" he said.

"You could just tell them. Tell them that he was in the car with you at the time of the murder," she said.

"I don't know that," he said.

"That's what you told me last night," she said. "You're just scared now."

"I am not scared," he said.

"Stubborn, then. Withholding. Vengeful," she said. She stood up and threw her bourbon down the drain.

Something had happened, though he hadn't a clue what it was, and they were back to square one. He said, "Okay, say I went down there and told them that Jonah rode across the country with me. Say I tell them the truth, which is I lost track of him out at a truck stop fifty miles up the road, I drove straight to Swan's

Knob right past all of the rescue squads already cleaning up the mess. So I say that to them, will they believe me? Who knows? Will they make up some other story about how Jonah hitched a ride with a faster driver? Who knows? Maybe they'll decide, hell no, Jonah's not the guy, so what about this other twerp here, he'll do just as well. Maybe they'll look up my record. Perfect. They'll see the drug charge. Just perfect. Jonah will be out of jail by midnight. You can take my car. Then the three of you can be back in Santa Fe before they can even find a judge to set my bail. Perfect. Let me go comb my hair. I'll go right down there."

"Let me add paranoid to the list," she said. "For Pete's sake, how are these guys going to find out about some two-joint drug charge, ten years old in New York State? That is not the reason you won't go down there. Come on, Harper, I know you're mad about this. Okay. I have a little experience in the area, don't forget. I'm not asking you to forgive me. I'm not asking you to forgive him. We will deal with that situation separately. But first, can you think of him as a human being? Someone we need to help?"

"I have noticed that he is quite successful himself with this kind of appeal," he said. "Remember that I am the human being who drove him across the country. Dumb me. Drove him right to you, it turns out. I am not sure that I care to oblige him further." Harper wished for more bourbon. Sullen, he sounded positively sullen—not at all pretty. Where had that other moment gone off to?

"Jesus, I didn't know he was coming to find me in North Carolina," she said, "I didn't know you were coming. If I had known the entire circus was following me, I would have picked another town, a town a little farther away from my mother and everyone she knows."

"That's the other little difficulty with all of this. Thanks so much for sharing your affair with your mother," he said.

"You told my mother about all of this?" she said.

"Not me," he said.

"Oh God," she said, and sat back down in the chair. "I should have never left Santa Fe. What did she say?"

"Nothing, not a thing," he said. "She just got this sweetie smile on her face every time she looked at Jonah, like she had a crush on him too." Sarah was looking very tired now, like someone had let the air out of her tires.

"Are you okay?" he said.

"Sure," she said. "Definitely better than Jonah."

She looked like she was getting the flu or something, probably sick with worry. This scene was not going down in his favor. Shit. They always loved the underdog.

"Okay," he said, "what about this? I'll call them. There is no way I'll go down there, but I will call the station and talk to the Man and I'll tell him what I know. We'll go from there. Okay?"

"Great," she said, taking in a big breath of relief, he noticed. "I'll look up the number for you."

Harper went over to the phone and dialed the number she dictated from the directory. The phone rang, he counted, ten rings. "No answer," he said. "It's a Barney Fife kind of jail. They all went home to Aunt Bee. So he'll be all right for tonight, then. Don't you think?"

"I guess so," she said. "I just hate for him to spend another night in jail when we could have helped."

"What else can we do? If I keep calling, all I'll do is wake him up again. We'll help first thing in the morning, babe," he said, hating her almost, hating the piteous look on her face, wanting to go over and stroke her hair.

∽

When Sarah was pregnant with Starling, most of her morning sickness had actually hit her during the evenings. So it didn't surprise her that one whiff of the bourbon going down the sink made her stomach begin to tumble. She was not about to lose it in front of Harper—one more discovery might send either one of them over the edge at this point, over the edge or out the door on another odyssey. She, for one, needed to spend the night in a bed. She could tell that Harper was wired—drinking did that to him. He could stay up for hours now. Maybe she could go up alone.

"All of the driving has made me exhausted," she said. "I'm going to bed. You're right. We'll call the station first thing in the morning. Straighten all of this out." Harper only waved as she went down the hall.

On the landing, she could see that Starling's room was dark. She was long asleep. Her mother's light was still on. She was probably listening on the other side of the door, waiting to hear Sarah come up the stairs. An ambush. She had been so breezy earlier in the kitchen, probably on account of Starling, but now she'd want a full explanation. Sarah was inclined to tiptoe on by, but she knew that Wilma had impeccable hearing. If she was waiting, she had already heard Sarah come up alone, and she would be knocking on her door in a moment. Get it over with, she thought, and tapped lightly on her mother's door. She didn't wait for an answer, but walked on in.

Wilma was in bed, still propped up on her pillows, but she was sound asleep. Her head had fallen to the side a little and rested on her shoulder in a way that was vaguely chilling. Sarah tiptoed across the room to turn off the light on her mother's vanity table, and feeling her stomach churn again, she hurried back out as fast as possible.

In the bathroom, she threw up with abandon and then soaked her face with a wet washcloth. She held it there, trying to breathe slowly, in and out. The little towel had the smell of her childhood in this house—the slightly metallic water, her mother's detergent, the musk of the linen closet. She draped the washcloth on the side of the tub, walked back to her bed, and tried to lie perfectly still, focusing on a tiny crack in the ceiling.

Despite everything that happened when Sarah was young, her mother had constructed for her an orderly life—a life so orderly, in fact, that Sarah had spent much of her adulthood creating complications, hoping for an entropy so dense that no single event could pull her life apart. Confusion to mask confusion. Noise louder than noise. And here was the thing, she had come back to the order after all, to the house where every pin had its place. In her coming back, though, she had brought disorder with her. It had spread out all through the world in front of her. She knew what she had done: She had screwed up every one of their lives—her own life and her little baby's, Starling's life, Harper's, Jonah's. She had to acknowledge now also, though she could not make the exact connection, that in Swan's Knob, for the exacting terms of the town, she had ruined Wilma as well.

Chapter Thirteen

*I*t seemed to Wilma that in the few days since the wedding, some of the paint had rubbed off Lily's house, that maybe they had all gone on vacation or someone had neglected to pay the light bill—whatever it was, Lily's house had lost its glow. Brown poplar tulips littered the front walk, and when she got up to the front door, Wilma couldn't hear even a footfall from inside. She rang the bell. She knew for a fact that at least Doris was there. She had talked to her on the phone not fifteen minutes before, asked her to let Lily know that she was coming by this morning. She regretted now not giving Doris the chance to respond, to go and see, as Doris had said, if Miss Lily was in any shape at all. Wilma straightened her waistband, adjusted the purse straps on her shoulder. Lily's version of being indisposed meant that she was wearing an *old* silk blouse. Doris answered the door just then. She was wearing her street clothes and carrying her own purse, like she had finished her cleaning and was ready to go home, even though it was only ten o'clock.

"Miss Wilma, she is in the den," said Doris, shaking her head. "I am leaving. She says that things around here are clean enough. To go on. So I'm going on. You tell her for me to call me if she needs me."

"Goodness, is she sick?" said Wilma.

"Not that I can tell," said Doris. "Tell her I hope she'll be all right. Tell her I'll be praying for her." Doris walked past her then and out the front door, continuing to shake her head as she went down the walk.

"Hang on, Doris. Doris?" Wilma had to say it loudly to get her to stop and turn around. "Have you talked to James? Do you know if he heard anything yet?"

Doris smiled when she heard her nephew's name and relaxed her grip on her purse. "Nothing, not a word, but we are all hoping it'll turn out good. Don't you think it'll turn out that they'll give it to him?"

"I do," said Wilma, though she was less certain as the days went by.

"We're all praying. His daddy most of all." Doris was in less of a hurry now, stood with one hip cocked up slightly, and seemed to consider Wilma for a moment. "You go on in," she said. "She could probably use some *female* company for a change."

Wilma felt a momentary pang. Maybe Lily had fewer friends than she had imagined. Then she realized what Doris was getting at. Best to play dumb. "Well, I suppose husbands can be tiresome," she said. "And Franklin's gone quite a bit."

"Yes, ma'am, they are leaving her left and right these days, yes, they sure are," said Doris, raising her eyebrows as she spoke, trying to see if Wilma caught her meaning. "I hope she can stay out of trouble. She's had about all she can take." Doris knew about Clem. She knew the whole thing. Of course she did.

Wilma felt herself flush. She wasn't sure if discussing the situation with Doris would help, and it might make things worse. Maybe she should try to talk to Lily first. "Well," she said, "you're certainly right. I guess most mothers feel at loose ends after a child's wedding. It is so hard to let your daughter go, even if she's going off to be a married lady."

Doris looked at her with confusion for a moment, and then Wilma thought she saw disappointment cross her face just before it reverted to a careful neutrality that invited no further conversation. Then Doris began making her way down the driveway.

There was nothing to do but go on in. Wilma used the elaborate brass handle to open the door. She crossed the threshold and stood still in the entrance hall for a moment, hoping to hear Lily call out for her. Surely she must have heard the front door open. Wilma moved slowly toward the arch that led to the center hall. She noticed that the console table against the back wall still held a small vase of wedding roses and the guest book, opened to the last page of signatures, "Best wishes, sweet Martha Jane. . . ." Toward the back of the house, she thought she heard a television. She headed down the center hall, treading heavily so Lily would know she was coming.

"Doris, Doris, you still here? Bring me a co-cola," Wilma heard Lily's muffled voice from the den once she was halfway down the hall.

"Doris's just gone," she said, just as she reached the den door. "Do you want me to get you something?" The heavy toile drapes were pulled shut in the room so that the television provided most of the light in the room. Of all things, it was a rerun of the *Andy Griffith Show*. Aunt Bee was going on a trip, worried about Andy and Opie's supper. Lily's den, like every other room in the house, was full of furniture. The décor on the best of days suffered from an overabundance of patterns. This particular room had an English gentleman's hunt club theme. There was a hunting party marching across the couch fabric, plaid wing chairs, a fox and a hunting dog on throw pillows, a lamp with a ceramic pheasant for a base. Adding to all of this was an inexplicable array of items left over from the wedding: baskets and vases full of drooping flowers, attendants' bouquets, gloves, candlesticks. Fragrance and theme colors—white and lavender—filled every available space.

Lily was curled up on the couch, huddled under a wedding ring quilt, likely purloined from Martha's gifts. She looked up at Wilma with raccoon eyes, alarmed, Wilma thought, for just a second, to see who it was, then somehow resigned. Lily looked back to the screen. "I just don't know how you're going to get along without me," Aunt Bee was saying. Wilma hovered around the threshold, hoping that Lily would tell her to come in. After a few moments, Lily said nothing, didn't even move, so Wilma walked on light feet into the room and sat down on the couch carefully, as if it were a hospital bed.

"Lily, are you sick? Is there something I could get you?" she said, knowing of course that this was no virus at all. "We'll get along just fine, mighty fine," said Sheriff Andy. Lily looked over at Wilma, seemed to study her for a moment. Even this morning her French twist was fully intact, and she had even made an attempt at makeup. Despite the near darkness, Wilma could see that she had on a thick coat of lipstick. However, mascara, liner and whatever else had already washed off her lashes and was layered in smudgy rings under her eyes. Lily had forgotten her earrings, Wilma noticed. Her earlobes were misshapen, with the holes elongated over the years from carrying tons of semi-precious gems and metals.

"What, for the love of God, are you doing here?" said Lily finally, without the least fanfare or warning, making Wilma jump in her skin. It was a perfectly valid question, but Wilma did not have a ready answer, and now it was her turn to watch the television show, where laundry and dishes were piling up.

"I came to check on you," said Wilma. There was of course no reason in the world for Wilma to check on Lily—there had never been an occasion for Wilma to even call on her over the past ten years, but somehow Lily took her explanation without any question.

"Well, as you can see, I am just fine. Just a little tired after all of the festivities," said Lily, finally moving now, pulling one shaky hand out from under the quilt and taking her glass among the array of shoes, jewelry and men's handkerchiefs that cluttered the lamp table. Lily closed her eyes as she drank down the last few sips from the glass. Poor thing. Wilma had to admit that she had started the morning out fairly well mad at Lily, downright perturbed at the woman for somehow, in some convoluted way, causing havoc once again in her life. She had to admit that she had trotted on over to Lily's house on this misguided mission to get to the bottom of it all, to see if maybe Lily had the information that would set her household back in order. Those rings around Lily's eyes told her that anything she had to say would only lead to further confusion.

Once again it occurred to Wilma—this was her week, the one week of her life for disconnected action, just like some kind of chicken in her mother's backyard halfway to Sunday dinner. This was her week to be that chicken, to just go on and act without one minute of forethought. Wilma found now that her ability for subtle discourse—that last and dying Southern woman's art—had also forsaken her. "I've come," she said, "to find out about Clem."

"Clem?" said Lily, turning suddenly back to Mayberry, where Opie was eating a cold breakfast.

"Yes, Clem. You know what I'm talking about," said Wilma.

"Clem? Poor Clem, so young," said Lily, with the tone of someone far, far away from the situation. This vague, movie-style response, almost a little melody, somehow flushed all the pity out of Wilma's body and replaced it with irritation.

"So young?" she said. "So young? Maybe that's one little thing you should have considered from the start of it."

"Start of what?" said Lily, becoming flushed now, looking at Wilma, Miss Melanie about to scold Scarlet. "Why whatever do you mean?"

"Now, Lily Mae, you know exactly what I mean. I am sorry but I happen to know that you have been involved with Clem Baker." The muffled sound of TV laughter filled the room as Andy made a futile effort to clean house wearing one of Aunt Bee's aprons. Strangely Lily laughed along with the TV, as if she hadn't heard a word. Wilma could take no more. She went over to the television and punched every knob on it until the thing was finally silent, then she turned around to face Lily. "This is serious this time," she said, fighting the urge to shake her finger at Lily. "You're in a lot of trouble. There's no telling who knows about you and Clem. Things have gone all to heck downtown. They've arrested a friend of Sarah's, some innocent boy, and Lord knows what else is going to happen. You've got to put a stop to it all."

Lily picked up the shoe that inexplicably sat on the lamp table beside her. It was one of the pair from the wedding, peau de soie dyed blue to match Lily's dress. Lily seemed to study it carefully, ran one finger up and down its side. "Miss Wilma, hon, you have finally lost your cookies," she said, still looking at her shoe. "Why on earth would you think such a thing? I have no idea. But even if such a thing were true . . ." She looked back up at Wilma finally, paused theatrically, looked directly at Wilma, made Wilma see all the way down into those round and lovely eyes, eyes that looked almost purple, supplanting for a moment all the flesh and bones that hung around them, making Wilma see clear on down to something that she had no business seeing. Then Lily snapped her little neck and closed her eyes, took them away, laughing again, saying, "Well, if such a thing were true, I would be the damn lucky lady, robbing the cradle like that. I tell you, you'd have to give me a little credit, wouldn't you?"

"He is dead," said Wilma, wondering suddenly if Lily might be dangerous.

"You think I don't know that?" said Lily. "Dead? Didn't you see me in my knockoff Chanel at the funeral along with everybody else? Dead? Dead? Killed?" She was shouting now, as if Wilma was somehow to blame for pointing it out. She began shrieking sounds more than words, louder and louder, and finally looked at Wilma full of fury. Wilma saw those eyes again, scarier than any she had ever seen, saw them for just a moment, before she had to duck down fast.

Lily had thrown her peau de soie shoe.

Wilma again found herself at a complete loss for words. The shoe had landed in a large centerpiece, narrowly missing the television tube. Lily was still huddled on the couch, her hands covering her face. Wilma had a great mind to simply excuse herself and run out the front door. Second time inside a week. She looked down at Lily, who was crying softly now, moaning annoyingly, "Clemmie, Clemmie, Clemmie." Wilma sat back down on the couch, knowing suddenly that despite the circumstance, Lily simply lacked the wherewithal to kill Clem Baker or anyone else.

They sat there for several minutes. Wilma briefly considered laying a hand on Lily's hunched shoulder, but decided sitting beside her was enough. In truth, Wilma found it hard to believe that she was there at all. She couldn't remember the last time she had been a guest in the house. Being the wedding accompanist didn't count. It was all very strange. Wilma had gotten the news about Lily, about her being Harry's sister all in the same week that Harry's father died in her guest room, the same week that Harry lost the business, the same week she had seen Harry cry over his daddy's grave, all of this news had come in such a lump that Wilma had never really untangled it. It occurred to Wilma that the woman sitting next to her had been, and really still was, her sister-in-law, family of some description. Wilma pondered this for a minute, waiting to see if she could feel some kind of thawing out of her feelings. Beside her, Lily's grief was reduced to ragged breathing and sniffling. She took one hand away from her face and neatly grabbed a handkerchief from the lamp table. Lily was dabbing her eyes, trying to remove the accumulated smudges, when the doorbell rang.

"Oh God, what now?" she said. "Let's just sit here and maybe they'll go away."

"We can't do that. My car is sitting in the driveway, plain as day. They'll know we're here," said Wilma. "Why don't I just go to the door? I'll send whoever it is away." She didn't wait for a reply from Lily before getting up from the couch and going out into the hall. She was immediately happy to be out of the closeness of the den, which was much warmer than the hall. As she walked toward the door, she took a strange and sudden pleasure in the formality of the rooms around her, in the stateliness of the front hall. She approached the large front door and peeped out the sidelight. Despite herself, she felt a little zing of happiness when the watery form of Roy appeared through the beveled glass. As she wrestled with the stiff works of the doorknob, a silly notion passed through her mind. Like some young schoolgirl, she imagined that this was her fine house, that Roy was her loving husband, and that now she opened the door to welcome him home after a long day's work.

✑

He knew she had gone to Lily's even before he pulled up in the driveway behind her familiar green LTD. Her granddaughter had told him on the phone. Roy had come over in a rush, afraid she had jumped the gun somehow and taken things into her own hands. He felt an enormous fear for her, unfounded most likely, but nonetheless he felt it intensely on the whole drive to the house, up the walk, onto the stoop, waiting for someone to answer the bell, listening inside, hearing nothing for a few moments, then footsteps, faint at first then louder and louder, and finally identifiable as hers.

By the time Wilma opened the door, he was downright breathless, and seeing her, he was flooded at once with relief—relief for her safety—which of course was assured the whole time, but still flooded with relief, and he didn't know what else, admiration maybe, almost adoration, if that were possible—for she looked at him so calmly and nicely, like she had opened the door to greet him a thousand times before and would a thousand times hence.

He did not even take in whatever she said to him in those first few seconds, but somehow made it across the threshold and into the hall and let her close the door behind him. That done, he reached over to her with both his arms and pulled her close up to his chest. He held on to her there for just a moment, just long enough for him to feel her hands rest in the small of his back. A small miracle and all done in a way that he could not have accomplished with weeks of planning.

"Is everything all right here?" he said. It was just the two of them in the hall. The rest of the house was quiet. He had created all kinds of wild scenarios on his way over.

"Pretty much," said Wilma. The color had come up in her cheeks.

Lily had to be around somewhere. Roy leaned over toward Wilma and whispered, "Whatever possessed you to come over here this morning?"

"I wanted to get to her before anyone else did," she said. "I need to figure this thing out, and I thought she was the best person to start with."

"And?"

"Roy, you can come see for yourself. She is a mess, torn up. But I can't really believe that she has sense enough to kill someone."

"I agree with you there, honey," he said, letting the endearment sneak out. "But I have been turning this thing around and around, and I think I have an idea about what might have happened. Maybe Lily can help."

"I seriously doubt it," said Wilma. "She is no more reliable than a two-year-old this morning."

"Can I try to talk to her, you think?" said Roy.

Wilma shrugged and motioned Roy through the door to the central hallway. He followed along and caught up to her. The hall was wide enough for them to walk side by side, and as they did Roy placed his hand lightly on Wilma's shoulders, then took it off again. As they neared the den door, Wilma paused a bit and took in a breath. She looked up a Roy, who tried to nod in reassurance as they walked into the den. Just inside the door, Roy was instantly overcome with the fragrant closeness of the room. It filled him with the feeling he had as a boy when he was forced to come to see some dead relative laid out in their parlor. It was a smell that he could never shake off. And Lily, Lily staring up at him from the couch looking as ghostlike as the day is long. Good God almighty, he had for just a second the strangest urge to run. Instead, he put on his manners—just nodded his head a bit and said, "Morning, Lily."

"Good morning yourself," said Lily, in an accent that didn't belong in such a house. "If you're looking for Franklin, he is not here. His business has taken him to Atlanta this week. You'll have to come back another time." She made an effort to sit on the couch and straighten herself up a bit.

"Well, to tell the truth, Lily, I've come to talk to you," said Roy. Wilma sat down, businesslike, on the couch beside Lily. "We both have, Miss Wilma and I." Standing alone, Roy had the feeling at once of being somewhere he did not belong, like he had landed in the middle of a baby shower or one of his mother's bridge parties. He felt very large. He stepped over toward the one chair that looked like it could hold him—a leather job with a lot of rivets—but he noticed once he got near it that some flower thing, a bouquet of some description, was in the seat. He lifted it up and put it on the floor, relieved that nothing fell off, and sat down finally. The chair turned out to be quite comfortable, and he was sorry to see that its companion footstool was inaccessible, across the room and covered with more wilted flowers. No wonder the place smelled like a funeral parlor.

Having gotten himself arranged, he looked back over at the two women on the couch. Time to take charge of the situation. He put what he considered a no-nonsense look on his face and cleared his throat. As he did so, a girlish titter escaped from Wilma, who covered her mouth but continued to laugh. Lily, still recovering from a near collapse, also suppressed a smile.

They're nervous, Roy thought. He pressed ahead. "Now, Lily, I guess it's no surprise why we have come over here this morning, Miss Wilma and I. This is a real bad situation, there's no way around it. I'm sorry to say that we know something of your, um, involvement with Clem Baker. Knowing what we do, there are some things that we just cannot ignore." He looked over at Wilma at this point to see if she would lend some affirmation here, but he was disturbed to discover that she was still tittering a bit. "And we have come here I think in the spirit of neighborliness. . . ." He stopped talking and looked at both women. "What?" he said, but they only laughed harder. He gave them a stern look.

That seemed to shut them up finally, and after a few moments of silence, Lily spoke up. "Roy, if you can refrain from blushing until you are plum purple, I will explain. I was just telling Wilma here before you came in that you are terrible mistaken about Clem."

"And I was saying that we knew otherwise," said Wilma.

"What would he want with me?" said Lily. "He is thirty-two years and I am . . . I am several years older than him."

"Thirty-two, and not thirty-three, maybe?" said Wilma, suppressing a laugh. Lily had to be in her late fifties. Wilma looked back over at Roy.

"Yes," said Lily, not catching on, "he won't be thirty-three until July. He was class of 1966, I believe. Not that I would know. But come to think of it, he was a football player and wasn't that 1966 when he played, Roy?"

"I don't know, Lily. He was your boyfriend."

"Would you stop saying that?" said Lily, throwing the quilt off her now, recovering from her near breakdown mighty fast. "I will admit that we did have a special friendship. That's sure allowed, ain't it? Franklin is gone so much these days. It doesn't hurt to have a little company from time to time."

"Company, you call it? Company come a-visiting on a blanket

in the woods?" said Roy, though he knew at once he shouldn't have said it.

Lily turned bloodred then, heaved her chest up and down, and made silent sputtering motions with her lips. Roy noticed Lily had big lips, swollen almost and blurred by some kind of slick, white lipstick. Beside her, it looked like Wilma was holding her breath. He saw from the worried look in Wilma's eyes that in every fiber of her body she really wanted to comfort Lily. Bless her heart, imagine that, she wanted to comfort this woman. Wisely, she was fighting her impulse—she knew when to keep quiet, which was a very admirable trait. Quite right to let Lily squirm a little bit, might get her to tell the truth. And squirming she was. She seemed to be adjusting her shoulders and the front of her blouse—to no avail, he noticed. She uncovered more than she covered up. She crossed her legs back and forth, smoothing her little trousers with her hands.

Finally she looked up at him sort of cutesy-like and smiled real sly, and to his surprise she giggled again. He would never understand women. Why would she do that? Had she lost her mind? This must have been what Wilma was thinking, because she was looking on with alarm. Lily said, "Why Roy Swan, what have you been doing with yourself? Have you been spying on me? Did you see something that you liked, hon?" With that she narrowed her eyes and flung her arms up in the air and bent them at the elbows wantonly and made a noise that was so suggestive that Roy felt himself going all red again. He thought for a minute that Wilma was embarrassed too, but then she hopped up and faced Lily. Roy could tell by the flash of her eyes that she was just plain mad.

"That is enough. That is enough," Wilma shouted, a little louder than necessary. She actually stomped her foot. Lily looked over at her like she had forgotten Wilma was in the room. Uh-oh, thought Roy, catfight.

"Listen, little lady, Roy has done nothing but mind his own

business. He was just out on a historic photo shoot and he stumbled on your little, your little, what's the word, *tryst*. Now if you're going to run around in the woods naked, Lily, what else can you expect?" Wilma was wound up now. She had already said too much, in Roy's opinion.

"This is all beside the point," said Roy, but as he feared, Wilma was not deterred.

"How dare you accuse him of being a Peeping Tom?" she said. "My God, who else might have seen you? There could have been some children playing in those woods—what if they had seen you and Clem running around naked?"

"Hon, as Roy has probably already told you, we were by no means running around. Isn't that right, Roy?" Lily gave him that sexy look again. "In fact, Miss Wilma, maybe he has done more than tell you. Didn't you say something about photographs?" This is what Roy had been afraid of.

"I only said he was photographing gravestones for historical purposes," said Wilma icily, "but now that you mention it, yes, Roy does happen to have photographic proof of your endeavors."

"Well, you two must have had a lot of fun looking over those," said Lily. She was trying to be flippant, but Roy could see that her hands were shaking.

"Hardly," said Wilma, reddening again.

"Okay, so you have me," said Lily. "Caught in the act. What are you going to do? I know you, Wilma, you'll find some way to lord this over me for the rest of my life. What do you want? Money? You two here to blackmail me?"

"Blackmail? Of course not," said Roy. It was time to take charge again. "We are just here to help figure out what happened to Clem."

"Oh, sure. Of course you are. You are so sorry about Clem, so sorry to come over here and rub my nose in my dirty deeds," said Lily, ready to tune up and cry again. She pointed at Wilma. "She's been waiting years to have a chance like this. A chance to get my money and to shame me all at the same time." She huddled into the quilt again, crying piteously.

Wilma rolled her eyes and sat back down beside Lily. There would be no talking to her until she calmed down a bit. Roy leaned back in the chair. He had not eaten a lot of breakfast and his stomach began growling. He shifted in the chair again, hoping that Wilma had not heard it. She seemed intent, however, on Lily.

"Lily, come on, Lily," said Wilma in a soothing voice. Roy could tell she had been a good mother. "I am not here to get you or your money. What would I want with that? Let me tell you why I'm here. They have arrested a suspect in Clem's murder."

"They have?" said Lily, looking up. "Was it the Indian?"

"I don't think he's actually an Indian," said Wilma, "but he's from Santa Fe. You know, New Mexico, where my Sarah lives. Jonah Branch. Yes, they arrested him last night."

"They think he did it, then?" said Lily.

"Yes," said Wilma, "but Roy and me here, we think otherwise. Right, Roy?"

"Right."

Lily's eyes got big. "Oh my God, you think it was me, don't you? Oh my God. Oh my God. Please. You can't think that. I loved Clem with all my heart. Truly I did. You have got to believe that I didn't kill him."

Maybe Roy was a complete sucker, but he could not help but believe her. He looked over, and Wilma was nodding solemnly at Lily, saying, "We know, Lily. We know." This brought on a new round of crying on Lily's part. Roy was almost getting used to it.

While they sat there waiting for the tide to go back out, Roy found himself studying the two women that sat before him. Other men might differ, but for all her efforts, Lily could not hold a candle to Wilma in his opinion. If the rumors were true, Harry Mabry had been a fool to mess with Lily. Roy did have to admit, though, it was hard to keep your eyes off that unbuttoned front of Lily's blouse, especially seeing as how she was so skinny on the rest of her body, it seemed a little unnatural to him, somehow. This also made him get to wondering about how Wilma might look with a few of her buttons gone. He thought about that for a few minutes, pictured her sitting in the wing chair by the window in his bedroom, with her pretty blue blouse, all pressed and clean. Despite himself, he started to grin, a wide grin directed at Wilma, who shot back a stern look. She had some idea what kind of thing he was thinking about, he was sure, for under the sternness he could see that she was a little pleased.

He sensed that Lily was getting near done, so he began again. "Lily, so let's say that of course you didn't have anything to do with Clem's shooting."

"Lord, I can't even shoot a gun, never could. My granddaddy tried to teach me when I was a kid, took me out in the yard and set up a row of gourds on sticks, but I flat-out refused to take the shotgun," she said.

Roy knew few details about Lily's upbringing, but now he pictured a sepia hillside and a cabin with a lopsided front porch. It was a far cry from this fussy den full of flowers. "Okay, granted, Lily. You were not the one. Let's think about who else might it be."

"Well, I have a very good idea," said Lily. "It's plain as day if you ask me."

"Who?" Wilma and Roy said it at the same time.

"Well, it wasn't any Indian boy, that's for sure," said Lily.

"Who?" said Wilma again.

"Ava, that's who, the woman scorched. She must have found out somehow and kerpow." Lily shot Roy with her finger, then blew on it. "Done."

"That sure is one theory," said Roy. "But do you have any kind of evidence? Any way to prove this?"

"She is a bitch, for one thing," said Lily. "Clem always told me that she was plumb mean to him. Wouldn't iron his uniforms, hardly ever fixed his supper, withheld wifely favors, that kind of thing. You can see why he turned to me."

"Bad housekeeping is hardly any kind of evidence," said Wilma. "Did Clem ever tell you that Ava knew what was going on?"

"Not as far as he said to me. We were real careful," said Lily. "The only thing I can think is last week he got on me a little because, afterwards, he had some little marks." Lily held up her hands to show them her long nails. "I must have scratched him a little bit around his shoulders, without meaning to, you understand, in the heat of passion." Roy noticed that Wilma was looking down at the floor. She wasn't accustomed to such talk. It must kill her to have to listen to such things from Lily.

"Let's think about this," he said. "If Ava killed Clem, that means she had to be out on the bypass in the middle of the night. How would she get there? Did she have a car?"

"Clem has a Pinto," said Lily. "He would drive in from their house over in Westfield to the police station and leave it there while he was on duty. I know because sometimes he would pick me up and we'd sneak out."

"Okay, if Clem had the Pinto, then how would Ava get out to the bypass?" said Roy.

"Could she borrow a car?" said Wilma.

"They're out in the country. Not many close neighbors, right, Lily?" said Roy.

"Right," said Lily. "The only time I've even seen Ava drive was once in her brother's truck. She was out looking for Clem, you know. He had just dropped me off behind the drugstore, and I came up the side alley just as she drove by. Looked mad as hell."

"This is not getting us anywhere," said Roy. He had eliminated Ava from his list just from what he knew of her. Sweet girl, really. Nice to everyone when you'd see her downtown. No match for Lily. He had another theory altogether. "I just don't think it adds up: Why would Ava shoot him out on the bypass?

How could she even get there? I just don't see it. Now, Lily, do you have any indication that Ava's brother, Avery, knew about you and Clem?"

"Avery? I don't think so. Ava and Avery are real close, being twins and all. That's what Clemmie always said. Said Ava would call Avery the very minute any little thing went wrong: scraped knee, lost kitty cat, bank foreclosure. It's all spooky to me, this twin stuff," said Lily. "Especially a boy and a girl twin like them. Different sides of the same coin. Sort of unnatural."

"Let's think here a minute," said Wilma, always quick on the uptake, Roy noticed. "Do you have any idea about how Avery could have found out?"

"Clem said Avery was always over at their trailer," said Lily. "He didn't never go to his own house, which is a hovel, by the way. Clem showed it to me. Four miles down the road from their place, some old leftover tenant farmer shack, barely any plumbing."

"Do you think Ava might have told him?" Roy said. It was hard to keep Lily on track.

"From everything Clemmie told me, Ava was like a little child, not real aware of things around her. A child spoiled rotten really. Now that I think about it, it was probably Avery who seen to that. Lord, Clem married Ava the week right after he got back from the army, pulled her out of a tobacco barn in the middle of priming season. Neither one of them knew what they was doing. Clem said Avery won't have allowed it had he been there. Said Avery came back from Fort Bragg on leave when he found out and pitched a big fit. Pulled up every bush Clem had planted in the yard, if you can imagine. Maybe you are right. Maybe Avery killed him, maybe he did it for Ava—kilt Clem for that spoilt child." This brought on a new round of tears, which Roy could almost ignore at this point. He could see the exasperation on Wilma's face too. This is what he got for trying to play detective, all kinds of details that proved nothing.

"Lily, you are going to have to get ahold of yourself or we cannot help you," said Wilma.

"You are not here to help me," sobbed Lily.

"Don't be foolish. We are here to straighten this whole thing out," said Wilma. "Somehow, this situation has gotten wrapped around each and every one of us, and I for one am not going to let it take me down. Now, come on. Think. Start here: Is there any evidence, and I mean evidence here, not tearful conjecture, of anybody knowing about you and Clem? Did you go to a hotel? Could somebody have seen you up at the Holiday Inn? Bootsey Milstone can be pretty nosy, you know."

"No, we never went to a hotel," said Lily. "Never. No restaurants, nothing like that. Clem said we couldn't. Not even over in Winston. We were mostly, well, you know, mostly out in the country or in the car, that kind of thing."

"Did anybody ever see you, that you know about?" said Wilma. Before the day was over, Roy vowed that he would burn his photographs and the negatives. Even just hearing Wilma's question, the images flashed through his mind like giant slides projected onto the living room wall.

"Well, until this morning, I didn't think anybody ever saw us, not a living soul. Now, well, who knows? For all I know, Roy's dropped off a few choice photos all over town. There's no telling, really." Lily looked pointedly at Roy again.

"No one's seen them except Wilma and me," Roy said. "I developed them myself." Lily did have a point though. If he had stumbled upon them, who else might have as well? "Is there any other way someone might have found out? Were there any letters or phone calls? How about something you might have dropped in his car or something you gave him?"

Lily shook her head. "The only time we talked on the phone, I think it was only once or twice, he was alone at the police station. And letters? He wasn't that kind of man—not one to write letters or even send a card. Me neither. I did give him something, though. I gave him a cigarette lighter last Christmas, a real pretty one I bought over at Schiffman's in Winston. I had his initials put on it, CB, Clemont Baker. Pretty name, don't you think? Have you ever known anyone else the name of Clemont? He looked all pleased when I gave it to him. Didn't say much, which was just like him, but acted real pleased, said I shouldn't have, how was he going to use it in front of everybody. In the end he kept it though, kept it in his police car so he could use it when he worked, and that way Ava never would get ahold of it." Of course this was the lighter that Chief Henry was waving around as evidence against Jonah just last night. Roy had a feeling that all the little pieces of the story were about to fall into place, if he could just get this confounded woman to be quiet so that he could think a minute.

"He was fixing to leave her, I think, I think he was going to even though he never said as much. It was hard for him knowing that I would never leave Franklin. I told him that. I was honest from the beginning. I told him that in this world a girl has got to consider her standing—without Franklin, I might still have money, you know all about that, Wilma—but honey, I wouldn't have no standing whatsoever in this town. So I wasn't about to leave. Of course, that's what you're here to take, you and Wilma. You're a man, Roy, so this probably hadn't occurred to you, but Wilma don't even care that I got her man's money. Oh, no, she's just mad that I got what come with it, social standing with all the right people in this town. And now that she knows, she'll take it all away directly—all she's got to do is tell my little story, whisper it one little time to Grace Snow or Mamie Brown at the Garden Club, and I might as well be living in that old shanty of Avery's out on Cook School Road."

Lily was right about one thing—Roy didn't have a clue what in the world she was talking about. All this about Lily having Harry's money and the Garden Club, what did that have to do with the price of rice in China? Good Lord. He had just about had it with this woman. Wilma must have been thinking the same thing because she was beet red again. It got quiet for just a second in the room, and Roy could hear Wilma take a big swallow, then a big breath. She spoke softly back to Lily: "This is going to be hard for you to understand, but I am not here to take anything from you, let alone what you call your 'standing.' Why would I want anyone to know what the two of us know, you and I? Why, you silly woman, you've already said too much." She looked over at Roy now. "As long as we're sharing secrets here, you might as well know."

"I know," he said right quick, not wanting for her to have to say it. Hadn't they already gone over all of this? Hadn't he been the one to mention it in the car the other night? "I know all about it. Miss Lily here and Harry, the same as her and Clem Baker." There, the less said the better now. No telling what would happen if these two got going on the subject. Already Lily was fixing to go into another spasm and Wilma, lady that she was, looked like she just might spit.

"You got it all wrong, though I can't say I blame you," said Wilma. "I may not give two cents for what the rest of the town thinks of me or my Harry, but I can't stand for you to think he was that kind of person."

"Honey, he is long gone. We don't have to think of him at all," said Roy—the "my Harry" bit stung a little. If Wilma still wanted to deny what had happened, he couldn't blame her. It had happened, he had taken that as fact, though he couldn't think what he had seen or heard at the time to make him so sure. How had they gotten off into the past again?

"I refuse to dwell on these things, so I'll just tell you and we'll be done," said Wilma. "Lily is Harry's half-sister. She is the product of goings-on between Harry's father and a woman from the yarn plant. When Harry's father died, he willed his entire estate to Lily, every last cent. So that's that, and so you see why Lily and Harry could not have been involved in that way, you know . . . like Lily and Clem."

Roy felt like he was back in some kind of odd math class, where a professor had just finished writing some complicated proof on the blackboard. He stared at Wilma's face for a minute, hoping to put it all together in his mind. Something did not seem right, but he couldn't put his finger on it. Meanwhile, he saw, Wilma was waiting on his response.

"I had no idea. I don't think anyone did. And I am so sorry," he managed and was happy to see Wilma lean back on the couch and give him a little smile of relief. Meanwhile, Lily had had nothing to say on the subject. She just sat on the couch, completely silent and still, with her shoulders hunched together and her face turned down, like she was trying to be as small a thing as possible, and no wonder. Now Roy understood all the ranting and raving about Mamie Brown and the Garden Club. Lord God, this was just the sort of thing that could keep people whispering through an entire growing season. He had always wondered what had happened to Harry—he didn't seem to be the kind of man to let the world get out in front of him. "This explains a lot of things, Wilma. I feel real bad about what you've had to bear."

"It hadn't been a picnic for me either, that's for damn sure." Lily was standing up now, folding up her quilt. "I'm going to get myself some iced tea. What can I get you two? Roy, you're bound to be getting hungry there. What about a pimento cheese sandwich?" It was such a rapid recovery that both Roy and Wilma just stared for a moment as Lily began picking up the collection of glasses and used Kleenex on the lamp table.

"Well, okay. That would be fine," said Roy as Lily headed out of the room. He could hear Lily making noise in the kitchen before he allowed himself to look back over at Wilma. His first impulse was to leave his chair and go sit beside her, maybe let her put her head on his shoulder, but when he looked, she was back to her old piano bench posture and he couldn't tell what she might be thinking. He supposed this was how she had done it—

this carefully composed stillness—this was how she had endured the news about Lily all these years, endured Harry's death, and Lord knows what other sadness. It broke his heart to think about her sitting up at the front of the church with that dignified look on her face, all the time probably sick with worry about how to put Sarah through college on piano-lesson money or how to keep the roof from falling in on her head. Despite himself, he got up and went over to her. He was about to put him arms around her when she whispered, "Roy, don't be nice to me right now. I can't stand it. Don't be nice. I would break into a million pieces."

"Okay, that's fine," he said. He knew just what she meant. There were times in the middle of the night when he woke up and wanted nothing so much as the warmth of another human being, but he was never sure what he would do if he had it, especially since he had been without it for so long. "Back to the present then," he said, though he was not sure that even this was a safe topic. "Maybe you and I can go over things for a minute before Lily comes back. What do we know?"

He ventured a look back at Wilma, who gave a quick sniff, but said, "Well, we don't know a thing for sure, but we can guess, can't we. . . ."

"Yes," he said, "let's say that Ava had it all figured out about Clem and Lily. Lily told us about her riding around looking for Clem. Let's face it those two couldn't have been very discrete."

"That's for sure," said Wilma. "We can also assume that if Ava knew, she told Avery at some point. Could it be this simple? Could it just be that Avery was furious that Clem had fooled around on Ava and went out and shot him? That's what you're thinking, aren't you?"

"Yes," said Roy. He could hear now just the slightest bit of excitement creeping into Wilma's voice. He felt a little giddy himself and just a tad guilty that his fantasy about the two of them was coming true.

"But the lighter," said Wilma. "How did Jonah end up with the lighter out at his campsite on the river?"

"Well, you've hit on the best clue," said Roy, trying not to sound too proud. "That was the thing that got me thinking last night. It was all too convenient, as they say on TV. I thought that the minute Chief Henry started bragging on it up at the Coach House. Why would anyone kill a policeman and then take his cigarette lighter?"

"So Jonah never had it, is that what you're saying?" said Wilma.

"Of course not. Avery was up there with them searching the campsite, remember? All he had to do was drop it in the grass and let one of the other men find it."

"You know, that makes all the sense in the world. It's the first thing that's made sense in a couple of days now. My goodness, then Chief Henry has gone and deputized the murderer himself. Well, you are Perry Mason," said Wilma in a way that was almost possessive.

"This is not fit for a TV show," said Roy. "It's more like one of the stories you find in those true-crime magazines they got down at the barbershop."

"We've got to go down and tell Chief Henry," said Wilma. "Do you think he'll believe us? How are we going to prove it all?"

"I have no idea," said Roy, hearing Lily's footsteps in the hall, "but if at all possible, I'd like to leave the whole notion of the photographs out of it."

"I don't see how you can," said Wilma, "but it's worth a try. The main thing is to go down and get this thing straightened out before something else happens."

"Here we are," said Lily, coming through the door with a silver tray that looked too heavy for anyone her size to carry. Wilma and Roy jumped up to clear more flower bouquets off the coffee table. Roy immediately picked up the Dixie cup full of iced tea and sat back down to drink it.

Wilma remained standing: "What a shame we can't stay," she

said. "Roy and I have to get down to the police station with all this information."

"What information?" said Lily. "Are you going to turn Ava in?"

"No, Lily. We've been over this. We don't think Ava did it. It was Avery," Wilma said.

"Lily's gone to all this trouble. Our news will keep long enough for us to eat," said Roy. Lily had toasted the bread for the pimento sandwiches just like he liked it.

Chapter Fourteen

Sarah woke up feeling sorry for herself and for the rest of the world. She lay in bed paging through the people in her life and the odd personalities she had run across in town—there was a certain hopelessness about every one them, she decided: her mother the keeper of secrets, Harper the weak, Jonah the prisoner, Clara from the drugstore, Chief Henry and his stupid deputies, even the tow-truck man with the sorry son. Every one of them was without much to hope for except for Starling, maybe, who was too young to be hopeless, and possibly that woman in the red pantsuit, whose life seemed to be going pretty well—though, come to think of it, she did have breast cancer and a broken windowpane. For her part, Sarah felt pounds heavier, as if a little extra gravity bore down on every inch of the bed, as if overnight she had been filled with the hormones of loathing.

As she managed to stand finally and throw on the pair of jeans that she found at the end of the bed, she could hear that the daily piano practice had begun downstairs. An older student with a certain flair for phrasing was playing "Fur Elise." This would stop soon, she knew, so that Wilma could scold the child for the sour notes that Sarah could hear in every third bar or so. After all these years, Sarah wondered if her mother could hear anything but missed notes. She wondered if she could do anything but squash the spirit of that child downstairs, squash her beautiful feeling for the music, squash it in favor of correctness. She was downstairs and halfway through a piece of toast before she realized that the playing had not stopped, that it had continued all the way through to the end. Even then, there was only a brief pause, and oddly Harper's voice saying, "Again," before the whole thing started over. Sarah tiptoed out to the front of the house. At the far end of the living room, she could see Harper through the arched doorway of Miss Wilma's music room. It was an old sunporch really, crowded with an ancient baby grand Steinway, a forest of houseplants, and neat shelves filled with sheet music.

Harper had his back to Sarah and his pupil was obscured by the open piano lid. Sarah walked quietly forward, hoping not to disturb the student's playing—on this second time through, most of the notes were corrected and the sound was almost pleasant. She could see that Harper was just out of the shower. The ends of his hair were still wet. He had put on a button-down shirt that he must have found somewhere in the house. Harper stood beside the piano, like an altogether legitimate music teacher, his head slightly cocked so as to hear every important note. The overall effect was so compelling that Sarah did not look up again at the pianist for a few more steps. Finally, around the end of the piano lid, Sarah had to look twice to know for sure that it was Starling at the piano. Starling sat easily on the bench with her head bowed slightly over the keys in the innocent morning light, her features beautiful and marked only by the music that swelled around her.

When Sarah and Harper arrived at the police station and stated their business, Chief Henry and one of the other policemen hustled Harper into the back of the station, to the chief's office maybe or to Jonah's cell. They assigned Sarah to a ladder-back chair in the front room of the police station. It creaked when she sat down and wobbled on its legs, worn down from a thousand nights of deputies leaning back against the wall. Sarah had been left to wait with Deputy Avery, who sat now behind a gray metal desk used most recently for the station's ham biscuit breakfast. The deputy looked at Sarah sullenly, just long enough to make her uncomfortable, and then went back to his cigarette and coffee.

"Where did your biscuits come from? The Coach House?" she said by way of breaking the silence.

"Drugstore soda fountain," he said in a short tone that let her know he had no intention of carrying it any further. He was pissed to be left out of the fun in the back, Sarah figured, pissed for being the low man on the totem pole. Story of his life, most likely. He looked like he was close to her age, maybe a bit younger. Had she known him in school? She studied his wide shallow face, clipped black hair, neck a little bit too long. He didn't look familiar. She gathered that he had only taken up with the force since Clem Baker's killing. He had more or less inherited the job. He was the dead man's brother-in-law, this kinship alone being adequate qualification in this neck of the woods. He had lived his life so far as some kind of millworker or farmhand, given the state of the fingers. This job was probably a step up, though no one had even bothered to give him a uniform. Instead he wore a filthy green vest, which undoubtedly looked some kind of official to him.

He stubbed out his cigarette in the overflowing ashtray and began opening and closing the desk drawers, pretending, Sarah thought, that he had some work to do.

"Do you think it will be much longer?" she said. Starling had been completely content to be left alone—she was planting a whole flat of annuals in the bed beside the house—but Sarah hated to be gone all day.

"I really can't say. Interrogations can last a few minutes or they can go on for days, ma'am," he said. He was a bit better spoken than Sarah would have thought, though he must have been quoting some television show. Questioning could go on for days? This proved he knew nothing.

"Maybe I'll just go across to the drugstore and get some tea while I wait for my husband to finish up," she said.

"I'm sorry, ma'am, my orders were to wait here with you, ma'am. They may want to question you next," he said.

"Call me Sarah," she said. He just stared at her in that creepy sullen way and went back to rummaging through the drawers.

"For Pete's sake. Let me go. I'll come right back," she said.

"Not an option," he said without bothering to look up again, like he was accustomed to handling such matters.

Sarah wished that she had eaten more than toast for breakfast. She looked around the room, which was dominated on one side by vending machines: a brand-new one for cigarettes lit up like a new Buick and a stone-age upright for drinks. There was even an honor-system box of Nabs and peanuts, but nothing that her churning stomach would even allow her to consider.

Deputy Avery slammed the last drawer shut and made his way loudly over to a row of filing cabinets. He was wearing what looked like combat boots.

"How about some water?" Sarah asked finally. The man's sigh was supposed to tell her that she was interrupting important police business. He stomped over to the drink machine, opened the vertical glass door and peered inside. Then he pulled a pocketknife out of his vest, poked it into the machine with one hand, twisted it a few times, and pulled out a Coke. It took two tries and several obscenities before he succeeded in removing the bottle cap as well. He handed the Coke over to Sarah. "Here, plenty of water in that," he said and stomped back to the files.

Sarah was afraid not to drink it. After a few sips, her stomach seemed grateful. She tried to relax for a moment in her hard chair, tried to forestall her fears about Harper and Jonah. Deputy Avery was not making it easy for her to relax, however. He was now attempting to open the filing cabinet drawers, one by one, but finding them all locked he began to go through the stacks of papers and files piled up on top of them. Sarah noticed he had a way of jiggling his knees even when he was standing upright. Now that his back was turned to her, Sarah could see a crude eagle drawn in magic marker on the back of Avery's green vest and the letters USAC: 5th Inf. So it was a uniform, then—all those pockets and loops and things on the front—flack jacket, it was called, like the ones the vets had worn at protest rallies back in the sixties. He was still hanging on to a war souvenir. Avery continued to ignore her, so she snuck another look: other things were written on the jacket, though they were fainter than the eagle. She couldn't read the words, but they looked like autographs, little lines of words written in various hands—and names signed—like entries in a high school yearbook. What could they say? "What a four years this had been" or "Once more into the . . ." or "See you at Carolina . . . ," "See you on the other side," "Don't forget the time we . . ." or "Friends 4 ever."

"So you were in Vietnam," she said, too casually. His body stopped all motion, then he carefully replaced the file he was perusing and picked up another one. She thought for a moment that he would ignore the question, wished he would. He turned toward her finally and looked down at his vest.

"Oh, the jacket. This jacket here was Clem's. He gave it to me a while back right after he got home. I was in the army too, but I didn't make it to Vietnam," he said, as if he had provided this explanation many times. "I joined up right out of high school, but by the time I made it through basic, they had pulled up the last helicopter ladder over the embassy. What about you?"

"Nowhere," she said. "Sorry."

"Yeah, sorry," he said, penciling something on the file, drawing some kind of bird. "Real sorry. To college, that would be where you went."

"Pardon?"

"I said, you went to college, unlike the dumb saps like me, dumbasses that actually volunteered. You and pretty boy having a fine time in college, just like everyone you knew, right? Probably protesting the war, the whole freaking time."

"Oh, no," said Sarah, "nothing like that. We wanted . . . we wanted . . ."

"You wanted . . . just what?" he said. He folded his arms over his chest. She looked back at him, looked straight into his eyes finally, and in them saw a bright flash of something akin to craziness, making any response she was about to muster dissolve into some kind of lame prayer for the door to the back to open, for Harper or Jonah or anybody else to walk through it. Before she could work up a real panic though, the man seemed to wipe the intensity off his face and replace it with a wide grin that let her know that he didn't really expect an answer.

"What year did you graduate? You must have been two or three years ahead of me." he said.

Sarah searched his face again and tried to rewind the features by ten or fifteen years. She could not remember him. " 'Sixty-eight."

"Right," he said. "I remember that you were in that play they had—it was Greek or Roman or something. . . ."

"Antigone," said Sarah, trying to picture this man at a play. "I played Antigone's sister. I hardly remember that myself."

"I went because my buddy Junior Freeman was going with Patsy Thomas." Avery seemed to be over the Vietnam remark now. He had gone back over to the desk chair. He sat swiveling the seat back and forth. "She was in the, what do you call it, the choir or something."

"Chorus," said Sarah. She did remember Junior Freeman. He had been a loudmouthed football player, one of the Industrial Ed boys who spent most of high school in the car shop class. She remembered Patsy from the play rehearsals, a cute blonde. "I remember both of them."

"They got married, you know. Have three children. Moved up to Kannapolis, I think." Sarah pictured three blonde children sitting in the back of an old car, waiting for their daddy to come out of second shift.

"What about you, who'd you marry?" she said.

"Me? Well, no one. You interested? Oh, that's right, you're married to the little man in there." He smirked at her like he was still in high school and went back to his files. Sarah studied his features for something familiar but couldn't really find anything. He could have been any one of the boys who clustered around the front sidewalk of the high school before the first bell. Those boys would smoke filterless cigarettes with their man-size hands while they watched Sarah and her friends come up the stairs. It was an unwritten rule that this gauntlet was to be ignored, and never to be remarked upon. She remembered the tiny charge she would feel from the frank eyes on her body, the muttered farmhand appreciation. Sarah could picture this man in that group, she could picture his dark eyes staring at her from underneath an overgrowth of black hair. He would have been what she considered dangerous in high school, far away from the in-town boys who bought her milk shakes at Setzer's drive-in, boys who rode around in their daddies' cars and not in the back of pickup trucks. Dangerous.

He had gone back over to the filing cabinet again, and she looked at the outline of his back. Of course, the jacket, the white T-shirt even. He was the guy from the Ararat River the other night.

"Oh, hey, I guess you're not married, for real," she said. "I saw you just the other night out at the Ararat. Dating a little high school girl, are you?"

She saw that she had said the wrong thing again because the man's eyes flashed alarmingly for just a second as he turned around, but he said only, "I don't know what in the world you're talking about," and went back to his desk. Sarah just sat quietly in her chair, tried not to feel hungry. It had been dumb of her to bring that up. Who, past high school, wanted to admit taking a date parking at the Ararat? After a minute, he said quietly, "So, if you don't mind telling me, what does your husband have to tell? I don't suppose he seen something?"

"No," she said, "he just knows they have the wrong man. You see, he was driving with Jonah—the man you have in jail in there—he was driving with him across the mountains on the night the policeman was killed, so there's no way he could have done it."

"I see," he said, turning intense again, staring her down. "And why didn't he come forward before now? Your husband has been in town a few days and he was there last night when we arrested him at your mama's house. Why didn't he say nothing then?"

"He was scared. I don't know. It's complicated," said Sarah, wondering why she had started talking at all.

"Scared of what?" The man had started jerking his knee up and down again, and looked at the closed door to the back room.

"I don't know. I guess he just didn't know what you fellows might do next, after arresting Jonah."

The deputy laughed quickly and looked at the door again. "I guess you have to be careful with all that long hair and all. They even gave your man a pretty hard time over at Squirrely's the other night."

"Do you think they might all be out soon?" Sarah said, willing the back door to open again.

"Who?"

"Well, Harper, my husband, that is, and I thought maybe they might be letting Jonah out too."

"Well, they aren't going to be letting Jonah out, that's for sure."

"Why not, if Harper clears him?" said Sarah.

"Well, he ain't here, that's why. They took him over to Dobson this morning to see the judge," said the deputy, nonetheless sneaking another look at the door.

County courthouse, in front of a judge. They had come to the wrong place, then. Sarah found herself on her feet, digging in her purse for car keys. She had a bad feeling, a complete urgency that she had not felt before to get to Jonah, to get him away from this place. She started toward the closed door, and Deputy Avery started over to stop her but they were still several feet away when the door burst open. Chief Henry, Harper and several other men rushed out.

Harper looked a bit like an elf standing among the beefy red-faced policemen, but Sarah was happy to see that at least he was not handcuffed. He looked purposefully at Sarah and said, "They've taken him over to—"

"I know," she said.

"I've got to go over to the court to testify," he said in an official tone. He marched out the door with them, trying to match their posture, she saw, tucking in his shirt.

That shirt, a blue oxford cloth, was four sizes too large for Harper. It must have been her father's, she decided, stashed these years in an upstairs closet.

Harper was in the police car and moving down the street before it occurred to Sarah that he had the keys to the car in his pocket. She stood out on the sidewalk with Deputy Avery, who, equally abandoned, stood with his hands on his hips and looked at the car's taillights as it stopped a block down at the Church Street light. When the light changed, Deputy Avery turned his attention back to the activity right in front him—he had been left to guard the fort, Sarah supposed, all five blocks of it. Two stores down, a group of children parked their bikes on the sidewalk and headed into the dime store. Across the street, Jimmy Belton was just opening his shoe store and the pool hall was still dark. Only Surry Drug was populated this time of the morning. Sarah could see two or three people drinking coffee at the soda fountain, craning their necks up over the magazine racks to see what was going on in front of the police station.

"I've got to get over there, you know," she said, though the deputy pretended that she had not directed the order to him. "You have got to take me to the courthouse."

The man shifted from one foot to the other and surveyed the street once again. "Ma'am, I can't take you right now. I'm on duty here. I can't just abandon my post."

"Your post? There are no more than four children and dogs combined down here this morning. What could happen?" she said, trying not to sound exasperated. "Look. You have no way of knowing, but this, this is an extreme emergency and I have to get over there. Now."

He looked at her warily and at the downtown street that didn't need him. "Okay," he said, to her surprise, and nodded toward the second-string police car. "Get in. I'll get the keys and lock up." Sarah looked at the car for a moment, wondering whether she should ride in the front or the back. She decided that the front would be better, even though she had to move a bunch of his junk down to the floorboard before she settled into the seat. She was surprised there weren't more things of an official nature in the car. There was nothing other than a two-way radio—which would be useless since there was no one in the station—and two big buttons, one for the red light, she supposed, and one for the siren.

Deputy Avery was now struggling to lock the front door of the police station, still searching for the right key, it seemed. Another car pulled up behind her, and Sarah heard two doors slam. She turned to see, of all people, her mother and that man Roy rushing up to the police station. Both of them stopped dead in the middle of the sidewalk when they saw that Deputy Avery had locked the door. Sarah realized that her mother had a concerned look on her face, and she wondered for a second if something was wrong with Starling. She rolled down the car window in time to hear Avery say, "I was just heading over to the courthouse in Dobson. You'll have to come back later," and brush past them in a big hurry now to get into the car.

Sarah's mother turned around and saw her then, looked at her stupidly, and yelled, "Sarah," in the voice that warned Sarah she was about to fall off the swing set. The fellow Roy gripped Wilma's arm then, which she shook off absently. Avery was in the car now, was starting it up, and Wilma ran toward her. "Get out of that car," she said, angrily. She reached for the door handle. "This minute."

Nothing made Sarah angrier than being treated like a child. She locked the door and gave her mother a murderous glare as she rolled up the window. Honestly, to put up with this kind of nonsense. Wilma rapped on the window now, the diamond ring from her decades-dead husband clanging on the glass.

"I thought you said this was some kind of emergency," said Deputy Avery, anxious to go now that her irrational mother was making a scene.

"Yes, I'm ready," said Sarah. "Just don't run over her when we pull out into the street." Her mother was running around the front of the car now, ready to make an appeal to the deputy. When he waved her out of the way, she understood finally that they meant to leave. Sarah thought then that her mother was going to let her go on, but at the last minute Wilma put her hand up to the deputy to stop him and then grabbed open the rear door and threw herself into the backseat.

"Anyone else?" was all that the deputy said, and when no one replied he began to make a U-turn across Main Street to put them in the direction of Dobson.

"Deputy Avery, this is my mother. Mother, this is Deputy Avery," said Sarah. "He has been kind enough to give me a ride over to the courthouse. Harper is going over to get Jonah out of jail." As they headed out of town, Sarah saw that her mother's friend Roy had somehow gotten his own car turned around and was following them, inches from the policeman's back bumper.

In the backseat, Wilma, red-faced from exertion and anger, regarded her with an expression that seemed oddly more fearful than anything else. Sarah could not fathom what real or imagined danger her mother had conjured up in this situation. Did it have to do with accepting rides from strangers? Or maybe it was the rule against a lady tearing off to a courthouse where her husband and her lover would appear simultaneously. She supposed in Wilma's book maybe this kind of exposure was tantamount to wearing a white dress without a slip. Thirty. Sarah was thirty years old, and if her memory served her correctly, there was exactly one slip in her drawer in Santa Fe. It was black.

∽

What flashed most prominently through Wilma's mind as she tried to catch her breath in the backseat—aside from the terrifying fact that she was, quite possibly, being driven down Main Street by a cold-blooded killer—was that she was missing her pocketbook. It was a silly thought really. She knew that she had left her bag in Roy's car, and after all, he was not more than ten feet behind her, riding the patrol car's bumper like he was in the demolition derby. But still, she couldn't help it, it was like being without an arm or something. Every few seconds she would automatically feel around for it on the seat and find it gone again. It was distracting, probably her mind's way of keeping her from going completely crazy. She knew she had to think of what to do before something awful happened. She needed somehow to signal Sarah that there was a problem with Avery.

This was not going to be easy, though. Sarah had barely even looked her way since Wilma got into the car. It was just like her teenage years when Sarah would act like she barely knew Wilma. Right now, Sarah was more than embarrassed, she was probably plain mad, figuring her mother was about to butt into her business. Well, Wilma certainly was getting into her business, but this was different—there was some real danger here, this was nothing imagined.

She turned around to check on Roy. He was gripping his steering wheel with both hands and staring grimly ahead. The patrol car slowed down as it reached the stoplight at Main and Vine. Wilma leaned her face toward the back window and caught Roy's attention. He gave her a look of wishful concern, and shook his head at her like she really shouldn't have jumped into that car. Now look what you've done, his expression said, I'm going to have to chase you all the way across the county. She waved at him sheepishly and shrugged her shoulders, signaling, what else could I have done with my daughter in his car? I had to go along. And he nodded back, he understood, he forgave her. He looked so sweet just then that Wilma had almost entirely forgotten herself, and she was about to blow him a kiss when she felt the patrol car jerk forward. Avery had stepped on the gas and the car roared through the intersection even though the light was red. Out the back window, Wilma saw Roy's startled eyes for only a split second before another car crossed in front of him. Avery had entered the intersection just ahead of several cars coming across from the left side of the intersection. The patrol car made it through safely, but they left Roy in the dust.

Wilma could feel the fear tingling in her scalp, worse than a carelessly timed permanent. She glanced up at Sarah to see if she had gotten the clue. Sarah looked a little stunned as they sped down Main Street, but by the time they passed Wilma's house, she was looking over at Avery and laughing conspiratorially. "You are bad," she said to him in a flirtatious voice. "Running a red light, speeding. What kind of cop are you?"

"One that don't like no old farts tailgating me, that's what kind I am," he said, cutting his eyes over at her. They came to the light at Key Street, and thank God, Wilma noticed that he did intend to stop at this red light before making a left to go to Dobson. The light turned green before they had fully stopped, and to Wilma's alarm Avery roared the car forward, saying to Sarah, "In fact, just to make sure he don't catch up, we'll just take us the shortcut to the courthouse." Wilma looked back to see if Roy's car was in sight. She was hoping he would see that they didn't make the turn and be able to follow them somehow, but she couldn't see him at all. They were all the way out to the bypass now. Avery was heading for Cook School Road. That meant he intended to go all the way to Dobson on Ararat Road, which was no shortcut for sure. Lord, they could be an hour or more. How could she stand it that long, if they made it at all, if this sly fellow didn't throw the both of them into the river when they came to it?

Wilma tried to put a lid on her fear. No one was going in the river. The two in front seemed content to ride in a companionable silence. She reminded herself that this would be a dangerous situation if and only if she said the wrong thing—if she let on to Avery that she knew the whole story. So all she had to do was keep her mouth shut. She tried to direct her attention to the passing scene, pretend she was on a Sunday drive.

There were lots of small tobacco farms out here, each with a cluster of houses, one for each generation, each successive house uglier and less able to withstand the test of time than the one before. There was the usual blight of trailers, rusty cars, tacky yard art. For all the prefab metal and plastic introduced by this latest generation, Wilma noticed as their car rolled over the gentle hills, the country itself was still beautiful. As they came around a little bend, Wilma looked over to the left, out over a tobacco field with its little plants just set out. Plain in the distance was Swan's Knob, the ancient foothill of the Blue Ridge, its familiar silhouette—a ridge sloping gently to the top, then a section scooped out, almost like ice cream, it had always seemed to her, a scoop of the mountain lifted up and dumped again on the other side. Just the sight of it made her want to cry. She felt like she could almost reach out of the car window and put her hand over that little knob, hold on to the rock at the base and feel the topmost trees brush her palm.

They passed down a little hill and into a grove of trees, blocking the view of the mountain. They were gradually descending now. In a few miles they would cross the Ararat River. After that, it was at least fifteen, twenty miles to Dobson. No one had spoken in a while now. Wilma began to get that creeping anxiety that you get in church or some other quiet place now and then, that bizarre almost animal impulse to shout or to bolt and run. She knew the only thing that she had to do was stay quiet, but suddenly that seemed like an almost impossible task. Murderer! she wanted to scream. You did it! Control, she said to herself, just stay in control.

She tried to remain as still as possible, though her breathing alone made that hard, and then once she had started to think about her breathing, even that task seemed to take on a new urgency. Somehow her lungs wouldn't work right, and she needed to breathe deeper. She noticed that her heart was beating faster, too, which just alarmed her further and sent a new shot of adrenaline through her heart and then out to her whole body. She started to perspire beyond all belief, and breaking her vow of complete stillness, she reached for her pocketbook to get a Kleenex, but of course her pocketbook was not there either. It was in Roy's Thunderbird, somewhere on the other side of the county.

They were going down a steep grade now, with tall trees on either side. Kudzu had grown in a wall from the ground all the way to the tops of those trees, hemming their car into the narrow road, sucking all the air and light from the landscape. It must have been at this point that she started making a little wheezing noise and thrashing around slightly in the backseat because Sarah turned around and looked at her with alarm.

"My God, Mother, are you all right?" she said.

Wilma found that she could not spare the oxygen to reply.

"Mother? Mother, can you breathe?" Wilma would have been pleased by her concern had she not been preoccupied with trying to breathe.

"Oh my God, she looks like she's having a stroke or a heart attack or something," Sarah said to Avery.

It seemed to Wilma that what she most needed was a little air.

"Stop," she managed, "fresh air."

"Mother, we can't stop now. We are in the middle of nowhere. We need to get you some medical attention. Where's the nearest real hospital? It's Baptist, right, all the way to Winston."

"Pull over," Wilma said. They were out of the kudzu and she would see the bridge over the Ararat just up ahead.

"Won't hurt none to stop and check her out," said Avery, her unlikely ally. He slowed the car and turned onto a little dirt road that ran parallel to the river, an old lovers' lane, if Wilma remembered right.

"Shit, shit this podunk town," said Sarah as she jumped out of the car and threw open Wilma's door.

As soon as Wilma got a breath of air outside the car, she knew that she would not die. Two breaths more and she felt her heart slowing down. Just nerves, thank God, though it was embarrassing to admit it. Sarah and Avery were staring at her intently, so she tried to think fast. "Carsick," she said. "Had it all my life."

"Are you sure, Mother?" Sarah did not look convinced and put her hand up to Wilma's brow. Avery just shook his head and turned to walk down to the river. Wilma stood up and walked away from the car so that she could watch him out of the corner of her eye. Sarah followed nervously at her elbow, fighting the impulse, Wilma thought, to take her arm.

"Are you going to throw up?" Sarah whispered.

"No, really, I'm feeling better," said Wilma, wishing that Sarah would move aside so that she could keep Avery in view.

"At least sit down a minute, for God's sake. You sounded like you were dying a minute ago." Sarah pointed to a group of old stumps and a bare log in a little clearing opposite the car. It looked like some kind of campsite. There was a small fire pit in the middle surrounded with river rocks and a little kindling stacked up nearby. "We used to come here in high school," Sarah said, adding her tight little laugh. "Looks like someone is still using it. Not the usual place to bring your mother."

Wilma tried to laugh along with her, though she was still too scared to say much. She looked around for a place to sit, decided on the highest stump. She concentrated on balancing on it, wondering vaguely if her hose would snag when she finally stood up. She checked on Avery again, who seemed to be doing nothing more than throwing stones into the river.

When she turned back to Sarah, Sarah seemed to be staring into an imaginary fire in the burnt wood and ashes in the center of the ring. She was sitting on an old log, closer to the ground than Wilma, slumped forward with her hands on her knees—the crumpled crouch of the young. For all her concern a moment earlier, she seemed oddly far away from Wilma now, thinking about something. She pushed a lock of hair behind her ears and traced it through with the tips of her fingers. She looked up finally at Wilma. "Better?"

"Much better. Fine," said Wilma. They would be leaving in a moment, and Wilma wondered if maybe she should try to warn Sarah while Avery was over by the river, but she quickly dismissed the idea—too much to explain, and even if she could tell Sarah, there was no sense in both of them having a nervous breakdown. She hoped that Roy was driving directly to the courthouse instead of searching the countryside for the patrol car. That way, maybe he would have time to explain their theory about Avery. Maybe he would have the whole thing straightened out by the time the patrol car arrived. It was too much to hope for, really. Even if he told them and even if they believed him, they were still likely to get all excited, and then Lord knows what might happen when Avery pulled up with Sarah and Wilma in the car. Wilma felt her heart beating again. Maybe she should say something to Sarah just to keep her back out of the way if there was gunfire or something at the courthouse.

"Sarah," Wilma whispered, "before we get back in the car, honey, there's something I want to tell you. It's important." Sarah looked up at Wilma and for just a second, Wilma saw her little girl again—clear eyes, brown as acorns, guileless in that moment, eyes waiting without blinking to see if Wilma intended to scold or to praise. Wilma paused, as she had on that day years ago, that day when she had been forced, however gently, however civilly, to introduce the obscene world to her daughter's heart. On her stump here years later, she found herself as mute as the day that Sarah's father had died, as reluctant perhaps, and then finally, as resigned: "Honey, when we get to the courthouse in a few minutes—now this may not make sense to you but I beg you to listen. When we get there, we just need to lay low. Do you understand me? We cannot jump out and go rushing around. We just need to calmly get out of the car and then get out of the way. Understood?"

Sarah blinked, in confusion maybe, and then looked quickly back at the fire pit, like Wilma had just delivered some kind of reprimand. Wilma braced herself for Sarah's cynical half laugh and the brush-off: "Really, mother, what are you talking about?" she was going to say. And she was way too old for Wilma to reply, "Never you mind. Do what I tell you. Trust me."

"Trust me," Wilma said out loud. "We've got to stay out of it."

Sarah did not look back at her, but put her face in her hands. "That's just it," she said. "I can't stay out of it. I'm right in the middle of it all." She began to cry. Wilma was wholly unprepared for this. She wondered wildly if Sarah knew the whole story and was somehow mixed up in it.

"Mother, I am so sorry," Sarah said, still crying, not looking at Wilma. "This whole mess is my fault. I am so sorry I have dragged you into it."

This was the way Sarah had reacted to the news about her father. "What did I do?" she had asked, first thing, and then weeks later, "What did you do?"

"Honey, all this trouble has nothing to do with you. You didn't murder the man," said Wilma softly.

"Oh, the policeman's murder, well, you're right about that, thank God," said Sarah. "It wasn't Jonah who did it, but that didn't stop his arrest on your front porch. And now Harper's had to go over to the courthouse to try and vouch for him. God knows who really did kill the man that night. I'm just sorry that me and all my trouble showed up in town at the same time."

"Trouble. You're not trouble," said Wilma automatically.

"Mother, I'm *in* big trouble," said Sarah, starting to cry again. "Isn't that what they used to say about a girl? She's 'in trouble.' That boy got her 'in trouble.' "

"In trouble? You mean you're pregnant?" said Wilma, hoping she had misunderstood, hoping she was not going to have to take this news and act right about it sitting out here on this stump.

Sarah looked up at her finally and just nodded her head, like a little girl again, hoping Wilma could fix it. She wiped tears away with the back of her hand.

"Well, that's not so bad," Wilma managed finally. "Starling will love having a brother or sister." She tried to manage a smile but couldn't because she had a hunch it was not that simple at all.

"Right," said Sarah, "everything's just hunky-dory. Great story for the bridge club, Mother." There was a silence while Wilma tried to absorb the return of the grown-up, angry Sarah, the return of her own not knowing what to say to make things right again. Wilma looked toward the river. Avery was way over on the bridge itself, looking down into the water.

"You always do this," said Sarah. She had picked up a stick and was breaking it into little pieces and throwing them onto the burned-out fire pit.

"Do what?" said Wilma "What did I say? Only that Starling would enjoy a sibling. What's wrong with that? Isn't that much true?"

"Half true maybe." Sarah was back to her nervous laugh again, but she couldn't stop the tears coming either.

"So the baby's Jonah's," Wilma ventured, but Sarah just dropped her head between her knees like the school nurse made you do if you felt faint. "Harper's?"

Sarah raised her head then and looked right into Wilma's face. When she did, Wilma was almost thrown off her seat—because in that first second and for several thereafter, it was not Sarah who was looking back at her. There he was, plain as day, Harry Mabry, looking at her from across the breakfast table, peering up over the business section on that last morning of his life. Not Sarah, Harry. It made Wilma want to cry, for she recognized that forlorn and quizzical expression. The lift in the left brow, the slight downturn of the eyes—she remembered it now precisely. How had she possibly forgotten it, how had she possibly hidden this memory, this very last glance that Harry had given her? It was hard to bear, both of them staring out at her through one pair of eyes, each wondering, trying to decide. This time, Wilma could see that there was a question curled up in the lip, bitten back by the teeth. This time it was Sarah, wanting to know—*Can I tell her? Can I possibly tell her?*

Yes, Wilma wanted to say, yes, you can tell me. She fought this time her animal need to look away; she did not even blink. She held her breath and leaned forward. Sarah leaned in too, finally. "I don't know," she said. "Either one of them could be the father. There's no telling which." Wilma was not sure whether it was sympathy or gratitude that kept her from speaking. Sarah dropped her head back down. Wilma leaned over to put her hand on Sarah's shoulder.

"Hey, I thought it was your mama that was sick." Avery was close enough behind Wilma that the sound of his voice made her jump.

"Go away. Can you just leave us alone here for a minute?" It was out of her mouth before she could stop it. She looked quickly at the man to see if she had set him off, but he looked as chastened as a third-grader who had not practiced her scales.

"All right, for Christ's sake. I just thought she was in an almighty hurry here," he said, flicking his head over toward Sarah. "I'll just wait in the car. You ladies come on when you're ready, I guess."

"Thank you so much. We'll just be a minute," Wilma called after him. Sarah kept her head down, trying to hide her crying. This was the place, right here, where Wilma would normally stand up, brush off her skirt, and give Sarah some pithy advice that involved ignoring plain facts, steering the course of her own life and moving right along. If that wasn't sufficient to fix things, then she might suggest a little heavy gardening or, God help her, a makeover. Beyond that, Wilma knew that she was generally relieved to be interrupted in such conversations, even by a known murderer. It was a sad fact that she would rather get back in the car with Deputy Avery than offer any real advice about this paternity business or anything else. But somehow, sitting here by this river with the raw edge of the stump scraping the back of her thighs, slap dab in the middle of this ridiculous situation, advice escaped her once and for all and she couldn't do a thing but sit by her daughter. Strangely, this seemed to help them both, for after a little time there, Wilma noticed, Sarah had recovered a bit and was wiping her face off with her sleeve and sniffing.

Avery climbed back into the patrol car and began to fiddle loudly with his keys. When this was all over, Wilma resolved, she would think what to say—just the right words of comfort this time, not advice. It was comfort that was always in short supply, really, and that was the thing about a child, about her child—her very presence in the world lent Wilma comfort. She would find a way to return the favor, maybe tell Sarah some big secret of her own, if she could think of one. In the meantime, Wilma realized, she could at least begin by leveling with Sarah about the little pickle they were in. She sat up straight and plastered a smile on her face and held it there for Avery to see. "Sarah, honey," she said, barely daring to move her mouth or change her expression in any way. "Listen real good to me, because we just have a second here. That man Avery is the one who murdered Clem Baker."

"What?" Sarah was about to stand up until Wilma put a hand on her knee.

"Shh. Don't move," Wilma said, still smiling and cutting her eyes over to the car, where Avery was trying out different positions for his hands on the steering wheel. "Just stay real calm and let me tell you what we're going to do. We'll just go to the courthouse with him and walk in like nothing's wrong at all. Like I said before, remember, all we have to do is stay out of the way."

"Are you sure?" said Sarah. "He really did this?"

"Pretty sure," said Wilma.

Avery had found the horn and laid on it for a moment.

"Oh God," said Sarah. "We're riding with him. This can't be right. Why are we riding with him?"

"You were in the car with him," said Wilma. "Remember? Back on Main Street. I tried to tell you. Come on now. We have to get back in." She stood up finally, glad at least to get off the stump, but Sarah remained planted on her campfire log.

"Wait," she said. "This is crazy. Let's just stay right here."

"No, we can't let him get wind of this." Wilma was hissing through her teeth now, still trying to maintain a smile. She grasped Sarah's hand and pulled her to her feet.

"Wait," said Sarah again. "You stay here. I'll go. I'll say you're still sick."

"He's not going to leave me here," said Wilma, "that wouldn't be right."

"God, Mother. He's got manners now?"

"Shh. Just do what I say," said Wilma quickly in a voice she hadn't used in a while. Sarah got to her feet finally and looked at her mother. As they moved toward the car, Wilma raised her voice and said, "Here we are finally, Deputy Avery, we're both okay. We're just hunky-dory. Let's go."

"Why did you get in the car anyway, whatever possessed you?" said Sarah.

Avery opened his door and got out again and began banging on the hood of the car. "Ladies. . . ."

"Because," whispered Wilma, taking Sarah's hand, leaning

against her as if she were still recovering from her bout of carsickness. "Because I'm your mother."

"I'll go in the front seat," Wilma said as they got to the car. She sat down before Sarah could object. "I'm less apt to get carsick up here." It was best that Sarah have a little time to get used to their circumstances sitting in the backseat. Besides, it was Wilma's job to keep a close eye on Avery, just to make sure that he behaved. They crossed the bridge over the Ararat. Wilma noticed that the river was wider than she remembered it—must be all the spring rains. It was amazing, now that Wilma thought about it, that most everybody, even the smallest child, had the capacity to carry on with life: to bake a cake, fold up a bath towel, add up a column of numbers, to climb right on back into a car—to do all these little normal things in the worst of times. You could do it even when you were scared out of your wits, even when your heart was breaking. Right after Harry died, people used to ask Wilma, how do you stand it? How can you keep going? She always wanted to ask them, well, what do you want me to do? Lay down on the floor and cry? She also wanted to ask, to ask Harry, how it was that somehow he got the lid off his life and couldn't get it back on.

Avery seemed to be in a more jovial mood now that they were on their way again. He hummed to himself for a few seconds, then turned around to them and said, "I wonder if either of you two ever heard how it was the Ararat River got its name?"

"From Noah," said Sarah. Thankfully she sounded fairly normal. "Mount Ararat is where the ark came to rest." Wilma thought that maybe, just maybe they could make it to the courthouse without incident.

"Naw," said Avery, "that's something different. My cousin told me this story. I'd forgotten it until I was standing up on that bridge. It seemed this old country fellow was a-fishing from the bridge one day, and another fellow, he came by and inquired as to what was biting. The fisherman answers him, says, 'I ain't had nary a fish on the line, my friend,' says he, 'I hadn't even seen a fish all morning, but I tell you I've seen dozens and dozens of big ole rats running on the banks of this here river.' And his friend, he says to the fisherman, says, 'Well, have you caught you ary a rat?' Get it? *Ary a rat.* The Ararat River, that's how it come to be named."

Avery laughed at his joke then, and looked over at Wilma, who would have laughed louder if she hadn't felt a little sorry for this ignorant man who was going to be locked up, God willing, within the hour.

"Ararat," Avery said again, checking his mirror to see Sarah's reaction. Sarah laughed quickly to appease him. "Did you see *ary* a one today?" he said, looked at the mirror again.

"Well," said Sarah, "I must say that I like that story more than Noah's ark, really."

"Now what does that have to do with Ararat, again?" said Avery. As Sarah began to recount the story of the flood, trying to distract the man, Wilma began to feel optimistic for the first time since she had gotten into the patrol car. They were, after all, only a few minutes from Dobson. She stretched her legs a bit and tried to cross them at the ankles, but her left heel knocked up against something heavy on the floorboard.

"There are still stories," Sarah was saying, "that the ark is still there, preserved in ice on the top of Mount Ararat." Wilma looked down and saw a black leather case. Sarah said, "But the mountain itself is so remote and the weather is so bad for most of the year . . ." After a moment, Wilma realized that the case wedged up against her foot in fact held a gun, a police service revolver. She jerked her foot away, thankful that the gun had not blown her foot off when she nudged it. She was not about to say a word to Avery—maybe he didn't even know it was there. They were driving into Dobson now, and Wilma said a quick prayer that cool heads would prevail at the courthouse. She looked around at Sarah, who smiled at her as if she were reassuring a child. As they approached the town square, Wilma herself wondered what was about to happen, and at the last minute, she thought of what to say. She turned and looked at Sarah. "I love you, honey," she said, and turned right back around as they pulled up in front of the courthouse. There was a little crowd on the sidewalk and Wilma could see Roy, Harper and Chief Henry among the men. At first Wilma was relieved to see that Avery had pulled the car up on the wrong side of the street, so that his side of the car was against the curb. This way, she thought, the chief can just open the door and grab him. Then she saw in a flash that four or five policemen were waiting on the other side of the street—they had expected for Avery to come up the street the other way and park legally. Oddly, this struck her as funny, and she was starting to laugh when she noticed all five men rush across the street with their hands on their holstered guns, their eyes wild with fear. In the seat next to her, Avery saw this too and understood immediately. Wilma could see the killer in him now, his whole body tensed with an animal anger.

"Sarah!" Wilma screamed. It was the only warning possible, for in that same split second, Avery dove down to the floorboard in front of her seat. The gun. He wanted the gun. There was no time to do anything, let alone think, and before she knew it she had kicked him, and kicked him again, just kicked the fire out of him, and he yelped and reared back and was holding his nose, and she heard Sarah screaming in the backseat. Then there were hands in the car, three or four pairs of them, pulling on Avery shirt and shoulder, hand and foot, yanking him out of the car. In the next breath, it was all over. He was handcuffed and gone.

After that, Wilma heard mostly a roaring in her ears. She could hear Sarah calling out from the back faintly, "What happened? What happened?" and she could hear Roy, asking if she was all right. She knew enough to nod her head for him, yes, she was okay, but everything seemed muted, covered with a blanket of white noise. She found that what she wanted to do most was just to sit where she was. She needed just a few moments to adjust. She saw that somehow Roy understood this and was holding back the Rescue Squad, the police, and God knows who else. Sarah, she saw, had been persuaded to get out of the car and was waiting for Wilma just outside her window. Wilma found now that she could smile at her Sarah and found too that it was no trouble at all to reach up and take her perfect hand.

Chapter Fifteen

*H*arper tried to stand as close as he could to the stone bench on the courthouse lawn where Sarah sat with her mother, tried to stay in Sarah's line of vision in case she needed him for something. At the moment, though, there were too many people hovering around Sarah and her mother, checking to make sure they weren't hurt, asking questions. Some brave fireman even attempted to put a blanket over Miss Wilma's shoulders, but he was quickly rebuffed.

The whole scene was a little out of control as far as Harper was concerned, but he had to admit there had been a few tense minutes before, waiting for the car. He was not entirely convinced that Roy had gotten his facts straight, but everyone else in the courtroom had jumped on the bandwagon the minute Roy had told his story. Harper was just relieved some redneck cop had not started shooting wildly when the guy had driven up to the curb with Wilma and Sarah in the patrol car. It was obvious these people did not handle real criminals every day.

There was a carnival-like chaos across the entire town square. The poor suspect—broken nose and all—had been led away by a contingent of five policemen several minutes ago, but still, things were not about to settle down. What most people in these parts would call a crowd gathered on the surrounding sidewalks: tired women with their children, car mechanics from the Chevy place in their coveralls, court employees, teenagers on bikes. That's what you got in a place where the last excitement downtown was the Christmas parade—people came out to enjoy the pageantry of a crisis.

Chief Henry loudly supervised the remaining policemen as they ransacked their own police car. "Everything is evidence, boys," he was saying. The Rescue Squad was standing by, each man smoking and adding his bit of detail to the tale of the big arrest.

For his own part, Harper was more relaxed than he had been in days. Sarah was safe—if she had ever actually been in danger—from this Avery character. What's more, Harper had to believe that Jonah would not be bothering them anymore. When Harper had appeared before the judge and told him, very convincingly he thought, that the dude had not even been in Swan's Knob at the time of the murder, that was the end of it. The judge had frowned real sternly at Chief Henry and the SBI boys, and then he had let Jonah go. Harper had to admit it: Jonah had been properly grateful to him. The minute they had taken the handcuffs off him, he had walked straight over to Harper. Under the circumstances, Harper found it easy to be gracious, especially since Jonah wanted to know where he could catch the first bus out of town. Hell, Harper had offered him an extra twenty for the road. He told the dude, sure thing, he'd give Sarah a message. Sure, he would tell Sarah that Jonah would see her back in Santa Fe. Jonah had walked out of the courthouse still rubbing his wrists. That was a full ten minutes before Roy had shown up with his story about this jealous twin brother.

Sarah was motioning for him now. She wanted something to drink and then she wanted him to call the house and check on Starling. Harper was happy, more than happy to oblige.

Roy had always wondered what it would be like to pack a bunch of kids in a station wagon and take off on a long vacation down to Florida. He felt a bit like that now—the big daddy with his big car driving the whole family down the highway. It was nice having Wilma and Sarah and Harper all packed in around him, safe and sound, especially after the scare they'd had. Wilma didn't have much to say, but she seemed to appreciate his efforts to get the climate control just right, to turn on the radio at a low volume. He sank contently against his nice leather seat—soft as butter, the salesman had said, like butter, like butter.

Wilma looked down at her cordovan Aigner pump. The shoe wasn't even scratched, but inside her big toe was still stinging. She felt a little bit bad about kicking the man so hard, especially when she saw them taking him away with his nose all bleeding down his face, but she knew in her heart that the first kick had been no more than a reflex, the second and third kicks, well, they had seemed necessary at the time. That man had been going to shoot them all. Sarah was right there. She was glad she had stopped him, glad that she hadn't even had time to consider what to do.

She was just happy that the whole thing was over and that she was riding home in Roy's car—she hoped she would never see the inside of a police car again. Roy was steering the car like a riverboat captain in a wide channel. He smiled at her from the driver's seat—nothing to worry about, folks—and leaned down to turn on his radio. It was tuned to a Mount Airy station that played easy-listening music. Unfortunately, floating along in Roy's hermetically sealed boat listening to string arrangements of Beatles songs was about as soothing as a trip to the dentist, as far as Wilma was concerned. She figured she must have about a quart of adrenaline still running through her veins because the sound of "Let It Be" played at half-tempo was making that Aigner pump feel like it would just punch through the floorboard.

To distract herself, Wilma tried to think about going with Roy on a weekend trip, the kind of thing where she might wear a smart pantsuit and maybe sunglasses. She pictured them driving down to Kitty Hawk, rolling the windows down as they crossed the last bridge over the Intercoastal Waterway, and driving straight out on the sand. She looked over at Roy, admired his profile (she had never minded a Roman nose). He sensed this somehow and reached his hand out for hers without looking away from the road. At first she felt soothed by the warm pressure of his grasp, but after a few minutes she was thinking about this hand and how it would feel pressed against her bare back, smoothing down her shoulders. This train of thought, rather than soothe her, began to make her jumpy again, made her feel the closeness of the space. She reminded herself that as recently as an hour ago she had experienced a full-blown anxiety attack, followed by what she would only call a brush with death. It was natural to want to thrash around in one's seat.

Shortly, even the floating motion of the expensive suspension system began to agitate her, and she was looking out at the road, hoping for a couple of railroad tracks or some rough pavement to break up the smoothness of it all, when she heard a new song come gliding into the car. "Let It Be" had somehow modulated itself into "Bridge Over Troubled Water" and an easy-listening choir was beginning the chorus, "Like a briiiidge ooover trou-uh . . ." Wilma dove on the radio tuning knob and crashed through ten seconds of static, preachers, and country music before finding the Wake Forest University station at the far end of the dial. This was the place where she usually found classical music, but today everything was haywire and they were playing jazz instead. She nearly turned the thing off, but after a few bars—it sounded like a little quartet with a saxophone out front—she decided this might be just what she needed.

Wilma did not listen to this music often, but once in a while she did turn on the clock radio late at night when she was having trouble sleeping. They had an announcer with a deep mellow voice and music like this piece that started out neatly with a simple melodic line that the musicians repeated among themselves, as if saying, "This, this is it. Do you get it?" It seemed to Wilma not so different from a symphony, an idea introduced, discussed, elaborated upon. But as she listened today in Roy's car with terror and relief running up and down her body and most everyone she loved or almost loved wrapped up safe in the car around her, she heard the music with a strange acuteness, as if it had been composed to accompany that very moment. The simple melody exploded there into a full-out jam and divided into a thousand pieces. Wilma could hear each fragment played out by one or another of the instruments. It was almost as if she could hear at once the minds of all the players following the music out to the ends of the earth, playing without one second's thought of finding their way back. She felt herself relaxing further and further into the music herself, waiting for the moment toward the end when they would, as they say, bring it all back home, which they did, of course.

Wilma looked over at Captain Roy, whose hands remained at ten and two o'clock on the wheel, whose smile had nothing to do with the music and everything to do with driving them all down the road in calmness and comfort. This calm was a good thing, judging from her daughter's pale presence in the backseat. It occurred to Wilma that Sarah hadn't eaten in several hours. This was not good at all, considering. No wonder she looked pale. Wilma pulled her compact out of her pocketbook—which had been in Roy's car the whole time. She snuck a look at her own face. Of course her lipstick was gone completely, and her forehead was as shiny as a headlight.

Sarah could feel a river of sweat pouring down the center of her back, a delayed reaction, she supposed, to all the mayhem back at the courthouse. She was still trying to get a grip on the entire situation. It had all happened so fast. One minute, she was sitting out by the river confessing to her mother, *her mother,* something she'd never intended to tell anyone, and then they were zooming up to the courthouse and kerpow—Wilma was pulling some wild kung fu maneuver, subduing an apparent murderer while half the county stood around with their mouths hanging open. And now, there was her mother, just sitting up in the front seat calmly patting this man Roy's hand. Sarah wondered if her confession had somehow escaped Wilma's memory in all of the shuffle. Surely she could have plenty to say later, though for a moment there at the river . . .

Wilma relinquished Roy's hand now, put it back in his lap with a quick smile and began fixing her hair like she had just come away from a windy croquet match. It was uncanny. Sarah had seen Wilma more upset over a run in her stocking. Now that she thought about it, though, this was typical of her mother—hysterics over a ruined pair of sandal foot Hanes, utter calm when one is attacked by a murderer, complete stalwartness when one's husband scatters his brains across the garden. Wilma was applying lipstick now, holding her mirror so Roy wouldn't catch her in the act, the gesture of a thousand car rides of Sarah's childhood. First, a careful coat of L'Oreal Luscious Berry to her top lip, up and around the cupid's bow, quick swipe of the full bottom lip, out of the corners, and then here it came, Sarah could see it in the mirror: press pucker, press pucker, press. Satisfied, Wilma tilted the mirror to survey the rest of her face, and then she slowly angled it to sneak a look into the backseat.

Their eyes met there in the mirror, and Sarah realized for the second time that day, neither of them looked away. It was just long enough for Sarah to register Wilma's sad smile that said *Oh honey, I have not forgotten what you told me and I am as sorry as I can be.* It was all there just for a moment, then her mother reset her expression into the life-goes-on-let's-get-on-with-it position. There, Sarah thought, I've caught her, I've caught her in the act. I've caught the whole and irreplaceable act of Wilma Mabry. For the rest of her life, Sarah would puzzle about which parts of this bizarre and arcane heritage she might herself embody. She did not think that she could take to wearing panty hose or opaque lip color, but she did hope that somewhere inside she would find her mother's ability to put one foot in front of the other. And all those layers of subterfuge—the politeness and the mirrors—she could use a little bit of that too right now, because she desperately needed to know what had happened to Jonah.

She could not think of a good way to ask about him. One of the policemen had said he'd been cleared—Harper had done that much—but she had not seen him in the crowd and no one at the courthouse seemed to know where he had gone to. While the rest of the assembled officials fussed over Wilma, she had walked all the way around the courthouse, hoping to find him waiting for her, tucked behind one of the old columns of the south entrance, perhaps. She hurried up the sidewalk, hoping to see Jonah among the stream of people that came out the doors in twos and threes, relieved of their business with the court, perhaps, possessing a new permit or a commuted sentence. She sorted through the pasty white faces, the black ones, the gimme caps, the crew cuts and the blondes—looking for his face, knowing it would shine out at her any moment. And when after a few minutes she didn't see him, she wandered back around the building and sat down on the marble courthouse steps. It was then that she knew finally that she had made up her mind—maybe she had known even before she left Santa Fe.

In the scheme of things, maybe it didn't matter where Jonah was off to. Maybe he would be waiting on her mother's front porch, maybe he was headed back out West. Maybe none of this mattered in the end, but still, she had to know. She looked over at Harper, who seemed mostly to be listening to the radio. It didn't seem right, after everything, to ask him directly, so she said,

levely, "So I guess everything went well in court? You cleared . . .
everything up for them?"

Harper had wondered when she'd ask. He tried to groove for
a moment on the Stan Getz number that was blasting through the
back speakers, hoping to stall until he could collect his thoughts.
At least they were out of Dobson and there was no chance of
spotting a forlorn lover waiting for the bus. Getz sure could sell a
song. Harper would bet the man could just blow in a chick's ear
and she'd follow him anywhere. He must be, in his fifties by now?
Just blowing in the chicks' ears.

He said, "I've gotten it all settled, babe. I just told them about
where we were that night. They asked me a few questions, the
name of the truck stop, what it was we ate. I even had the gas re-
ceipt. The judge just looked mad. He frowned at the chief and
ordered him to let Jonah go."

"And Jonah?" said Sarah. She was looking out the window.
Harper couldn't see her face, so he couldn't tell if she was just
faking the casual tone. He didn't dare look at her either.

"Oh, Jonah was relieved the whole thing was over. He was in
a real hurry to split town, which is what he should have done in
the first place, if you ask me."

"So did he go? I think he left his backpack at Mother's house,"
she said. "Maybe he'll stop by to get it."

"Doubt it. He asked about where to catch the next bus out."

"Oh," she said quietly, "did he say anything else?"

"Anything?"

"Did he say anything, like a message to me or where he was
going?" An expression crossed her face just then, one that he had
not seen for a long time. Her forehead smoothed out, her eyes
sparked open with the kind of bare hopefulness that you see only
from the very young. This warmed him briefly, until it sunk in that
all that energy and expectation was for the other guy, the one who
would do her no good, the one who would take her away.

Harper took a deep breath and stared straight into all that expectation, and said, "A message? No, no message. He didn't say where he was going, really, just said he was going to split pronto." Every bit of it a lie, Harper knew, but a strategic one. And it had a high probability of success.

In that moment, Sarah discovered that she had in fact in ten years of marriage learned something after all: the truth was always plain as day on Harper's face. All you had to do was ignore every word that he said. Jonah's departing message was written in the twitch of Harper's jaw and in the first barely-visible wrinkle that was crossing his forehead just now. Jonah had given him a message, all right, and it was one that Harper would not deliver. And Harper's lie . . . well, it occurred to Sarah that she had been waiting for quite some time for a lie like the miserable specimen he had just told. Here she had been spending her days traveling in the mountains, brooding in her mother's house, swimming around in the cold soup of the psyche, trying to figure out what to do, when all she really needed was for this man to make her good and mad just one more time.

Here she had been waiting for some big revelation, when in truth Harper had been gone from her—or maybe they had left one another—quite a while back. She had been on the lookout for a cataclysm, some single hideous act to pin on him. She had just failed to notice the real death knell, the slow leak of his departure. All of the struggle, the Sturm and Drang, had been replaced over time by a subtle absence, one in which Harper had drifted in and out of town, quietly getting up at dawn, gone to the Hopi lands with his tape recorder, back down the next day through the Shawnee country, and without incident over to the casinos on to Albuquerque, then back home reading the paper and listening to who knows what on his earphones (music he had picked up along the way? old jazz masters? torch songs? She had stopped asking), until three in the morning, bothering no one, and then out at dawn again and again without a harsh word or inopportune event, taking nothing, leaving nothing behind.

Wilma felt sorry, in a way, to hear that Jonah had gone and a little disappointed that he had left without fighting for Sarah. What a sad moment for Sarah. Here Jonah had come all this way for her, full of ardor, but in the end he hadn't been able to follow through. In the backseat, Sarah said nothing, what could she say? Wilma admitted this to herself, though: all in all, Jonah's departure was a tidier outcome. Sarah may not see it this way now, but here was her chance to move on. She would get over it, and she could concentrate on having a healthy pregnancy. Then Sarah would have the baby, and it would be Harper's baby now, by default. There would be no question about that, if she played her cards right. Still . . . What was wrong with her? She felt horribly disappointed for Sarah, really. She realized that somehow over these past few days, she had begun rooting for Jonah, wanting him for her daughter. Surely that was not the proper response, breaking up a family—what was she thinking?—there was Starling, the new baby. . . .

Butter, butter, soft as butter. Roy thought he would take them all out to dinner tonight. The Coach House, it was fish fry night. No, Ray's. He would take them up to Ray's Starlight. Was there a combo there on the weekend these days? Maybe he could persuade Wilma to dance with him. It had been a rough day, to be sure, but, hey, maybe this would get her mind off of things. He would put his arms around her and pull her close. He'd whisper in her ear and tell her what he'd been thinking about all day.

Sarah felt Harper's arm reach around behind her. He cupped her shoulder with his hand and began to massage it slowly with his palm and fingers. Harper leaned his body into hers and began to breathe lightly on her neck. Years ago, this secret gesture would have made her melt in the seat. Even last week she would have seen it as a return to tenderness and put a mark in the column in Harper's favor. But at this moment, after everything, it seemed ridiculously presumptuous. Harper leaned his head over toward her like he might actually want to kiss her now. And suddenly, every bit of Harper, the heat of his body and his breath, was as unwelcome as the big sweaty man with greasy hair who had forced himself in the seat next to Starling last week on the bus when Sarah was in the bathroom. Sarah had gotten the sleaze-bag out of the seat with a single evil stare, but she had smelled him for the rest of the trip. Here next to Harper, she had an identical reaction: she wanted to get to her mother's house, get out of the car and wash the remnants of his scent down the drain. She knew from that moment on, he was poison—every word, every gesture. She was done. It was no longer a matter of choosing. Jonah or no Jonah, Harper was gone. Done.

"Honey," said her mother, "do we need to stop and get you something to eat? I remember early on when you were expecting Starling you needed to eat every hour or two or you felt sick."

Wilma knew the second she asked the question that she had gone and let the cat out of the bag. There was complete silence in the backseat. She didn't dare turn around. She thought for a moment about how she might qualify the question so that no one would get the wrong idea, but it was too late.

"Well, there's some news I didn't know," said Roy. "Sarah making you a grandmother again, is she? Well, isn't that fine." Wilma closed her eyes. She never did this sort of thing, never, never, and surely not to her own daughter. She was always the one to think poorly of someone who put her foot in her mouth.

Harper did not realize the force of his grip on her shoulder until Sarah let out a muted "Ow" and shrugged his hand away. He looked quickly at her belly and then up to her face. There was nothing in either place to give him a clue. Shit. Roy looked over his shoulder at Harper and winked. "Hoping for a little-leaguer?" he said.

It took him a minute to take it in. Déjà-fucking-vu. Shit. Could this woman ever get her biological act together? That was what came to him first, because for Christ's sake the whole thing with Starling had been when they were kids, really, easy to get things mixed up. But now he had to wonder how this sort of thing could happen by accident. There were pills and things. He looked back over at Sarah. Had he misunderstood? That part of her face that he could see was flushed and she would not look at him, even when he ducked down in front of her to catch her gaze. Panic—pure and simple—began rising from the middle of his gut. By the time it reached the base of his neck and began creeping in the form of pinpricks up his scalp, he had made the old calculation. It was not impossible. In fact, it was entirely possible, damnit. Déjà-fucking-vu, he could almost hear the tune that went with the words now. Déjà, déjà, déjà. He could write the song, hell, he could play it on the spot. It played right there in his head. He could play it all day and he would come back to the same place he had been those ten years ago: he would not back out on her. What was a little uncertainty, a little indiscretion, right? Shit, why not? He had done it before. Why the hell not? This might be just what they needed to pull the whole thing back together.

"You a baseball fan?" Roy was grinning.

"Absolutely, a little-leaguer would be just great," said Harper. "Only it would be just fine with me if he had a little more height on him than me and maybe a better arm."

"You can always hope," said Roy.

Sarah could not believe it. After years of discretion, nothing but discretion in Wilma's past, really—years of tight lips, tongue biting, cryptic pleasantries, oh dear, yes, I see, what next, what is this world coming to really, and my goodness, I see, well, I see, uh-huh, uh-huh, well, well I see—her mother had been perfectly discreet. But now, here—she opens her newly Luscious Berry'd lips—and this. This, only minutes after Sarah thought she had glimpsed the depth and breadth of her mother. Up in the front seat, Wilma sat stone still with perfect posture, but Sarah could feel in the very air a distinct electric charge. It held her mother's mortification. Wilma had caught her mistake the moment it exited her mouth. Sarah tried to work up the energy to be really deeply angry with her, but she could not muster it. In the continued silence she was aware mostly of the encroaching presence of Harper, who was literally vibrating in the seat next to her, bending like a dancer in an effort to catch her eye, every inch of him absurdly vibrating in time to the jazz tune that was heating up on the radio.

She shifted in the seat and tried to look out the window, to count the trailers and yard art. Harper would want, she knew suddenly, to fix up the situation. He would want to say something to make it all better, to lead her back home to Santa Fe. He would want for them to forgive each other as children forgive negligent parents—hoping, always hoping for the worst to be gone, for a new fancy and perfect life to be starting, for all the bad old bears and broken glass to be gone forever. Sarah saw it clearly now. In this moment Harper possessed all of the hope and willingness of a child, but he was no more capable of providing real sustenance than the crazy old bear of her childhood. Harper might love her, he surely loved Starling and maybe even this inconvenient baby, but Sarah knew now that sooner or later, in one way or another, he would leave them to fend for themselves.

Harper had finally tired of trying to get her attention. He had settled back in the seat and was staring out the window, absently fingering notes on an invisible trumpet. Always practicing. They had crossed back over the Ararat River bridge now and would soon be back at her mother's house. Starling would be waiting for them—Starling, of the soulful eyes, dark brown eyes copied directly from her father (Sarah had thought when she wanted to comfort herself). Starling had a way of focusing on a person, looking deep into your eyes when she wanted something badly— candy, a new blouse, or permission for a sleep-over. Harper had that same look, and whether Starling had inherited or acquired it through living with Harper, it was difficult for Sarah to resist in either of them. Sarah could not fathom truly leaving Harper if she thought simultaneously about those eyes. The simple memory of Starling's face pulled Sarah inexorably into the simple arithmetic of family: mother, father, child. Starling was their pivot point, once and forever their child. Sarah would not change that, Starling would see. They would always be her parents, but this much would change—Sarah was going to leave Harper.

Roy rolled his Thunderbird up in the driveway. The crunch of his tires on the gravel satisfied him mightily. Maybe this was not the time to bring up dinner and dancing at the Starlight. Wilma had been quiet most of the way back. Of course she had to be tired out after her ordeal. He was glad at least he had been able to supply some comfortable upholstery for the ride home.

Tomorrow morning, Sarah decided, the three of them would pack up the car and leave Swan's Knob. This much they would do quietly, without a fuss. She and Harper would take Starling and they would leave this place. Along the way, Sarah would make them see that it was all for the best. Sarah unfolded herself from the backseat—it seemed she had spent several days in a car and now was destined to spend several more. Harper looked around the side of the house and up into the yard a bit warily, but Jonah was not waiting there. This was as she had expected, but it stung a bit anyway. She put one weary foot in front of the other, up the steps. As she crossed the front porch, she noticed. There were two flat stones—smooth and oval from the river, sitting right by the front door. One perched perfectly on top of the other. She knew at once who had left them there.

✎

After dinner, Wilma found Sarah out in the yard near the back fence, fingering the new green shoots on the Don Juan rosebush. The Don Juan was a climber planted years ago when Sarah was a baby. Wilma could remember standing near this same spot with the garden hose, holding Sarah on her hip, tending to the bush and tickling Sarah's toes with the water. Sarah had been a serious child, but this would always make her giggle. The bush arched across the whole back fence now. In a month or so there would be nothing but a mass of red blooms.

"We're leaving tomorrow morning," said Sarah, "finally getting out of your hair."

"You've been no trouble, really," said Wilma, unable to help herself.

"Like the plague," said Sarah, then laughed.

"Like horseflies," said Wilma. The rare light of dusk in the backyard filtered through the first leaves and the mist and settled on their skin, and rendered them beautiful, the two of them after all, standing there listening to the crickets. "So you're leaving with Harper, then? You and Starling?"

"Yes, together just for the trip, Harper and I. Then, that's it. Finito." Sarah studied her then, trying to see how she would take it.

"I see," came out of Wilma's mouth on its own, involuntarily followed by a laugh. "No, I mean, I do see, really. And it's not funny at all, considering Starling and the rest, but I think I understand," she said.

"You're not surprised, then. You're not thinking I'm a poor thing like Wanda Stone teaching ladies to putt up at the country club?"

"Heavens no," said Wilma. "This may have nothing to do with it, but I did get a good long look at your friend Jonah sitting out here on my garden bench the other morning."

Sarah rewarded her with a near giggle. "There is that," she said.

They walked across the yard to the center bed. It was coming along. Both the La Tosca and the Symphony bushes had promising buds, but unfortunately an aphid was hiding under one of the brand-new leaves of the Summer Damask. Wilma pinched the bug and threw it on the ground. She looked up at Sarah and found that it was easy just to lean over and hug her neck. Dividend, she thought, for all the horseflies, for the plague of aphids to come.

"Mother," her child asked, "when you found Daddy out here, you know, that day, did he say anything to you, you know, about why?"

Involuntarily, Wilma's eyes searched out the spot, the very blades of grass trampled by his fall, the soil nurtured by blood. Gone. "No, honey, he didn't say anything. He was already gone."

"Then did you ever know why?"

"No," said Wilma. "I never did, thank God." This was mostly true. He had breathed, she thought, one or two times after she got to him, but that was all.

∽

And Roy, Roy didn't remember right away. In fact, it may have never again entered his mind at all if they hadn't started offering a Sunday dinner buffet up at the Holiday Inn. Roy took Wilma the first chance he got, though Wilma had to play the postlude for the eleven o'clock service, which meant that by the time they got there there was only well-done roast beef and none of the medium rare that Roy liked. Still, they had run into the Moody kid, the student of Wilma's, and his entire family, eight or ten of them sitting around a big table in the back eating banana pudding. They had just come from church themselves—the AME service tended to go longer than First Methodist's. Everyone was all dressed up and celebrating, it turned out, the boy's music scholarship to Greensboro College.

When the boy's father saw Wilma walking by with her salad plate, he had stood right up and pointed at her and said, "There she is, there's his piano teacher. Thankye, thankye, Miss Wilma." He had said this loud enough for everyone to hear, and there had even been a little clapping from nearby tables. Roy had been able to stand right there beside her while she smiled modestly at the whole crowd. Roy had been the one who got to follow her back to the booth. He had been the only one who knew just from the way she fumbled with her fork that inside she was about to bust. He was the only one who knew that she was proud as proud could be of the boy and that she would follow him whatever he did until the day she died.

So, they had thoroughly enjoyed themselves and left the restaurant, gently debating whether it was proper after eating to use a toothpick in public, especially when there was a little dish full of toothpicks right by the cash register. It had been a nice and pleasant day for late July, and Roy had walked out toward his car with his hand almost casually now in the small of Wilma's back. He was almost used to it now, though if he thought about it at all he would think on to this evening maybe or some other night soon when he would leave his car in his own driveway and sneak on down the street to her house and find the back door unlocked like she said it would be. He could conjure it all up out in the broad daylight of the parking lot: the creak of her stairs, the glow of her bedside lamp, her graceful hand reaching up to turn off the light. He could feel all of these things and more tingle in the small of her back. He would have said that he was in that moment as fully content as any man could be, and maybe he would've never thought another thing about the whole business between Harry and Lily again if he hadn't by chance looked up to see a couple coming out of a room on the second floor of the motel.

They were nobody he knew—middle aged, the man wearing a golf sweater, the woman with bright lipstick and a little scarf tied around her neck. Tourists, probably, stopped on their way up to the Blue Ridge Parkway. Roy opened Wilma's door, and as she was getting herself settled in the seat, he looked up to see the couple walking along the open hallway that ran across the front of the motel. The woman carried their only piece of luggage, a little blue train case, the kind of thing used for makeup and curlers and things. Somehow, that brought it back to him—Lily's case had been red. He wondered why he had not remembered before, that picture from years ago: Lily and Harry coming out of one of those same rooms, neither of them bothering to look around, Lily walking pretty as you please down that hall, swinging her red train case. The memory was so vivid suddenly that Roy felt compelled to shut Wilma's door and hurry around to his side of the car lest she would somehow see the apparition that had just appeared to him.

It was an act of will just to stay calm as he got into his seat and found the key to start the car. He fought the urge to throw it in gear and peel out of the parking lot. Instead, he smiled as best he could at Wilma and turned his AC on full blast. The strong whoosh of the fan slowed up his pulse to where he could reason with himself. The tourist couple had emerged from the building now, and he could see them getting into a white Nova behind him. South Carolina plates. Roy, buddy, he told himself, get ahold of yourself. It is an old memory, maybe even a dream. Even if he did remember it just right—Lily swinging that train case—who was to say why they had been in that room. Maybe Harry had some estate papers for Lily to sign. Why, there could have been legal papers in that case of Lily's. Roy navigated his beautiful Thunderbird through the parking lot and turned out toward Highway 52. The car was getting cool now.

Roy looked over at Wilma. There was a peaceful, Sunday-drive expression on her face. There was no easy way, Roy thought, to find out what had really happened, no way to ever know or to prove what had come to pass between Lily and Harry. No way to know. Roy knew, however, just what he would do with his suspicions. He lowered the electric window on his side of the car and threw his toothpick out into the street.

"What do you say, sugar," he said, "let's take a spin up on the Blue Ridge Parkway. There's a little house with a pretty view that I want you to see."

ACKNOWLEDGMENTS

My sincere thanks . . .

To my family: Ann and Vann York, Beth Schiff, Greg York, Greg Cranford, and my patient and inspiring children, Anna Lee and Will.

To my teachers: Betty Adcock, Darnell Arnoult, who first shepherded this book, Wallace Kaufman, Keith Yokley, and most especially, Lee Smith.

To the many friends and fellow writers who inspired, advised, employed, lent their houses and their expertise, and provided all manner of support: Roy Ahn, Margy Brehmer, Ron Carlson, Dexter Cirillo, Cathy Chiesa, Kathy Dorran, Michael Dupree, Danny Gotham, Shirley Henly, Charlie Holloway, Silas House, Haven Kimmel, Tina Montalvo, Bill Roche, Susan Rogers, David Vintinner, Charles Waldrup and the other members of the Roger Flourish writers group, and John Warasila. Also to Anderson Ranch Arts Center, Julie Comins and the folks at the Aspen Writers Foundation, and Weymouth Center for the Arts & Humanities.

To Jane Danielewicz and John McGowan, Megan Matchinske and David Brehmer, who believed from the beginning, and supplied courage and enjoyment as needed.

To Virginia Boyd and Pamela Duncan, the members of my writing group, who know the secret recipes for writing and for life, and who, as true friends, have been willing to give them out to me on a weekly basis.

To the incredible Suzanne Gluck, who opened the gate, Eugenie Furniss, and my most talented and enthusiastic editor, Kelly Notaras, and all of those at Plume who helped to publish this book.

ABOUT THE AUTHOR

Lynn York was born in the North Carolina piedmont to a family of car dealers. She grew up in Pilot Mountain and High Point, North Carolina, and was educated at Duke University and the University of Texas at Austin. She worked in the international telecommunications industry in Washington, D.C., until the promise of decent vegetables and a yard with grass brought her back to North Carolina in 1995, where she found *The Piano Teacher* waiting for her. She lives in Chapel Hill with her two children, Anna Lee and Will.